6-19
DATE DUE

JUL 10

AUG 0 8 2008

Who Slays the Wicked

Center Point
Large Print

Also by C. S. Harris and available from
Center Point Large Print:

Why Kill the Innocent

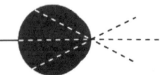

**This Large Print Book carries the
Seal of Approval of N.A.V.H.**

Who Slays *the* Wicked

A SEBASTIAN ST. CYR MYSTERY

C. S. HARRIS

CENTER POINT LARGE PRINT
THORNDIKE, MAINE

The text of this Large Print edition is unabridged.
In other aspects, this book may vary
from the original edition.
Printed in the United States of America
on permanent paper.
Set in 16-point Times New Roman type.

ISBN: 978-1-64358-220-7

Library of Congress Cataloging-in-Publication Data

Names: Harris, C. S., author.
Title: Who slays the wicked : a Sebastian St. Cyr mystery / C.S. Harris.
Description: Large Print edition. | Thorndike, Maine :
    Center Point Large Print, 2019.
Identifiers: LCCN 2019013151 | ISBN 9781643582207
    (hardcover : alk. paper)
Subjects: LCSH: Large type books. | GSAFD: Mystery fiction. |
    Historical fiction.
Classification: LCC PS3566.R5877 W47855 2019b | DDC 813/.54—dc23
LC record available at https://lccn.loc.gov/2019013151

In memory of KitKat:
with us for such a short time

Evil shall slay the wicked, and they that hate the righteous shall be desolate.
                                                   —Psalm 34:21

CHAPTER 1

London: Friday, 1 April 1814

Bloodred and splayed wide as if in panic, the dried handprint stood out clearly against the white, freshly painted inside panel of the town house's front door.

Jenny Crutcher was crossing his lordship's grand black-and-white marble-tiled entrance hall, humming to herself, when she saw it. She drew up, one fist clenching around the handle of her broom as she glanced in dismay at the golden glow of the rising sun filtering in through the fanlight above the door. A housemaid in any normal gentleman's establishment would have been shocked by such a discovery. But Jenny had worked in Viscount Ashworth's Curzon Street residence for six years now. Little shocked her anymore.

She was a slight, underfed woman with a pinched face and dull, straight fair hair that combined to make her look older than her twenty-six years. Once not so long ago, folks had called her a pretty little thing. But Jenny didn't mind her fading looks too much. Fresh-faced young housemaids had a tendency to catch his lordship's eye, and Jenny had more than enough trouble in her life already. Frowning at the blood, she hurried off to fetch a bucket of water and a rag. She didn't have time for this; she'd been working since before dawn, and there was still so much to do before the master came down.

"Blast," she muttered when water splashed over the rim of the bucket as she set it down on the marble tiles. More work. It wasn't until she was on her hands and knees, wiping up the spilled water, that she noticed the blood on the door's handle. She cleaned that too, surprised to realize the door was unbarred. His lordship's aged butler, Mr. Fullerton, always made a big show of ceremoniously lowering the bar on the front door every morning. But the old man wasn't up yet.

In a normal household, it would also be the butler's responsibility to bar the door at night before retiring. But that task was often delegated to his lordship's valet for reasons Jenny understood only too well. *Forgot something, did we, Digby?* Jenny thought, allowing herself a faintly malicious smile. She was not fond of the nasty little valet.

Leaving the bucket of bloody water for later, she scurried off to work her way through the rooms of the first two floors, throwing open curtains, collecting dirty wine and brandy glasses, and straightening the disorder left from the night before. She worked in concert with the second housemaid, Alice, the two women dividing the tasks between them in a familiar routine they'd developed over the years. By the time they climbed the stairs to the floor where the Viscount kept his bedchamber, it was already past ten o'clock. Fortunately, his lordship was never up before noon, so they should still have plenty of time to sneak into his room, quietly make up the fire, leave fresh water, and be away before he stirred.

They'd almost reached the master's door before they realized it was standing ajar. The room beyond gaped dark and quiet.

"Reckon he's up already?" whispered Alice, hesitating.

Jenny shook her head. "Can't be. He didn't ring for Digby."

Alice shifted her grip on the heavy coal scuttle she carried. "So why's the door open?"

"A draft coulda pushed it." Yet even as she suggested it, Jenny was remembering the bloody handprint on the unbarred front door. Something tingled up her spine, and she clutched the water pitcher she carried more tightly to her chest. "Maybe we shouldn't go in there."

"We have to," said Alice. Nudging the door open wider, she took one step into the room.

And screamed.

CHAPTER 2

Anthony Marcus Ledger, Viscount Ashworth, only son and heir of the Marquis of Lindley, lay sprawled naked on his back in the rumpled depths of his vast silk-hung bedstead. His eyes were open but sunken flat, his handsome young face ashen, his lips oddly purple in contrast. One did not need to look at the raw, hacked mess that had once been his chest to know he was dead.

"Ghastly sight," said Sir Henry Lovejoy, one of three stipendiary magistrates attached to Bow Street's famous Public Office. A small balding man with the appearance of a respectable merchant and the demeanor of a stern cleric, he was careful to stand well back from the gore-splattered bed. There'd once been a time when Lovejoy was indeed a merchant, and a moderately successful one at that. But the death of his beloved wife and daughter some thirteen years before had caused him to reevaluate everything from his religious beliefs to his purpose in life and devote his remaining days to public service.

Now pressing a clean white handkerchief to his lips, he let his horrified gaze drift from the blood-soaked fine linen sheets beneath his lordship's mutilated body to the sprayed arcs of blood that showed quite clearly against the champagne-colored silk of the bed's hangings. Silken red cords tied the dead man's widespread hands and feet to the bedstead's stout wooden posts. "I believe we can safely surmise that his lordship was killed here," said Lovejoy.

Beside him, a young constable with thin shoulders and a pockmarked face swallowed hard. "That's an awful lot o' blood, sir."

"It is, indeed."

The heavy curtains at the windows overlooking the street had been hastily yanked open, flooding the elegant bedchamber with the dazzling light of a fine spring morning. Tucking away his handkerchief, Lovejoy turned in a slow circle, taking in the new Aubusson carpet, the gleaming rosewood chests, the gilt-framed paintings of highbred hunters and racing hounds. To all appearances, Ashworth's life had been one of rare privilege and refinement. And while Lovejoy knew only too well that in this instance appearances were in some ways deceptive, the fact remained that the violent murder of the handsome young son of one of the wealthiest noblemen in the kingdom would both shock and terrify the rarefied world of the haut *ton*—and seriously rattle the palace.

Troubled by the thought, Lovejoy went to stand at the window. Curzon Street lay in that part of London known as Mayfair, home to the fashionable, the titled, the wealthy, and the powerful. There'd been no official announcement yet of his lordship's death, but word of ghastly murders always managed to spread quickly. A dozen or more murmuring gawkers had already gathered in the normally quiet street. Soon there would be more. Many more.

"No answer yet from Brook Street?" said Lovejoy, his gaze on the growing crowd below.

"Not yet, sir."

Lovejoy had already set half a dozen of his constables to searching the house and interviewing the dead man's servants. But he was waiting for someone else, someone to whom he had sent word as soon as news of Ashworth's death reached Bow Street: Sebastian St. Cyr, Viscount Devlin, only surviving son and heir of the Earl of Hendon. There'd been a time not so long ago when Devlin had been on the run for a murder he didn't commit, with Lovejoy determined to bring him in. But in the years since then, an unusual friendship had developed between the two men, an affinity based on profound mutual respect and a shared determination to see murderers brought to justice.

Yet that was not Lovejoy's sole reason for involving Devlin. For just seven months ago, the dissolute, dangerous man now lying dead in that blood-soaked bed had married Lord Devlin's beautiful young niece, Stephanie.

14

CHAPTER 3

"Reckon 'e's really dead?" asked the boy in a tight voice as Sebastian guided his curricle and pair through the crowd gathered in front of Lord Ashworth's Curzon Street house. "I mean, really, *really* dead?"

Sebastian glanced back at the sharp-featured young groom, or tiger, who clung to the perch at the rear of the curricle. "There doesn't seem to be any doubt."

Tom nodded, his eyes haunted by a dark, painful memory. "I hope so."

Sebastian drew in close to the kerb. But for a moment he paused, his gaze on the boy's tense, troubled face. Ashworth hadn't been directly involved in the hours-long nightmare the boy had endured last September, but the nobleman's complicity was as significant as it was impossible to prove. "Are you all right, lad?"

"Aye."

Sebastian nodded, taking the boy at his word. "Walk them if I'm too long."

Tom scrambled forward to take the reins. "Aye, gov'nor."

Dropping to the pavement, Sebastian let his gaze drift over the town house's classical facade. The last time he'd been here, seven months before, there'd been subtle signs of neglect—the area steps unswept, the paint on the entrance door dull and peeling. Now, as one of the constables stationed to keep back the crowd leapt to open the door for him, Sebastian noted the gleaming fresh black paint, the newly repaired iron railing. Lord Ashworth's financial situation had obviously improved considerably since his marriage. But then, thought Sebastian as he followed a second constable up the town house's elegant staircase, that was precisely why Ashworth had finally agreed to wed and beget an heir—because his father, the Marquis of Lindley, had cut off his son's generous allowance and refused to reinstate it until he did.

Sir Henry Lovejoy was waiting for Sebastian at the top of the stairs, his habitually grave face even more somber than usual. "My apologies for sending such news with one of the lads rather than coming myself," he said with a bow.

"Understandable," said Sebastian as the two men turned toward the large chamber at the front of the house. From somewhere in the distance came the wail of a woman crying hysterically. "There's no doubt it's murder?"

"None at all, I'm afraid." Lovejoy stood back to allow him to enter the room first. "Look."

"Good God." Sebastian's step faltered on the threshold as he took in the gore-splattered bed and the naked, spread-eagled man who lay within it. The cloying smell of blood and death hung heavy in the air. "Who found him?"

"Two housemaids, shortly after ten this morning. The younger of the two—Alice, I believe is her name—has been weeping uncontrollably ever since."

"I'm surprised they're not both in hysterics after seeing this." Going to stand beside the bed, Sebastian let his gaze travel over the pallid, blood-streaked corpse of his niece's debauched husband. He'd been a good-looking man, Anthony Ledger, with even, sensuous features enhanced rather than marred by a thin scar high on one cheek. His eyes were a light gray, his honey-colored hair artfully disheveled. Like Sebastian, he'd been in his early thirties. A dedicated sportsman, he was tall and well toned, his shoulders broad, his abdomen hard.

His chest was a pulpy, ravaged horror.

As a cavalry officer for six long years, Sebastian had seen more men die—most of them horribly—than he could remember. Yet it didn't seem to make any difference; he typically still found the sight of sudden, violent death profoundly disturbing. *Any man's death diminishes me,* John Donne had written, *because I am involved in mankind.* But as he stared down at what was left of Anthony Ledger, Sebastian felt only relief.

Relief, and a vague, niggling fear he hoped desperately was misplaced.

"Lovely," said Sebastian, his eyes narrowing as he studied the multiple gaping wounds. Whoever killed Ashworth had struck him in the chest with a sharp blade over and over again, so many times that it was nearly impossible to distinguish one blow from the next. "What did the killer use? An ax?"

"It looks that way, doesn't it? We haven't found anything that might be the murder weapon yet, although my men are still searching the house. Perhaps an autopsy will give us a better idea of what we're looking for. I've sent for a shell to have the body transported to Paul Gibson."

"Good," said Sebastian. No one could read the secrets a murder victim had to tell better than the former army surgeon.

Lovejoy cleared his throat uncomfortably. "I am informed by his lordship's staff that your niece, Lady Ashworth, does not reside here."

"No, she doesn't," said Sebastian, his gaze drifting to where the dead man's boots, finely tailored coat, cravat, shirt, doeskin breeches, and small clothes lay strewn from the door to the bed as if they'd been stripped off in the frenzied heat of passion. "The house was in such a state of disrepair at the time of their marriage that Ashworth suggested she stay with his father and maiden aunt at Lindley House in Park Lane while the place was being refurbished."

Lovejoy cleared his throat again. "She's with child, yes?"

"She was. She was safely delivered of twin boys early last month."

"Ah," said Lovejoy, who could do sums as well as the next man. "It's certainly understandable that she should be reluctant to relocate at such a time."

Sebastian suspected that wasn't her only reason, but all he said was "What have you learned from Ashcroft's servants?"

"Not as much as we'd hoped, I'm afraid. It seems it was not unusual for his lordship to, er, entertain females in the evening. On such occasions, the servants would retire early, with only his lordship's valet—a gentleman's gentleman by the name of Edward Digby—waiting up to see to his needs."

"And what does Digby have to say about last night?"

"Unfortunately, we've been unable to locate the man."

Sebastian had crouched down to study the splotches of blood on the carpet beside the bed, but at that he looked up. "Perhaps he's our killer. What do you know of him?"

"I gather he's not precisely well liked by the other members of the staff. But no one seems to believe him capable of"—Lovejoy paused as if searching for the right word—"this."

"People can reach a breaking point and snap," said Sebastian. "Particularly when they work for a man as vicious as Ashworth."

"True."

Pushing to his feet, Sebastian squinted up at the blood-splattered silk-lined tester that arched over the bed. "Jesus," he said softly. "Whoever did this must have been covered in blood."

Lovejoy nodded. "There's blood on the inside handle of the bedroom door and another streak smeared along its frame. I'm told there was also blood downstairs on the door to the street, but one of the housemaids unfortunately washed it off before the body was discovered."

Sebastian nodded toward the pale-figured carpet. "Interesting there are no bloody footprints leading back to the door. How the devil do you hack a man to death and keep from tracking his blood all over the place?"

A gleam of white peeking out from beneath the bed caught his eye, and he reached to pick up what turned out to be a woman's white silk stocking, gossamer fine and quite new. He held it up to the morning light streaming in the window. "Any idea as to the identity of the woman Ashworth was entertaining last night?"

"We're told the valet, Digby, might know."

"And he's making himself scarce." Sebastian found himself staring at a black leather whip that lay half-tangled in the blood-drenched bedding and felt his throat tighten. Ashworth had a well-known taste for sexual games—vicious games of pain and humiliation that sometimes turned deadly. "If ever a man deserved to die like this, it's him."

Lovejoy gazed woodenly at a far wall. "You still believe he was a part of what we discovered last year out at Clerkenwell and Bethnal Green?"

"Yes." Seven months before, Ashworth had been implicated in a string of brutal murders targeting vulnerable, homeless youths snatched off the poorest streets of London. Sebastian had killed one of the men responsible. But he hadn't been able to prove Ashworth's involvement even though he'd kept working on it ever since, searching for evidence he might have missed and keeping a watchful eye on the nasty son of a bitch.

Keeping an eye on Stephanie.

Something about Lovejoy's silence told Sebastian he understood only too well the drift of Sebastian's thoughts. "Do you know of anyone who might have wanted him dead?" asked the magistrate quietly.

Besides me? thought Sebastian. After all, the thin scar on Ashworth's cheek had been left by the tip of Sebastian's own swordstick. Aloud, he said, "No one I can name offhand. But men like Ashworth do tend to accumulate enemies. And they—" He broke off, leaning forward to study the knot in the twisted silk cord that held Ashworth's nearest wrist lashed to the bedpost. "That's odd," he said, circling the bed to study each cord in turn.

"My lord?"

"These knots aren't as tight as you'd expect. Even if the cords weren't tied tightly to begin with, surely they would have been pulled tight when Ashworth struggled against them as he was being killed."

"You think he was tied up *after* he was murdered?"

"I don't know what to think."

A shout echoed up from the entry hall below, followed by an aged, imperious voice demanding, "Let me pass this instant! How *dare* you? That is my son lying up there dead, you fools."

"Oh, dear," said Lovejoy. "My colleague Sir John volunteered to go to Lindley House and personally inform the Marquis of his son's death. But surely he must have advised his lordship not to come here?"

"I doubt the Marquis would listen."

Footsteps sounded on the stairs. Then Alexander Adrian Ledger, the Third Marquis of Lindley, appeared in the doorway shadowed by a harassed-looking constable who threw Lovejoy an apologetic look.

In many ways, the Marquis was an older, thinner version of his son: white-haired but still tall, square jawed, and handsome despite his eighty-plus years. Yet there was a distinctly kinder, gentler cast to the elderly man's expression that his son had lacked. Now deep lines of shock and grief etched his face.

"My lord," said Sebastian, stepping forward to block the old man's view of the bed. "You don't want to see this."

The Marquis met Sebastian's gaze, his light gray eyes blazingly fierce and drowning in a father's pain. "Let me pass."

Sebastian hesitated, then nodded and stood aside.

At the sight of Ashworth's savaged, bloody corpse, the old man checked for an instant, his nostrils flaring. Then, swallowing hard, he tightened his face as if guarding against any betraying signs of emotion and forced himself to approach his dead son. The effort required for him to put one foot in front of the other was painful to watch.

"Dear God," he whispered, one hand reaching out to grasp the nearest bedpost as his knees half buckled. *"Anthony."* He stared down at the dead man, his face a frozen mask of horrified disbelief. Then he swung toward them, his voice gruff, almost accusatory. "Who did this? Have you no idea?"

"Not yet, my lord," said Lovejoy with a deep bow.

Lindley turned back to the bed, a spasm of revulsion quivering over his aged features as he stared at the silken cords wrapped around his son's wrists and ankles. "A woman, obviously. Surely the servants must know who she is?"

"We are still conducting interviews, my lord."

He dragged a shaky hand down over his face. "Yes. Of course. I beg your pardon."

"When was the last time you saw your son, my lord?" asked Sebastian.

The question seemed to confuse the old man. "I don't know. . . . It's been several days. Why?"

"Did he mention anyone with whom he'd quarreled recently?"

"Not that I recall, no." He sucked in a deep, ragged breath and gave a faint shake of his head. "Poor Stephanie. She's visiting her mother this morning, so she wasn't at home when the magistrate came to tell us what had happened. I've sent a message to Lady Wilcox—it seemed best that she be the one to break the news to her daughter, but . . . This will be so very hard on her."

"Yes, undoubtedly," murmured Lovejoy.

Sebastian himself remained silent. He wasn't certain how much Stephanie had known about Ashworth's unorthodox sexual interests when she married him. But her continued residence in her father-in-law's Park Lane mansion suggested she'd learned enough by now to stay far away from her new husband.

It was a thought that should have reassured Sebastian. Yet, for some reason he couldn't quite name, it did not.

CHAPTER 4

"How long must we put up with this?" demanded the Crown Prince, his plump face red with annoyance.

His Royal Highness George August Frederick, Prince of Wales and for three years now Regent of the United Kingdom of Great Britain and Ireland, stood at an upper window of his Carlton House palace overlooking Pall Mall. The object of his revulsion—a beautiful, exotic-looking young woman with a wide smile and flashing dark eyes—was seated in an open-topped barouche passing below. The cheers and huzzahs of the crowds thronging the street to greet her wafted up to the opulently furnished room in roaring waves. For a prince who was inevitably met with boos and hisses wherever he went, it was a painful spectacle to witness.

"How long?" he snapped again.

The question was addressed to his adviser, confidant, and distant cousin, Charles, Lord Jarvis. A brilliant and ruthlessly cunning man, Jarvis had successfully steered the kingdom through every hazard from republican fervor and endless war to royal madness and princely incompetence. He might be both brutally determined and utterly amoral, but he was also genuinely dedicated to protecting and promoting the interests of both the monarchy and Britain. The House of Hanover would have crumbled long ago without him.

In age he had just turned sixty. Decades of attendance on his dissolute, hedonistic prince had added extra pounds to Jarvis's tall frame, but he was still an attractive man, with an aquiline nose and surprisingly sensual lips that could smile with a disarming—although generally insincere—sweetness. He cast a dismissive glance at the flamboyant occupant of the carriage below. "She has only just arrived, sir. The hoi polloi's enthusiasm for her will dissipate soon enough."

"I wish I could share your confidence." The Prince turned away from the aggravating spectacle. "Why the devil has she come so early?"

The object of the Prince's annoyance was Grand Duchess Catherine of Oldenburg, the recently widowed and best-loved sister of Tsar Alexander of Russia. With the allied armies advancing ever closer to Paris, it was becoming obvious to all that the decades-long war with France would soon be at an end. And so the Regent had invited the Allied Sovereigns to convene in London that summer for what he envisioned as a grand, weeks-long victory celebration. But the celebration wasn't until June, and the Tsar's favorite sister had already arrived.

Her explanation for her early presence—to prepare for her brother's impending visit—was laughably suspect. Jarvis had several theories about her true motives, but he had no intention of sharing them with his agitated prince.

"I don't trust her," said the Regent, going to fling himself in a gilded, silk-covered chair fashioned to look like a lotus blossom. As far as the Prince was concerned, all women (with the exception, of course, of his own beloved mother) were either silly, annoying featherheads or scheming vixens. The formidable Grand Duchess Catherine obviously fell into the latter category. "She's up to something. I know it."

"Perhaps," said Jarvis soothingly. "But there's no need to distress yourself, sir. Have you given any more thought to having Lawrence paint a new portrait of you for the Allied Sovereigns' visit?"

The Regent's petulant expression relaxed into a smile, for he was always easily distracted by his favorite conversation topic: himself. "Life-sized, don't you think? And in one of my uniforms. Perhaps against the backdrop of the Battle of Talavera?" The Prince had never been anywhere near a battle in his life. But that didn't stop him from amassing a collection of splendid uniforms and entertaining dinner guests with fanciful tales of his supposed feats of courage and brilliance on the field of arms.

"Talavera?" said Jarvis as the cheers for the Grand Duchess receded into the distance. "Or would you prefer Vittoria?"

CHAPTER 5

Sebastian walked out of Lord Ashworth's house to find Curzon Street packed with street hawkers and apprentices jostling tradesmen and shopkeepers and what looked like more than a few of the dead man's curious aristocratic neighbors.

What he didn't see was his curricle.

He eventually discovered his tiger watering the chestnuts at a trough outside a pub at the corner of Clarges. The boy was simply staring into space, his gaze fixed unseeingly on nothing in particular.

"M'lord," said Tom, collecting himself with a jerk when Sebastian walked up to him. "I didn't see ye! I'm that sorry, I am. I shoulda—"

Sebastian leapt up to the curricle's high seat and collected the reins. "It's all right, Tom. Believe it or not, I am capable of walking a couple of blocks without suffering undue fatigue."

The boy scrambled up to his perch. "Is 'e—is Ashworth dead?"

"Very."

"Ye know who offed 'im?"

"Not yet."

"Ye ask me, whoever killed 'im done the world a favor, gettin' rid o' that cove."

"I'm inclined to agree with you."

"So ye ain't gonna bother tryin' t' figure out who done it?"

Sebastian turned his horses toward his sister's house in St. James's Square. "Unfortunately, the brutal murder of a marquis's son is something the authorities can't simply ignore. That means they're going to need to arrest someone. And if the palace gets too insistent, it won't matter if the person they finger is guilty or innocent, as long as he hangs." He paused, aware of the quiet but insistent whisper of a disturbing possibility, and added, "He, or she."

Sebastian's relationship with his sister, Amanda, the Dowager Lady Wilcox, had never been easy.

Of the four children born to the marriage of the Fifth Earl of Hendon and his beautiful, errant Countess, Amanda was the eldest. If she'd been a boy, she would automatically have become Viscount Devlin and heir to Hendon's vast lands and titles. Instead, as a girl, she'd watched that honor go first to her brother Richard and then, after his death, to Cecil. Sebastian knew she'd resented both Richard and Cecil, although she'd never hated either of those two long-dead siblings the way she'd always hated her youngest and only surviving brother, Sebastian. But then, she was twelve years his senior, which meant she'd been old enough to know some painful truths about Sebastian's birth that had until recently eluded him.

A widow now for three years, she lived in an elegant town house on St. James's Square that technically belonged to her son, Bayard, the current Lord Wilcox. But the young Baron was a troubled soul still firmly under the control of his mother. Knowing what he did of Bayard Wilcox, Sebastian suspected that was a good thing.

Her ladyship's impressive front door was guarded by a grim-faced butler named Crowley who bowed to Sebastian and said stiffly, "I beg your pardon, my lord, but I still have orders not to admit your lordship to the house."

"I know." Sebastian handed the man his hat anyway. "Is Lady Ashworth with my sister?"

"She is, my lord. There's been"—the butler hesitated, the hat clutched in both hands as he obviously debated how much information to divulge to his employer's estranged brother—"an incident."

"I am aware of Ashworth's murder, if that's what's worrying you. I'll wait while you inform my sister and niece that I have some information they urgently need to hear. I suspect you'll find Lady Wilcox changes her mind about seeing me."

The butler looked doubtful but showed Sebastian to a small withdrawing room and went off to convey his message to her ladyship. On his return, he bowed again and said, "This way, my lord."

He led Sebastian to a pleasant morning room

where Amanda and her daughter sat near a window overlooking the rear gardens. The remnants of a half-eaten breakfast littered the table before them, as if Lindley's message had interrupted their meal.

Amanda was well into her forties now. Like their mother, the beautiful but infamous Countess of Hendon, she was built slim and graceful, her golden hair still little touched by gray. But her blunt facial features were those of her father, the Earl, as were her startlingly blue eyes. Lately she'd taken to wearing gowns of silver or the pale gray of half mourning in honor of her dead husband, a nasty man she'd intensely hated and certainly did not miss.

Her nineteen-year-old daughter, the newly widowed Lady Ashworth, sat with her hands gripping the delicate arms of her chair.

Like her mother, Stephanie was golden-haired and elegantly built, with the same intensely blue St. Cyr eyes. But unlike Amanda, the girl had avoided inheriting Hendon's less attractive features. Instead, she looked startlingly like her errant grandmother—ethereally beautiful, alluring, and recklessly wild to the point of self-destruction. Studying her pale but tightly composed face, Sebastian found himself wondering not for the first time about the exact nature of the sequence of events that had led her to marry Ashworth seven months before.

"If you've come here simply to gloat," said Amanda without any greeting, "you can turn around right now and leave."

Ignoring his sister, Sebastian met his niece's gaze and said, "I won't pretend to be sorry he's dead, Stephanie. But I am sorry for any distress his death causes you."

"Delicately put, Uncle," said Stephanie. "Do you know how he died?"

"Yes. Do you?"

She shook her head. "The Marquis's message to Mama was tactful to the point of abstruseness. I take it that's because the truth is rather lurid?"

"I'm afraid so."

"Oh, stop being so namby-pamby and tell us," snapped Amanda.

"Very well. He was found bound hand and foot to his bed, naked. It's a bit hard to tell at this point, but from the looks of things, I'd say someone took a hatchet to his chest."

"Good God," said Amanda. "What a fool to put himself in such a vulnerable position."

Sebastian watched his niece. Her chest lifted with a quickly indrawn breath, but otherwise her expression didn't alter. He said, "You don't appear surprised."

She met his gaze squarely. "I know what he was like."

Since neither woman had invited him to sit, he went to stand before the hearth, one arm resting along the mantel. "Do you have any idea who might have killed him?" he asked Stephanie.

"Someone who disliked him?" she suggested, her nostrils quivering with a pinched look. "That should narrow the list of suspects down to virtually everyone who ever dealt with him."

The faint, niggling whisper of misgiving Sebastian had experienced earlier now flared into full-blown concern. She was too calm, too . . . prepared. "Where were you last night, Steph?"

"Merciful heavens." Amanda pushed to her feet and took several steps toward him with a haste that set her silver mourning gown to swishing about her ankles. "Precisely what are you suggesting?"

Sebastian kept his gaze on Stephanie. "You know the question is going to come up," he said softly. "Where were you?"

Her hands spasmed on the arms of her chair. "Home. Asleep."

"Can anyone verify that?"

Her chin came up. "I was alone, if that's what you're asking."

Amanda's hand flashed through the air in a sharp, dismissive gesture. "Seriously, Devlin? She's barely a month out from childbirth. What do you mean to imply?"

"The twins sleep with their wet nurses?" he asked Stephanie.

"Yes."

Amanda's lips curled into a sneer. "You don't seriously think my daughter would turn herself into a milk cow?"

It was a barb directed at Sebastian's own wife, Hero, who had nursed their young son herself. He ignored the taunt and said to Stephanie, "When did you last see your husband?"

"It must have been a week ago, at least—if not more."

"You're certain?"

"Yes."

"I would caution you to be careful not to lie. Not when the subject is murder."

"I am not lying. Ashworth married me to satisfy his father's increasingly insistent demands for an heir, and as soon as he learned I was with child, he was as happy to ignore me as I was to be left alone. And I am now frankly quite overjoyed to be a widow."

"A truth I suggest you keep to yourself."

Stephanie tilted her head to one side, a strange smile tightening her lips. "Really, Uncle? And yet you just advised me not to lie."

"About your movements, never. But I believe your joy at widowhood can be safely concealed."

Amanda let out a huff of disgust. "You aren't seriously suggesting anyone would dare suspect Stephanie? *Stephanie?*"

"I'm afraid it's highly possible, given that Ashworth appears to have been killed by a woman." He watched Stephanie's eyes widen and said, "That frightens you. Why?"

"Of course it frightens me. Mother might believe I won't be suspected, but I fail to share her confidence."

Her voice cracked when she said it, giving him a glimpse of the quiet terror she was struggling so valiantly to keep hidden. And he felt momentarily overwhelmed by a rush of his lifelong affection for this beautiful, vibrant, troubled young woman. He said gently, "If you know anything—anything at all—that might shed some light on what happened to Ashworth, you must tell me."

She pushed up from her chair and went to stand staring out at the garden, one hand resting on the windowsill. "I don't know anything."

He studied her half-averted profile. "I'll help you in every way I can, Stephanie. But you must be honest with me."

"We don't need your help," said Amanda, going to give the bell a sharp tug. "One of the footmen will show you out."

Sebastian met his sister's stony gaze. "I hope to God you're right." To Stephanie, he said, "If you need me, you know where to find me."

She stared back at him, and he saw something flicker in the shadowy depths of the girl's vivid blue eyes.

Then she turned her face away and said nothing.

• • •

Sebastian went next to the Grosvenor Square residence of Alistair James St. Cyr, the Fifth Earl of Hendon, for many years now Chancellor of the Exchequer and the man known to the world as his father. But according to Hendon's butler, the Earl had departed for Oxford two days before.

After leaving a carefully worded note, Sebastian drove back to his own house in Brook Street. "Stable them for now," he told Tom, handing the boy the reins. "And grab yourself something to eat while you're at it. I have a feeling this is going to be a long day."

"Aye, m'lord."

Sebastian watched the boy drive off, then turned to mount the steps to the house. "Is Lady Devlin in?" he asked his majordomo, handing the man his driving coat, hat, and gloves.

"I believe she's in the library, my lord," said Morey.

"Ah. Thank you."

Sebastian found his wife, Hero, leaning over the library table, so focused on the map she had spread out to study that she didn't hear his approach. He paused for a moment in the doorway, a faint smile playing over his lips as he quietly watched her.

She was an extraordinarily tall woman—nearly as tall as he, with a Junoesque build, warm brown hair, and strong, slightly masculine features. She was also one of the most brilliant people he knew, fiercely logical and passionately devoted to identifying and righting the injustices of their world. For some time now, she'd been writing a series of articles on the poor of London—an endeavor that profoundly irritated her father, the King's omnipotent cousin, Charles, Lord Jarvis. As the real power behind the Prince of Wales's fragile Regency, Jarvis terrified nearly everyone in the kingdom. But not Hero.

She'd been Sebastian's wife for going on two years, but she was still a wonder to him. She'd come into his life at a particularly dark period, when he'd lost, first, the woman he'd loved for years, and then his own sense of who and what he was. Now he couldn't imagine his world without her. Sometimes in the haunted darkness of the night, the fear of losing her or their young son, Simon, could come upon him out of nowhere with a ferocity that took his breath and scared the hell out of him. He suspected it always would.

She looked up then, saw him, and smiled.

"New project?" he asked, pushing away from the doorframe.

"I'm thinking about writing an article on the street scavengers—mainly the pure finders and rag-and-bone pickers, but perhaps also the night-soil men, if I get up the nerve." The night-soil men were the laborers who emptied the city's hundreds of thousands of cesspits and privies, and always reeked of their occupation.

"Sounds lovely," said Sebastian, going to pour himself a brandy.

"Is it true?" she asked, watching him. "Ashworth is dead?"

Sebastian eased the stopper from the brandy carafe. "He is. Hacked to death while tied naked to his bed. They'll never keep that tidbit out of the papers."

"Poor Stephanie. How is she taking it?"

"With unnerving aplomb."

Hero watched him set aside the decanter and reach for his glass. "You can't seriously suspect Stephanie of murder?"

He took a slow sip of his brandy and felt it burn all the way down. "I wish I didn't."

"Is she capable of that sort of violence?"

"If pushed? I think so. I imagine a man such as Ashworth would drive almost any wife to want to murder him."

Hero walked over to take a sip of his brandy, then handed him back the glass. "I'll never understand why she married him."

"Because she was three months gone with child and couldn't bear to face the consequences."

Hero gave a wry smile. "That I can appreciate. I suppose what I can't understand is why she involved herself with such a man in the first place."

"Well, he was a marquis's heir, extraordinarily rich, and undeniably handsome in a rakish, dangerous sort of way. He could also come across as quite charming when he wanted to."

Hero made a face. "I suppose."

He took another sip. "According to Stephanie, the list of people who wanted Ashworth dead is virtually endless."

"No doubt. Where do you propose to start?"

"With someone who knew the man well and yet somehow still managed to like him."

"I suppose there must be someone."

"Oh, there is." Sebastian drained the rest of his drink in one long pull and set the glass aside. "I went to school with him."

CHAPTER 6

His name was Sir Felix Paige, and he'd been a friend of Ashworth since the two were boys together at Eton. Sebastian had been at Eton at the same time, but he'd never called either man a friend.

Unlike Ashworth, who'd been born into his position as his father's heir, Paige began life as the younger son of a younger son. At the age of seventeen, rather than going off to Oxford or Cambridge, he'd bought a pair of colors with his uncle's assistance and headed to India to make his fortune. Instead, he'd nearly died there—first of fever, then from a nasty head wound acquired at the Battle of Assaye. Sent home to recuperate, he'd had the good fortune to bury, in short order, his father, his uncle, his uncle's childless only son, and his own unmarried elder brother. Having thus unexpectedly acceded to the family's title and fortune, the new Baronet immediately sold out and settled permanently in London, visiting his estates only during hunting season.

Like Ashworth, Sir Felix was a Corinthian, a sportsman with a reputation as a bruising rider who spent hours at both Angelo's fencing academy and Jackson's boxing saloon in Bond Street. It was there that Sebastian found him going a couple of rounds with Gentleman Jackson himself.

Sebastian stood for a time leaning against a nearby wall as the two men sparred. Paige was a tall, lanky fellow with sandy hair, a high forehead, and a mobile, expressive face that habitually seemed to be breaking into a broad smile—although the smiles rarely reached his pale blue eyes, which were watchful and assessing.

Sebastian was impressed with the Baronet's footwork and science and the way his intense focus on his opponent never wavered. But Sebastian could tell the man knew he was there, and that he resented the scrutiny. When the last round ended, the Baronet looped a towel around his neck and walked up to him.

"I take it you're here for a reason," said Paige, his face gleaming with sweat and his chest lifting with his labored breathing.

Sebastian pushed away from the wall. "You've heard about Ashworth?"

Something flickered across the Baronet's rawboned features, an unreadable expression that was there and then gone. "I have."

"So, you know why I'm here."

"Do I?"

"You were one of his closest friends, were you not?" Sebastian paused a perceptible moment, then added, "Especially now that Rowe is dead."

"I never knew Rowe well. But Ash and I were friends, yes. Old friends." The Baronet's words were as guarded as his eyes.

"Who do you think killed him?"

Paige brought up a hand to swipe one end of the towel across his sweaty face, then turned toward the dressing rooms. "I have no idea."

"No?" said Sebastian, keeping pace with him. "Yet you must have some idea who his enemies were."

Paige glanced sideways at him. "I didn't exactly keep a list, if that's what you're asking."

"Were there so many?"

"Most men have enemies."

"But Ashworth had more than a few?"

Paige shrugged.

Sebastian said, "When was the last time you saw him?"

"Yesterday afternoon, actually. At Tattersall's. Why?"

"Did he happen to mention how he planned to spend the evening?"

"Not so's I recall, no. Sorry."

"How did he seem?"

Paige stripped off his sweaty shirt and went to pour water into a basin. "Meaning—what?"

"Was he nervous? Angry? Upset?"

Paige shook his head. "Hardly. If anything, I'd say he was in good spirits. He usually was."

"You heard how he was found?"

42

Paige's mouth thinned into a flat line. "I heard."

"You're familiar with the sort of games he liked to play?"

"Vaguely."

"Do you like to play those games too?"

Paige froze in the act of washing his hands. "No."

"I can find out, you know."

The Baronet's nostril's flared on a quickly indrawn breath. "Suit yourself. But call me a liar again, and you'll meet me for it."

"If you found his activities so distasteful, then why stay friends?"

"That was none of my affair."

"I suppose that's one way of looking at it." Sebastian watched Paige bend over the washbowl and splash his face. "You wouldn't happen to know the name of the woman Ashworth was with last night, would you?"

"Sorry, but no."

"There wasn't anyone in particular he'd been involved with lately?"

Paige looked up, his face dripping.

"I take it there is someone?" said Sebastian.

Paige reached for a clean towel and dried his face. "Ash always did like dangerous women. He saw them as a challenge."

"So who was his most recent 'dangerous woman'?"

They were alone, but the Baronet still cast

43

a quick look around and lowered his voice. "You've heard about this Grand Duchess who's in town?"

There was only one Grand Duchess in London who mattered: Catherine of Oldenburg, the attention-loving, Russian-born sister of Tsar Alexander. "You aren't seriously suggesting that Ashcroft was involved with Grand Duchess Catherine?" said Sebastian. "She's only just arrived."

Paige shook his head. "Not her; one of her ladies. Ivanna is her name; Princess Ivanna Gagarin. She's been here for weeks."

Sebastian studied the other man's face, looking for some evidence of subterfuge. He saw none. "You're certain?"

"That she was with Ash last night? No, of course not. I've no idea. But I understand she does like to play his kind of games."

Sebastian watched Paige pull a clean shirt over his head. "Who else has he been playing his games with lately?"

"That I couldn't say."

"Can't, or won't?"

Paige gave a faint smile and reached for his cravat.

Sebastian said, "Out of curiosity, where were you last night?"

"Me? White's. Why?"

"Until when?"

"Two? Maybe three."

"And then you went home?"

"Yes. I made an early night of it." The Baronet kept his gaze on the mirror, his focus on the intricacies of his neckcloth. "Please tell me you aren't seriously suggesting that I might have had something to do with what happened to Ash. I understand your compulsion to try to protect your niece, but you won't do it by shifting the blame to me. Believe me, you'll have far better luck with Princess Ivanna."

"Oh? Why's that?"

Paige turned from the mirror, his eyes now crinkled with genuine amusement. "Look into her. You'll see."

CHAPTER 7

Sebastian pondered the Grand Duchess's presence in London as he drove toward the Pulteney Hotel.

Her Imperial Highness Grand Duchess Catherine Pavlovna of Russia had taken London by storm. Gorgeous, incurably dramatic, and just twenty-five years old, she possessed a knack for playing to the crowds that greeted her with roars of acclaim whenever she drove through the streets or showed herself on the balcony of the Pulteney Hotel—which she had hired in its entirety for a vast sum. Yes, she was haughty and demanding, with an inordinately excessive opinion of herself. But she responded to the people's cheers with smiles and a wave of her hand, and they loved her for it.

Sebastian had heard that George, the Prince Regent, despised her.

Part of the Regent's animosity, Sebastian knew, stemmed from the simple fact that he hated anyone the people loved, including his own eighteen-year-old daughter. But Sebastian suspected that didn't explain all of it—or the fact that the antipathy was reportedly mutual. The two royals were said to have despised each other on sight.

The problem was, Sebastian couldn't begin to imagine how or why Ashworth could have become involved with the Russians. There'd been a time when his father, the Marquis of Lindley, had played an influential role in government, having served first as Master-General of Ordnance and then as Foreign Secretary. And Sebastian had heard that despite his age, the old Marquis still felt duty bound to take his seat in Parliament whenever it was in session. But, unlike his father, Ashworth had never shown any interest in public affairs, preferring to spend his time gambling and riding to hounds and playing his nasty bedroom games. So of what possible use could such a man be to the Tsar's wily sister or anyone in her retinue? It made no sense.

But that didn't mean it wasn't true.

The Pulteney Hotel stood on the corner of Piccadilly and Bolton Streets, overlooking the gentle acres of Green Park. It occurred to Sebastian as he sent his card up to Princess Ivanna Gagarin that the Pulteney was less than two blocks from Ashworth's house on Curzon Street.

A lady traveling in the household of Her Imperial Highness the Grand Duchess didn't receive just anyone. But no member of a diplomatic delegation to the Court of St. James was going to turn away the son and heir of the Chancellor of the Exchequer. Princess Gagarin received Sebastian in a pleasant parlor overlooking the hotel's cobbled mews. She was attended by a hatchet-faced older woman in black who sat silently tatting in the corner and a barrel-chested, mustachioed colonel in the green-and-white uniform of the elite Imperial Guard.

"Lord Devlin," said the young Princess, greeting him with a wide smile. "What a pleasant surprise. How kind of you to call and make us feel welcome."

Sebastian bowed low, acutely aware of the stiff, unsmiling officer watching them from his position by the hearth. "Thank you for seeing me."

Like her mistress, the Grand Duchess, Princess Ivanna Gagarin was somewhere in her twenties, slender and of above average height, with gleaming dark hair and milky white skin. There was a distinctly Slavic cast to her features, her face flat and wide, her cheekbones pronounced, her nose small. She was not a beautiful woman, but she was undeniably attractive, with a raw earthiness that somehow managed to be both subtle and powerful.

She introduced the burly, full-faced officer as Colonel Nikolai Demidov. The colonel clicked his heels, gave a jerky bow, and grunted. She did not introduce the older woman. The Princess then offered Sebastian wine, which he politely refused, and invited him to sit, which he did. The colonel simply remained standing by the hearth,

48

a silent but unforgettable presence. And all the while they went through the rituals of polite society, Sebastian was conscious of Princess Ivanna quietly assessing him, her eyes half-hidden beneath thickly lashed lids.

She had unusual eyes, he noticed; almond shaped and of a light frosty gray that made him think of the steppes of Asia in winter. If those eyes were anything to go by, he decided, she was more than capable of tying a man to his bed and turning his chest into a bloody mess.

"I know why you are here," she said, fingering the lace edging of her elegant silk gown's low neckline in a way that drew his attention—as he knew it was meant to.

"You do?"

"Mmm. We're told you have a reputation for investigating murders, and Viscount Ashworth has just been murdered—quite spectacularly, yes?" She spoke good English, with a pronounced French inflection rather than a Russian accent. But then he had heard that many Russian woman of her class spoke no Russian at all.

He said, "Do you mind if I ask how you knew him?"

"We met at a loo-party given by Countess Lieven." Countess Lieven was the wife of the Russian ambassador to London, Kristofer Anreyevich Lieven, and if rumor was to be believed, she had slept with a goodly percentage of the most powerful men in the British government.

"And you quickly became . . ." He paused, searching for the right word, and finally settled on, "Friends?"

"That surprises you?" She leaned forward ever so slightly, her fingers still playing with the lace edging of her bodice. She had full, high breasts, and her gown was cut to show them to advantage. "I enjoy beauty in all its many forms, and Lord Ashworth was an undeniably attractive gentleman. Handsome and intriguing."

"When did you last see him?"

"Just yesterday. In the afternoon."

"For any particular reason?"

"He called to return a book he had borrowed."

"And did you see him again last night?"

She tipped her head to one side. Her lips were still smiling, but the expression in those exotic eyes was utterly unreadable. "I did not. Are you suggesting I might like to play Viscount Ashworth's games, my lord?"

The question was both an abrupt attack and a telling revelation. He glanced at Colonel Demidov, but the Russian was staring woodenly into space, his face set in stiff, hard lines.

Sebastian said, "You know about Ashworth's . . . games?"

"I have heard of his tastes, yes."

"Was that one of the things that . . . intrigued you?"

He expected her to take offense—or at least pretend to. Instead, she relaxed back in her chair and smiled. "You could say that."

The colonel by the hearth never moved, while the silent woman in the corner kept her attention on her tatting and might have been deaf for all the heed she seemed to be paying to their conversation. Sebastian chose his next words carefully. "Would you happen to know of other women who . . . found Ashworth intriguing?"

She shook her head. "Sorry; no."

"Do you know if he'd quarreled with anyone recently? Or if there was someone who might have threatened him or wished him harm in any way?"

A faint frown puckered her high white forehead. "Actually, he did mention some beastly shopkeeper who's been more than tiresome. But if he gave the man's name, I fear I do not remember it."

"A shopkeeper?"

"A shopkeeper or a tradesman. I don't recall precisely. But I gather the man was becoming quite a nuisance. He actually threatened him."

"Threatened him? How?"

"I don't believe Ashworth said. He—" She broke off as the door from an adjoining room opened and a vision in black silk and exquisite lace swept into the room with an air of theatrical grandeur worthy of the stage.

Even if Ivanna Gagarin had not hastened to present him, Sebastian would have had no difficulty recognizing the new arrival as Her Imperial Highness Grand Duchess Catherine. He'd heard her described as a strikingly attractive woman, and she was, with curling dark hair, brilliant flashing eyes, and the overbearing manner of someone who expects to be the center of attention—and doubtless sulked spectacularly when she was not. But then, she was the daughter of one Tsar, the sister of another, and the widow of a German Prince. Sebastian suspected she'd been indulged and catered to her entire life. She was dressed in deep mourning for her late husband, Prince George of Oldenburg, although it occurred to him that her bereavement didn't prevent her from traveling widely or attending the numerous banquets and balls given in her honor.

"I have met your father, the Earl," she said in French as Sebastian bowed low. "He is a shrewd man, but very cautious, yes?"

"I'd say that's a fair assessment, yes, Your Highness," said Sebastian.

She let her gaze travel over him in open appraisal. "You look nothing like him."

"I am told I resemble my mother."

"You must." She did not sit, but prowled restlessly around the room, as if requiring the movement as an outlet for her boundless energy.

"I take it you are here because of this ghastly murder we are hearing so much about. Is it usual, in England, for noblemen to involve themselves in such matters?"

"Not usual, no."

"Yet you do?"

He found himself wondering why the sister of the Tsar of Russia was here, now, asking probing questions about an investigation into the murder of a man she must have barely known, if at all. But he kept that thought to himself. "As it happens," he said, "the dead man was my niece's husband."

The Grand Duchess exchanged a swift, surreptitious glance with her noble lady-in-waiting, then said, "But his murder is not the first you have chosen to investigate, no?"

"No, Your Highness."

She raised one carefully arched eyebrow. "You have many murders in London?"

"No more than most large cities, I suspect."

"It is a very large, busy city, this." Her nose wrinkled in disgust. "We were advised that the Pulteney is a hotel of the greatest gentility. But, *ppff,* it is noisy. First, I was given a room overlooking the mews, only to be awakened at half past six by carts with men ringing bells and shouting, 'Dust-ho.' Then came more carts with rattling pewter pots and bawling vegetable sellers. So I moved to rooms overlooking Piccadilly, only to discover that from midnight until past five, a steady stream of carriages goes back and forth always. And there is this watchman person who endlessly announces the hour and weather—as if anyone trying to sleep cares. Why must they do this thing?"

She looked at him in a way that told him she both expected a response and considered the obvious answer—that the calls were intended for those *not* sleeping—to be irrelevant. He said, "I suppose because it has always been the custom, madame."

"Ppff," she said again in disgust. "You English have customs the most strange."

There seemed no reply to that, and so he bowed again to the ladies and the silent colonel, and took his leave. To his surprise, Ivanna Gagarin walked with him to the parlor door.

"Lord Ashworth told me he was related to you by marriage," she said, stopping him on the threshold.

"Did he? Why was that, I wonder?"

"He said you'd threatened to kill him."

"On more than one occasion, actually."

She rested a hand fleetingly and ever so lightly on his arm, and he was surprised to feel his skin crawl. His reaction to her was that powerful, that visceral. She said, "It makes for an interesting dynamic, does it not? For you to investigate the murder of a man you yourself threatened to kill?"

He held himself perfectly still. "If nothing else, I suppose it gives me some insight into the motivation of his killer."

A calculating, malevolent gleam showed in the depths of those wintry eyes. But all she said was, "Perhaps. Or perhaps not."

And then she turned and left him without a backward glance.

CHAPTER 8

Sebastian wasn't prepared to take anything Princess Ivanna Gagarin told him at face value. But on the off chance there might be something to her tale of a "beastly shopkeeper," he decided to pay another visit to Curzon Street. If an angry merchant had been personally dunning Ashworth, his staff would know about it.

Ashworth's butler, Fullerton, was an ancient, wizened relic with watery, myopic eyes, wispy white hair, and liver-spotted, palsied hands. His demeanor was that of an elderly family retainer, and Sebastian had always wondered why Ashcroft hadn't pensioned the old man off long ago. Now he thought he understood: a tired, indulgent, doddering old man would likely remain ignorant of—or at least choose to overlook—behavior and incidents that would drive away a younger butler.

"Sir Henry and the constables have all gone, my lord," said Fullerton, blinking, when he opened the door to Sebastian. "And we've instructions from his lordship to keep everyone out of the Viscount's chamber until his lordship overcomes his grief enough to deal with it. Locked up, it is."

"Actually," said Sebastian with a pleasant smile, "I was wondering if I might have a moment of your time. There are a few questions I'd like to ask you."

Fullerton took a step back. "Me, my lord?"

"Mmm. Has Ashworth's valet turned up yet?"

"No, my lord." He ushered Sebastian to a seat but insisted on remaining standing himself, his hands folded together behind his back.

"What was the valet's name, again?" asked Sebastian.

"Digby, my lord. Edward Digby. It's most curious," added the old man with a shake of his head. "Can't think where he's taken himself off to. Most improper to disappear like this without warning."

"How long has he been with the Viscount?"

"Five or six years, my lord."

"And how long have you been with his lordship?"

"Me?" The old man allowed himself a faint smile. "Why, I've known his lordship since he was born. Used to be down at Lindley Hall in Devon, you see. The Marquis, he was al! for having me retire, but then Lord Ashworth offered to take me on here."

"That was very kind of him," said Sebastian, who doubted Ashworth had ever deliberately done a kind thing in his life.

"I'm not one to want to spend my last years sitting in a chair by some cottage fire," said the old man, his jaw jutting out.

"I can see that," said Sebastian. "Who do you think killed his lordship?"

"Me?" Fullerton looked surprised by the question. "As to that, I couldn't say, my lord."

"No?"

"No, my lord."

"What about Ashworth's valet, Digby? Could he have done it?"

"Digby?" The aged butler indulged himself with a faint sneer. "Wouldn't think he had it in him, my lord. Thing is, the paltry fellow can't abide the sight of blood. Cut his lordship one day while shaving him and fainted dead away. Wasn't worth much the rest of the day either." Fullerton leaned forward and dropped his voice. "You did see the state of his lordship's bedchamber this morning?"

"I did."

Fullerton nodded and straightened with a creak. "You ask me, it looked more like an abattoir than a gentleman's bedroom. Digby would've crumpled into a sniveling puddle if he'd seen it."

"So where do you think he's gone?"

"Well, he has people down in Kent. Mayhap he's taken himself there, although I've no notion why he'd go off like this without telling anyone."

Sebastian could think of several reasons, but all he said was "Do you know of any shopkeepers or tradesmen with whom Ashworth might have quarreled recently?"

Fullerton held himself quite still. Only the faint widening of his eyes and a spasm along his jawline betrayed him.

"There is someone," said Sebastian, watching him.

The butler brought up a hand to pull at one earlobe. "His lordship had a long-standing belief that tradesmen, shopkeepers, and merchants should consider themselves honored to be given the privilege of serving him. Saw their demands for actual payment as something of an insult, he did."

"I wouldn't imagine very many of them agreed with that philosophy."

"No, my lord."

"So who amongst those his lordship 'honored' with his patronage has complained recently?"

"Most complained for a time. Those who kept at it and didn't give up sometimes got half of what they were owed." He paused. "Eventually."

"Anyone not satisfied with that?"

"We—ell." Fullerton looked thoughtful. "There's a fellow over on Long Acre who sold his lordship some furniture last September. Cut up something fierce when his lordship refused to pay for any of it."

"How large of a bill are we talking about?"

"Three thousand guineas, I believe."

Sebastian was surprised into making a low whistle. "That's a hefty sum." A housemaid in a gentleman's establishment rarely made more than fifteen pounds a year.

Fullerton nodded. "At one point, his lordship

offered the fellow eight hundred, but he refused to take it. He's been following his lordship around, demanding the entire sum—quite loudly. Even stood outside White's one day, telling anyone and everyone who'd listen that his lordship was a dishonorable cheat. His lordship threated to call the authorities on him."

"Did that stop him?"

"Not for long. Showed up here just a few days ago, he did, threatening to make his lordship pay—'One way or another,' he said." The butler's eyes widened in that way he had, as if seeing something for the first time. "You think he might be the one who did that to the Viscount?"

"It certainly sounds possible. What's this fellow's name?"

"McCay, my lord. Lawrence McCay."

"When was this, exactly?"

"That he last came around? Must've been Tuesday or Wednesday, I'd say."

"How did Ashworth react?"

The butler's thin nose twitched. "Laughed in the fellow's face, he did. Told him to go ahead and try."

By the time Sebastian reached Long Acre, the afternoon was still fine, the blue sky above only faintly hazed by the smudge of coal smoke and dust that normally hugged the city. But it was late enough that the light soaking the upper stories of the old brick shops and houses had taken on the golden, tea-colored hues of approaching evening, and the raucous muddle of carts, wagons, carriages, donkeys, and barrows clogging the street already lay in shadow.

There'd been a time long ago, in the days when Henry VIII seized this area along with the convent gardens to the south that became known as Covent Garden, that Long Acre had been a simple lane cutting across fields and pastureland belonging to Westminster Abbey. Building here didn't begin in earnest until the arrival of the Stuarts. For a while, the district had been prosperous and fashionable, but the street was now given over to coach makers, wainwrights, upholsterers, and cabinetmakers. Sebastian suspected it would be difficult for any of these businesses to sustain a three-thousand-guinea loss to a spoiled, arrogant marquis's son who viewed tradesmen's bills as impertinent insults unworthy of payment or even notice.

McCay & Sons, Fine Furniture Emporium, sprawled across a row of three old brick houses on the corner of Long Acre and Cross Lane that probably dated back to the days of Charles I. It was an impressive establishment that included, besides the front showroom, or "ForeWare Room," a "glass room" for mirrors, a joinery shop, a marble hall, a chair-making workshop, an upholstery room, and a gilding room. When

Sebastian pushed open the showroom door, a bell jingled, and a dark-haired young woman who'd been reading a newspaper spread out atop an elegant rosewood chest straightened and turned toward him with a welcoming smile. "May I help you?"

Sebastian handed her his card. "I'm looking for Lawrence McCay. Is he in?"

She fingered the card, her smile fading as she read it. But then, given the establishment's recent experience with Ashworth, Sebastian supposed a certain amount of hostility toward a random viscount was to be expected. "I'm sorry; he's just stepped out." She paused, then repeated with a marked reduction in enthusiasm, "May I help you?"

Sebastian let his gaze drift around the nearly empty showroom. From the looks of things, Ashworth's default had forced McCay to sell much of his display stock to stay afloat and pay the tradesmen who worked for him. "I understand Viscount Ashworth was one of your customers."

She shifted to stand behind the chest, as if she felt the need to put some sort of barrier between them. She was an attractive woman probably in her early twenties, built small but strong, with a square chin, short nose, and shrewd brown eyes narrowed with hostile suspicion. "Why are you here asking about him?"

"He's dead."

"I know." She nodded to the open newspaper. "I was just reading about his murder."

"Oh? How much detail do they go into?"

"A great deal. Is it true? Was he really found tied to his bed and hacked to death?"

"Essentially, yes."

She gave a curt nod of approval. "Good. I hope he suffered. Maybe he even thought about the way he cheated us as he lay dying—although I doubt it."

Sebastian studied her pretty, hard-set face. Nothing missish about this young woman. "I understand he owed Lawrence McCay money."

"He did. More than three thousand guineas." She shook back her hair. "What do you think our chances of recovering it from his heirs are?"

"From what I'm hearing, they can't be worse than your odds of recovering such a sum from Ashworth himself."

A succession of emotions chased one another across her features, comprehension and chagrin followed instantly by fear as she realized that Lawrence McCay made an obvious suspect and that the bluntness of her speech had not been wise.

Sebastian said, "You're Lawrence McCay's wife?"

"Daughter." Her gaze strayed for one telling instant toward a corridor that opened onto a rear woodyard and sawpit—now standing idle—and a curtained alcove that probably led to a private office. She looked away again quickly, but he had heard it too: the soft approach of a man's footsteps, followed by the faint breathing of whoever was standing there listening.

Sebastian said, "The sign reads 'McCay and Sons'; you've brothers?"

"Not anymore. They're both dead."

"So it's just you and your father?"

"Yes. Why?"

Rather than answer, Sebastian said, "Tell me about your dealings with Ashworth."

She shook her head, her gaze hard on his face. "What is your interest in all this?"

He came to rest his hands on the edge of the chest that lay between them and leaned into it, his gaze holding hers. "Anthony Ledger was my niece's husband, but I am under no illusions as to what manner of man he was. He was a vile, dangerous hedonist who harmed more people in his life than we will ever know. Like you, I am glad he's dead. But his father is a wealthy, powerful nobleman, which means that someone will be arrested for Ashworth's death, whether truly guilty or not. If you have nothing to hide, you would be wise to cooperate with me."

He could see the pulse beating wildly in her slim white neck; her eyes were huge. "Why should we trust you?"

"Let me put it this way: Your father's name has

already been mentioned, and he is likely to come under scrutiny from Bow Street whether you cooperate with me or not. But believe me when I tell you I mean you no harm and that if I am able to help you, I will."

"I don't believe you."

He shoved away from the chest. "If you should change your mind, my address is on the card."

He was reaching for the door when a middle-aged man he took to be Lawrence McCay hurried into the showroom and said, "Wait."

Like his daughter, McCay was built short and solid. His once dark hair had faded mostly to gray, and the years had scored deep smile lines beside his eyes and mouth. Lines that now seemed out of place in a gravely troubled face.

"Mr. McCay?" said Sebastian, turning.

The man nodded. The fear in his eyes was impossible to miss, but his jaw was clenched. "I didn't kill the bastard. I won't deny I wanted to, but I didn't do it."

Sebastian said, "But you did threaten to make him pay—'one way or another'?"

"I did."

The girl came from behind the chest in a rush. "Papa—"

He put out a hand, stopping her. "There's no sense in me trying to deny it, Julie. There's more'n enough heard me say it. But I didn't mean I would kill him. I just wanted him to pay what he owed me, and, failing that, I figured I'd do my best to make damned sure everyone knows what he does. How he hurts people—little people, like us."

"I know what he was like," said Sebastian.

McCay's daughter made a harsh, scoffing sound in her throat. "Do you? Ashworth came close to ruining us. He did it as deliberately and casually as a normal person might step on a bug. Men like him, they think their wealth and lineage give them the right to do whatever they please to anyone weaker or poorer than they are. And you know why they think that way? Because it's true—they always get away with it. Always. No one stops them. No one dares to stop them. And there's no real way for those they harm to fight back."

"Someone obviously stopped him," said Sebastian.

"Good," said McCay. "I'm glad someone finally had the courage to do it. But it wasn't me."

Sebastian studied the older man's closed, hard face. "Where were you last night?"

"Here. We live upstairs."

"You didn't go out?"

"No."

"Can you prove it?"

McCay glanced toward his daughter, then shook his head. "How can a man prove he was in his own bed, asleep? My wife's been dead these thirteen years."

"When did you last see Ashworth?"

McCay rubbed his forehead with a splayed thumb and forefinger. "Must've been Tuesday or Wednesday; I'm not sure which."

"You went by his house on Curzon Street?"

The merchant nodded. "I was delivering an invoice. At first, I used to just send them, but the last few months, I've taken to delivering them myself."

"Why?"

McCay twitched one shoulder. "Hoping he'd see me. Hoping maybe I'd see him, so I could tell him what I thought of him."

"Perhaps even follow him to White's, shouting at him the whole way?"

Another twitch of the shoulder. "Look—there's only one way somebody like me can make a man like him pay, and that's by hurting his reputation. Shouting what he's done to the world."

"There are other ways," Sebastian said quietly.

"Maybe. But I'm not a violent man. You can ask anyone; they'll tell you. I might lose my temper and shout, but I've never been one for brawling."

Sebastian had no trouble believing that. The problem was, Ashworth hadn't been killed in a brawl. Whoever murdered him was either a woman frightened by one of the bastard's erotic "games" or someone who executed him in a cold and calculated revenge.

"He's telling the truth," said McCay's daughter.

"My father may be stubborn, but he's never hurt anyone. There must be scores of shopkeepers and tradesmen who've been ruined by Ashworth."

Sebastian studied her set, angry face. "Can you name others?"

McCay said, "Anyone that bastard did business with, he cheated if he could. It was like a game with him—a matter of pride, a way to show that he was the one with the power, while the rest of us . . ." His face spasmed. "The rest of us were like nothin' to him. He liked to toy with people. Walk all over them. Make them hurt and then crush them. He was an ugly human being and I'm glad he's dead, but I didn't kill him. Not because it would have been morally wrong, because it wouldn't have been. I'm just too much of a coward. But I'm grateful to whoever finally had the courage to wipe him from the face of the earth, and I pray to God that bastard burns in hell for all eternity."

Sebastian let his gaze drift around the nearly empty showroom. "What furniture did you sell him, anyway?"

Father and daughter exchanged glances. Neither spoke.

But Sebastian knew. "One of the pieces was the bed, wasn't it?"

Julie McCay simply stared back at him. But her father sucked in a deep, shaky breath and nodded.

CHAPTER 9

"Troublesome," said Sir Henry Lovejoy as he and Sebastian walked along the terrace of Somerset House. "I find it odd that none of the servants said anything to my constables about a furniture maker shouting threats to the Viscount in the streets."

"Not as odd as one might think," said Sebastian, pausing to stare out over the sun-sparkled Thames. There was a chill in the air as the sun sank toward the west, painting the sky with splashes of pink and purple reflected gloriously in the multicolored water. "Given the way Ashworth treated shopkeepers and merchants, I suspect it was a relatively common event. It probably didn't occur to them to mention it."

Sir Henry's lips flattened in disgust. "Is Ashworth's valet still missing?"

"Last I heard, yes."

"Perhaps he is our killer after all."

"According to the butler, he faints at the sight of blood."

Lovejoy glanced over at him. "You think that eliminates him as a suspect?"

"Maybe not. I won't deny I'd like to know more about him."

"I'll set one of the lads to seeing what he can

learn about the fellow," said Lovejoy as they turned away from the river. "Have you spoken to Paul Gibson?"

"No. Why? Has he finished Ashworth's postmortem already?"

"He has. Seems the Viscount wasn't attacked with an ax after all. He was stabbed, probably with something like a butcher knife."

"A knife? How many times would you need to stab a man to make that kind of a mess of his chest?"

Lovejoy lifted his face to the growing wind, his eyes dark and troubled. "Apparently too many to count."

Sebastian's friendship with the Irish-born surgeon, Paul Gibson, dated back to a time when both men wore the King's colors and fought the King's wars from Italy and the Peninsula to the West Indies. Even after a French cannonball took off the lower part of his left leg, Gibson had stayed with the regiment. But the rigors of the campaign—combined with the phantom pains from his missing limb and the opium he used to control them—eventually proved to be too much. And so he'd come here, to London, to teach at the hospitals of St. Bartholomew's and St. Thomas's, and to set up a small surgery on Tower Hill in the shadow of the city's ancient Norman castle.

By the time Sebastian reached Tower Hill, the

daylight was fading fast. This was one of the oldest sections of London, its low stone or timber houses dating back to the days of the Tudors and beyond. In times gone past, it had been the site of execution for nobles fallen out of favor with the king and rebels caught on the battlefield. For some, death had come quickly with the hiss of a falling ax. But most had been forced to endure agonizing, hours-long tortures so hideous that Sebastian fancied he could sometimes still catch the echoes of their screams reverberating through the ancient alleyways and lanes.

For some reason he could not have named, he found himself thinking about those long-dead victims as he knocked at the door of the old stone house Gibson shared with a mysterious Frenchwoman named Alexandri Sauvage. She had lived with Gibson for more than a year now, although she steadfastly refused to become his wife. And she both disliked and distrusted Sebastian for reasons he had to admit were more than valid.

"Ah, it's you," she said when she answered his knock. She was a small woman perhaps a few years older than Gibson, fine-boned and thin, with pale skin, a head of luxurious flaming hair, and eyes that told Sebastian she had not forgotten— would never forget—that he had killed her lover four years before in the mountains of Portugal.

She took a step back to allow him to enter, then

closed the door behind him with a snap. "You know where to find him."

Sebastian turned to look at her. "Still? I thought he'd completed Ashworth's autopsy."

"He has."

Gibson performed his autopsies in a stone outbuilding at the base of what had not long ago been an overgrown, vaguely sinister yard. But he also used the building for surreptitious dissections performed on cadavers filched from London's overcrowded churchyards by gangs of body snatchers known euphemistically as resurrection men. Sebastian assumed the Irishman must be working on some new "specimen." But when he reached the dank single-roomed building, he found Ashworth still lying on the elevated stone slab that stood in the center of the room. Gibson was bent over him, doing something in the cadaver's abdomen that Sebastian had no desire to look closely enough to identify.

"I thought you were finished with him?"

"With the postmortem," said the surgeon, looking up with a grin. He was in his mid-thirties, although he looked older, his dark hair heavily touched by gray, his face gaunt, and his frame leaner than it should have been, thanks to the opium. But he was still the most brilliant anatomist Sebastian knew, and he'd made death and its effects on the human body his specialty.

"I was just taking a wee look at a few things. No point in letting a perfectly good cadaver go to waste."

"It's getting dark," said Sebastian.

"Unfortunately." Gibson laid aside his scalpel with a sigh. "I wish to God I had your bloody eyesight."

Sebastian starred down at the raw, pulpy mess that Ashworth's murderer had made of his chest. "You're certain this was done by a butcher knife?"

"Either that or something like it." The surgeon reached for a rag and wiped his hands. "It wasn't a hatchet or an ax, if that's what you're thinking. The killer stabbed him over and over again—and then hacked at him a few dozen more times, just for good measure. Your killer obviously wanted to make damned sure he was dead."

"I suppose someone might do that if they were very frightened."

"Either frightened, angry, or just plain crazy."

"Any whip marks on him?"

"No, none. Why?"

"There was a whip mixed up in his bedclothes."

"It wasn't used on him."

Sebastian shifted his gaze to the Viscount's calm, handsome face. "He died quickly?"

"Quickly but not instantly—at least not from all the blood I'm told was splattered over his bed. One of the first stab wounds must have hit a major artery rather than the heart itself. So the heart kept pumping, sending the blood everywhere. Unless you know what you're doing, the heart itself is hard to hit. Too protected by the sternum and ribs."

"So he—or she—kept stabbing, trying to get the heart to stop beating."

Gibson nodded. "And then just kept stabbing and stabbing. I'm surprised he didn't break the knife."

"I'm wondering if the killer brought the knife with him or found it in his lordship's bedchamber."

"Well, this is Ashworth we're talking about."

"True."

Sebastian went to stand in the open doorway, looking out over the yard. Little more than a year ago, this had been a wasteland of dying weeds and the occasional inexplicable mound of raw earth. But over the passing months, Alexi Sauvage had managed to turn it into a place of peace and beauty, with clumps of sweet-smelling gillyflowers, tulips, wallflowers, and peonies, their blooms now showing pale and ghostlike in the gathering gloom.

Unfortunately, her attempts to rescue Gibson from himself had been less successful.

"How is your niece taking this?" asked Gibson, watching him.

"To be honest, she's grateful he's dead—as is

74

virtually everyone who knew the bastard except, I suppose, his father. And maybe one very indulgent old butler."

"You still think Ashworth helped kidnap those street children out at Clerkenwell and Bethnal Green?"

"Yes."

"So maybe someone connected to one of them did this."

Sebastian watched him reach for a sheet to cover the dead nobleman's corpse. "Now, that's a possibility I hadn't considered. Except how would they know to blame him?"

Gibson shook his head. "That I can't explain."

"Hang on a minute." Sebastian came to crouch down beside the body, his gaze on the dead man's left wrist. He went next to check the other wrist, then pushed the sheet aside to look at the ankles. Someone had cut away the silk ties that once bound him, and it was as if they had never been. "I don't see any sign of abrasions on either his wrists or ankles from the cords that tied him to the bed frame."

"There aren't any."

Sebastian looked up. "There's no doubt in my mind that he was murdered in that bed. But he must not have been tied down until after he was killed."

"Maybe. Except the only blood on his hands was splatter, and there are no defensive cuts or bruises of any kind, the way you'd expect if he were fighting someone off. Those first stab wounds didn't kill him. So if he wasn't tied down, why wasn't he grabbing at the knife and trying to stop whoever was killing him?"

"I suppose he could have been drugged."

"He could have been. Although it's just as likely he simply passed out drunk, and whatever frightened woman he was abusing took advantage of his stupor to kill him. He had enough alcohol in him that you can still smell it."

Sebastian leaned forward and sniffed. But all he smelled was blood and death.

He straightened and went to stand at the doorway again, his hands on his hips, his gaze on the darkening sky. The light had almost vanished from the day, leaving a world of death-haunted shadows and secrets.

"You're worried about something," said Gibson, watching him. "What?"

Sebastian glanced back at his friend. What could he say? *I'm afraid because this bastard's twisted evil was too close to my family, and even though he's dead, I'm not convinced he's done hurting them. I'm afraid because the darkness within men like this seems to seep into everything and everyone they touch. I'm afraid because it's not beyond the realm of possibility that a vulnerable, fragile young woman I love might actually have done this.*

But, of course, he couldn't say any of those things.

He saw light flicker in the kitchen of the medieval house, and the slender form of a woman passed on the far side of the ancient mullioned window. Gibson said, "How about a pint before dinner?"

Sebastian let out a long breath. "Sounds good." But as the two friends walked back across the yard, he thought for one suspended moment that he caught the echoing scream of a long-dead man.

And the roar of the crowd that had once assembled for the joy of watching him die.

CHAPTER 10

By the time Sebastian made it back to Brook Street, night had long since fallen, bringing with it a haze that wreathed the rows of streetlamps with pale, misty haloes.

He sent Tom off to the stables with the horses, then paused for a moment, his gaze on the wind-tossed trees in the distant square, his thoughts far, far in the past. He was remembering a sunny day long ago when he'd been a young man about to go off to war and Stephanie a child of perhaps eight. He'd taken her out for an afternoon of simple pleasures—a regatta at Chelsea, ices at Gunter's, a walk in the park. She'd been so absurdly delighted, so obviously grateful for his attention, that it cut him to the quick to realize how lonely her life must be. And it grieved him too to realize how oblivious he had been to the pain and want of a niece he professed to love.

At one point, while they watched the regatta, she had frightened him by teetering on the edge of the quay with the deadly rush of the river beneath her, the wind blowing her hair and her face alive with the heady delight of it all. He'd been shaking when he pulled her back to safety, but she'd only laughed. And he'd known then that there was more than a wildness to her.

78

She possessed deep within her an urge to push boundaries and walk on the thin, ragged edge of destruction, as if compelled to tempt fate or even welcome it.

"I wish I could go with you," she'd said later that afternoon, when he was driving her home.

He'd laughed. "To war?"

"Yes."

"Unfortunately, there's more to war than handsome uniforms, magnificent horses, and the glory of homecoming."

She'd turned her head to look at him, her eyes solemn with a wisdom that didn't belong in a child. "You think that's what appeals to me, Uncle? The uniforms and horses and chance for glory?"

"Evidently not," he'd answered, suddenly serious. "My apologies for underestimating you. So, what does?"

"They say it's the ultimate test of one's mettle, don't they? A chance to experience life at its most raw, when it's most . . . real. And then . . . die."

He'd felt a chill wash over him. "You want to die, Steph?"

A strange smile played about her lips. "Doesn't everyone?"

"Actually, no."

She'd stared at him a moment before turning her face away. "Then they're luckier than they realize."

It was a conversation that had haunted him ever since. And he felt again, now, that sense of having failed her, of never quite grasping the elusive pain that drove her hurtling through a troubled life. He was missing something, he thought as he turned to mount his front steps. He'd always missed something.

But what?

"Ah, there you are, my lord," said Morey as he opened the door.

Sebastian's gaze fell on a familiar hat and cane resting on the hall table. "Hendon?"

"Yes, my lord. He's with her ladyship and young master Simon in the drawing room."

Sebastian swung off his driving coat and handed it with his own hat and gloves to the majordomo. Then he mounted the stairs to find the man known to the world as his father sitting beside a cheerful fire and dangling fourteen-month-old Simon on one knee.

Alistair St. Cyr, the Fifth Earl of Hendon, was nearing seventy now, his thinning hair long since gone white, his heavyset, once-tall frame beginning to stoop. He was laughing when Sebastian entered the room, the little boy's hands clinging to Hendon's thick, blunt fingers as he bounced his knee up and down. For a moment, Sebastian paused, conscious of a warm tightening in his chest as he watched them. Technically the child was only distantly related to Hendon through his grandmother. But that didn't stop the Earl from loving Simon with a fierceness that was impossible to miss.

Then Hendon looked up and saw Sebastian, and the laughter faded from his blunt-featured face. "I came back to town as soon as I heard," he said, grasping the little boy around his sturdy waist and setting him down on his feet.

Simon's face crumpled, and Hero, who had been standing nearby, stepped forward to swing the little boy up into her arms as he began to cry. "I think someone's ready for bed. Say good night, then."

Hendon made a big show of wishing the child pleasant dreams. But as soon as Hero left the room, he turned to Sebastian and said, "Is it true, what they're saying in the papers? That Ashworth was found tied naked to his bed?"

"Yes. With red silk bonds."

"Bloody hell." Hendon watched Sebastian walk over to pour two glasses of burgundy. "Any idea yet who did it?"

"None whatsoever, although there was a black leather whip mixed up in the bedclothes."

"Bloody hell," said Hendon again, taking the drink Sebastian held out to him. Hendon rolled the wine in its glass, his gaze on the swirling ruby liquid, his lips pursed. "You've spoken to Steph?"

"I have, yes."

He looked up. "And?"

"She says she didn't do it."

Sebastian expected Hendon to explode at him, to insist that *of course* she hadn't done it; that only a fool could think even for a moment that his granddaughter might have committed murder. Instead, he took a deep swallow of his wine and said, "You believe her?"

"I honestly don't know."

Hendon nodded, his face strained. "I wouldn't blame her if she did."

Sebastian went to stand beside the hearth, his gaze on the small blaze. "Neither would I."

"Is she in danger of being accused?"

"Not yet."

"Please tell me you've at least found other suspects."

Sebastian looked up. "There's a shopkeeper who had good reason to kill the bastard, and I might even be inclined to think him guilty if Ashworth had been found in an alley with his head bashed in. But under the circumstances, I'm afraid we're looking for a woman—probably someone who took fright at what Ashworth was doing to her. I suppose it's technically possible that someone just happened to find him passed out and tied to his bed and took advantage of the situation to murder him. But it seems rather doubtful."

"There's no one else besides this shopkeeper?"

"I'm looking into a woman he was involved with. And his valet is missing. If we're lucky, he'll be found and confess to the murder before anyone has enough time to start thinking that Stephanie might have done it."

Hendon pushed to his feet and went to stand at one of the windows overlooking the darkened, misty street. "I saw Ashworth myself just a few days before I left for Oxford."

"Oh? Why?"

Hendon stood with his hands clasped behind his back, his jaw working silently in that way he had when he was thoughtful or troubled. He was the kind of man who never allowed himself to be hurried into speech, who chose his words carefully and deliberately. And so Sebastian swallowed his impatience and waited.

After a moment, the Earl said, "It was utterly by chance. I was in Swallow Street, looking at the demolitions they've started for Nash's New Street."

"It's really going to happen, then?"

"Oh, yes. There's talk of calling it 'Regent Street,' although I suspect the Prince is optimistic that by the time it's actually under construction, it'll be called 'George the Fourth Street.'"

"Nothing like hopefully anticipating your own sire's death." Sebastian took a sip of his wine. "So, what was Ashworth doing in Swallow Street?"

"I don't know. I actually didn't speak with

him myself. I'm not certain he even saw me. John Nash has a young associate, a Welshman named Russell Firth. He's a bright, personable fellow—I knew who he was because I'd met him before, when he and Nash were making their presentations before the Commissioners of Woods and Forests. That's who Ashworth was talking to—arguing with, in fact."

"Firth?" Sebastian had met the young architect himself through Hero. "What were they arguing about?"

"I couldn't hear. But there's no doubt their words were heated. I wouldn't have thought much about it, except . . ."

"Yes?"

Hendon swiped one thick, blunt-fingered hand across his lower face. "I'd just seen the fellow— Firth—a few days before, with Stephanie. They were standing by the Serpentine in Hyde Park."

"Doing what?"

"Simply standing together by the water. Talking. Laughing."

Sebastian studied Hendon's troubled face. "Stephanie might not be the insufferable snob her mother is, but somehow I find it difficult to believe she's suddenly taken to consorting with some random architect-builder. There's probably a simple explanation."

"There could be." Hendon shook his head. "Except . . ."

"Yes?"

Hendon let out his breath in a heavy sigh. "It was the way she was looking at him that caught my attention." He hesitated, then pushed on. "I may be an old man, but I recognize that expression. She was looking at him the way a woman looks at a man who interests her. And he was looking right back."

"Hendon thinks Stephanie is having an affair with Russell Firth?" said Hero later that night when Sebastian finally had an opportunity alone to tell her about it. "An architect? *Stephanie?*"

She was curled up in a chair beside their bedroom fire with Sebastian seated at her feet. He tipped back his head to look up at her. "I agree it sounds improbable, but Hendon isn't given to flights of fancy. Even if Steph isn't actually having an affair with the fellow, there must be something there for Hendon to have been struck by it."

"You think that's why Ashworth was having words with Firth? Because he suspected the man was sleeping with his wife?"

"Possibly."

Her lips parted as she drew in a troubled breath. "If Hendon saw them and leapt to such a troubling conclusion, other people must have as well. This isn't good."

"No," said Sebastian. "No, it isn't."

CHAPTER 11

Saturday, 2 April

"We used t' live in Swallow Street when I was a wee tyke," Tom said the next morning as Sebastian guided his horses east toward the doomed street.

The day had dawned cool and overcast, the air heavy with the smell of coal smoke and horse droppings and the promise of rain. Sebastian threw a quick glance back at his tiger. The boy rarely spoke of the days when his father was still alive, of the life he'd lived before his mother was transported to Botany Bay and his brother hanged for theft at the age of thirteen. "You did?"

Tom nodded. "Are they really gonna tear it all out so's they can put in some fancy new street?"

"Most of it. Or at least that's the plan."

The Prince Regent's grand project to plow a new avenue through London had been sparked by the reversion to the Crown of a stretch of rural parkland known as Marylebone on the northwest outskirts of the city. Originally, the scheme simply called for the construction at Marylebone Park of a palatial summer residence for the Prince surrounded by several dozen villas amid what he wanted to rename "Regent's Park."

But the vision was soon expanded by a proposal to punch a magnificent new artery through the preexisting neighborhoods on the edge of the West End, thus creating a sweeping avenue of high-end shops and houses that would connect the Prince's new summer residence to his existing palace of Carlton House on Pall Mall. This "New Street" would have the added happy benefit of dividing the wealthy, privileged inhabitants of Mayfair from less fashionable, fading areas such as Soho and Golden Square, and the even more insalubrious stretches of London that lay to the east. The Regent's favorite architect, John Nash, was overseeing the vast project. But so great was its scope that Nash was forced to bring in other builders and architects such as James Burton and young Russell Firth.

Firth was still in his late twenties, but he'd already made something of a name for himself. The son of a successful Cardiff builder, he'd won a scholarship to Cambridge at the age of sixteen and then received the university's prestigious Worts Traveling Bachelorship, a stipend that enabled him to spend three years studying antiquities in Asia Minor, Greece, and Italy. It was a unique background that combined a solid grounding in classical architecture with a builder's grasp of the realities of construction. If the Regent's grand rebuilding scheme ever came to fruition, Sebastian suspected it would owe more to Firth than to the Prince's favorite architect, Nash.

As he turned in to Swallow Street, Sebastian at first found it difficult to believe the street was slated for demolition. The roadway was thronged with carts and wagons; pedestrians passed back and forth on the pavement; children shouted and laughed; dogs barked. But then he noticed the stretches of already empty shops, the windows of their upper stories blank. What had once been an aged public house on a far corner was already being reduced to rubble, and Sebastian spotted Firth himself deep in conversation with the foreman of the work crew.

"I shouldn't be long," said Sebastian, pulling in close to the kerb and handing the boy the reins.

The architect was just turning away from the half-demolished building when Sebastian hopped down and walked toward him. He was attractive in a quiet, unassuming way, of above average height and slim, with lightly curling fair hair and even features. When Sebastian had seen him before, at the Royal Society, his dress had been that of a respectable, relatively affluent man of affairs. But today he looked like what he was—an architect-builder not afraid of getting his clothes dirty on a construction site.

At the moment, his attention was focused on a notebook he held in one hand. Then he looked up, caught sight of Sebastian, and paused, his eyes narrowing and his face smoothing into a blank mask as he let Sebastian walk up to him.

"Good morning," said Sebastian. "I don't know if you remember—"

"I know who you are. And I can guess why you're here."

"Oh?"

Firth held his head at a proud angle, his eyes hooded and wary. "I saw the newspapers. I don't imagine you've randomly decided to take a break from investigating the murder of your niece's husband simply to come and have a look at our progress on the Regent's New Street."

"Fair enough. Then let's be blunt, shall we? You were recently seen arguing with Ashworth. Here, actually. Just a few days before he was killed. Care to tell me why?"

The air filled with a clattering bang and an explosion of dust; someone in the distance laughed. Firth threw a glance over his shoulder at the demolition, then said, "Is there a reason I should?"

"When it comes to murder, cooperation is always a good idea. Unless one is guilty, of course. Then I suppose a semblance of cooperation is probably the best way to go."

Firth stood with his hands on his hips, his jaw set hard. "You can't seriously think I killed him. Why would I?"

"I don't know. Why were you arguing with him?"

He went to toss his notebook on a nearby rough worktable and began sorting through a stack of papers held down by a brick fragment. "We weren't arguing, exactly. Ashworth was interested in hiring me to rebuild the facade of some manor house of his down in Kent. I refused."

"Why?"

Firth glanced over at him. "Why what?"

"Why did you refuse?"

"Because the bastard has—had—a well-earned reputation for not paying people who work for him. I was pretty blunt about my reasons for turning him down, and he got a bit nasty as a result."

It all sounded believable. Except of course it did nothing to explain the private interlude with Stephanie that Hendon had witnessed beside the Serpentine in Hyde Park.

Sebastian said, "I understand you know Lady Ashworth."

For one telling moment, Firth paused at his paper shuffling, then resumed it almost at once. "I do, yes. We met at a lecture I gave last spring on the Greek temple of Poseidon at Sounion."

"Stephanie attended a lecture on ancient Greek architecture?"

"You say that as if it surprises you. You obviously don't know your niece as well as you think you do."

"Obviously not," agreed Sebastian. "But I

gather that wasn't the only time you've met her."

Firth gave up fiddling with the papers and swung to face him. "No. No, it wasn't. But I hope you're not suggesting that somehow implicates me in her husband's death."

Sebastian studied the younger man's smooth, tense face. "Who do you think killed him?"

Firth gave an incredulous laugh. "How would I know?"

"You must have some theory about what happened."

Firth shook his head. "He was an arrogant, nasty bastard who cheated and abused everyone. And do you know why? Because he was always—*always*—allowed to get away with it."

"Someone evidently decided not to let him get away with it anymore."

"Good," said Firth. "It's too bad it didn't happen long ago. But it wasn't me."

"Where were you last night?"

"Home. Asleep."

"Any way to verify that?"

"No." His gaze shifted to a couple of workmen stacking stones from the half-dismantled public house into a wagon. And for one unguarded moment, the man's facade of angry belligerence cracked, allowing a glimpse of the yawning fear that lurked behind it. Firth carefully set the brick on his papers again, his attention all for his task.

"You know something," said Sebastian, watching him. "What is it?"

Firth looked up, his face strained.

"Tell me."

The architect gave an uncomfortable shake of his head, as if disturbed by what he was about to say. "It may be nothing, but I did hear he was being blamed for the death of a young woman. Seems he forced himself on her, and she killed herself because of it. Word is, the mother vowed to make him pay for the rest of what she promised would be a short life."

"What was the woman's name?"

"I don't think I ever knew. Or if I did, I don't recall it."

"Who told you this?"

"I overheard it at a Royal Society lecture. I wasn't familiar with the people who were talking, but I caught Ashworth's name and it drew my attention."

"Because of your friendship with his wife, you mean?"

Firth looked suddenly, unexpectedly young and vulnerable. "I don't know if I'd call us friends, exactly."

"Oh? What word would you prefer? 'Acquaintances'?"

"Something like that, yes."

"You're not doing yourself any favors, you know," said Sebastian. "Trying to hide whatever is between you and my niece."

Firth stiffened in a way that reminded Sebastian that while the man might be young, he had the kind of courage and fortitude necessary to travel alone for three years through war-torn Europe and the wilds of the Middle East. "I don't know what you're talking about."

"Oh, you know," said Sebastian, and walked back toward his curricle.

Half an hour later, word came from Sir Henry Lovejoy that Ashworth's valet had been found. Dead.

CHAPTER 12

The naked body of Edward Digby lay sprawled against the soot-stained wall of a rubbish-strewn alley not far from Ashworth's Curzon Street house. He was turned almost onto his left side, face out, his arms flung up over his head, eyes wide and staring. In life he'd been a plump little man with thinning dark hair, a simpering, superior manner, and fastidious ways. It occurred to Sebastian, looking at him, that the valet would be mortified if he could see himself now, lying amidst mushy cabbage leaves and reeking puddles of urine, the pasty white flesh of his body smeared with the alley's muck. Something—probably either a foraging pig or rats—had been nibbling at the man's feet. But except for a faint trickle of dried blood beside his mouth, there was no hint as to how he'd died.

"Who found him?" asked Sebastian, hunkering down beside the dead man.

Sir Henry Lovejoy stood near a pile of broken crates, his hands in the pockets of his greatcoat, his shoulders hunched against the cold, damp wind that was kicking up. "A baker's boy who ducked into the alley to relieve himself."

Sebastian touched the valet's hand. He was utterly cold, and when Sebastian carefully moved the dead man's arm back and forth, he found the stiffness of rigor mortis nearly gone. A faint greenish hue was even beginning to creep into the dead man's face and neck.

"Gibson will know better than I," said Sebastian, "but it looks to me as if Digby might have been killed the same night as Ashworth."

"Telling, I suspect," said Lovejoy. "Although I'm not sure what it tells us."

Sebastian pushed to his feet. "Have you had a look at his back yet?"

"Not yet." Lovejoy nodded to one of his constables, who stepped forward to roll the dead man onto his stomach.

Digby landed facedown in the muck with a soft plop, his right arm flinging out in a way that for one horrible instant came close to imitating life.

"*Ooff,*" said the constable, his breath leaving his lungs in a rush as he leapt aside. The dead man's back was ripped and crusted with dried blood.

Lovejoy stepped forward, peering over the rims of his spectacles. "So he's been stabbed. Not with the same violence as Ashworth, but a fair number of times."

Sebastian cast a thoughtful glance around the narrow alley with its piles of stinking rubbish. "I wonder what the hell he's doing here, a couple of blocks from Ashworth's house?"

"It's hard to believe he could lie here for a day

and two nights without someone seeing him," said Lovejoy. "Except why would anyone kill him, keep his body someplace else for thirty-six hours, and then dump him here?"

Sebastian brought his gaze back to the once prim and proper man now lying naked at their feet. "And where the hell are his clothes?"

Lord Ashworth's aged butler, Fullerton, had a cold. His nose was red and running, his eyes more watery than ever. He sat in a chair before the fire in the servants' hall, a shawl wrapped around his shoulders and a cup of hot tea cradled in both hands.

"My lord!" he exclaimed when Sebastian was shown into the basement by a flustered footman. "What was Alan thinking, bringing you down to the servants' hall like this? Let me just—"

"No, please, don't get up," said Sebastian as the old man struggled to heave himself out of the chair. "The footman told me you weren't well, which is why I had him bring me here. I have some questions I need to ask you about Lord Ashworth's valet."

Fullerton settled back in his chair. "Edward Digby?"

"That's right."

The old butler sniffed. "Heard he's been found dead in an alley up the street."

"Where did you hear that?"

"From the kitchen maid, Nell. She had it from the baker's boy."

"Ah." Sebastian settled into a nearby chair. "I'd like to know more about Digby. You said he was originally from Kent?"

"Aye. Still has family there, I'm told—although he didn't have much contact with them that I could tell."

"He's been with the Viscount five or six years?"

"Five. I gave it some thought and realized it was only five. A little less, actually."

"Do you know who he was with before he came to his lordship?"

Fullerton frowned. "I did know. Let me think on it. It might come. I seem to recall the fellow died."

"Five years is a long time. He and Ashworth got on well?"

"Well enough," said the old family retainer, more guarded now that the conversation was circling back to Ashworth.

"What manner of man was he?"

"Digby?" Fullerton drew a handkerchief from his pocket and wiped his nose. His movements were slow and deliberate, as if he were using the time to choose his words. "Can't say I knew him well. Kept pretty much to himself, he did. Bit uppity, you see."

"Yet over the course of five years, a butler with your experience in dealing with servants must have formed a measure of the man."

"True, true." Fullerton sat up a bit straighter. "Very careful of his dignity, was Digby. Considered himself above the touch of everyone else in the hall, he did—and he wasn't the least hesitant to show it either. Always let everyone know he was in the master's confidence in ways the rest of us weren't. Lorded it over the others, he did, casting hints about how he knew things no one else did."

"What sort of things?"

Fullerton looked away, his watery eyes blinking rapidly. "His lordship's appetites were . . . Let's say they were prodigious and unusual."

"His sexual appetites, you mean?"

"All his appetites. Believed in living life to the fullest, did his lordship."

"Did Digby form a friendship with anyone in the household?"

"Digby? Hardly. Like I said, weren't any of us up to snuff, as far as he was concerned. Added to which, of course, nobody liked him."

"Because he was proud and disdainful?"

Fullerton threw a quick look around as if to make certain they were alone in the hall. Then he leaned forward and lowered his voice. "Wasn't just that. He was a sly, sneaky thing. You never knew what he was up to, that one."

"Oh? Do you think he was the sort someone might have bribed?"

Fullerton gave a snort. "If somone'd offered him enough money? Of course."

Sebastian studied the butler's aged, wrinkled face and sunken eyes. "I'm told the front door was found unbarred the morning after Ashworth was killed."

Fullerton nodded and settled more comfortably in his chair again. "That's what Jenny said."

"Jenny is one of the housemaids?"

"Mmm. Jenny Crutcher. Said she found the bar down and a bloody handprint on the door's inside panel. Time was, I always locked up at night myself. But Digby's been doing it more and more for the past few years. And he always handled it on those occasions when his lordship was entertaining a female guest."

"So Digby would put the bar in place after he'd escorted his lordship's lady friend from the house?"

The butler nodded.

"What sort of females did his lordship 'entertain'?"

Fullerton wiped his nose again. "I was never privy to his lordship's confidences in that regard," he said with great dignity. "But . . ."

"But?"

"Digby did like to talk, you see. To hear him tell it, his lordship's tastes varied at a whim, from ladies of quality to bits of muslin or whatever pretty young shopkeeper's assistant might catch his eye and take his fancy."

"Did Digby say anything about the woman

Ashworth planned to entertain the night of his death?"

The butler sneezed hard and blew his nose. "I don't recall it, no, my lord."

Sebastian pushed to his feet. "I think I'd like to have a word with the housemaid you say found the door unbarred yesterday morning. Jenny, wasn't it?"

Fullerton nodded. "Jenny Crutcher. But I'm sorry, my lord; she's not here anymore."

Sebastian knew a quiet bubble of concern. "Are you saying she's missing too?"

"No, my lord; she quit."

"Quit? When?"

"Yesterday evening, my lord. Packed her things and left, she did, without even waiting for the wages that were owed her."

"She's the one I heard screaming hysterically yesterday?"

"No, my lord; that was Alice. She's always been more than a tad harebrained, has Alice. Jenny's nothing like that."

"Do you know where I might find Jenny?"

Fullerton scratched his cheek with the nail of one middle finger. "Can't say's I do, my lord. But I can ask the staff if you'd like. One of them might know."

"Yes, please do."

Sebastian was descending the front steps of Ashworth's town house when an elegant carriage

100

drawn by four highbred bays and with a familiar crest on the door drew up before him with a rattle of chains and a clatter of hooves. The near window was let down with a bang.

"Fortuitous," said the King's powerful cousin Charles, Lord Jarvis. "Climb in. I wish to speak with you."

Sebastian looked up to meet his father-in-law's hard gray eyes as a liveried footman hurried to open the door and let down the steps. "Why?"

"Do you seriously expect me to shout what I have to say in the street for all to hear?"

The relationship between Sebastian and Hero's father had always been strained, but never as much as it was now, thanks to the events of the previous September. Sebastian was tempted to tell him to go to hell. Instead, he said, "Wait while I tell my tiger to follow us."

Sebastian turned to have a word with Tom, then came back to leap up into the carriage. The footman was still closing the door when Jarvis said, "What the devil were you doing talking to Grand Duchess Catherine of Oldenburg?"

Sebastian studied his father-in-law's full, still-handsome face, the arrogant aquiline nose and sensitive lips that were so disconcertingly similar to Hero's. "I presume you've heard Ashworth is dead?"

"Of course I've heard," snapped Jarvis. "What has that to do with the Grand Duchess?"

"Nothing that I know of. But there's a Princess Ivanna Gagarin in the court of the Tsar's decidedly colorful sister. I'm told she arrived in London some weeks ago to prepare for Her Imperial Highness's visit."

"She did, yes."

"How much do you know about her?"

"She's the widow of Prince Mikhail Gagarin, who fell at the Battle of Borodino. The Gagarins were once the sovereign rulers of Starodub and are still highly influential in Russia. I hope you don't mean to insinuate that she had something to do with the death of your niece's unpleasant husband?"

"It's not beyond the realm of possibility, given that she is said to share at least some of Ashworth's more unusual sexual interests."

Jarvis withdrew a pearl-studded gold snuffbox from one pocket. "Something I trust you intend to keep to yourself—for your niece's sake if nothing else."

Because you care so much about Stephanie, thought Sebastian. Aloud, he said, "If your dear cousin were still alive, we could add him to our list of suspects. Fortunately, he's not."

Eyes narrowing, the older man flipped open his snuffbox, lifted a pinch to his nostrils, and sniffed. His movements were slow and unruffled. But Sebastian knew his father-in-law well; knew by the tightening of his lips that Sebastian had touched a nerve.

"I won't have you causing an international incident by involving the Tsar's sister in some tawdry murder." Jarvis closed his snuffbox with a snap. "Leave the Grand Duchess and her delegation alone."

Sebastian signaled the coach driver to pull up. "I'll keep your concerns in mind," he told his father-in-law. Then he pushed open the door and hopped down, ignoring the footman who was rushing to let down the steps.

"I mean it," said Jarvis, leaning forward.

Sebastian turned to look back at him. "I've no doubt that you do."

CHAPTER 13

They called them "bone pickers," "rag gatherers," "rag-and-bone men," or sometimes simply "street finders." A thousand-strong army of grimy men and women, they fanned out across London every day from sunup to sundown, carrying tattered bags bulging with their finds and sticks with spikes or hooks they used to turn over heaps of refuse in their search for the rags and bones that formed the bulk of their trade.

"It's a good enough livin'," said Bill Mullet, the rag-and-bone man who'd agreed to talk to Hero for a shilling. "Good as most, I reckon."

Because of the damp, cold wind, they stood in the protective lee of the high brick walls of a sprawling brewhouse that fronted the Thames not far from St. John's Churchyard. Hero's coach and two footmen waited beside them, for this was a gloomy section of the City of Westminster, crowded with almshouses, bridewells, charity schools, woodmongers, and wharfs. And yet just a short walk up Millbank Street and Abingdon lay Old Palace Yard and the Houses of Parliament.

"I don't ever see children doing this," said Hero, her notebook braced against her ribs as she scribbled notes.

"That's 'cause they really can't, m'lady," said

Bill Mullet. He was a sandy-haired, lean man somewhere in his forties or fifties, with blood-shot eyes, unshaven cheeks, and an unhealthy yellowish cast to his skin. His ragged coat and breeches were greasy from the bones that formed the bulk of his stock-in-trade, and his shoes were so broken down that Hero noticed he limped when he walked. "Bag's too heavy."

"How heavy does it get?"

He kicked the bulging sack he'd set down for their interview. "Can weigh as much as forty pounds by the end of the day, I reckon. You see some women doin' it if they're strong. But it ain't easy, walkin' twenty t' thirty miles a day, haulin' a load like this."

"How many hours a day do you work?"

"Get up before dawn, I do, and keep at it as long as there's light. Then I go home and sort what I got in me bag."

"Sort it?"

"Aye. Got t' sort the rags," he said in a tone that suggested he thought her a bit slow, not to know something so obvious. "The rag shops and marine-store dealers, they'll give ye two t' three pence a pound fer white rags. But if they're colored, or even if they're white but dirty, ye'll only get tuppence fer five pounds of 'em."

"So how much do you earn in a day?"

"On a good day, I can get as much as twelve, maybe fourteen pence—as long as it don't rain.

Ye can't sell wet rags." He squinted up at the ominously gray sky and shook his head.

"That must make things difficult in winter," said Hero.

"Oh, aye. That it does, m'lady. But folks eat more meat in winter, so I tend t' find more bones then." He gave a sudden grin, displaying a mouth containing swollen gums and no more than half a dozen teeth. "Once I found a handkerchief with two shillings tied up in the corner. That was the best day I ever had."

Hero felt a painful ache swell in her chest. "What sort of diet do you typically consume?"

He looked confused. "Diet?"

"What do you usually eat?"

"Oh. Well, I have me bread about midday. Then I'll have a bit more bread fer me supper."

"Just bread?"

"Sometimes a householder'll give me a bone with some meat on it, so I'll save that and have it with me supper."

Good Lord, thought Hero. Aloud, she said, "How long have you been a rag-and-bone man?"

"Oh, long time. Me da used t' work on the docks, only he died when I was a wee lad. At first, I couldn't do much more'n run errands, but then I got big enough to do this. Course, I couldn't carry much in them days, so I was only making four or five pence a day." A cloud of apprehension shadowed his features. "It's the same way when ye get old. Ye cain't walk as far nor carry as much."

"Do you pick up anything else besides rags and bones?"

He gave another grin. "If'n I find somethin' I can sell, t' be sure. I see cigar ends, I always pick 'em up and put 'em in me pocket till I get enough t' sell. I'll pick up anything if I can sell it."

"Have you ever been married?"

A faraway look of sadness crept into his eyes. "Once, long ago. Her name was Marie, and she was the prettiest little thing you ever did see. But—" His voice caught, and he had to swallow before he could continue. "She died one winter, and that was that."

"I'm sorry," said Hero, her own throat tight.

He nodded and swiped his sleeve across his nose. "Had a wee babe, we did. A little boy. But he didn't last much longer than his ma."

"Did you ever . . . Did you ever think of doing anything else?"

"Besides bein' a street finder, ye mean?" He considered the question a moment, then shrugged. "I guess when I first started, I figured I'd do it fer a little while and then move on t' somethin' different. But the years jist slid away from me and somehow it never happened. Now I can't even remember what it was I thought I wanted t' do." He wiped his nose on his sleeve again and reached to pick up his bag. "Can I have that shilling now, please, m'lady? I'd best get movin' before it comes on t' rain."

Hero was standing beside her carriage and watching Bill Mullett limp down the lane, when she was surprised to see Devlin walking toward her. He was wearing a buff-colored driving coat with a cascade of capes at the shoulders and had his high-crowned hat tipped at a rakish angle, and she found herself smiling.

He nodded to where the ragged man was stooping to pick up some new treasure and stuff it in his bag. "So is he a bone picker or a pure finder?"

"A bone picker. You can tell because he carries a bag rather than a basket."

"Oh."

She said, "Were you looking for me? Has something happened?"

He drew her hand through the crook of his arm and turned their steps toward the river. "I want your opinion."

They walked up Mill Bank Street toward the horse ferry landing, where a line of pollard oaks and beeches beckoned like a leafy oasis at the edge of Westminster's foul warren of dirty, squalled lanes.

"Your father just went out of his way to track me down and threaten me," said Sebastian.

"He threatened to kill you?"

"He didn't specify."

"Ah." She kept walking. "Then it was probably meant simply as a general first warning." She glanced over to find him smiling. "What's so funny?"

"You say that as if it were an everyday thing, for a woman's father to threaten to kill his daughter's husband."

"Huh," she said.

He laughed out loud. "I was under the impression the Prince and the Tsar's sister did not exactly hit it off."

"They didn't. I'm told the antipathy was instant and intense, although I haven't heard the reason."

"So why is Jarvis so anxious to keep me away from the Grand Duchess? I mean, I can understand a general desire not to displease the sister of one of the Allied Sovereigns. But somehow I had the impression there was more to it than that."

"If there is, I don't know about it." They'd reached the river now, near where a single row of decent houses had been built facing the water. Beyond that stretched open country with market gardens scattered amongst wasteland and marshes where tall grasses and cat's tails danced in the wind. Hero paused and drew the cold, wonderfully fresh air deep into her lungs. "I could pay a visit to Jarvis House. See what I can learn."

"He won't tell you anything. Not now that he knows I'm interested."

"No. But if I go early this afternoon and catch my dear cousin Victoria alone, she might."

Sebastian glanced over at her but wisely chose to say nothing. Hero's attitudes toward her cousin Victoria were . . . complicated.

They paused to watch the horse ferry pull away from the far bank and work its way toward them across the gray, wind-whipped water. Hero said, "Did you speak to Firth?"

"I did. He claims the quarrel Hendon observed grew out of Ashworth's attempts to hire him to redesign the facade of some manor house."

"Do you believe him?"

"Not exactly. He was definitely lying about something. I'm just not sure about what. But he did give me one piece of information that may prove useful: He says Ashworth forced himself on some girl who later committed suicide."

"That doesn't surprise me."

"No," he agreed. "Supposedly the young woman's mother vowed to make him pay."

"Does Firth know her name?"

"He says no."

"Ah. So how do you go about finding something like that out?"

He watched the ferry as it drew closer. It was near enough now that they could hear its ancient timbers groaning as it plowed through the rolling water. "If it's well enough known that Firth has heard the whispers, then surely Ashworth's good friend, Sir Felix Paige, will have heard about it."

She looked over at him. "Yet he didn't mention the woman to you before, when you asked him who might have killed Ashworth."

"No, he didn't. And I can't help but wonder why."

It was still unfashionably early when Sebastian reached Sir Felix Paige's town house on Cork Street—far too early for a gentleman to be receiving visitors. The Baronet's fastidious butler tried to deny him, but a few carefully veiled insinuations convinced the man to go off and see if his master would receive him.

Sir Felix was seated on a low stool in his dressing room, clad only in breeches and an open shirt while his valet bustled about shaving him. "I trust this is important," said the Baronet, not even bothering to glance toward the door when Sebastian was shown up by a nervous footman.

Sebastian went to stand beside the window overlooking the street. "It is if you consider murder important."

"Still on that, are you?"

"Yes."

The Baronet kept his head perfectly still as the valet eased the razor up one soapy cheek. Only his eyeballs slid sideways. "And you think I might have acquired some useful information in the last twenty-four hours? I haven't, you know."

"No new theories?"

"None."

"Tell me about the girl Ashworth raped. The one who recently committed suicide."

Sir Felix shifted his gaze to the far wall. The silence filled with the scrape of the valet's razor sliding across his master's face.

"I take it you did hear about it?" said Sebastian.

"I heard the talk. Didn't believe it, of course."

"You didn't? And here I thought you knew Ashworth well."

Sir Felix's jaw flexed. "He wasn't as bad as people thought."

"Actually," said Sebastian, "he was far worse."

When Sir Felix remained silent, Sebastian said, "The young woman—what was her name?"

"I've no idea."

Sebastian watched the valet use a cloth to carefully wipe the last traces of shaving soap from his master's face. "Leave us," Sebastian said to the man.

The valet's eyes widened as he looked from Sebastian to his master. Sir Felix sat forward. "Seriously, Devlin? You can't go around giving orders to another man's servants."

Sebastian pushed away from the window. "I thought you might not want your man to hear what I have to say. But if you don't mind it spreading all over town—"

Sir Felix caught his valet's eye and nodded toward the door. "Go." He waited until the man left, then came up out of his chair in a rush with his fists clenched. "If you ever try something like that agai—"

Sebastian caught the Baronet by the front of his shirt and swung him around to slam his back against the wall with a thud that rattled the pictures in the room. Sir Felix bucked, then went still when Sebastian shoved one forearm up under his chin and leaned into his windpipe. "Don't. Don't even think about threatening me."

"What the d—"

"Your dear friend Ashworth used to help Sir Francis Rowe kidnap, rape, and kill street children. *Children.* Do you expect me to believe you didn't know that?"

Sir Felix made a faint gurgling sound.

"Shut up," hissed Sebastian, leaning in harder. "For all I know, you helped them too. Did you? *Did you?*"

"Can't . . . breathe," gasped the Baronet.

Sebastian eased up on him a bit. "Understand this: I'm going to find the answers I need, even if it means destroying you in the process. *Now, what was the name of the young woman who killed herself?*"

"I don't know," croaked Sir Felix.

Sebastian started to lean in hard again, but the man gasped and said, "Wait! I honestly don't know. All I know is that there was some scandal about a French fortune-teller at a soiree a few weeks ago. I'm surprised you didn't hear about it—it was quite the *on dit* at the time. I wasn't there, but you can surely find someone who was."

"What soiree?"

"At the home of the Marquis of Egremont."

Sebastian took a step back and let him go. "If you're—"

He broke off as Sir Felix came away from the wall in a lunge, leading with a right hook that grazed Sebastian's chin before he could bring up his forearm in a sweeping block.

"Bloody hell," swore Sebastian, burying his fist just below the Baronet's sternum.

The air left Sir Felix's lungs in a *whoosh* as he doubled over and went down on one knee. Sebastian grabbed the man's shoulders and slammed him back against the wall again. "When I asked you yesterday who you thought might have killed him, you didn't say anything about some French fortune-teller."

"I didn't think about her, damn you. For all I know, the story about the girl killing herself is just that—a story."

"If the fortune-teller exists, I'll find her," said Sebastian, who had an aunt known to be close friends with the Dowager Marquesa of Egremont. "If not, I'll be back."

CHAPTER 14

Born Lady Henrietta St. Cyr, the elder sister of the current Earl of Hendon, the Dowager Duchess of Claiborne was officially although not technically Sebastian's aunt. But neither Sebastian nor the Duchess had ever allowed that technicality to interfere with their relationship.

She was in her seventies now and had been a widow for five years. But she still lived in the grand Park Lane mansion to which she had come as a bride of eighteen. On those occasions when her son, the current Duke of Claiborne, to whom the house actually belonged, came up to London, he stayed with his family in a much smaller house in Half Moon Street. It occurred to Sebastian as he climbed his aunt's steps that the St. Cyr women seemed to make it a habit of maintaining possession of their late husbands' houses even in widowhood. But whereas his relationship with his half sister, Amanda, had always been strained, he adored his aunt Henrietta.

She was a large, dignified woman, white haired, with her brother's bulky build and a massive bosom. She resembled Hendon too much to ever have been pretty, even when young. But she had a tall, magnificent carriage and stately presence, and she had always possessed superb taste in clothes.

He found her seated beside the fireplace in her morning room, wearing a round circassian robe of emerald velvet decorated at its high waist and hem with rows of silver and emerald tassels. She'd been reading a book but laid it aside when he entered. "Well, I suppose I should thank you for not coming to visit me at some ungodly hour for a change," she said.

"Reading again, dear aunt?" He bent to kiss the rouged cheek she turned up to him. "If you're not careful, people are going to start calling you a bluestocking."

"Not for reading Byron. Everyone is mad about him these days." She pulled a face. "The poetry is pleasant enough, I suppose, if you enjoy that sort of thing. But he's still shockingly bad *ton*." Aunt Henrietta's opinion of Byron had never recovered from the night she encountered him relieving himself in a potted plant in the lobby of Steven's Hotel.

She leaned forward now as she stared at Sebastian, and he realized she was studying his chin. "Good heavens, Devlin, have you been engaging in fisticuffs?"

Sebastian put up a hand to finger the swollen graze on the side of his jaw. "Not exactly."

"Huh." She settled more comfortably in her chair. "I assume you're here because of Stephanie?"

"You've heard about Ashworth?"

116

"I doubt there's anyone in London who hasn't heard about Ashworth. I won't pretend I'm sorry he's dead, but I do wish he could have found a way to achieve that happy result in a less sensational manner."

"Have you seen her? Steph, I mean."

The Dowager shook her head. "Not yet. Poor girl. Can't think what she was about, getting mixed up with such a bounder. But at least she's managed to be rid of him quickly. Amanda must be crushed. She was positively besotted with the idea of her daughter becoming a marchioness."

"She can console herself with the thought that her firstborn grandson will someday be a marquis."

"There is that," she agreed. "Now, out with it. Why are you here? And don't even think of trying to bamboozle me into believing it's because you've suddenly been overcome by a hankering for the pleasure of my company. I know what you're like when you're investigating a murder." She paused. "At least, I assume you're trying to find out who killed him—although I can't think why. If you ask me, it's good riddance to bad rubbish."

"I agree. Unfortunately, there's a distinct possibility that Ashworth was killed by a woman."

"Oh, dear." She sat perfectly still, one hand coming up to press against her lips. "Not—oh, surely not Stephanie?"

"I honestly don't know. Did you by chance attend a soiree given by Lord and Lady Egremont a few weeks ago?"

"I did, yes. But what has that to say to anything?"

"I'm told they brought in a fortune-teller to entertain their guests."

"They did, yes; a card reader. They've become shockingly popular, you know. It beggars belief how many otherwise perfectly reasonable people can swallow such nonsense."

"Do you remember this particular fortune-teller's name?"

The Dowager frowned. "I should. Give me a moment. She's French—or at any rate she did a good job of pretending to be. And she has a rather pronounced limp. Supposedly her leg was crushed in one of the Revolutionary *journées*, although goodness knows if that's true."

"Ashworth was there?"

"He was, yes. That I do recall, because the fortune-teller singled him out specifically. At first, he was a good sport and played along with her. But then she started talking about some girl who'd killed herself because of him and supposedly laid down a curse that would hound him to hell. Needless to say, the atmosphere in the room changed markedly. He tried to laugh it off, but people were looking at him, and there was more than a bit of whispered speculation. He left soon after."

"Was Steph with him?"

"No. I believe it was not long after the twins' birth. Although the truth is, I don't think anyone has seen them together for months."

"She tells me they agreed to go their separate ways if she was delivered of an heir."

"Then she was lucky; not only an heir but a spare as well, both in one fell swoop." The Dowager was silent a moment, her plump, beringed fingers absently playing with the tassels on her gown, her face thoughtful. Then she shook her head. "I keep thinking the woman's name is on the tip of my tongue, but I can't seem to grasp it. I guess my memory isn't what it used to be. I'm afraid I'm getting old."

"Nonsense. You can remember every scandal that has rocked the *ton* in the last fifty years. But given your conviction that fortune-telling is all a farrago of nonsense, I suspect you didn't pay much attention to Madame Whatever-her-name-is."

"Blanchette," said Aunt Henrietta suddenly in triumph. "Madame Marie-Claire Blanchette."

Leaving the Dowager's house some minutes later, Sebastian paused at the top of the steps, his gaze on the rolling green expanse of Hyde Park on the far side of Park Lane. The rain that had begun just after noon had ended, leaving the grass sodden and the trees dripping. He was turning toward his waiting curricle when a lady's barouche dashed past, drawn by a team of dapple grays. He caught a quick glimpse of its occupant's flawless profile and guinea gold hair beneath a black widow's bonnet. Then she was gone.

"Wait here," he told Tom. "I shan't be but a moment."

The barouche was already slowing down before the stately detached house that took up all of the next block. By the time Sebastian reached Lindley House, the carriage had stopped and a footman was letting down the steps. Sebastian held out his hand to his niece. She hesitated a noticeable instant, then put her hand in his and let him help her alight.

"Uncle," she said with a bright smile that didn't come close to reaching her eyes. "This is unexpected."

She was wearing a deeply somber black gown made high at the neck and without a touch of adornment. Her bonnet, gloves, and shoes were all black. She looked every inch the grieving young widow, and it was all—all—for show.

"How are you, Steph?" he asked, drawing her out of earshot of the footman and abigail who were assembling armloads of paper-wrapped purchases. "Honestly."

Her color was high, her eyes brittle with what he realized was quietly seething rage. "Honestly? I just spent two hours in Bond Street shopping for mourning clothes while everyone stared at me as if I were a two-headed giraffe. No one actually came up and asked me to my face if I killed Anthony or ever let him tie me naked to the bed. But they didn't hesitate to whisper about it to one another—and quite loud enough for me to hear."

"You could leave town for a while," he suggested. "After the funeral."

"You mean run away and hide?"

"Until the tattle-mongers move on to something new. They will, you know. Eventually."

"Eventually."

He searched her strained, tightly held face. "How is Lindley taking it?"

"To be honest, I'm worried about him. His doctor has been warning him about his heart for months and giving him all kinds of potions that don't seem to do any good. I'm afraid Ashworth's death is going to kill him. It must be unbearable, burying your own child—however horrid that child may be. And Lindley has already buried three."

"I didn't know he'd had other children."

She nodded. "A younger son who died at fifteen, and two little girls he lost as infants." Her face relaxed with a hint of a smile. "He worries about the twins constantly. He's always climbing up to the nursery just to check on them. If anything is going to get him through the pain of losing his son, I suspect it'll be the boys. I couldn't take them away from him simply so that I could go hide in the country."

"He could go with you. It might do him some good as well."

She let out a soft sigh. "I can try. But I suspect he takes his responsibilities in Parliament far too seriously to leave while they're still sitting."

Sebastian watched a young nursemaid shepherd her charges across the street toward the park. What he had to ask his niece wasn't just delicate; it was potentially insulting, and he wasn't quite sure how to go about bringing it up.

He came at it sideways. "I didn't realize Ashworth had an estate in Kent."

"He does, yes. It's small but pleasantly situated near Brighton. A maiden aunt left it to him." She paused. "Why?"

"I'm told he was interested in redoing the facade."

Sebastian saw the flare of raw panic in her vivid blue St. Cyr eyes before she half lowered her lashes and turned her face to stare out over the misty park. "I believe he was, yes."

"Do you recall the name of the architect he was interested in engaging?"

Her breathing was rapid enough now to flutter the black ribbons of her bonnet where they lay against her throat. "You don't seriously imagine that Ashworth would discuss such things with me, do you, Uncle? That's not what women are for—at least, not in his mind."

"I did warn you not to lie," Sebastian said softly. "Not when you're talking about murder."

"Are we talking about murder? I thought we were discussing architecture."

"Firth. The architect's name is Russell Firth. And don't try to pretend you don't know him, because you've been seen together."

She took a step back, her nostrils flaring, her eyes wide. "All right. Yes, I know him. He's brilliant. But he had nothing to do with Ashworth's death. To suggest otherwise is ridiculous."

"Is it?"

"Ashworth was killed while tied naked to his bed with red silk cords, and his clothes were strewn all over the room. You know the kinds of games he liked to play. You should be looking for the woman he was 'playing' with that night rather than casting nasty aspersions on a fine architect."

"Actually, I'm doing both."

She started to turn away, but he laid a hand on her arm, stopping her. "One more question, Stephanie. Do you know anything about a young woman who is supposed to have committed suicide after Ashworth raped her?"

"I'm told there was some incident involving a card reader at Lady Egremont's soiree a few weeks ago. I wasn't there, but there's not a tattletale in London who could resist making certain I'd heard of it."

"You don't know anything more about it?"

"No. Anthony and I didn't discuss his latest rapes." She glanced toward Lindley House and said calmly, "I really must go, Uncle."

He took his hand from her arm but touched her cheek ever so gently before letting it fall. "I wish you'd trust me, Steph."

"Trust is a dangerous luxury I learned to do without at the age of seven," she said, then walked away, a tall, seemingly self-possessed woman whom he now knew to be far more fragile than he'd ever realized.

CHAPTER 15

It didn't take Sebastian long to track Marie-Claire Blanchette to rooms in a Stuart-era building on the south side of Golden Square. The fortune-teller was obviously better known than he'd realized.

At one time, Golden Square had been the height of fashion and home to bishops, noblemen, and diplomats. Now it was one of the "fading" districts fated to fall on the wrong side of the Regent's New Street.

Madame Blanchette answered the door herself, a small, straight-backed woman with thick, iron gray hair, relatively unlined olive skin, and the kind of pronounced bone structure that meant she was still striking, even in her fifties. She wore a lavender brocade gown made in a style popular perhaps twenty-five years before, with pearl-drop earrings and a pearl-studded cross that looked like something that might have been brought back from Byzantium by a member of the Fourth Crusade. She stared at him a moment, her dark eyes unblinking and thoughtful, as if she were assessing him to see how he measured up to her image of him. Then she said, "I expected you sooner," and stood aside for him to enter.

"Saw it in the cards, did you?" said Sebastian,

his gaze drifting around a room that seemed oddly dislocated in time and space. Several of the chests and one of the chairs were dark and medieval-looking, a table inlaid with mother-of-pearl reminded him of something from Damascus, while the paintings on the wall were strange scenes of tempest-driven seas, wind-tossed moons, and one bizarre image of a man hanging upside down. Everywhere he looked, there were groupings of crystals and candles and bells and other strange objects he couldn't begin to identify.

Her eyes narrowed with what looked like amusement. "You don't believe in the cards, *monsieur le vicomte*?"

So absorbed was he in his inspection of the room that it took him a moment to realize she was responding to his own question. He hadn't introduced himself, but then, there appeared to be no need. He said, "I neither believe nor disbelieve."

"A man with an open mind. You've no idea how rare that truly is." Limping badly, she led the way to a small settee covered by a worn, early eighteenth-century tapestry, asked him to sit, then took the chair opposite—an ancient thing of dark wood whose high back was carved with mythical creatures and naked men writhing in either ecstasy or pain. "But to answer your question, no, I did not need the cards. There are times when simple reasoning ability suffices to tell us all we need to know."

Her English was very good, fluent and easy but pleasantly inflected with what sounded like a genuine French accent.

"Yes, I really am French," she said, as if he had spoken the thought aloud. "I have been in your country since 1805. Which makes it . . ." She paused, as if doing the sums. "Nine years now."

"Impressive. Why do you use cards if you can simply read minds?"

"People find the cards more believable. And they do help to focus one's thoughts." Again that gleam of amusement in the depths of her dark brown eyes. "But you said that facetiously, yes?"

"Perhaps."

She leaned back in the chair, her hands resting lightly on wooden arms carved into the shape of lions' paws, her gaze on his face. "You're here to learn about Giselle?"

"Giselle is the woman you accused Ashworth of raping?"

"Giselle was my daughter."

She rose awkwardly and disappeared with her halting step into an adjoining chamber. She returned a moment later with a small framed portrait of a young woman. "She was sixteen when this was painted three years ago," said Madame Blanchette, turning the painting to face him. She did not hand it to him.

The girl was lovely, with luxurious dark hair, deep-set brown eyes, a small chin, and a seductive mouth. Looking at her, Sebastian felt a surge of sadness mixed with rage—rage at men like Ashworth, whose wealth and privilege enabled them to career through the world, taking what they wanted, utterly heedless of the lives they were destroying in the process. Rage at the society that allowed such things to happen. Rage at the senselessness of it all.

"The anger this stirs within you?" said Giselle's mother. "Multiply that by infinity, and you'll have some concept of how I feel."

"How did it happen?"

She set the portrait with loving care atop a nearby bureau. "Giselle worked as a shopkeeper's assistant at a jeweler's on Bond Street. Ashworth saw her there and decided he wanted her."

Sebastian drew a heavy breath. He was remembering what Ashworth's butler had told him. *His lordship's tastes varied on a whim, from ladies of quality to bits of muslin to whatever pretty shopkeeper's assistant happened to catch his fancy.*

"At first he tried to seduce her. He could be a most charming man, you know. Giselle was no fool; she knew what he wanted. But because he was a wealthy nobleman, she needed to be careful. She couldn't go too far in discouraging him without risking her job. And good positions are so difficult to find these days."

"Which jewelry store was this?"

"Vincent's," she replied without hesitation. "I asked him later why he didn't protect my daughter. I expected him to say he hadn't known about Ashworth. But you know what Mr. Vincent said to me? He said, 'You can't seriously expect me to have risked alienating a potential customer.'"

"Mr. Vincent obviously didn't know about Ashworth's habit of not paying his bills," said Sebastian. "And now his potential customer is dead."

"That he is. But I did not kill him." She tipped her head to one side, her gaze still hard on his face. "That is why you are here, is it not?"

"Tell me what Ashworth did to her," said Sebastian.

A spasm of pain crossed the Frenchwoman's face before being smoothed away out of sight. "Very well. As I said, first he sought to woo her with flattery and presents; he even promised to set her up in fine rooms as his mistress. She never wavered. So one evening last October, he caught her in the shop when she was alone, pushed her into the back room, and forced himself on her there. Took her bent over a counter like a dog."

"Why do you think he was so obsessed with her?"

"Because he wanted her, but she kept telling

him no. I don't think it happened to him often. He was so very rich and handsome."

"And charming."

"Yes, most charming."

Madame Blanchette settled in her strange chair again, her hands folded together in her lap. The pose looked relaxed and at peace, but it was not; her hands were clasped together so tightly, the knuckles were white. There was a crackle of energy about her that hadn't been there before; a kind of hard, lethal purposefulness that was nearly palpable. And he found himself thinking, *This woman could kill.* In fact, he knew somehow with a deep certainty that she had killed in the past.

"I have killed men in my life," she said, again fallowing his thoughts with eerie accuracy. "One I stabbed. Another I pushed to his death off a cliff. But that was years ago, in France, in self-defense. I won't deny that I wanted Ashworth dead. But I did not kill him."

Why not? Sebastian wanted to ask. Instead, he said, "Your daughter killed herself?"

Madame Blanchette nodded. "In December. I did everything I could to help her come to terms with what he had done to her. But she couldn't shake the overwhelming sense of shame and degradation he'd made her feel. And then she realized she was with child by him. She felt as if she had been impregnated with the devil's

130

spawn—that the child she was carrying could someday grow up to be a monster, just like its father. So she threw herself in the Thames."

The sudden silence in the room was like a hum in his ears, a hum both punctuated and oddly accentuated by the sound of his own beating heart and the slow, strained breathing of a grieving mother.

After a moment, Madame Blanchette said, "The coroner was kind. The inquest concluded she must have lost her way and fallen into the water in the heavy fog. Death by misadventure, they called it. But I knew the truth."

"So she was given a Christian burial?"

"She was, yes. At St. James's churchyard in Piccadilly."

"I think I would have killed him," said Sebastian.

The faintest suggestion of a smile hovered about the Frenchwoman's dark, knowing eyes. "I've no doubt you would have. But death is easy—a moment of heartsick, frightened realization that all is about to be lost, and then nothing. I wanted him to suffer longer. Far longer."

"Not all deaths are easy," said Sebastian. In his six years of war, he had seen countless men die after screaming in agony for days. Countless men, and one innocent woman of God whose suffering still haunted him . . .

"True," she said. "But mere physical pain

wouldn't have been enough. I wanted him to suffer social ostracism. Humiliation. Degradation. The loss of everything he held most dear. I had only just begun. Whoever killed him robbed me of my revenge."

Sebastian felt a whisper of unease that was like a cold breath on the back of his neck. "So, who do you think killed him? Did you ask your cards?"

Rather than answer him, she said, "If I gave you a name, now, would you believe me?"

"No," he admitted.

She smiled. "There is a man—a man named Sid. Lord Ashworth used to pay this man to do his dirty work. He is dangerous, but Ashworth in his hubris alienated him. Infuriated him."

"Sid—what?"

"That I cannot tell you."

Sebastian noticed she didn't say she did not know. "You're suggesting this 'Sid' killed him?"

"Perhaps. Perhaps not. But I suspect you will find him interesting for more than one reason."

"Meaning?"

"When you find him, you will understand." Madame Blanchette pushed to her feet and went to open the door for him. Their conversation was at an end.

"What if I don't find him?" asked Sebastian, pausing at the door.

"You will. And afterward, we will talk more."

132

CHAPTER 16

After returning home, Hero spent some time writing up the notes from her morning interview before sharing a pleasant nuncheon with Simon in the nursery. And then, planning her timing carefully, she ordered her carriage and set out for her father's house in Berkeley Square.

As the carriage pulled away from Brook Street, she rested her head against the back of the tufted leather seat, her heart heavy with thoughts of the past. It had been more than six months now since her mother's short illness and unexpected death. Six months. And yet somehow a part of Hero still couldn't quite absorb the reality of her loss. Simon would do something clever or funny, and Hero would think, *I must remember to tell Mama.* For one fleeting instant, she would smile in anticipation of her mother's pleasure. Then would come the crushing realization that she would never be able to share anything with her mother again; never again have the joy of watching her mother smile lovingly at her grandson; never again hear her mother's gentle laughter or be able to seek out her quiet, simple wisdom.

Hero had lived with the crushing ache of this loss for months. But going to Jarvis House, knowing her mother would not be there, always gave that ache a painful twist.

She was aware of the coach drawing up in Berkeley Square, of the footman opening the door to let down the steps. And still she hesitated. Her father, she calculated, should be at Carlton House with the Prince Regent. But then she was here not to see Jarvis but her cousin Victoria Hart-Davis.

The two women were related through their mothers' grandparents, which Hero supposed made them second cousins. But since Victoria had grown up in India, they'd never met until the previous September. Although only a few years older than Hero, Victoria had lived an adventurous life that carried her to Ireland, South America, and the Peninsula and had seen her bury two husbands. The first, Lieutenant Lester Boyne, died of fever in the Maratha Wars, while the second, Captain John Hart-Davis, son and heir of Lord Hart-Davis, had been killed last summer at the Siege of San Sebastián. It was when she'd been newly widowed for the second time and on her way from Spain to stay with her dead husband's family in Norfolk that Victoria had stopped in London to visit her cousins. She'd been at Hero's side when Lady Jarvis died.

Hero's aged, arthritic, foul-tempered grand-mother, the Dowager Lady Jarvis, rarely left her rooms these days and was incapable of taking up the burdensome task of managing Lord Jarvis's large household. And so, Cousin Victoria had kindly offered to stay and help. Six months later, she was still there.

The young widow was crossing the entry hall, her focus on a sealed missive in her hand, when a footman opened the door for Hero. Looking up, she saw Hero and immediately turned toward her, a delighted smile sweeping across her face.

"Oh, what a lovely surprise!" she cried, quickly enfolding Hero in a warm embrace. A beautiful, exquisitely tiny woman with angel-fair hair, soft blue eyes, and porcelain skin, Victoria was so small—and Hero so tall—that even standing on tiptoe she could barely reach to kiss Hero's cheek.

She drew back, the smile in her eyes fading to gentle concern as she searched Hero's face. "We heard about Ashworth. How is Stephanie?"

"She's handling it as well as can be expected," said Hero, choosing her words carefully.

Victoria cast a quick glance at the footman and drew Hero upstairs to the drawing room.

"The poor, poor girl," said Victoria as they settled before the fire. "Married less than a year and left with not one but two tiny babes. Are they all right? The twins, I mean. I'm told they were born dreadfully premature."

"Amazingly healthy, considering," said Hero, and left it at that. The two boys had come earlier than expected, but not nearly as early as most believed.

"Well, thank goodness for that at least. She doesn't need any more grief. This dreadful murder! Any idea yet who might have been responsible?" Her words tumbled out in a rush the way they always did, for Victoria Hart-Davis came across to the casual observer as a vivacious young woman who was good-natured and gay but not particularly deep or intelligent. The impression was misleading, for she was a woman who read the works of Plato and Cicero in their original Greek and Latin and was fluent in half a dozen modern languages as well. Her mind was quick and clever, her reasoning ability acute. Yet few would ever guess it by listening to her happy chatter. Hiding away her strength and intelligence, she showed the world a face that was not real. In essence she was an actress playing a part, and she was very good at it. It was one of the reasons Hero could never feel comfortable around her, even after all these months.

"Devlin is looking into it," Hero said carefully. "But it's early days yet."

They ordered tea and talked for a time of fashion and the Season, which was now in full swing. Only then did Hero casually bring the conversation around to the purpose of her visit, saying, "Have you met the Tsar's sister yet?"

"Not yet," said Victoria. "Although I did see

her driving up Bond Street this morning in her barouche. I'm told she always drives with the top down so she can wave to the crowds. They adore her, of course. Jarvis says the Prince is quite put out about it."

Hero took a slow sip of her tea. "I wonder why she's come to England so far ahead of the others?"

"It's curious, isn't it? Did you hear she rejected the cutter Prinny sent to pick her up from Holland? She was beyond insulted—seems a paltry naval cutter is quite beneath the dignity of a Tsar's daughter. Fortunately, one of the Royal Dukes came to the rescue by lending his frigate to the cause."

"Charming. So that's why they dislike each other?"

"Well, that was the beginning. The Prince then made the mistake of hurrying around to the Pulteney Hotel to meet her so quickly after her arrival in London that she hadn't had time to change, with the result that he encountered her on the stairs in all her travel dirt."

"And she was outraged by this as well?"

"Mmm. She treated him as if he were an overweight, aged buffoon, and he resented it."

"Fancy that."

Victoria let out a soft laugh, a gay melodic ripple of amusement that brought an impish smile to her face. "I understand everyone is all agog to see her up close at the Russian ambassador's ball tonight—particularly since Countess Lieven is said not to be one of her admirers." She paused, her head turning slightly at the sound of the front door opening below, followed by the low murmur of a man's familiar voice in the entry hall and his heavy footsteps upon the stairs.

"Jarvis?" said Hero, feeling like a cat caught amidst the pigeons. "Already?"

He appeared in the doorway, his gaze fixed on Hero, his expression as inscrutable as ever. "This is a surprise."

"Jarvis." Victoria glanced over at him, her amusement still animating her face. "We were just gossiping about all the interest in the Grand Duchess. Countess Lieven's ball tonight will doubtless be a dreadful squeeze."

"It should definitely be more entertaining than the usual such fare," he said. For one brief instant, his gaze met Victoria's, and a silent message passed between them.

The exchange was meant to be private, but Hero caught it. And she knew her father well enough to understand that whatever Jarvis's interest in the Grand Duchess, Cousin Victoria knew about it. And she'd just reassured him that she had given nothing away.

CHAPTER 17

Sebastian stood beside the library fire, his gaze on the slowly kindling flames. He was trying to decide how he would react if a child of his killed herself as a result of some man's rape. Would he be able to bide his time, skillfully spinning out a long, sadistic revenge? Or would he simply kill the bastard?

Sebastian suspected he'd probably kill the bastard.

If Madame Blanchette had indeed been the one who hacked Ashworth's chest into a bloody pulp, Sebastian would find it hard to blame her. It would be an impossibly long walk from Golden Square to Curzon Street and back again for a woman with a badly crushed leg. But she could have taken a hackney. And London's hackney drivers were all licensed and answerable to Bow Street.

Sebastian was still pondering the possibilities of this when Sir Henry Lovejoy stopped by Brook Street.

"Something has come up that may or may not be relevant to Ashworth's murder," said the magistrate, accepting Sebastian's invitation to settle in one of the chairs before the library fire.

Sebastian took the seat opposite him. "Oh?"

"Thursday night, just before dawn, a wherry-man was heading back toward Lambeth after dropping a passenger at the Westminster Steps when he chanced to look up and see a young woman standing on the bridge, near the center of the river. She was well dressed enough that it struck him as odd for her to be out alone at that time of night. Then he realized there was another woman standing behind her."

"And?"

"One of the women had a bundle in her arms. As he watched, she held it out over the water and let it go. He assumed it must be a babe—says he's pulled more dead infants out of that river than he cares to remember. So he rowed to it as quickly as he could and managed to haul it into his boat before it went under."

People were always throwing newborns into the Thames. How great must a person's poverty, desperation, and fear be, Sebastian had always wondered, to do such a thing?

"So was it a babe?"

Lovejoy shook his head. "It was a bundle of women's clothes: a fine woolen cloak, a muslin gown beautifully embroidered around the hem with birds and flowers, and undergarments. All were covered with blood. He thought about it for a day, and finally decided it was strange enough that he brought them to us."

Sebastian felt a curl of apprehension so sudden

and intense, he wondered if it showed on his face. "The wherryman said the women were young?"

"He said one of them was, at least—the one who threw the bundle in the river. The other was hanging back, and he didn't get as good a look at her. The night was so dark and misty, he says he probably wouldn't have seen them at all if they hadn't been standing by a lamp, but he thought the one in front had dark hair."

Not Stephanie, then, thought Sebastian. Although he wished he knew for certain that her abigail was fair too.

"Obviously," Lovejoy was saying, "there could be a simple explanation for it that has nothing to do with Ashworth's murder. But I've set one of my constables to taking the gown around to the city's various fashionable modistas. If there were any identifying signature marks on it, they've been removed. But it's distinctive enough that whoever made it should be able to recognize her own work and identify the customer she made it for."

Undoubtedly, thought Sebastian. *But would a fashionable modista identify the owner of a blood-covered gown brought to her by Bow Street, and thus risk losing an important customer?* Unlikely. Aloud he said, "The gown could have been purchased from a secondhand shop."

"There is that. And unfortunately, such proprietors are considerably less likely to cooperate with us." Lovejoy looked at him expectantly. "Have you discovered anything of interest?"

Sebastian found himself reluctant to mention his morning encounters with either Russell Firth or Madame Blanchette. "Nothing definite," he said vaguely. "Although I've been thinking we might try checking with the city's hackney drivers. See if any of them picked up or let off a fare in the area that night."

"Mmm. Good idea," said Lovejoy, reaching for his hat as he rose to his feet.

Sebastian stood with him. "Have you ever heard of a ruffian called 'Sid'? I don't know his surname."

Lovejoy thought for a moment. "Not that I can recall. Sorry. Why? You think he might be involved?"

"It's possible. I'll have to ask my valet if he knows of him."

Lovejoy looked vaguely startled. "Your valet?"

"My valet," said Sebastian without elaborating.

Sebastian's valet was a slim, fair-haired gentleman's gentleman named Jules Calhoun. Calm and unflappable, he possessed a rare genius for repairing the damage Sebastian's more unorthodox activities sometimes inflicted on his wardrobe. But Calhoun's talents with boot blacking and brush hid a dark and unusual past, for he'd been raised in one of London's most notorious flash houses. His infamous mother's connections to the city's underworld were both vast and highly useful.

"Sid?" said Calhoun with a frown when Sebastian asked him. "Can't think of anyone by that name offhand. But I can ask around if you'd like."

"Yes, thank you," said Sebastian.

After Calhoun had gone, Sebastian went to stand, thoughtful, at the front window. The rain might have ended, but the day remained dark and blustery. He was still standing there when Hero's yellow-bodied barouche drew up before the house and she came in, bringing with her all the scents of a wet spring afternoon.

"Good, you're back," she said, her color high.

"So, how was it?"

She tore off her very fetching ostrich-plumed hat and tossed it aside with what sounded suspiciously like a smothered oath.

Sebastian said, "That bad?"

Stalking over to where he kept a brandy carafe and glasses, she poured herself a drink and took a long swallow. Then she took another before looking over at him, gray eyes sparkling with outrage and something else—something he couldn't quite identify. "I have the most lowering suspicion that my cousin is sleeping with my father."

Sebastian walked over to pour himself a brandy. "I've been wondering that myself for some time now."

She stared at him. "You have? Why didn't you say anything to me?"

"Because it's always been just a guess on my part; I've never seen or heard anything to confirm it." He paused. "Why? What happened?"

She went to fling herself into one of the delicate chairs near the bay window, the brandy glass cupped in her hand. "I asked Victoria about the Grand Duchess. She was very chatty and effusive in that way she has that makes you think she hasn't a calculating thought in her head, when in reality nothing she says isn't completely thought out ahead of time and fashioned to have precisely whatever effect she wants it to have. At any rate, she says the Prince Regent irritated the Tsar's unbelievably demanding sister by attempting to transport her across the Channel in a cutter."

"What's wrong with a cutter?"

"Quite beneath Her Imperial Highness's dignity, I'm afraid. It seems a Tsar's daughter requires at least a frigate."

"Charming."

"Very. And then, to make matters worse, the Regent compounded the affront to Her Imperial Highness by arriving at the Pulteney Hotel to meet her before she'd had a chance to change out of her travel clothes."

"That's it?"

"I gather she was decidedly rude to him when he encountered her by chance on the hotel's stairs. That—combined with the way the London crowds cheer her—has quite put up his back."

"In other words, we're talking about two incredibly selfish and wholly self-absorbed royals, each believing themselves treated shabbily by the other."

Hero nodded. "If you care to see more of her, the Russian ambassador and his wife are giving a ball tonight in her honor—although I'm afraid we already sent our regrets."

"Frankly, once was enough." He studied her strained, set face. "Jarvis was there?"

"Yes. He surprised me by coming in unexpectedly. I think he guessed my mission, by the way."

"Probably."

Her eyes narrowed, and he realized she was staring at his face. She said, "What happened to your chin?"

"Sir Felix."

"He planted you a facer?"

"More like a grazing blow than a facer, I'd say."

"Huh."

He waited for her to say more. When she didn't, he said, "What makes you suspect Jarvis is sleeping with your cousin?"

She took a slow sip of her brandy and grimaced. "It wasn't any one thing, exactly. It was more just . . . something about the way they were in tune with each other . . . the easy way they communicated without words. I know that sounds nebulous, but the reality was so intense that once I became aware of it, I wondered how I could possibly have missed it before. It was that powerful."

He went to stand behind her chair, his hands on her shoulders. He kept trying to think of something to say, something that might comfort her. But all he could come up with was *I'm sorry,* and that was so hopelessly inadequate that it seemed better left unsaid.

Hero tipped back her head to look up at him. "I don't know why I'm so surprised. In some ways, Victoria is exactly the kind of woman Jarvis has always admired: tiny, fair-haired, and pretty. In fact, she looks very much like the portraits I've seen of my mother when she was young. The difference is, my mother was given the typical but shockingly poor education considered proper for girls in her day. She was taught to sing, sew, dance, sketch, and converse in French and Italian, and that was about it. Her mind was quick—or at least it was until she suffered that dreadful apoplexy after her last stillbirth. But because she was so uneducated and had been taught to hide her intelligence, I don't think my father ever realized she wasn't the idiot he thought her to be."

"You mother was no idiot, even with her health weakened."

Hero gave a faint, sad smile. "The odd thing is, he's always claimed he likes women who are ornamental rather than educated. Yet while Victoria affects a kind of chatty, cheerful mindlessness in public, she's never made any attempt to hide either her intelligence or her learning from Jarvis. I wouldn't have expected that to appeal to him, but it obviously does."

"People's tastes can change over the years."

"Dear Lord," said Hero suddenly, as if a thought had just occurred to her. "I don't even *like* her. What am I going to do if he marries her?"

"Get a lot of practice at smiling dissemblance."

She gave a hoarse laugh and set the rest of her brandy aside unfinished. "Morey said Sir Henry was here?"

Sebastian nodded and told her about the bundle of clothes fished from the Thames. "Of course, it could have absolutely nothing to do with Ashworth's murder," he said.

"A coincidence?" She looked over at him. "I thought you didn't believe in coincidences."

"I am skeptical of them, at least when it comes to murder. And yet they do happen."

"They do."

"If there is indeed a link, it lends credence to

the theory that this murderer is a woman. Which is interesting, given that I've discovered Firth's tale about the young woman who killed herself because of Ashworth is true."

"Oh, no."

"Her name was Giselle Blanchette. Her mother's a tarot card reader."

"You mean Marie-Claire Blanchette?"

He looked at her in surprise. "You've heard of her?"

"Mmm. There are some who say she's a French spy."

"Oh? Is she?"

"I've no idea. I didn't get that from my father, if that's what you're asking. To be honest, I'm not entirely certain where I heard it. It could very well be nothing more than a vile rumor. You know what people are like."

"Well, she's definitely French."

"That doesn't mean she's a spy."

"No," agreed Sebastian. "But if she's not, it does make me wonder who started the rumor—and why."

CHAPTER 18

Later that afternoon, as a weak sun sank lower in the cloud-filled sky, Sebastian walked through the ancient piazza of Covent Garden. Most of the vegetable and fruit sellers were gone by now, their stalls shuttered, the cobbles underfoot mushy with spoiled fruit and cabbage leaves mixed with dung. The air was filled with the cooing of the pigeons strutting along the pediment of the church of St. Paul's and the laughter of a gang of ragged street children playing chase amongst the shuttered sections of the market. Soon the district's theaters would be opening, and the focus of Covent Garden would shift from produce market to evening entertainment. Only the flower sellers were still here, their section a colorful collage of sweet-smelling lilies, daffodils, violets, and tulips.

He came across Kat Boleyn, the woman he was here to find, selecting a bunch of white violets near the piazza's northern arcade. She was a strikingly attractive woman with luxurious auburn-lit hair, a wide, sensuous mouth, and brilliant blue eyes of the same distinctive shade as Stephanie's—the famous blue St. Cyr eyes Kat had inherited from her natural father, the Earl of Hendon.

She was the toast of London's stage, as acclaimed for her acting ability as for her beauty. But when Sebastian first met her, she'd been a young unknown actress of sixteen and he barely twenty-one. Their ill-fated love had haunted him for years, while the discovery of her parentage— so tangled up with his—had nearly killed him. There'd been a time when he believed he'd never come to terms with it all. But they'd eventually managed to forge a new kind of relationship with an affection much like that of the sister and brother they'd once thought themselves.

She looked up then, saw him, and smiled.

"Do you come here every day before your performance?" he asked, walking up to her.

She laughed and handed the flower seller the coins for her posy. "When I can."

They turned to walk through the banks of fragrant flowers toward the Strand. "I saw Hendon," she said, holding the posy to her nose and breathing deep. "He tells me you're trying to find who killed Ashworth."

"Trying. You'd be amazed at the number of people who wanted to murder him—and for very good reasons."

She glanced over at him. "Frankly, I'm glad he's dead."

"That seems to be a common sentiment shared by almost everyone I've spoken to so far, with the notable exception of his father and best friend."

"The father, I can understand. But what kind of man has a monster like Ashworth as a friend?"

"Someone who's a bit of a monster himself, I suspect. Although Sir Felix hides it better than most."

"Hendon is afraid people will start to suspect Stephanie."

"So am I."

They walked on in silence for a time. The shadows were beginning to deepen with the approach of evening, and he could smell the briny tang of the sea on the incoming tide as they drew closer to the river. He said, "Are you familiar with a tarot card reader named Marie-Claire Blanchette?"

"Yes, of course; she's quite well-known. Why?"

"Ashworth raped her daughter. When the girl discovered she was with child by him, she killed herself."

"Dear God. Surely you aren't suggesting Madame Blanchette might have murdered him in revenge?"

"I think it's certainly possible."

"I'd have expected such a woman to find a more creative way to make him suffer."

"You know her?"

"Not well. But I have met her."

"Is there any truth to the rumor that she passes information to Paris?" The question was not as odd as it might have seemed to someone who didn't know Kat, for there'd been a time when she herself had spied for the French. She was no longer active, but he knew she kept in contact with some who were. Her allegiance was not to France but to Ireland, the conquered land of her mother's people, and he'd never been able to hold it against her. How could he, when he knew what England had done to Ireland?

What they'd done to Kat's mother.

"I don't believe so, no," she said.

"But you don't know for certain?"

Kat was silent for a moment. They had reached the Strand now, and the breeze was stronger here. She put up a hand, holding her hair back from her face. "How much have you heard about her background?"

"Virtually nothing. Why?"

"I don't know anything about her early life. But at some point during the Directory, she read Josephine Beauharnais's cards and predicted she would marry a handsome young officer who would someday become emperor."

"Surely the tale is apocryphal?"

"Perhaps. But there is no doubt that Josephine set great store by her predictions. As a result of her patronage, Madame Blanchette became enormously popular. And then, shortly after Napoléon crowned himself emperor, Josephine badgered Madame Blanchette into reading his cards. She didn't want to, but how could she refuse?"

"So what did she tell him?"

"She told him he had the capacity to achieve greatness, to bring freedom and peace to all of Europe. But she also warned him against trying to exceed the fame and conquests of Alexander the Great, saying he would ultimately fail and die in disgrace."

"That can't have been popular."

"It wasn't. Napoléon was so enraged that she had to flee France."

Sebastian watched a boy dart past, shouting something he didn't quite catch. "It does seem unlikely that she would now be spying for him—unless of course he's forcing her to cooperate by threatening family members still in France."

"It's possible. But I suspect the rumors are simply malicious, begun by someone who wanted to discredit her—someone she angered or frightened. She often knows things about people that they think they've managed to keep hidden. Whether she 'sees' the information with the help of her cards or acquires it from talkative servants, it doesn't really matter, does it? Knowledge can be a dangerous thing."

She turned her head as a shout went up farther down the Strand, a huzzah that rippled through the crowd around them.

"What the devil?" said Sebastian.

And then they saw her: Grand Duchess Catherine, waving to the people from her open-topped barouche, her smile wide, her luxuriously dark curls fluttering beneath the poke-fronted bonnet that people were beginning to call "the Oldenburg" in her honor. Beside her, Princess Ivanna Gagarin looked both smaller and more subdued, and yet still managed to be a forceful presence. The mustachioed Colonel Demidov sat on the bench facing them, his arms crossed at his chest, his expression alert as the Grand Duchess played to the crowd, turning to acknowledge first one side of the street, then the other. Watching her, Sebastian found himself wondering if someone had told the Tsar's sister how much the crowds' cheering of her infuriated the Regent, so that she now encouraged it simply to annoy him.

Kat remained silent as the Russian women rolled past. Then she said, "I hear she arrived in London early as part of a scheme to catch herself a new husband."

Sebastian looked over at her. "Not one of Prinny's fat old brothers, surely?"

"Hardly. I believe her intended target was the Regent himself."

"But Prinny already has a wife—however much he might despise her."

Kat raised her eyebrows. "Inconvenient wives are easily eliminated if one is ruthless enough. And the Grand Duchess is reputed to be quite ruthless. Her lady-in-waiting, Princess Ivanna, is said to possess a special talent for poisons."

"She does?"

"Mmm." Kat was still staring after the Tsar's sister. "I wonder if the Princess of Wales realizes how lucky she is that Her Imperial Highness has taken such an instant, intense dislike to the Regent."

Sebastian studied her faintly smiling profile. "I won't ask how you know all this."

She gave a soft laugh and turned their steps back toward the theater. "No, don't."

Paul Gibson was in his surgery tending a boy's broken arm when Sebastian arrived at Tower Hill.

"Ah," said the Irishman, glancing over at him. "I was hoping you'd stop by. Give me a moment to finish up here; I want to show you something."

The boy's name was Alan, and he looked to be about fourteen. A butcher's apprentice, he was big and strong and grim faced as Gibson set the arm and wrapped it up. "Be smart and don't try to use that arm for six weeks," Gibson told the lad. "If you listen to me, you shouldn't lose it."

"Ole Grimes won't like it."

"Tell Ned Grimes he'll have to answer to me if he gives you any trouble."

"And what will you do to 'Ole Grimes' if he ignores your warning?" asked Sebastian after the boy had taken himself off.

"Refuse to treat his gout," said Gibson with

a smile. He picked up the flickering oil lamp that rested on a nearby table, for darkness was beginning to fall. "I finished your dead valet right before the lad, Alan, showed up."

"And?" said Sebastian as Gibson's lantern cast wobbly patterns of light and shadow across the yard.

Gibson unlocked the outbuilding's door and pushed it open. "I think you'll find this interesting."

Edward Digby lay facedown on the stone table in the center of the room. Gibson hung the lantern from the chain suspended over the slab, and for a moment it swung back and forth, the golden light playing over the dead man's back. The gaping knife wounds and startling purple-and-white patterns of lividity—caused by the way his blood had settled—were rendered hideous by the shifting shadows.

Gibson put up a hand to still the lantern. "From the looks of things, I'd say it's more than likely he was killed the same night as Ashworth—maybe even by the same knife."

"Huh," said Sebastian, walking around the body.

"He wasn't attacked with quite the same fury as Ashworth, but whoever did it wasn't very neat or experienced."

"You think the killer kept stabbing to make certain he was dead?"

"It's definitely a possibility." Gibson pointed

to the purple-red and white splotches discoloring the dead man's back. "What I wanted to show you was this. See the evenness of the pattern? It suggests he was lying flat on his back for quite some time after he was killed."

"But he wasn't found on his back. He was on his side, propped against the alley wall."

Gibson nodded. "That's what the fellows who brought him here told me."

Sebastian looked up. *Bloody hell.* Why move the man's body hours after he was killed?"

"That I can't tell you. But I can tell you this: He wasn't naked when he was killed. There were threads in his wounds."

"So he was killed and then stripped and moved? That's even more bizarre."

"I'd say so, yes. Given that he was left not far from Ashworth's house, it isn't as if the killer could have been hoping the body might not be identified."

Sebastian went to stand in the doorway, his gaze on the dark, deceptively peaceful garden beyond. If he were the type to leap to conclusions, he'd probably assume that the valet's death—and the bizarre circumstances surrounding it—meant that this murderer couldn't possibly be a woman. But Sebastian had learned long ago the danger of hasty deductions, particularly when his thinking was clouded as it was now by his own emotional involvement.

When he was desperate to find something—anything—that could point the finger of suspicion away from the niece he loved.

He swung around abruptly to stare at the shrouded form lying on one of the wide shelves that ran across the old building's rear wall. "That's Ashworth?"

"Yes."

He went to draw back the sheet, exposing the dead nobleman's waxen face. "You said there's no way to tell if he was poisoned?"

"Depends on the poison. The effects of some are so violent, it's hard to miss. And sometimes with cyanide, you get a faint, almond-like smell, although not always. The fact is, the world is full of poisons, and we've no reliable way to detect any of them."

"What about a drug that would leave a man alive but unable to move or fight back?"

"A large enough dose of laudanum would do that. Was he an opium eater?"

"I don't know. It wouldn't surprise me, though."

"You're back to thinking Ashworth might have been drugged rather than simply passed out?" Gibson looked thoughtful. "There are other substances that would have an effect similar to laudanum, but in a small enough dose that it might conceivably have been slipped to him. A purer tincture of opium, perhaps. There are others, but I don't know that much about them."

"Know anyone who does?"

"Alexi, actually. She's off delivering a babe at the moment, but I can ask her about it."

Sebastian drew the sheet back over Ashworth's face, conscious of a rising tide of anger and frustration thrumming through him. "The bastard caused such untold pain and suffering in life. Now he's dead, and he's still causing it."

"At least he's dead," said Gibson.

"Yes. And yet the killing goes on."

CHAPTER 19

Hendon was looking over *The Quarterly Review* in the reading room of White's, a glass of brandy on the table at his elbow, when Sebastian came upon him.

"Take a walk with me?" he asked.

The Earl looked up, his eyes narrowing. "What happened to your chin?"

"It ran into a fist."

Hendon set aside his paper with a noncommittal grunt and rose to his feet.

Outside, a wind was kicking up, the air growing colder, the night alive with voices and laughter and snatches of music. This part of London was considered the gentlemen's pleasure haunt, a land of exclusive men's clubs, ruinous gaming hells, fashionable supper rooms, and the kind of women a man of birth and breeding was not supposed to take to wife.

"I hear Ashworth's missing valet was found dead this morning," said Hendon as they pushed their way through the well-dressed crowds thronging St. James's Street.

"Gibson thinks he was killed the same night as Ashworth. Perhaps even by the same knife."

"Pity. I was hoping he'd be found to be the killer and put an end to this nightmare." Hendon brought up a splayed hand to rub his eyes. "Why kill the valet? It makes no sense."

"It does if Digby—that's the valet—could have identified the murderer."

"Yes, I suppose; I didn't think of that."

"Unfortunately, it doesn't explain some of the more bizarre circumstances surrounding the body's discovery."

Hendon looked over at him. "Such as?"

"He was stripped naked and the body moved after he was killed."

"Dear God."

Sebastian said, "I've heard it suggested that the Grand Duchess arrived in London so far in advance of the Allied Sovereigns because she had hopes of contracting a marriage alliance with the Regent. Do you think that's true?"

Hendon stared out over the somber redbrick walls of the Tudor palace that seemed to squat at the bottom of the street. Beyond it the trees in the park were no more than dark, shifting shadows. "I suppose it wouldn't be surprising if she did have such aspirations. After all, it's no secret that Prinny has spent the last ten years trying to divorce his wife. But if that was her ambition, nothing will come of it now. She took an instant dislike to him, and the feeling is quite mutual."

"So why is she staying in town? Her brother isn't expected for another two months or more. Why not go on an extended tour of the Lake

District or Scotland and come back to London when the Tsar arrives?"

Hendon started to say something, then hesitated.

"What?" asked Sebastian, watching him.

"It's not going to be easy, putting Europe back together after more than twenty years of war and revolution and republican fervor. We're looking at months and months of tricky negotiations before it's all sorted out. Grievances will need to be forgotten or at least buried and old alliances reaffirmed—and new ones forged."

Sebastian studied the Earl's troubled face. "What exactly are you saying?"

Hendon cast a quick look around and noticeably lowered his voice. "Word is, Russia is unhappy with the prospect of a strong British-Dutch alliance—especially one cemented by the marriage of Princess Charlotte to William of Orange."

"Hence the Russians' interest in a possible marital alliance between the Regent and the Tsar's sister?"

Hendon nodded. "But with that now out of the question, they might be looking for some other way to interfere with the British-Dutch alliance."

"Such as?"

"I wish I knew."

They walked on in silence for a time. The night air was dense with the smell of hot lamp oil and coal smoke and horses, the pavements of Pall Mall splashed with light from the tall, classically fronted buildings that rose up on either side. The crowds of half-inebriated men were nearly as thick here as on St. James's, and as he looked out at that sea of gay, laughing faces, Sebastian felt himself for one suspended moment to be oddly apart from it all, as if he were a witness rather than a participant. But then, perhaps he was. These men were here on a quest for life's pleasures, or at least a semblance of such, whereas his thoughts were on the dead and the hidden darkness of those who had made them so.

Hendon said, "Why this sudden interest in the Russians?"

"It seems Ashworth was playing his erotic games with one of the Grand Duchess's ladies."

"Good heavens. What could it mean?"

"I don't know. To my knowledge, the only thing Ashworth cared about was his own pleasure, not foreign alliances and diplomatic maneuverings. But I think I may have just changed my mind about not attending the Russian ambassador's ball tonight."

"We already sent Countess Lieven our regrets," said Hero, who was dressing for dinner when he told her of his plan.

"I know."

She looked over at him and laughed.

• • •

Invitations to Countess Lieven's balls were always amongst the most coveted prizes of the London Season. Technically it was her husband, Count Lieven, who represented the Tsar at the Court of St. James. But people in diplomatic circles liked to joke that Russia actually had two ambassadors in London, and that by far the shrewder and more capable one was Lieven's wife, Dorothea. Born into a noble Baltic family, she'd married at the age of fourteen and was now just twenty-eight years old. Despite having been in London only a year, she'd somehow managed to conquer the heights of society and reigned as one of the powerful patronesses of Almack's.

Arriving shortly after eleven, Sebastian and Hero found the ambassador's residence ablaze with light and throbbing with music and laughter. A red carpet stretched from the front door to the street, with constables holding back the crowds of gawkers who typically gathered to enjoy such spectacles, their necks craning as they jostled for glimpses of the Quality in all their finery.

"Cousin Victoria says Countess Lieven is not a fan of the Grand Duchess," said Hero quietly as they waited their turn to be announced. It was late enough that the worst of the crush of arrivals had already passed, but it still took some time to wind their way up the stairs.

"Not surprising," said Sebastian, leaning in so

that his lips were close to her ear. "Two highborn Russian women famous for their allure, wit, and enormous self-regard in one foreign capital? The mind reels."

Hero smothered a soft laugh. "It's a good thing Her Imperial Highness will be gone in a few months."

"Hopefully."

Countess Lieven's husband stood at her side, receiving guests. But all eyes were on her, not the ambassador. She was an attractive woman, striking rather than beautiful, with an unusually long neck, dark, fashionably cropped hair, a firm chin, and a saucy mouth. Graceful and elegant despite her rather bony figure, she had a haughty manner that effectively conveyed her contempt for anyone she considered her inferior—which was virtually everyone. Even those who called themselves her friends admitted there was nothing amiable about her. She was neither intellectual nor bookish, but she was extraordinarily clever and calculating, and utterly ruthless.

"Lord Devlin," she said with a glittering smile as Sebastian bowed over her hand. "What a nice surprise. For some reason I had the idea you and your wife sent your regrets."

"Fortunately, we had an unexpected change in plans," said Hero with a smile every bit as false as that of their hostess. "We knew you'd be thrilled."

The Countess's eyes narrowed, but her smile never changed. "Just so."

"Point, counterpoint," said Sebastian softly as they eased their way into a ballroom ablaze with the light of hundreds of candles shimmering over polished crystal and reflected by vast, flower-banked mirrors. The air was heavy with the smell of hot wax and hot, tightly pressed bodies.

"It truly is an abominable thing to do," said Hero. "To refuse an invitation and then come anyway. But she's such a detestable person, I can't seem to dredge up the least shred of compunction. I'll never understand why she is so successful in society. No one actually likes her."

"It's because she's the female version of a bully. No one might like her, but an amazing number are willing to accept her inflated sense of her own self-worth."

"Yes. But why?"

He scanned the crowd of bejeweled, silk-clad women and sweating men. "That I don't know."

Hero unfurled her fan in a feeble attempt to stir up some breathable air. "Why exactly are we here?"

"To watch. And listen. And leap to wild and probably faulty assumptions."

"I don't see Her Imperial Highness," said Hero, scanning the dancers.

"No, but there's Princess Ivanna Gagarin." He cast a seemingly casual glance toward a square of couples near the musicians, then looked pointedly away. "The striking young woman in white crepe over pale pink satin."

"Pale pink satin and nothing else, from the looks of it," said Hero, watching the Russian noblewoman move through the figures of the cotillion. "I think she's even dispensed with the scandalous option of dampened petticoats."

"Interesting choice of partners," said Sebastian as the dancers promenaded.

Hero shifted her attention to the young gentleman opposite the Grand Duchess's lady-in-waiting. "Who is he?"

"An up-and-coming relative of the Foreign Secretary."

"Interesting, indeed. Didn't she tell you she met Ashworth at one of Countess Lieven's loo-parties?"

"She did, yes. Suggestive, isn't it?"

Sebastian waited until the dance ended and Ivanna Gagarin retired with her partner to a nearby refreshment room.

"Excuse us for a moment," said Sebastian, walking up to her escort with a hard stare that had the young buck backing away fast.

"That was clumsy," said Ivanna, taking a sip of her champagne.

"But effective."

"Are you so very anxious to speak with me again, my lord?"

"I am, actually. I'm hearing that the real reason the Grand Duchess came to London so far in advance of her brother was in hopes of securing a new husband—the Prince Regent, to be specific."

He expected her to deny it. Instead, she gave a laugh of what sounded like genuine amusement and said, "Ironic, is it not? Obviously, nothing will come of that now."

"You do realize, of course, that the Regent already has a wife."

"Wives are easily dispensed with."

"You mean by poison?"

She kept her smile in place, but it definitely tightened. "That is one method, I suppose. Although a simple divorce is generally sufficient."

"The Prince has tried that approach—several times. Without success."

"Perhaps. Although I suspect that with the coming of peace on the Continent, Princess Caroline will find continued residence in England much less attractive."

It was common knowledge in certain circles that the Princess of Wales was growing restless. Her daughter, Charlotte, was terrified her mother would be tempted to leave England once peace was declared—an unwise move that would make Prinny's dream of a divorce considerably easier to obtain.

Sebastian said, "None of this explains why

Her Imperial Highness has decided to remain in London for the next two months while awaiting her brother's arrival."

Ivanna gave a negligent shrug. "She finds the London Season . . . amusing."

Sebastian looked out over the ballroom, where couples were still assembling for the next dance. "Yet she chooses not to dance?"

"The Grand Duchess is not fond of music."

"That must make it difficult to enjoy the Season."

"There is more to the Season than music and dance." Ivanna took another sip of her champagne. There was an air of coiled alertness about her that reminded Sebastian of a serpent preparing to strike. "I seem to recall Ashworth mentioning that his young bride is quite fond of dancing. How unfortunate that he should die at the beginning of the Season, thus depriving her of her fun."

Sebastian found it profoundly disturbing, the thought of Ashworth discussing Stephanie with this woman. "He spoke to you of his wife?"

"Not a great deal. Although I assume you are aware of her affair with that young Welsh architect. What's his name again? Ah, yes, Russell Firth."

She started to turn away, but Sebastian put out a hand, stopping her. "Did you get this from Ashworth as well?"

"Not exactly."

"Then what? 'Exactly.' "

"He's not the one who told me." Her lips quirked up into a taunting smile. "Now you must decide whether you believe me."

Sebastian searched her beautiful, quietly triumphant face. "Why were you involved with him? Truly."

"I told you: He intrigued me. I'd never met anyone quite like him."

"There are more than a dozen dead street children buried up at Clerkenwell who would agree with that last part, at least."

She gave a disbelieving laugh. "Street children?"

"You would have me think you didn't know?"

"I've not the slightest idea what you're talking about."

"Torture. Rape. Murder."

"I think you exaggerate."

"The dead don't exaggerate."

"Then perhaps their translators do. All I know is that I'm sorry I never had the chance to get to know Ashworth better."

"Most people would consider that a blessing."

"Perhaps. But then, I'm not like most people."

And with that she glided away, a sensuous slip of a woman in pink silk that clung to her exquisite form like a shimmering second skin.

Sebastian was pushing through the tightly packed mass of Countess Lieven's perspiring guests, looking for Hero, when Colonel Nikolai Demidov, his dress uniform dripping with gold braid, cut him off.

"Vhy are you here?" demanded the colonel in a fierce growl. Unlike the Grand Duchess and her noble lady-in-waiting, Demidov spoke English with a heavy Russian accent.

"Ah, he speaks," said Sebastian. "I was beginning to wonder."

The colonel's eyes narrowed. He looked to be in his late thirties, with dark hair, heavy dark brows, and the traditional thick, military-style mustache of the Imperial Guard. "You vill leave the Princess Ivanna alone."

"Or you'll—what? Hack me to bits in my sleep? Stab me in the back and leave me as food for foraging pigs in some noisome alley?"

"You laugh." The colonel leaned in closer, his breath washing over Sebastian's face as he made a heavy *tssk-tssk* sound with his tongue and teeth. Then he turned and walked away.

Sebastian was still staring after him when Amanda came to stand beside him and demand in a low, harsh voice, "What are you doing here?"

Sebastian brought his gaze to his sister's face. He was really in no mood for this. "Dear Amanda. You're the second person in as many minutes to ask me that. What do you think? That I'm here for some nefarious purpose?"

"Of course you are." She was wearing an elegant

V-necked gown of silver silk edged with dainty white lace, a silk dowager's turban crowned with a towering white ostrich plume, and the famous Wilcox diamonds. The effect was awe-inspiring.

He said, "Why are you here? Aren't you supposed to be in mourning for your daughter's dead husband? True, he's only a son-in-law; but surely he should get at least two weeks?"

She ignored the question, as he'd known she would. "Your presence here is making people talk."

"If the subject is Ashworth, then they'd be talking whether I was here or not. There's something about being found dead tied naked to your bed that tends to provide fodder for gossip."

"Will you keep your voice down?" she hissed. "I swear, if I didn't know better, I'd think you were actually enjoying this."

"I'm not the least bit sorry he's dead, if that's what you're suggesting. But I never 'enjoy' investigating murders. It isn't about the hunt, or the winning, or in fact anything about me. It's about stopping someone who is dangerous. And in this instance, it's also about protecting someone I love."

"I told you, you're being ridiculous. No one with any sense would ever think to blame Stephanie for this."

Her words did not match the tight, worried anger in her face. He kept his voice low. "Was

172

Steph having an affair with someone, Amanda? Do you know?"

"Now you are going beyond ridiculous," she snapped, and turned away.

He was still gazing after her when Hero walked up to him. She said, "Amanda is not pleased, I take it."

"Not hardly. She thinks my presence here is making people talk."

"It is. And by confronting you like that, she just gave them more fodder for gossip."

On the carriage ride home, he told Hero of his conversation with the Grand Duchess's lady-in-waiting.

"You think Ivanna Gagarin is telling the truth?" said Hero. "That Stephanie is having an affair?"

"Ironically, it's one of the few things she's told me that I'm inclined to believe."

"Because it reinforces what Hendon chanced to witness in Hyde Park?"

"Partially. But also because Princess Ivanna claimed Ashworth wasn't the one who told her about it. If her intent was to deflect my suspicions away from his strange Russian connection and toward some tawdry romantic triangle, then it would make more sense for her to say she'd had it from him."

"But you probably wouldn't have believed her, then."

"Perhaps not."

Hero was silent for a moment, her gaze on the darkened, quiet shops and rows of softly glowing streetlamps sliding by in the night. Then she said, "People are already whispering about Stephanie. If she was having an affair and word of it gets out, it won't look good."

He took Hero's hand in his and laced his fingers with hers. "You know Firth better than I. Could he have done this, do you think? Hacked two men to death?"

"I don't know him that well. Have you asked Stephanie herself about him?"

"Yes, and she pretended she hardly knew him. But then, she would, wouldn't she?"

CHAPTER 20

Sunday, 3 April

Early the next morning, Sebastian took his Arabian mare for a ride in Hyde Park. It was early enough that the mist still hung in the upper branches of the plane trees lining Rotten Row. The air was fresh and cool, the park a tapestry of mellow browns and hazy greens carpeted with endless drifts of dew-dampened bluebells. He trotted up and down the Row, waiting.

She arrived just as the clock towers of the city were striking eight, a golden-haired, solemn-faced young woman mounted on a big bay gelding. Her neat black riding habit was more somber than usual, but she still wore her little shako cap at a defiant angle.

"Uncle," said Stephanie, reining in beside him. The bay moved restlessly beneath her, eager to stretch its legs, for she had only recently returned to riding again after her confinement. "Do I take it this meeting is not by chance?"

He turned his horse to walk up the Row beside hers, her groom following at a discreet distance. "There's something important I need to ask you, and it's delicate enough that I thought it best to broach the subject in as private a setting as possible."

"This sounds ominous. Are you going to ask if I killed my husband again? I didn't, you know."

"Actually, it's about the Welsh architect, Russell Firth."

He watched her carefully, saw her throat work as she swallowed before she turned her head to stare straight between her horse's ears and affect a casual, almost bored voice. "What about him?"

"To be blunt, Steph? I'm told you're having an affair with him. Is it true?"

"No!"

He studied her pale, strained face. "I wish I could believe you. But I can't."

She looked at him again, her vivid blue eyes snapping with anger. "Then why bother to ask?"

"I hoped you might be honest with me."

She urged her horse into a fast trot. He caught up, and a silence stretched out between them filled only with the creak of their saddle leather and the rhythm of the horses' hooves beating the soft earth of the track. Finally, she said, "I was with child until recently, in case you've forgotten. Exactly when do you imagine I indulged in this affair? Hmmm?"

"You met him last spring, did you not?"

"Good God." She reined in hard. "Now what are you suggesting?"

He drew up and swung his horse to face her. But he couldn't quite bring himself to put the worst of his suspicions into words. Instead, he said, "Do you know anything about Ashworth's involvement with a Russian noblewoman attached to the household of the Grand Duchess?"

She stared at him a long moment before answering. "If you mean Princess Ivanna Gagarin, I'm aware of the whispers. But are they true? I don't know. She's a nasty woman. From what I hear, she and Ashworth deserved each other."

"Oh? What have you heard?"

Her brows twitched together in a frown. "She likes to say her husband was killed at the Battle of Borodino, but that's not strictly true. He was wounded there and carried to a nearby inn. She arrived a day later with great show to nurse him back to health although everyone said it was unnecessary, that his wound was minor and he was expected to make a quick recovery. And then he . . . died."

"Men die of seemingly inconsequential battle wounds all the time."

"Perhaps. But there's a reason everyone suspected her of poisoning him. He wasn't the first person to die inexplicably around her." She made a soft, throaty sound that might have been a laugh. "There would be a certain poetic justice to it, don't you think? For Ashworth to die at the hands of someone like her?"

"But why would she kill him?"

"You assume she needed a reason. You're

always so logical, Uncle. You have this idea that people do everything for a *reason,* that they never act without carefully thinking their actions through. But that's not actually true of most people. Perhaps she simply enjoys killing."

He had to admit this was one possibility he had not considered—that Ivanna Gagarin could have stabbed Ashworth over and over again simply for the sheer pleasure of taking another human being's life. Given her affinity for Ashworth, it made a certain kind of twisted sense.

Stephanie put up a hand to brush a loose strand of hair from her face. "I hear the inquest is tomorrow."

Sebastian nodded. "At eleven."

"What's the point, when they have no idea who killed him?"

"It's necessary before the body can be released for burial."

"Ah. Well, I must say I'll be glad when he's buried. He's evil." She glanced over at him. "Where do you think it comes from? That terrible, twisted evil that lurks inside men like him."

He met her gaze. "I don't know. A vicar would tell you that evil comes from Satan."

"Do you believe that?"

"No," he said honestly. "I met an Egyptian holy man once who told me they believe evil has no existence in and of itself but is simply a lack of good—the same way darkness is a lack of light. That makes more sense to me. But I still can't say I agree."

They rode on in silence, walking their horses, the wind slowly blowing the mist clear of the trees. He wanted to ask her when she had realized that Ashworth was fundamentally, irretrievably evil. He wanted to ask if her husband had discovered she was being unfaithful to him, thus setting in motion the series of events that ended with his hacked, bloody corpse tied naked to his bed. But the words would not come. And so he simply rode beside her, with the breeze damp against his face and the sweet sound of morning birdsong somehow accentuating the ache in his heart.

Half an hour later, he was in his dressing room, changing out of his riding habit, when Calhoun said, "I believe I may have identified that ruffian named 'Sid' you were asking about, my lord."

"Oh?" said Sebastian, going to pour water into the washbowl.

"There's a blackguard called Sid Cotton who has a reputation as a thief, but word is he's willing to hire himself out for other purposes."

Sebastian looked up from washing his face. "Murder being one of those 'other purposes'?"

Calhoun handed him a towel. "They say if the offer is good enough, he doesn't turn down anything."

Sebastian dried his face. "Where would I find him?"

"He generally frequents at a tavern called the Black Rose, in Seven Dials. Keeps a room there."

"Seven Dials? How the blazes did Ashworth ever get mixed up with such a fellow?"

"I'm told Ashworth used his talents more than once."

Sebastian glanced over at the fine linen shirt, doeskin breeches, and exquisitely tailored coat he'd been about to put on. "I think perhaps I need something less . . . conspicuous."

By the time Sebastian reached Seven Dials, the day had turned gray and wet, with rain that dripped from the eaves and collected in malodorous puddles in clogged gutters.

Dressed now in greasy leather breeches and an old coat, with a black kerchief at his neck, he had his hackney driver drop him at the end of Long Acre. Then, with one hand resting on the small, double-barreled pistol in his pocket, he plunged into the area known as Seven Dials. Sandwiched between Long Acre and Broad Street, this was considered one of the most wretched, dangerous neighborhoods in London. It had been laid out like a starburst late in the seventeenth century by a speculator, its name derived from the multifaced sundial column that had once stood at the juncture of the seven converging streets. But the streets had been made too narrow, so that the area rapidly deteriorated. The column was long gone, and the dark lanes were now crowded with gin shops, bawdy houses, secondhand dealers, and a colony of astrologers who found the streets' layout symbolic. Filthy, ragged children swarmed everywhere he looked; tattered washing flapped from upper windows of low lodging houses so crowded that people lived eight to ten to a room. The entire area reeked of overflowing bog houses, rot, disease, and despair.

The Black Rose was a miserable brick hovel just two stories tall plus a garret. It stood at the apex of two of the converging streets, and even at this hour of the day was crowded with ragged, unshaven men with bloodshot eyes and gnarled hands that shook as they raised tankards to cracked lips.

A dozen pairs of eyes watched Sebastian cross the foul-smelling, low-ceilinged, smoke-blackened room. His was a strange face in a neighborhood wary of strangers. His clothes might have come from a secondhand stall, and he'd rubbed grease and ashes into his hair to obscure its stylish cut. But he could do little to hide his cleanly shaven face or the tall, leanly muscled build that gave silent witness to a lifetime of good, nourishing food.

He ordered a tankard of ale from the slatternly matron behind the battered old bar and turned to survey the pub's patrons. No one was looking at him anymore—at least not directly. Calhoun had been able to give Sebastian only a general description of Sid Cotton: late thirties or early forties, dark hair beginning to show signs of gray, and a head like a fish.

"What do you mean, a head like a fish?" Sebastian had asked.

"I don't know. That's all she said: 'A head like a fish.' "

Setting aside the fish-head part, Sebastian could see several men in the Black Rose who fit that description. Two were engaged in an earnest conversation at a table near the base of a steep set of stairs and seemed convincingly oblivious to Sebastian's continued presence. The third man was by himself, nearer the door. He wore a battered brown corduroy jacket and sat in a way that hunched his shoulders and threw his face into shadow. But there was something about the slant of those shoulders, something about the shape of the man's narrow head, that stirred within Sebastian a memory of snowy streets and stealthy footsteps and the deadly rush of an assassin closing in fast.

As if aware of Sebastian's focus upon him, the man looked up. For one intense moment, his eyes met Sebastian's—oddly uneven gray eyes Sebastian had seen before.

Then the man pushed up from his chair fast enough to send it crashing over and bolted for the door.

CHAPTER 21

Sebastian tore after him, slamming into a blue-smocked chairman who was just coming in the door and tripping over a roasted-potato seller's barrow on the narrow flagway.

It was raining harder now, a cold patter that splashed in the dirty puddles of the gutters and stung Sebastian's cheeks as he chased Cotton down one of Seven Dials' grimy narrow spokes. The miserable weather was thinning the rookery's usual crowds, but not by much. Sebastian was able to follow the fleeing man by the wave of angry hisses and shouts that rose up as Cotton trod on an upended umbrella filled with knitted nightcaps for sale, clattered into a stall selling patched tin saucepans, then smacked into an old man hawking rat poison from a rusty tray slung from a strap around his neck.

With a panicked glance thrown over one shoulder, Cotton darted across the lane, cutting between a cart and a brewer's dray. Sebastian swerved after him and lost his hat to the drayman's whip.

"Bloody hell," he swore, the rain running down the back of his neck as he veered under a broken gutter to avoid a man mending cracked china and dodged a woman crouched against a wall with a basket of dried herrings.

The two men ran on, feet sliding on the wet, muck-smeared paving stones as they pelted past a stinking soap boiler's shop, a ballad printer's, a line of stalls selling penny-pies and peas soup and sheep's trotters. As they rounded the nearest corner, Cotton grabbed a ladder from a passing workman and turned to swing it at Sebastian's head. He swerved, and the ladder hit the shoulder of a large woman sitting behind a pickled-egg stall. With an angry bellow, she rose up and threw her stool at Sebastian. He tried to duck, but his foot landed in a fresh pile of manure, and he went down on one knee, barely catching himself on outflung hands.

"Ho!" shouted Cotton, laughing, his face wet with rain as he took off again.

Sebastian pushed up and raced after him.

The man was surprisingly quick and agile, but Sebastian was gaining on him. Breathing heavily now, Cotton ducked into the yawning mouth of an alley and snatched up first a broken crate, then a worn-out broom handle to throw back at Sebastian on the fly.

Leaping the back of a foraging half-grown pig that Cotton tripped over, Sebastian drew close enough to slam the man in the small of the back and send him careening into a tower of barrels that shuddered and collapsed around them with a rolling clatter. As Cotton flung up his arms to protect his head, Sebastian grabbed the man by his ragged coat and spun him around to slam him up against the soot-stained wall of the brewery that ran alongside the alley.

"Why the 'ell ye chasing me?" demanded Cotton, bucking against him.

"You know why." Sebastian yanked the pistol from his pocket, pressed the twin muzzle against the side of the man's head, and calmly pulled back the first hammer.

Cotton froze.

"Good idea," said Sebastian, breathing heavily. The rain poured around them.

Cotton's breath was coming hard enough to make his chest shudder. He was a strange-looking man, his unshaven cheeks sunken, his head unnaturally long and narrow, his lips full. His eyes were oddly mismatched, one larger than the other and not quite even with its partner. He licked his protuberant lips, his eyes rolling sideways as he tried to get a better look at the pistol digging into the flesh just above his ear. "Wot ye want from me?"

"I hear you were angry with Lord Ashcroft about something—angry enough to want to kill him. Why was that? I wonder."

Cotton gave a weak excuse for a laugh that was almost lost in the pounding of the rain. "Wot would a cove like me have to do with some bloody Marquis's son?"

"A great deal, from what I'm hearing. Why did you want to kill him?"

"I ain't the one who done for him! I swear to ye."

"Why the blazes should I believe you?"

"Because it's batty, thinkin' I coulda done it. Why, the way I hear it, his lordship was found tied to his own bed. How you reckon I got in there to do that?"

"You'd have me believe you don't number housebreaking amongst your many talents?"

"We-ell . . ."

"Stubble it." Sebastian tried to blink the rain out of his eyes. "You're a talented man by all reports. You could have done it."

Cotton looked faintly aggrieved. "Ain't my style. Now, if'n you'd found the bastard in some back alley with a knife between his shoulder blades, ye could by rights be thinkin' maybe it was me. But I hear it didn't happen that way."

"An interesting observation, given that his valet was found stabbed in the back in a nearby alley."

Cotton's eyes widened. "That weren't me. I don't know nothin' 'bout that."

"Why did you want to kill Ashworth?"

Cotton licked his lips again, then pressed them tightly together. The rain ran down his unshaven face in irregular rivulets.

"Come on," said Sebastian. "Out with it."

Cotton swallowed hard, his labored breathing beginning to ease. "His lordship, he hired us to do a job fer him—me and my mate, Joey. Only, then he refused to pay up."

"What did he hire you to do?"

A sly grin slid across the man's face, revealing a mouthful of brown and broken teeth. "Kill somebody."

"You mean me?"

Cotton laughed out loud. "Think I'd tell ye if'n it was?"

"You don't need to tell me. I couldn't see most of your face last January in Fleet Street because of the scarf. But I remember your eyes."

Cotton's grin slid away.

Sebastian said, "Given that I'm still alive, you didn't actually do the job Ashworth hired you for. So I'm not surprised he refused to pay you."

"I keep tellin' ye, it didn't have nothin' t' do wit ye. He cheated us over somethin' else."

"You don't strike me as the sort of man to take being cheated."

"Nobody cheats me and gets away wit it," Cotton said with some pride. "I won't deny I was plannin' on killin' the bugger. But somebody beat me to it."

"Perhaps it was your mate, Joey."

Cotton shook his head. "Joey is dead."

"I thought your dead mate was named Jack."

"That was me other mate. Got lots of mates, I do."

"So how did Joey die?"

Cotton peered at him through his thatch of

matted, graying brown hair. "Wot's that matter t' you?"

Sebastian said, "It's been two months since Ashworth hired you to kill me—"

"I never said he did. If'n somebody tried to kill ye, it weren't me."

"Two months," said Sebastian again. "Seems to me that's plenty of time for you to have killed him, if you were so inclined and if—"

"See! I keep tellin' ye it weren't me."

"—if you were planning to simply stick a knife in his back on a dark night. But if you were planning something considerably more elaborate, that might take time."

"I don't believe in complicated or fancy. Fancy gets ye killed. Stick a knife in their backs when they ain't lookin' and run. That's me motto."

Sebastian wasn't inclined to believe much of what the man had told him. But that had a ring of truth to it.

"Who told ye about me, anyway?" Cotton demanded, his eyes narrowing with vengeful purposefulness.

"The moon and the stars and a hanged man," said Sebastian, stepping back and letting him go.

"Wot?" Cotton sagged against the wall, one hand coming up to cup his ear. "Wot's that mean?"

But Sebastian simply backed away, the pistol in his hand, every sense alert to the dangers of the deadly neighborhood around him.

CHAPTER 22

This time, the door to Madame Blanchette's strange rooms on Golden Square was opened by a thin servant girl of perhaps twelve or thirteen. She was a fey thing, with hair so fair it was nearly white, a pale face, and wide, childlike eyes that nevertheless seemed to possess an aura of age-old wisdom that Sebastian found disconcerting.

She said, "Madame is waiting for you in her *cabinet d'études*."

"Of course."

He followed her to the small room he'd once assumed was a bedchamber but now realized was devoted to something far different. Yards and yards of deep red cloth draped the walls, giving it a tentlike effect. There was no window, only another door that must open back onto the corridor, presumably to allow those having their fortunes read to leave unseen by anyone who might be waiting their turn in the parlor. The only illumination came from a pierced brass Moroccan lantern that hung above an inlaid table that was a larger version of the one he'd noticed in the parlor. Madame Blanchette occupied one of the two stools flanking it; the other stood empty, waiting. The air was dense with exotic scents: frankincense and myrrh and something else he couldn't quite identify. An articulated skeleton stood grinning in one corner; stuffed bats hung on thin wires from the ceiling, and an owl sat on its perch. He assumed it was also stuffed until he saw it blink.

"Atmospheric," he said.

A faint smile touched her lips. "Image and illusion are important in my business."

"At least you admit that it is a business."

She gave a Gallic shrug. "We must all live somehow."

"True."

She spread her hands in a gesture that took in the opposite stool. "Please. Sit."

"I'm all wet."

"So I see. But it was considerate of you to clean the muck and manure of Seven Dials off your boots before coming to visit me. Thank you."

Sebastian felt a faint prickling at the back of his neck. "I tried."

"You are angry, I take it?"

He wiped the sleeve of his secondhand coat across his dripping face and sat. "You don't think I have a right to be?"

"Anger is sometimes useful. But more often it is a handicap."

"How the bloody hell did you know Ashworth hired Sid Cotton to kill me two months ago?"

"Perhaps I saw it in the cards."

"No you didn't. It doesn't work that way."

"At least you acknowledge that it does sometimes work."

He studied her smooth, calm, ageless face. "Why give me his first name but not the last?"

"I did not know it at the time."

"But now you do?"

"Yes."

"He says he didn't kill Ashworth."

"And you find him an honest and forthright fellow?"

"Sid Cotton is a conscienceless killer. I've no doubt he wanted to murder Ashworth. But that doesn't mean he did."

"Because you think a knife in the back on a dark night would be more his style?"

Sebastian found his hands clenching against his thighs and forced himself to open and press them flat on the tabletop before him. "Did you see that in your cards too?"

Rather than answer, she reached for the worn tarot deck that lay before him. "You are thirty-one?"

"Yes. Why?"

"Your favorite color?"

"Blue."

She handed him the cards. "*Coupez*."

He hesitated a moment, then cut the deck. She took the first card, laid it faceup to one side, and said, "*Encore*."

Again and again he cut the deck, with her drawing the first revealed card, until she had arranged thirty-six cards in four rows of nine each across the tabletop. Sebastian had seen cartomancers at work before. Their tarot desks were typically printed in black and white on matte cardboard with the crude images then colored in. But these were exquisite individual works of art that reminded him of the strange pictures he'd seen on the walls of her parlor. All were doubtless by the same hand.

"Who did these?" he asked.

"Does it matter?" She studied the selected cards for a time, the patterns of shadow and golden light cast by the pierced lantern overhead lending a mysterious aura to her features. When she spoke, he found her accent more pronounced; at times she slipped completely into French. "You have seen this done before?"

"Yes."

"Then you know that few cards are either all good or all bad. Their meaning alters depending on how they fall in relation to one another."

When he remained silent, she tapped the fourth card in the first row, an image of a beautiful young woman standing on a jagged rock above a storm-tossed sea, the wind blowing her glorious long, fair hair. "If you were a woman, this card would represent you. But because you are a man, it represents a woman in your life. She is very strong, and her intentions toward you are only good. But she is . . . conflicted."

Sebastian's gaze met hers across the card-covered table. "Given that you know who I am, you obviously must know who she is as well. You don't need the cards to tell you the source of her . . . conflict."

The Frenchwoman lowered her gaze to the cards, her expression never changing as she pointed to an image of a knight, his helm held beneath one arm, a magnificent black stallion prancing at his side. "The man is you. You see the card beside it? The scythe? It is a warning that you are in danger. You must take heed and be cautious when you visit unsafe places or associate with dangerous people."

"You mean places such as Seven Dials and the likes of Sid Cotton?"

Rather than acknowledge his sarcasm, she simply moved on to the image of a coiled snake that lay beside the scythe. "Because the snake can shed its skin, it sometimes represents change and renewal. But here the serpent signifies more danger, except this danger is hidden. Be especially wary of those you think are your friends or whom you assume are well-disposed toward you. They may not be."

"Always wise advice in a murder investigation."

At that she did look up. "You make light of what I tell you. You should not." She turned her attention to the last row, to an image of an ancient illuminated manuscript resting half open at the entrance to an enchanted grotto. "The book represents a secret of great importance." Her eyes narrowed as if she were seeing something unexpected. "A secret that relates not to the murder of Ashworth but to you, *monsieur le vicomte*. It is an old secret that has long lain hidden despite your attempts to unveil it. But the unmasking of deceptions can be dangerous. You must understand well the perils of this personal quest upon which you have embarked."

Sebastian felt his face grow hot with what he knew was an old, old shame. It mattered not that the originating sin was of others' making; the resultant shame was still his to bear, and it always would be. He told himself she didn't know—she could not know. He told himself that all men have secrets. Easy enough to hint at one, watch for a betraying reaction, and then move in closer for the killing thrust.

He schooled his features into a mask of calm insouciance. And yet he knew by the flare of awareness in her eyes that she saw right through him. She might not grasp the ugly details of the deepest, darkest secret of his existence, but she now knew he hid a torment with the power to drive him from his bed in the darkest hours of night in search of an elusive peace that never came.

For one intense moment, she held his gaze. Then she dropped her attention again to the cards, her fingertips skimming over an image of a Spanish galleon in full sail, the winds billowing its sun-struck canvas as it cut through a raging sea. She frowned but kept going, her hand coming to rest on an image of two soaring birds, their dark wings silhouetted against a stormy sky. "Birds were once considered messengers from the gods to mankind," she said softly. "They can represent wisdom and freedom of the spirit. But as with so many cards, their meaning can alter depending on where they fall. Here they mean . . . adversity. Your life is approaching a period of great strife that will test you. Whether you survive without permanent loss or damage is up to you." She leaned back on her stool, folded her hands in her lap, and looked at him.

He had to fight a powerful urge to ask whether the looming "adversity" came from his attempts to reveal Ashworth's murderer or arose in some way from his quest to unravel the secret to which she had just alluded. He wanted to ask her if he would ever know the truths now hidden from him. Except of course he did no such thing because she was a charlatan, a fraud, a trickster, and he believed in none of this.

None of it.

She said, "I don't know if you will discover the truth you seek. But I can warn you that you must be certain you can accept whatever you will learn. Otherwise you must not seek it."

He stared at her. "Why are you doing this?"

She gave a small shake of her head, as if not understanding the question. "Doing what?"

He wafted one hand over the cards on the table. "This."

"Perhaps for the same reason you seek justice for those deprived of their lives through murder. We feel driven, you and I, to help those who need it most." She nodded toward the skeleton that stood in one corner of the red-shrouded room. "Much of what I do is for show—for the amusement and titillation of bored, wealthy men and women who like to play at touching the mysterious unknown from the safety of their drawing rooms." Again, that little shrug. "Francesca and I must eat and have a roof over our heads."

"Francesca?"

"The girl who met you at the door." She paused, and he thought she meant to say something more about the strange child. Instead, she said, "You have a gift for discerning patterns, for understanding motives and piercing deceptions." She began collecting her cards. "My gift is for this. When I can help, I do."

"You think it helps? Foretelling the future? It seems to me it could have unintended consequences."

"It can. I try to be careful with what I relay. What I see is only a possibility. Unfortunate outcomes can sometimes be averted if one is forewarned and wise."

"But not always."

For one brief instant her hands trembled, and he found himself thinking of an innocent young woman desperate enough to throw herself and her unborn child into the Thames. All the knowledge and foresight Madame Blanchette claimed to find in her cards hadn't been enough to save her own daughter.

He said, "Where did you learn to use the cards?"

She assembled the deck into a neat stack and set it aside. "My father was a minor government functionary in the Rouergue. When I was twelve, my parents sent me to a convent in Conques where the nuns were perhaps not as vigilant as they should have been. I befriended an old Gypsy woman. It was she who introduced me to the tarot."

He found himself wondering about the years in between, all the dangerous years of revolution and war that had taken a young girl from a convent on the Dourdou to the gilded halls of the Tuileries and then exile. Had the cards helped her navigate those treacherous times? Or had they provided her with only an illusion of control?

"Sometimes even illusions are helpful," she said, and he felt a chill pass over him that had nothing to do with his wet clothes.

He pushed to his feet, not surprised to realize that Francesca had silently appeared in the doorway, ready to show him out. But at the entrance, he looked back at the woman, who remained seated on her stool. He said, "You still haven't told me everything you know."

For a moment her gaze met his. And he saw in the dark depths of her eyes a lifetime of pain and fear and sorrow without end. "If the tarot has taught me anything," she said quietly, "it is the dangerous limitations of what I think I know."

He was tempted to pay a visit next to Vincent's, the Bond Street jeweler in whose shop Ashworth was said to have raped Giselle Blanchette. But it was Sunday, and raining, and he remembered he was still dressed to blend in with the riffraff of Seven Dials rather than the exalted residents of Mayfair.

He hailed a hackney and headed home.

He turned in to Brook Street to find a gentleman in a caped greatcoat and fashionable beaver hat standing at the base of the front steps of Sebastian's house. The slowing hackney briefly drew the man's attention. But he evidently failed to recognize the scruffy individual paying off the jarvey, because he started to turn away, only to stop, swing back toward the front steps, and hesitate again.

"Looking for me?" said Sebastian.

"Devlin. Good heavens." Russell Firth blinked against the rain. "Why are you dressed like that?"

"It's complicated." Sebastian squinted up at the weeping sky. "Shall we go inside? Or did you plan to keep pacing back and forth on the flagway all afternoon?"

A faint flush crept into the architect's cheeks. "I was trying to decide precisely what to say to you."

"You've seen Stephanie, I take it?"

Firth nodded.

"Then please, let's continue this conversation over a brandy in my library. I don't know about you, but I'm damnedably wet."

Sebastian led the way into the house and poured two generous measures of brandy. "Have a seat," he said as he turned to throw more coal on the fire. "I appreciate your coming, and I'll give you credit for being more honest than my niece. Or perhaps you're simply clever enough to realize that the jig is up."

Firth perched uncomfortably on the edge of one of the chairs facing the hearth. "It's not what you think."

"Oh?" Sebastian stood and turned to look at him. "Then tell me what it is."

Firth thrust up from the chair and went to gaze out the front window at the rain. "It happened much as I told you: I met her when she came to a presentation I gave on Sounion. For some reason, the temple captured her imagination in a way that I think caught even her by surprise. She came up to speak to me afterward, and—" He broke off and shook his head. "I knew it was hopeless from the beginning. We both did. But we were helpless to stop what was happening."

"Hopeless because of the disparity in your stations, you mean?"

Firth blew out a long breath. "That probably should have made a difference, but it didn't. The thing is, my wife was still alive then."

Sebastian stared at him. "I'm sorry, I didn't realize you were married."

"To my cousin, Elizabeth. She . . . she found herself in difficulty several years ago. We'd always been close, ever since we were children—more like brother and sister, actually. I couldn't simply leave her to suffer alone the consequences of what she'd done."

"She was with child?"

Firth nodded. "The father was long gone by the time she realized she was in trouble. Her own father, my aunt's husband, disowned her. She had no one else to turn to. So I married her."

He paused for a moment, and Sebastian waited until the Welshman was ready to continue. "Elizabeth was never well, and the emotional turmoil combined with bearing the child took a terrible toll on her. The little boy died within hours of birth, and she never really recovered. The doctors said sea air might do her good, so I hired a house for her down in Brighton and engaged a companion to keep her company and take care of her while I continued with my work here in London."

"When did she die?"

"Last October." Firth drew a crooked elbow across his rain-soaked face. "I don't mean to imply that the circumstances of my marriage excuse my allowing my affections to stray elsewhere, because they do not. But it may perhaps explain it. Elizabeth and I were never more than dear friends."

"When did you and Stephanie become lovers?"

"We didn't. Never."

Sebastian took a slow sip of his brandy. Firth might be marginally more honest than Stephanie, Sebastian decided, but it was still only a matter of degree. "A man like Ashworth wouldn't take it lightly if he found out his wife was in love with another man—even if he could somehow be convinced that the affair remained unconsummated."

Firth shook his head. "He didn't love her. He never did. He only married her because his father refused to give him another groat until he set about providing a legitimate heir for the succession."

"Perhaps. Except that even if he didn't care

for her, she was still his wife. And as far as most men are concerned, that makes a woman his possession. Something meant for him and him alone."

Firth started to say something, then simply raised his glass to his lips with an unsteady hand and drank deeply.

Sebastian said, "You realize the damage it will do if knowledge of the friendship between you gets out? People are already speculating that she might have killed him."

"But she didn't do it!"

So, what about you? thought Sebastian, his gaze hard on the younger man's face. *Did you kill Ashworth for her? Ashworth, or at least Digby?* He didn't voice the accusation aloud, but then, he didn't need to. It hung there in the tense atmosphere between them.

Firth swung away to look out the window again at the gray, wet street. "Ashworth made her existence a living hell. You . . . You've no idea what he was like."

"Actually, I have a pretty good idea. I'm not surprised she refused to live with him."

"He didn't want her there. He was always bringing home women, everything from titled ladies to whores hired off the street. If you ask me, that's who killed him—some poor woman who didn't understand the abuse she was letting herself in for and fought back."

"Except that Ashworth was the one tied to the bed."

Firth turned to stare at him for a long, unblinking moment. Then he set his drink aside unfinished. "The inquest is tomorrow?"

"Yes."

"Perhaps something will come out then."

"I doubt it. But I suppose it's always possible."

For one intense moment, the two men's gazes met. "She didn't do it," said the architect again, his jaw set at a stubborn angle.

Sebastian drained his own glass and gave an unexpected shudder. *I hope to God you're right,* he thought.

But he remained unconvinced.

CHAPTER 23

That night, Sebastian dreamed of ancient manuscripts written in blood, of shadowy caverns beckoning him with dangerous promises of secrets to be revealed. He saw a ship, its sunstruck sails billowing in a fair wind, and a familiar, golden-haired woman, ever young, her head thrown back in joyous laughter.

He awoke with his throat tight, his breath coming hard and fast. He was aware of a heavy ache of yearning in his chest and eyes so dry they hurt. Beside him, Hero shifted, murmuring in her sleep.

Gently so as not to wake her, he drew her to him and buried his face in the sweet warmth of her hair.

Monday, 4 April

The inquest into the murder of Lord Ashworth was held at the White Hart in Clarges Street. Because no official venue for such inquiries existed, inquests were typically convened in whatever nearby pub or inn was large enough to accommodate the crowds so often attracted by the titillating opportunity to view a bloody, mutilated corpse.

Viscount Ashworth, his skin beginning to take on a waxy, greenish hue, lay faceup on a battered table in the center of the room. The bodies of murder victims were typically displayed naked. At the insistence of his lordship's father, the Marquis of Lindley, a folded sheet had been draped over the victim's groin. But his lordship's savagely hacked chest was in full view of anyone who cared to wander in out of the rain and gawk at it.

"I never thought I'd be attending my own son's inquest," Lindley told Sebastian as the two men stood together waiting for the coroner to arrive. It seemed to Sebastian, looking at him, that the Marquis had aged a decade in just three days. He'd always been thin, but there was now an air of increased fragility about him, a slowness to his movements that hadn't been there before. It was as if his sorrow over his son's death were a brutal weight bearing down upon him. And it was visibly crushing him.

"Look at them," said Lindley, staring out over the pushing, malodorous crowd, all vying for a chance to peer at the dead man. The air was thick with a foul stench of wet wool, sweat, tobacco, and ale. "It's a rare day's entertainment for them, like a cockfight or a bearbaiting—with my son's mutilated body as the central spectacle."

"You don't need to stay for this," Sebastian said quietly.

"Yes, I do. I owe him that. And then—" The old man's voice broke, and he had to swallow and start again. "And then I'll take him home." He cleared his throat. "Lovejoy tells me you've agreed to help try to find the killer. I can't tell you how grateful I am for that. Are you making any progress at all?"

Sebastian shook his head. "I wish I could say I was, but . . . not really. I'm sorry."

" 'For this child I prayed,' " quoted the old man softly. " 'And the Lord hath given me my petition that which I asked of him. Therefore I have lent him to the Lord.' " Lindley sighed. "Samuel 1:27 to 28." He paused again, then said, "If there's anything I can do—anything—you'll let me know? I keep going over and over everything I can recall him saying these last few weeks, hoping I'll come up with something that might explain this. But I can't."

"He didn't seem nervous or upset or pre-occupied in any way?"

"Anthony? No. He wasn't the type, actually. They don't come any cooler or steadier."

Sebastian wasn't convinced such a characteristic was entirely admirable. In his experience, men who lacked the capacity to feel fear or nervousness were all too often missing other emotions, valuable attributes such as empathy, compassion, and remorse. He said, "Do you know if he'd quarreled with anyone recently? Or if there was someone he might have angered or frightened?"

The old Marquis thought about it a moment, then shook his head. "Not that I'm aware. Although to be honest, I didn't see much of him. I'd hoped marriage to your niece might settle him down. Change him. A wife and children typically have that effect, don't they? But not with Anthony." A quiver passed over his aged face. "I've outlived them all now—my wife, all but one of my sisters, and all four of my children. A man dedicates his life to preserving the proud heritage entrusted to him by his father—building up the family estates, protecting the honor of the family name—thinking one day he will pass on the sacred obligation to his own son . . ." His voice trailed off; then he swallowed hard and said, "Thank God for the birth of those two little boys."

"They must be a source of great comfort to you."

A faint spark of joy glimmered through the pain shadowing the old man's eyes. "Have you seen them? They're fine lads, as lusty and strong as you could wish. My only regret is that they'll never have the opportunity to know the man who was their father."

Personally, Sebastian thought that was just as well for the children's sake. But he kept that opinion to himself.

There was a stirring near the door that suggested the imminent arrival of the coroner. The Marquis glanced over at the commotion and said, "We had someone from Bow Street at Lindley House this morning, talking to the servants. Do you know anything about that?"

"No. Sorry."

Lindley fixed him with a hard stare. "Please tell me they don't suspect Stephanie."

A constable could be heard near the entrance barking, *"Make way! Make way there!"* as the coroner tried to push into the overcrowded public room.

Sebastian said, "I don't think they suspect her, exactly. But you must see that they feel the need to investigate every angle, no matter how delicate."

"I suppose, yes. But it's hard on the poor girl. She has enough to bear without Bow Street Runners throwing her abigail into hysterics."

"When were they there?"

"This morning, right before I left to come here. Something about a bundle of clothes some wherryman fished from the Thames."

Sebastian had expected the inquest to also cover the death of Edward Digby. But the coroner—a wispy, white-haired former reverend named Lamar Liddell—had declined to save the purses of the parish ratepayers by doubling up. It wasn't often a coroner was given the opportunity to preside over the murder of a viscount, and Sebastian suspected Liddell didn't want some mere valet distracting from the importance of the event.

But apart from the silent, inescapable presence of Ashworth's mutilated, bloody corpse, the inquest was something of a disappointment for those who'd crowded into the public room to enjoy it. The coroner's voice was so breathy and soft that he was difficult for many to hear. The most potentially interesting testimony came from Lovejoy, but the Bow Street magistrate did his best to deliver his evidence in dry, unsensational periods. His lordship's butler, Fullerton, could only explain apologetically that he'd slept through both the murder and the discovery of the body, and was quickly dismissed. Alice, the housemaid who'd first walked in on the blood-splashed murder scene, was weeping so hysterically that her testimony was virtually incoherent. And the second housemaid, Jenny Crutcher, wasn't there at all, since no one had been able to locate her in order to serve her with a summons.

"Havey-cavey thing to do," muttered the coroner when told of the woman's absence. "Going off like that right after a murder."

Sebastian glanced over at Lovejoy, who gave an almost imperceptible shake of his head. Lovejoy had assigned two of his Runners to track down the housemaid as soon as they discovered she'd bolted. At first, they'd been inclined to ascribe her hasty departure to nerves. But the discovery of Edward Digby's naked, bloody corpse raised the ominous possibility that Jenny Crutcher might somehow have been involved in Ashworth's death, or that she at least knew something.

Something that had put her life in danger.

The coroner's jury returned a verdict of bloody murder by person or persons unknown. Afterward, Sebastian sat with Lovejoy in a coffeehouse off Piccadilly. The day was wretchedly gloomy, with a heavy cover of thick gray clouds and endless, drizzling rain.

"The palace is not going to be happy," said Lovejoy, sipping cautiously at his hot chocolate. "They want someone arrested and remanded for trial. Quickly."

Sebastian wrapped his hands around his coffee mug. "Any luck finding a modista able to identify the bloodstained clothes recovered from the Thames?"

"Unfortunately, no." Lovejoy cleared his throat uncomfortably. "One of my lads, Constable Gowdy, took the clothes 'round to Lindley House this morning and asked Lady Ashworth's abigail if she could identify them. Pushed the girl rather hard, from what I understand. You'll be relieved to hear she denied they belonged to her mistress."

"But?" said Sebastian, watching his friend's face.

"Constable Gowdy says he doesn't believe her. He's convinced the abigail was lying." Lovejoy paused, then continued, his voice low. "I hesitate to even suggest it, but might Her Ladyship be capable of doing such a thing, do you think?"

Sebastian took a moment to answer. It was a question he'd been asking himself for three days now. He chose his words carefully. "Ashworth was an ugly, dangerous human being. I suspect someone like that could drive almost anyone to murder, particularly if they feared for their life. But stabbing a man in the back, the way Edward Digby was killed? That's something else entirely. I can't see Stephanie doing that." *Although she could have had an accomplice,* Sebastian thought. *Someone like Firth who loved her enough to try to clean up behind her.* But he kept that possibility to himself.

Lovejoy looked relieved. "Yes, that's my reading of the situation as well."

"Where are the clothes now?"

"With Constable Gowdy."

"Have him send them to Brook Street, why don't you? I'd like to take a look at them myself."

"Of course." Lovejoy took another sip of his hot chocolate. "We've also had no luck yet in finding a hackney driver, although we're still looking."

Sebastian leaned back in his seat. "I've had

211

two different people tell me Ashworth sometimes picked up streetwalkers and brought them home to play his 'games.' It might be worth looking into that too."

"You think that's what we could be dealing with here? A woman off the streets who didn't know what she was letting herself in for, took fright, and killed him?"

"Either took fright, or took revenge, depending on the sequence of events and the character of the woman."

"And Digby?"

"Perhaps he ran after her and tried to stop her. So she killed him too."

"Except that Digby was stabbed in the back."

"True. But I can envision several scenarios that would explain that. Although how he then ended up naked in that alley is a bit more problematic."

Lovejoy looked troubled. "If this woman does exist, it's not going to be easy finding her. Unlike hackney drivers, London does not license its whores."

"No." Sebastian paused. "Of course, there is another possibility."

Lovejoy shook his head. "What?"

"That Ashworth was with a whore that night, but she's not the murderer. She's a witness. And . . ."

"And?"

Sebastian pushed his coffee aside. "And by now she might well be another victim."

CHAPTER 24

Sebastian went next to Bond Street, where he intended to pay a visit to Vincent's and ask the jeweler about Giselle Blanchette. Except he found the shutters up and the bell off the shop door.

"Where's Mr. Vincent?" he asked a passing delivery boy.

"He's dead," said the boy, a lad of perhaps fifteen or sixteen with wide, staring eyes and a small chin.

"Since when?"

The boy shrugged. "A few weeks, meybe."

"What happened to him?"

"Somebody bashed in his skull as he was closin' up fer the night."

"It was a robbery?"

The boy shook his head. "There weren't nothin' taken. But whoever it was sure enough killed him. Killed him dead."

More troubled than ever, Sebastian arrived back at Brook Street to find a paper-wrapped bundle awaiting him. He stared at it a moment, but before opening it, sent for Calhoun.

"Do you know anything about the murder of a jeweler in Bond Street a few weeks ago?" he asked the valet. "A man by the name of Vincent."

Jules Calhoun shook his head. "I know it happened, but nothing beyond that. I can ask around if you like, my lord."

"Please. Also, it's possible that Ashworth hired a prostitute the night he was killed. She could be anything from a highflier to a common streetwalker, but if she exists, I need to find her. Think that's possible?"

Calhoun grinned. "I'll try, my lord."

After the valet left, Sebastian untied the paper-wrapped bundle from Bow Street and spread its contents across the library floor. Then he stood with his legs set widely apart, his arms crossed at his chest as he stared down at the dark blue, fine woolen cloak, fashionable muslin gown, linen petticoat, chemise, and lightweight, short corset.

The gown's scooped bodice and puff sleeves, combined with the delicate embroidery around the neckline and flounced hem, suggested it had belonged to a young woman. The quality of the materials and workmanship told him she was either wealthy or on good terms with someone who ran a high-end secondhand clothing shop.

The bloodstains were . . . curious.

From the pattern of the stains, he suspected the woman—whoever she was—must have been wearing the cloak when she somehow or other ended up covered in blood. Only the central front of the gown was stained, as if its sides had been protected by the open cloak. The blood on

214

the gown was heavy enough that it had soaked through to the petticoat, chemise, and short corset beneath. There were some faint traces of blood around the hem of both the gown and the petticoat, but most of the stains were higher up, mainly on the bodice and midriff sections.

It was entirely possible the clothing had absolutely nothing to do with Ashworth's death. Nothing at all. And yet . . .

The sound of a child's laughter drew his attention to the doorway. He heard Simon squeal with delight and shout, "Mm-ga-ga-gee." Then a long-haired black cat with a magnificent long, thick tail streaked into the room and went to ground beneath one of the chairs by the fire.

"You'd better hide," Sebastian told the cat, smiling.

"Mm-ga-ga-gee?" said Simon, drawing up perplexed at the entrance to the room.

Sebastian said, "I think perhaps Mr. Darcy wants to take a nap."

Hero appeared behind the boy, laughing as she swung him up into her arms. "I know someone else who needs a nap."

"Mm-ga-ga-gee," said Simon, one arm reaching out toward the chair where Mr. Darcy's magnificent tail was just visible.

"You can play with Mr. Darcy after you and he have a nap," said the boy's nurse, coming to take him from Hero. "Off we go."

"I thought you were planning to do another interview this afternoon," said Sebastian as the nurse carried the boy off.

"I am." Hero came to stand beside him, her gaze on the bloody clothes spread across the floor. "What's all this, then?"

"The contents of the bundle pulled from the Thames. The gown and underthings were wrapped in the cloak, which fortunately kept them quite dry."

She hunkered down beside the clothes, a faint frown drawing two parallel lines between her eyes. "This is a lovely cloak. And the gown is of the first stare—'all the crack,' as they say."

"Yet Lovejoy's constable took it to every fashionable modista in town, and none identified it as her own work. That could be because the maker feared betraying a valued customer, or . . ."

She looked up at him. "Or because the gown was made on the Continent."

"I'll admit that was my first thought."

"There are other explanations."

"There are?"

She pushed to her feet.

"The gown could have been made by a provincial modista. They may have a reputation for dowdiness, but the truth is that there are some very talented women working in places such as Brighton and Bath—or even Edinburgh."

Sebastian pursed his lips and blew out a harsh

breath. "Which means that unless someone remembers actually seeing a woman wearing this dress, it's a dead end . . . apart from the possibility it might not have anything to do with Ashworth's death anyway."

"I don't know about that. The fact that the clothes were thrown into the Thames in the middle of the night is rather suggestive. I mean, if all were innocent, why not simply have the clothes washed? That would only be out of the question if the young owner had something to hide, because even with the cooperation of her abigail, it would be virtually impossible to keep the other servants from seeing and asking awkward questions about all that blood. Much simpler in that case to drop the clothes off a bridge in the dark—particularly if she could afford to do so."

"I'd say it's a safe bet that whoever owned this cloak and gown has wardrobes full of other clothes." He watched as Hero bit her lip in thought. "What is it?"

"No shoes or stockings?"

"No. I checked with Bow Street, and they confirmed there weren't any with the bundle. But then, there was a woman's stocking under Ashworth's bed, remember?"

"Any blood on it?"

"No."

"So, assuming this is the killer's clothing, she

had her shoes and stockings off, but not her dress and cloak? That's odd."

"It is, indeed." He nodded to the embroidered muslin. "What does the gown tell you about the woman who wore it?"

"That she's quite young—or is trying to appear to be, at least."

"Well, that would exclude Madame Blanchette—apart from the fact that she dresses like an elegant ghost from the eighteenth century anyway. What else?"

"Wealthy, obviously. Either that, or she makes her own clothes, has access to fine materials, and is extraordinarily handy with her needle."

"I suppose Julie McCay could be hiding superb sewing skills. But I'd be surprised."

"How was she dressed when you saw her?"

He had to think about it for a moment. "In no way remarkable."

Hero reached to pick up the gown and held it against her own body. "Whoever owned this dress is quite slender. And taller than average, although not excessively so."

"That would also eliminate Julie McCay and Madame Blanchette. But not a certain Russian princess."

He didn't say, *Or Stephanie.* But then, he didn't need to.

Hero fingered the delicate stitching around the gown's neckline. "If the killer is some unknown woman Ashworth was 'entertaining' the night he was killed, then these clothes suggest you're looking for a lady rather than a woman he picked up off the streets."

"Which narrows things down to—oh, I don't know; how many young, wealthy, tallish ladies would you say there are in London? Five hundred? More? Less?"

Hero looked vaguely troubled. "If she killed him because of what he did to her that night, it seems wrong to expose her and make her suffer for it. She's suffered enough already."

"You're forgetting about what was done to Edward Digby."

"Yes. But he was complicit, was he not?"

"I suppose he was." Sebastian stared down at the woolen cloak. The bloodstains on the gown and undergarments had been well preserved by being wrapped in the cloak. But the cloak itself had been heavily saturated with water, making the pattern of the stains on the dark wool difficult to read.

"What?" asked Hero, watching him.

"I just wish I had an idea what the bloodstains on the cloak looked like before it was soaked." He reached for the large sheet of brown paper in which the clothes had been delivered from Bow Street.

"What are you going to do?" she asked, watching him bundle the clothes up again and tie the string.

"Show these to Stephanie and decide for myself whether she's lying."

Stephanie was curled up on a window seat in the music room of Lindley House, a book lying open but forgotten on her knee, when Sebastian was shown up to her.

"Uncle," she said, the book tumbling to the floor as she rose to her feet. She wore a simple muslin gown dyed black and stripped of all adornment, and she looked so young and vulnerable that it broke his heart. "You're quite grim today." Her gaze fell to the bulky paper-wrapped bundle he held tucked under one arm. "What's this?"

He set it on the tea table between them. "Open it."

She hesitated a moment, then came to untie the string and pull open the brown paper. The blood-soaked gown was folded on top, and she gasped at the sight of it, one hand coming up to press against her chest as she took a quick step back. "Dear God. Why did you bring these to me? Someone from Bow Street was already here this morning, badgering my abigail about them. She told him they're not mine."

"I know," said Sebastian, conscious of a yawning sense of concern. He had come here hoping to prove to himself that his suspicions were all wrong, that Stephanie had had nothing to do with the bloody carnage someone had wrought in Ashworth's bedchamber. Instead, he found himself studying her pale, strained face. "What I'm wondering, Steph, is how you knew these were the same clothes."

He saw a flare of panic in her eyes as if she realized her mistake. But she had always been quick-witted. Her chin jerked up, her hand curling into a fist as it dropped to her side. "It's a logical assumption, is it not? Surely there aren't two sets of bloody women's clothing floating around London at the moment?"

He walked away to stand by the fire, his gaze on the blaze crackling on the hearth. "Russell Firth came to see me yesterday," he said. "He swears you've never been lovers, although he made no real attempt to deny that he's in love with you." He looked over at her. "You lied to me, Steph."

She spun away, her hands clenched together against her midriff, her back held painfully straight.

Sebastian said quietly, "Ashworth found out about Firth, didn't he, Stephanie?"

"No." She swung to face him again. "No. But it wouldn't have mattered to him even if he had found out. He never loved me. Why would he have cared if he found out I loved someone else?"

"He might have cared if he suspected his newborn sons were not his."

Her head snapped back as if he had slapped her. "You're wrong," she said fiercely, color riding high in her cheeks. "Do you hear me? You're wrong."

"Am I, Steph? I keep trying to come up with another reason you might have married him, but I can't. Last September, I thought you were infatuated with him, that you'd fallen under the spell of his charm and the allure of his wealth and title. But that wasn't true; you were in love with another man. And yes, Firth was married to his cousin. But you knew she wasn't well. Why in the hell would you marry Ashworth?"

"Because I was carrying his child!"

"Were you, Steph? So, I suppose my question then becomes why? Why put yourself in that position when you were supposedly in love with another man?"

"You really want to know what happened, Uncle? All right; I'll tell you. It was at Lady Cowper's ball last June. I made the mistake of stepping out onto the terrace for some air. I was feeling faint from the heat, and I didn't expect to find it deserted, although it was. I'd been flirting with Ashworth earlier. I won't deny I found him attractive and entertaining in a rakish, dangerous way, and the ball was a bit of a bore. But I didn't mean anything by it; truly I didn't. Only, he read it all wrong. He followed me out onto the terrace, pushed me into the shadows, and started kissing me. I tried to laugh it off, told him he'd quite misunderstood the situation, and tried to pull away. He wouldn't let me go."

She paused, then continued, her voice a broken whisper. "He . . . he accused me of leading him on. Said he could tell I wanted it—that he knew what I was like just by looking at me, that I was asking for it. Then he shoved himself inside me and took me there up against the house wall with Lady Cowper's hundreds of guests dancing and laughing just a few feet away."

"My God, Steph. How could you marry him after that?"

"How?" She gave a ragged laugh. "I suppose because deep down I believed him. I thought I somehow deserved what he'd done to me—that I really had asked for it by smiling at him and 'playing the coquette' with him."

"Oh, Steph."

"After all, it was the same excuse my father gave for raping me from the time I was seven years old."

A hollow pit opened up low in Sebastian's gut. *Oh, God. Oh, God, no.*

"Anthony was far more gentle and solicitous when it was all over than my father ever was," she was saying. "He told me he loved me, and I eventually convinced myself he did, that it had all been a misunderstanding, that he wasn't really, truly horrible. After all, what choice did I have?

The man I loved was married to someone else, and it didn't take me long to realize I was with child. I desperately needed to marry someone."

"Does Firth know?"

"That Anthony raped me? No. He spent last July and August in Brighton."

"I wish you had told me."

"And what would you have done, Uncle?"

What would he have done? Sebastian wondered. Tried to convince her that it wasn't her fault—that it had never been her fault? That wishful thinking was never going to reform a monster like Ashworth? But he couldn't say any of those things to this fierce, fragile girl. And so he asked, "Does your mother know?"

"That Ashworth raped me? I told her, but her reaction was much the same as Ashworth's— she's convinced I must have done something to lure him into thinking I wanted it. As for my father, I never told her."

Sebastian noticed she didn't say that Amanda didn't know. And he thought that he had never despised his sister as much as he did in that moment.

"The point is," said Stephanie, "even if Ashworth did find out how I felt about Russell, he wouldn't have cared. All he cared about was acquiring an acceptable wife and an heir to seal the deal with his father. I suspect he'd have been perfectly happy if he never had to see either the twins or me again. He wasn't like normal people. You can't assume he would react to anything the way you'd expect someone else to react."

Sebastian felt a heavy ache of sadness settle in his chest. He wanted to believe her. He wanted desperately to believe her. But the sense that she was still hiding something persisted. He said, "Would you do me a favor and hold the dress up against you, Steph?"

"Why? So you can see if it would fit?" She turned to the pile of bloodstained clothes. Only, rather than doing as he had asked, she closed the paper wrapping with swift, jerky motions and retied the string. "Uncle," she said, holding the bundle out to him, her jaw set.

"I guess that tells me what I need to know."

Rather than answer, she simply stared back at him, those familiar blue St. Cyr eyes blazing with a strange light that was part defiance, part entreaty.

He reached out to touch her cheek, then thought better of it and let his hand drop. "I wish you'd be honest with me, child."

"I'm not a child anymore."

"No," he said, turning toward the door. "No, you're not."

CHAPTER 25

The old woman was shuffling down Skinner Street toward the top of Fleet Market when Hero spotted her. Dressed in rags, with broken-down shoes tied on her feet with cords, the woman had the handle of a covered basket slung over one arm and the telltale black glove of her trade on her right hand.

This was a section of London dominated by the reeking stockyards and slaughterhouses of Smithfield to the north and, nearer at hand, the ominous presence of Fleet Prison and Newgate and the constant spectacle of public hangings in the Old Bailey. All of which made it a good hunting ground for various types of scavengers.

"Draw up here," Hero told her coachman.

The basket and glove marked the woman as a "banter" or "pure finder," one of that army of desperate souls who eked out a miserable living picking up dog feces to sell to the tanneries of Bermondsey, where they were used to dress the skins of calves and lambs. It was called "pure" because, thanks to the feces' astringent and alkaline properties, it could be used to scour and "purify" the leather.

The woman blinked when Hero walked up to her and explained why she wanted to interview her. Her back was bent from years of stooping, her gray hair matted, most of her teeth either rotted away or sold to dentists. She said her name was Gussie Spilsby, and though she looked eighty, she claimed she was only sixty-two.

Fortified with a meat pie, a cup of tea, and the promise of a shilling, she agreed to sit on the steps of the porch of St. Sepulchre and tell Hero about her life.

"Have you always done this?" Hero asked, her notebook balanced on her knees, the reek coming from the woman's basket making her eyes water.

"Oh, no. My second husband used to be a barber," said the woman, sipping her tea with a daintiness that surprised Hero as much as her accent and relatively careful diction. "But he lost his right arm after he got knocked down and run over by a noblewoman's carriage, so he couldn't do that anymore. We managed for a time by selling what we had. But when there wasn't anything left to sell, we took to pure finding. With the two of us collecting, we could make a fair amount a week. Course, the tanners used to pay more in those days."

"How much can you make a week now?"

"Maybe five or six shillings, at least in summer, when the light lasts a long time—and if I find good stuff."

"What's the difference between 'good stuff' and everything else?"

"You get the best price for the dry, lime-looking stuff. It works better. Some pure finders mix old mortar with their pure, but I never do. It's a kind of stealing, isn't it? And I've never been a thief." She paused, then said, "In some ways, it's easier being a pure finder than a rag-and-bone picker. You only find rags and bones in back alleys and courts. But dogs go all over, don't they? Even down a busy street like this one. Mind you, I won't deny it was hard to bring myself to do it at first. But you get used to it." She paused, a gleam of amusement lighting her watery brown eyes, so that Hero wondered what the old woman had seen in her face. "You don't think so, I can tell. But it's true."

Hero cleared her throat and consulted her notes. "You said your second husband was a barber. Can you tell me about the first?"

The old woman finished her tea and handed the cup back to the stall's boy. "He was a sailor, worked on a barge that ran between London and Greenwich. Peter was his name. I met him when I was just fourteen. My father used to own a windmill, you see, but he died when I was twelve, and the man my mother married . . . Well, let's just say he didn't like me too much. So when I met Peter, I never looked back. We were very happy."

"How long were you and Peter together?"

"Seventeen years. Life was good then. He

wasn't away from home for long, and the money he brought in was enough to keep us comfortable. But then one day, the press gang got him. He managed to send me a letter from Rio, telling me what'd happened to him. They say it was just a few days later they ran into a bad storm and a spar fell on him. Killed him."

"I'm sorry," said Hero, painfully aware of the woeful inadequacy of her words.

"Those were hard times," said the old woman, her voice catching for a moment. "But then I met my George and things were good again. Until the accident." She nodded toward the malodorous basket that sat beside her. "He died doing this. I knew he wasn't feeling well even though he insisted on coming out with me every day. Then one morning he bent down to pick up a pile and just fell over dead. He was a good man, honest and hardworking and generous to a fault. He didn't deserve to die in a back alley with a dog turd in his hand."

Hero stared across the street to where a new row of low brick buildings had recently replaced the old, burned-out warehouse that once stood there. She found she had to swallow several times before she could keep going. "You never had any children?"

"Oh, no; I had eight. One of them, my Sylvia, made it all the way to thirty before she died in childbirth."

Hero was afraid to ask. "And the others?"

"All dead." The old woman squinted up at the heavy gray sky above. "It's just me now. I don't know what I'm going to do when I get too old to pick up dog droppings. It gets harder every year, walking fifteen, twenty miles a day, carrying this stinking basket, bending over time and time again. Some pure finders, they don't use a glove. They say their hands are easier to keep clean than a glove. But I can't do that. I've always had to use a glove."

She paused as a dusty mail coach rattled past, its horses lathered and wet with sweat, the guard shouting for an ostler as the coach swung in through the courtyard gate of the ancient inn that stood just to the west of St. Sepulchre's crowded churchyard. "Sometimes my legs and back hurt me so bad, I can't sleep at night," she said, shifting her weight on the cold stone steps with a sigh. "I lay there and wonder where I went wrong in my life, to end up like this. When I was a little girl, I used to work ever so hard in school. I was good at it all too. The teachers told my papa that if I'd been a boy, I could've become a clerk or maybe even something better. I married two good, hardworking, clean-living men; birthed eight beautiful children. And here I am, a ragged, lonely old woman sitting on church steps and telling some strange lady about my life, with a basket of dog turds at my side. If I get sick or hurt, what'm I going to do? I'll just starve to death. I keep trying to figure out what I should've done differently. I know there's no use in thinking like that—I mean, it won't make a difference now, will it? But for some reason I feel as if I should be able to see where I went wrong. And I can't. I just can't."

"You didn't do anything wrong," said Hero, her voice tight with an old, gut-deep anger. "Nothing."

"Must've done something wrong," said the woman, her eyes narrowing as she continued to stare at the arched entrance to the coaching inn's yard. "Do you know that fellow, my lady? The one there, in the brown corduroy coat with a squished-looking face? He's been staring at us ever so long."

Hero shifted to get a better look at the sagging facade of the Saracen's Head next door. A man was leaning against one of the old inn's dark upright timbers. He wore a brown corduroy coat, greasy breeches, and a battered slouch hat tilted back so that the light fell full on his unshaven face. He was a tall, gangly fellow with an oddly narrow head and a protruding mouth that reminded her of a fish. Her gaze met his, and rather than look away he nodded, an insolent smile curling his fish lips in a way that told Hero his study of her was neither casual nor innocent.

"No; I don't know him," she said, stowing her

notebook and pencil in her reticule. "But I think I'll ask him why he's so interested in what we're doing." She pressed five shillings into Gussie Spilsby's hand. "Thank you for agreeing to speak with me."

"Said I'd talk to you for a shilling," said the woman. "You don't need to be giving me more."

Hero closed the woman's hand around the money when she would have given some of it back. "No. Please. Keep it."

Tightening her grip on her reticule, Hero strode purposely toward the odd-looking man. She thought he might turn around and walk away, but he didn't. He simply stayed put, watching her come at him.

She drew up some five feet from him. "Why are you watching me?"

He readjusted his hat as he pushed away from the wall. "Been watchin' ye fer a while. Ye just noticed?"

"That doesn't exactly answer my question, now, does it?"

"Yer husband threatened to blow me brains out yesterday."

She blinked. "You're Sid Cotton?"

"Told ye about me, did he?"

"He said you tried to kill him last winter in Fleet Street."

Cotton's full lips pulled away from his rotten teeth in a big grin. "Me? Nah."

"Why are you here now?"

"Curious, I guess."

"About what?"

He stared at the jumbled assortment of carts, wagons, and carriages passing in the street, those oddly uneven eyes squinting thoughtfully. "Yer husband, he thinks I killed Lord Ashworth, but I didn't. Not sayin' I wasn't plannin' on it, mind ye. But somebody beat me to it. So I guess I feel like I got what ye might call a proprietary interest in wot was done to him."

"A proprietary interest?"

"That's right. I ain't gonna dance the hempen jig fer somethin' I didn't do."

"You mean hang?"

"That's wot I said, ain't it?" Cotton turned his head to spit a glob of yellowish phlegm into the gutter. "Ye see, I know a thing or two his lordship don't."

"Oh? So why didn't you tell him when he spoke to you last night?"

Sid Cotton looked at her as if he were affronted. "Ye reckon it's easy, thinkin' with a gun pressed to the side o' yer head? Well, let me tell ye, it ain't."

"What do you claim to know that his lordship does not?"

Cotton scratched the back of his head. "I been thinkin' his lordship might want t' take a look at a fellow name o' McCay. Lawrence McCay. Got a shop in Long Acre, he does."

Whatever she'd been expecting him to say, it wasn't that. "How do you know about McCay?"

The foul stench of his breath washed over her as he leaned in closer in the manner of a man imparting a secret. "He was annoyin' Ashworth somethin' fierce, ye see. 'Vociferously dunning' him, his lordship said."

" 'Vociferously dunning'?"

"That's right. He was always throwin' big words like that at me and smirkin' when he done it, thinkin' I'm thick as two short planks."

"You know what it means?"

"Course I know. It means Ashworth didn't pay this McCay what he owed him. That furniture maker wanted his money, and he weren't being quiet about it."

The man's eyes weren't simply off-kilter, Hero realized; one was noticeably larger than the other. She said, "Why would Ashworth discuss his unpaid bills with you?"

" 'Cause he wanted me to off the cove, that's why."

"He wanted to hire you to kill Lawrence McCay?"

"That's what I just said, wasn't it?"

"And did you agree to 'off' the man for him?"

"Nah."

"Why not?"

"It's like I told yer husband. Ashworth already bilked me once. I weren't gonna sign up t' get

234

cheated a second time." He glanced up as Hero's yellow-bodied coach rolled to a stop beside them. The coach had been waiting by the church, and Hero wondered what her coachman had sensed that compelled him to draw nearer.

"Thing is," said Cotton, "I been thinkin' about it, ye see. And it occurs t' me that meybe Ashworth hired somebody else to off the cove."

"McCay is still quite alive."

"I know that. M'point is, what if McCay knowed that Ashworth was tryin' to have him killed? What if McCay decided to kill Ashworth first?" He raised his eyebrows up and down in a gesture that might have been comic if the man didn't ooze evil. "Mmm?"

Hero kept her expression blank. "If Ashworth did decide to hire someone else to kill McCay, who would he turn to?"

"How'm I t' know?"

"Birds of a feather and all that."

He smiled again, a gleam of what looked like genuine amusement this time that slithered across his face and then was gone. "Won't deny I know a lot more'n some'd give me credit for. Ye might warn yer husband o' that." He tipped his hat in a mocking gesture. "Ma'am." And then he strolled away, whistling between the gaps in his broken teeth. It took Hero a moment to place the tune.

It was the Kyrie from Mozart's Requiem.

CHAPTER 26

Lawrence McCay was alone when Sebastian pushed open the door to the showroom.

The furniture maker was shifting the position of a delicate Adam-style chest and had brought in an array of mirrors from the glass room, presumably in an attempt to make the stripped space appear less pathetic. At the bell's cheerful jingle, he looked up, his face lighting with a leap of hope that drained away when he saw Sebastian. "Not you again."

Sebastian closed the door behind him. "I'm afraid so."

"But . . . why?"

"Are you familiar with a man named Sid Cotton?"

McCay looked puzzled. "Cotton? I don't believe so, no. Why? Who is he?"

"A thief, murderer, and general all-around unpleasant character."

He gave the chest a final scoot. "Then I'm glad I don't know him."

"He knows you."

"How?"

"Ashworth tried to hire him to kill you. You didn't know that?"

The furniture maker's heavily lined face sagged. "You're not serious?"

"I wish I weren't."

"Who told you this?"

"Cotton."

"Perhaps he made it up."

"It's possible. Although that does beg the question: If so, then how did he come to know your name?"

McCay tightened his lips back from his teeth in the manner of a man wrestling with a difficult question. "I don't know."

Sebastian watched him carefully. "You do appreciate the implications, don't you?"

"Of course I do. You take me for a fool?" McCay stood with his hands dangling at his sides as if unsure what to do with them. "You're suggesting it gave me an additional reason to kill him, aren't you?"

"If you knew."

"But I didn't! How the hell could I?"

"He could have threatened you."

"Ashworth did threaten me—said he'd make me sorry for 'bothering' him. But I thought he meant he'd take legal action against me. I never dreamt he meant he'd have me killed. Who does something like that?"

"A man who has no problem killing his fellow beings. You don't seem to understand the nature of the man you were dealing with. This is someone who used to abuse and kill street children. For fun."

McCay stared at him, his eyes flooding with a disbelieving horror. Then his gaze shifted to the window overlooking the street. An instant later, the bell jangled as Julie McCay pushed open the door.

"Papa, you won't believe what—" She broke off at the sight of Sebastian, the smile sliding off her face. "Why are you here again?"

"Miss McCay," said Sebastian, bowing politely. The first time Sebastian visited the emporium, Julie McCay's clothing had barely registered on him. But he paid attention now. Her white muslin gown was fashionably high-waisted but plain, with only a simple piping of green ribbon around the neck and hem. Respectable, but neither high style nor elegant. Not only that, but she was even smaller than he'd remembered—probably less than five feet. The blood-soaked gown retrieved from the Thames could not possibly have been hers.

She slammed the door behind her with a bell-jarring crash. "Why can't you leave us alone?"

It was McCay himself who answered her. "He says Ashworth tried to hire some fellow to kill me."

She stared at Sebastian, her face hard and inscrutable. There was a flintiness about her, a determination that arose from a deep and powerful anger that he suspected was not new. "Is that true?" she asked.

"Yes."

She went to stand beside her father. "So it isn't enough to ruin us financially? Now you nobs must take to murdering us as well?"

"Not all of us; just Ashworth."

"You think you're so different from him? You come here and treat us like dirt, secure in the knowledge that we can't even resist, let alone fight back. You lot can do anything you want to us, and we can do nothing to you. *Nothing.*"

"Julie," warned her father softly.

She ignored him. "It won't always be like this, you know," she told Sebastian, her head held high. "Someday it will be different. Someday you and your kind will pay."

"The way they did across the Channel?" Sebastian said softly. "Be careful what you wish for. Revolutions are easy to start but impossible to control."

"She didn't say nothing about no revolution," said McCay, his face gray with concern.

"No, she didn't," agreed Sebastian. He turned toward the door, then paused to look back. "I'm not your enemy, you know. Not if you're innocent."

Lawrence McCay stared back at him. His face looked tired and clouded with the wary fear of those who know—who have always known—that power rests with others and that everything they hold dear can be taken from them at any moment by a grinding system they are helpless to resist. "And who'll decide if I'm innocent? Many a man judged innocent by God has breathed his last at the end of a rope outside the Old Bailey."

It was an assertion no one familiar with the British legal system could honestly deny. Sebastian didn't even try.

"Surely if she knew her father was guilty of murder," said Hero later as she and Sebastian took Simon for a stroll along the gravel paths of Grosvenor Square, "she wouldn't have been so brazen as to basically tell you she'd like to see your head on a pike?"

This was a private, gated garden maintained by the occupants of the houses that surrounded it, its once-formal eighteenth-century geometric plantings having given way some years ago to naturalistic clumps of saplings and flowering shrubs. Their walk was extraordinarily slow since their pace was set by Simon, who not only had short legs but also felt compelled to stop and inspect every interesting rock, flower, and random bug that caught his attention.

"It does seem counterintuitive," Sebastian admitted.

"If she weren't so short, I might suspect her of killing Ashworth herself."

"We don't know that the clothes pulled from

the Thames had anything to do with Ashworth's murder," Sebastian reminded her.

"So maybe she did do it. And then she—or her father—killed Digby, after which the father stripped him and dragged him into an alley to hide the body."

"It's possible." Sebastian watched Simon hunker down to stare in wonder at a small green lizard. "Leaving aside Digby's strange death for a moment, I think there are probably three possibilities for what happened to Ashworth that night."

She looked over at him. "Three?"

He nodded. "The most obvious is that Ashworth passed out drunk, and the woman he was 'entertaining' that night killed him— either in a panic because he frightened her or in revenge for his humiliating her. Although it's also possible she's as twisted as he was and did it for kicks. Or she could have drugged him and plotted the whole thing ahead of time in revenge for something he'd done in the past."

"That's four possibilities."

He huffed a soft laugh. "That was only the various permutations of the first possibility." He sobered quickly. "And although it grieves me to say it, I think we still need to include Stephanie in there. The second scenario involves someone with a grudge—say, McCay or Cotton, or maybe even Steph again—who managed to slip into the house while Ashworth was busy 'entertaining' his female guest and killed him."

"If that's true, then what happened to the woman Ashworth was 'entertaining'?"

"Presumably she ran screaming into the night while the killer was busy hacking Ashworth's chest to a bloody pulp."

"After grabbing all of her clothes? That shows enormous presence of mind."

"Perhaps she hadn't taken them all off yet. And she did leave one stocking."

"What's the third possibility?"

"That something more complicated and devious was going on. Something I can't even envision yet, but which would also explain what happened to Digby."

They'd reached the grassy platform at the center of the garden and drew up as Simon gazed openmouthed at the towering, gilded equestrian stature of George I in Roman dress before him. "Have you considered that Ashworth might have been entertaining two women?" said Hero.

"No, that hadn't occurred to me. And it should have. Knowing what we know about Ashworth, it could be two women in any combination. Two highborn ladies; a lady and a prostitute; two prostitutes, or even a lady and a shopkeeper's assistant."

"Or a shopkeeper's daughter."

Sebastian met her troubled gaze. "Or daughter."

• • •

"There you are, my lord," said Morey when they returned to Brook Street. "Calhoun is looking for you. He's found that bit of muslin you were interested in."

"Ah, good," said Sebastian as Hero carried Simon up the stairs.

"Not exactly, my lord. He says the woman is dead."

CHAPTER 27

The dead woman's name was Sissy Jordan, and she'd kept a room in a cheap lodging house just off the Haymarket.

A broad thoroughfare running from Pall Mall north to Piccadilly, the Haymarket was a lively area crowded with coaching inns, taverns, coffeehouses, hotels, supper houses, and shops of every description. Thanks to the presence of the King's Theatre, it was also home to a shifting population of opera dancers, Italian singers, and so many prostitutes that "Haymarket ware" had become a synonym for practitioners of the occupation.

"How did you find her so quickly?" Sebastian asked his valet as they climbed the musty, battered staircase to the third floor of a ramshackle building that had been erected atop an old tennis court dating from the days of Charles II.

"My mother is acquainted with her roommate."

"I take it she's in the same business as Sissy?"

"Not 'she.' He. Giovanni Perosi. He used to be an opera singer until someone ruined his vocal cords by garroting him with a strap."

"So they were lovers?" Many prostitutes kept lovers or even husbands and practiced their trade on the side.

"No. Just friends," said Calhoun as they reached the dark, narrow corridor of the third floor.

At his knock, the nearest door opened with a jerk to reveal a tall, extraordinarily thin man with unusually long limbs and the smooth, unbearded face of a boy. He looked to be perhaps thirty or thirty-five, with dark hair and big brown eyes and the strangely ethereal, almost angelic beauty of a *musico*, also sometimes known as an *evirato* or *castrato*. Emasculated as boys before their voices changed, the *castrati* never went through puberty, thus retaining forever a boy's vocal range while joining it to the lung power and breath capacity of a man.

"I look out the window and see you come in the building," said the *castrato* in a whispery, ruined voice still heavily accented with his native Italian. His gaze darted to the empty, dusty corridor behind them before he opened the door wider. "Come in quickly, before anyone see you. You are certain no one follow you?"

"Who do you think would follow us?" asked Sebastian, squeezing into the garret room.

"The killer." Perosi closed the door and stood with his back pressed against it, his arms wrapped around his middle as if his stomach were hurting. He wore a respectable pair of breeches and a decent shirt open at the neck. But his face was haggard, his eyes looking bruised from lack of sleep and fear.

"You mean Sissy's killer?" Sebastian let his gaze rove over the narrow room. Divided down the middle by a ragged curtain, it contained only two low beds, a blackened washstand, and several changes of men's and women's clothing hanging from hooks on the wall. A small cracked window overlooked the court below.

"*Sì*," whispered Perosi.

"Do you know who he is?"

Perosi licked his lips. "No."

"Tell his lordship what you do know," said Calhoun.

The Italian perched on the edge of one of the lumpy straw mattresses and ran a trembling hand through his dark, wavy hair. "I don't know where to begin."

"Tell us about Sissy," said Sebastian. "Was she from London?"

Perosi shook his head. "She come up from Hampshire, two years ago. Her parents, they die. She say she hope to go into service, but she have no references, and her clothes, they ragged, so no one hire her. When I meet her, she keep herself alive the only way she can, by selling herself on the street."

"How old was she?"

"Then? Thirteen."

Dear God, thought Sebastian.

"I notice her one rainy night—she curled up in a doorway across the court, trying to stay dry. She remind me so much of my little sister, Caterina, that I can't leave her there. So I bring her up here. She . . ." His ruined voice cracked, his lower lip trembling, and he squeezed his eyes shut and brought up a fist to tap against his mouth. After a moment, he swallowed and said, "She a child in so many ways. She learn a woman's lures and the ways of the street, but beneath it all, she still a child—bighearted, loving, funny. I cannot believe she's dead."

"When was she killed?"

"Last night." The Italian drew in a ragged, shaky breath. "She tell me for days that someone follow her. Watch her. I think she being silly, letting what happen to that lord in Mayfair get to her. But it's him, yes? Whoever kill that lord come after her too. And he get her."

"What did she tell you about last Thursday night?"

The Italian hunched over, his hands thrust together between his knees, his entire body now rocking back and forth.

Sebastian's gaze met Calhoun's over the ruined singer's head. "You'll be safer once his lordship knows what you know," Calhoun said gently. "Do you understand that?"

Perosi nodded.

Sebastian said, "Did Ashworth come here, to the Haymarket, to hire her that night?"

"No. The valet, Digby. He hire her."

"You know Digby?"

"Everyone around here know Digby. Sometimes Ashworth, he come to pick out his own women. But usually he send Digby. He know what his master like."

"The young and pretty ones," said Sebastian. "The younger the better."

Perosi nodded again, his features strained. "I know other girls who go with Ashworth or Digby, before. I warn Sissy she no want to have anything to do with him. But she too excited to pay attention to Giovanni. All she think about is riding in a carriage and seeing the inside of a lord's house." He swallowed. "She no listen."

"She went there in Ashworth's own carriage?"

"No. The valet take her in a hackney. She disappointed about that, but the lord's house was a wonder to her. Digby take her to his lordship in the drawing room."

"That's unusual, isn't it?"

"Not for him. She tell me she nervous, remembering the things I warn her about. But she say I wrong. His lordship kind and charming; give her wine. But then someone knock at the front door below."

"Who was it?"

"She not know. The valet, he come to the drawing room and whisper something in his lordship's ear."

"Could she hear what he said?"

248

"No. She tell me, whatever it is, Ashworth is annoyed. He tell her to sit and wait for him—and not steal anything while he gone. But then Digby come back, give her a guinea, and tell her to go away—that her services aren't needed anymore."

"She left?"

"Yes. She happy to get the money without having to work for it. She come home laughing about it, thinking it's all a lark. For hours, she talk of nothing but his lordship's marble floors and gilt mirrors and grand chandeliers. And then the next morning we hear he found dead in his bed."

"She didn't think of going to Bow Street to tell them what she knew?"

Perosi's eyes widened. "*Dio*, no. She terrified they think she kill him."

"When did she notice someone watching her?"

"That day, or maybe the next. I no think she ever see anyone. It's just a feeling she has. She so scared." He bowed his head and laced his fingers behind his neck. "And I laugh at her. God help me."

Sebastian said, "Where was she killed?"

"They find her body in an alley near here."

"Stabbed?"

"Yes. In the chest."

"You saw the body?"

Perosi looked up, showing a ravaged face. "I identify her."

"Where is she now?"

"They take her to the deadhouse in St. Martin's."

"Did Sissy know if it was a man or a woman who came to the door while she was with Ashworth?"

Perosi shook his head. "No. She in a panic the next morning when we find out Ashworth dead. She afraid she be blamed for it, and she afraid the killer come after her, thinking she know who he is. But she know nothing."

"She knew that someone knocked at the door, that the valet came to tell Ashworth, and he then went downstairs to talk to the new arrival."

"Yes. But that is nothing."

"Did she notice a carriage or hackney waiting when she left the house?"

"I no think so. Digby give her money to take a hackney, but she save it and walk home."

"What time was this?"

"Midnight? Somewhere around there." He let his head fall back, his eyes wide and hurting, his ruined voice grating. "*Dio.* I wish I listen to her when she tell me she afraid."

"You didn't know this was going to happen," said Sebastian. "You didn't know, and you couldn't have stayed with her every minute of every day even if you did. You tried to stop her from going to Ashworth that night. You can't blame yourself."

Yet even as he said it, Sebastian knew it was useless. Giovanni had already picked up his burden of guilt, and he would carry it with him to the grave, if not beyond.

No one wanted to end up in one of London's deadhouses.

Typically located in churchyards or attached to workhouses and hospitals, some deadhouses were little more than toolsheds. They were the penultimate destination for the numerous drowned bodies pulled from the river or the unidentified dead picked up from the street. Here too came the paupers from the city's poorhouses as well as the insane asylums, hospitals, and prisons. Murder and accident victims and suicides were also often brought to deadhouses to await inquests.

Sissy Jordan had been taken to the deadhouse tucked away in a corner of the St. Martin's workhouse. Although situated on the institution's ground floor, it was reached by climbing a flight of crumbling stone steps, for the workhouse had been built atop an overflowing churchyard that bulged a good four feet above the street. Dank, gloomy, and noisome, the place seemed to throb with all the horror and despair of the endless procession of forgotten dead that passed through it.

"Yeah, we've got 'er," said the slovenly

attendant when Sebastian and Sir Henry Lovejoy inquired after the dead girl. "Over here."

"Merciful heavens," said Lovejoy, one hand pressing his handkerchief to his nose and mouth as he took in the overflowing horror of the room: Every slab, every shelf, was piled with two or three bodies, and far too many of them were children.

"A boy come into the workhouse a few weeks ago with the measles," said the attendant, shuffling ahead of them toward the back of the foul room. "It's taken off pret' near 'alf the young 'uns, it has, and more'n a few of the older ones too. We can't keep up with burying 'em."

Sissy lay on one of the slabs atop the emaciated cadaver of a middle-aged man in hideous rags. A flaxen-haired little boy of perhaps five or six lay on top of her. Seen in the dim light, both Sissy and the dead child she cradled might simply have been sleeping. She looked like a child herself, her features even and winsome, her light brown hair fine and softly curling. For a moment, Sebastian could only stare at her, his throat thick, a powerful rage pounding through him.

"Why kill her, damn it?" he said at last, his voice tight. "She didn't know anything. Not a bloody thing."

Above the white folds of his handkerchief, Lovejoy's eyes were dark, painful smudges. "Someone was afraid she did." He gave a heavy sigh. "He's very ruthless, this killer. I hope if there's anyone else out there he thinks can identify him, we get to them before this madman does."

Sebastian turned away to go stand in the open doorway and draw a breath of relatively fresh air into his lungs. "If that missing housemaid wasn't actually involved in any of this, then Sissy was probably our last link to the killer. Unless the killer took a hackney that night, in which case we need to find that jarvey."

"I'll tell my men to redouble their efforts in that direction."

Sebastian glanced back at the dead girl on the crowded slab. "If he exists, his life is in danger. And unlike Sissy, he probably doesn't even know it."

CHAPTER 28

That night, Sebastian dreamed of a winsome girl with delicate features and soft brown hair. She floated just beneath the surface of a quiet forest stream, her eyes closed, her hair billowing out around her. He reached for her in a hopeless attempt to save her, only to feel her slip wet and cold from his grasp. Then his vision expanded, and he realized the banks of the stream were crowded with children—scores and scores of ragged, painfully thin children, as far as he could see. They stared at him as if in silent reproach. But their faces were red with fever and their sunken eyes were dead.

He awoke with a gasp, his heart pounding in his chest, his eyes scratchy and achy as he stared into the darkness.

He felt Hero stir beside him, her hand sliding up his arm to touch his cheek. "Bad dream?"

He took her hand in his and pressed a kiss to her palm. "Sissy Jordan shouldn't have died. The killer only just got to her. If I'd started looking for her sooner . . ."

She brushed his lower lip with her fingers. "You told Giovanni Perosi not to blame himself. Yet you're blaming yourself?"

He smiled faintly against her hand. "I suppose

I am. The problem is, I'm missing something—something that should be obvious."

"Such as?"

He sat up abruptly and swung his legs over the side of the bed, his hands coming up to rake his hair back from his forehead. "Thanks to Sissy, we now have a vaguely better idea of what happened in Curzon Street that night. We know Ashworth sent his valet to pick up a young girl from the Haymarket and then plied her with wine in his drawing room."

"You don't find that odd?" said Hero, sitting up herself. "Obviously I'm not familiar with how these things are typically done, but I would have expected him to have the girl brought directly to his bedchamber."

"From what Giovanni said, I gather Ashworth often did it that way. I suspect it had something to do with deepening the girls' ultimate pain and humiliation. He met them in his drawing room, awed them with its opulence and wealth, and offered them wine as if they were simply his guests. He was probably at his most charming, making them feel special, perhaps even hopeful that something wonderful was about to happen to them. Then he'd take them upstairs and . . . brutalize them."

Hero was silent a moment, her gray eyes a luminous silver in the night. "The man was mad. Horribly, dangerously mad."

"Was he? He was definitely cruel, arrogant, and stunningly selfish. But at what point do those characteristics shade over into madness?"

She shifted to wrap her arms around him and lean against his back. "Who do you think came to the door that night? Whoever it was, Digby must have recognized them, since he let them in and went to inform Ashworth."

"Given the fact that Ashworth was found naked in his bed, one presumes the new arrival was a woman—or perhaps even two women. But I'm having a hard time envisioning a woman being responsible for what happened to Digby—and then later luring Sissy into an alley and stabbing her there—without an accomplice. An accomplice, or a hireling."

Hero propped her chin on his shoulder. "So Princess Ivanna Gagarin and her nasty colonel?"

"Perhaps. Or Stephanie and Firth, God help me. Or even Julie McCay and her father, if that bloodstained dress from the Thames has nothing to do with any of this. Or the mystery woman could be someone we don't even know about yet." He rested his head against hers. "The thing that bothers me is, the only person who knew the identity of the girl Digby hired that night was Digby. And he's dead."

"Ashworth knew."

"I doubt it. I'd be surprised if he even bothered to learn her first name. So, out of all the tens of thousands of prostitutes in this city, how did the killer know to go after Sissy? Digby must have told him—or her."

Hero was thoughtful for a moment. "I suppose it's possible the killer forced him to give up the girl's name before he killed him."

"He could have. Or Digby could have provided the girl's name quite willingly. I'm beginning to wonder if the valet might have played a more important role in Ashworth's death than I've been giving him credit for—Digby, and perhaps the missing housemaid as well."

"Jenny Crutcher? Bow Street still hasn't been able to trace her?"

"Not last I heard. Which strikes me as rather ominous. It might be worth spending some time in Curzon Street tomorrow. Someone must know what happened to her."

"You could try talking to the crossing sweeps. They stand on their corners all day, watching everyone who comes and goes, yet no one pays them any more heed than they do the neighborhood cats."

He found himself smiling at her in the darkness, and she said, "What?"

He speared his fingers through the heavy fall of her hair, drawing it back from her face. He felt the heat of her skin against his hands, breathed in the lavender-sweet scent that was all her own, watched her lips part. "God, I love you."

She gave a soft gurgle of laughter. "Because I consort with the likes of crossing sweeps and pure finders?"

He laughed with her and lowered his lips to hers. "That too."

Tuesday, 5 April

Ashworth's town house stood on the south side of Curzon Street, not far from the corner of Half Moon Street. Thanks to the proximity of both Shepherd's Market and the residence in nearby Chesterfield Street of Beau Brummell, this was a lucrative area for those pauper children who made their living as crossing sweeps. Every morning, a horde of wealthy aspirants to fashion—including frequently the Prince Regent himself—would trek to the dandy's boudoir for the honor of watching the Beau make his toilette and tie his famous cravats.

As a result, every corner up and down Curzon was manned by a pair of grubby, ragged children, one stationed on each side of the street, clutching their brooms and watching hopefully for largesse. In a sense it was a form of begging, although there was no doubt the children performed a service and worked hard at it.

The morning had dawned cloudy and dry, with a cold wind that gusted up unpleasantly, which meant the crossing sweeps weren't doing much business. But Sebastian was still surprised to find only one boy at the corner of Half Moon Street. At Sebastian's approach, the lad came trotting over from the far corner, his broom in one hand, elbow cocked skyward as he held a battered hat to his head with the other. Sebastian took a shilling from his pocket and held it up. "This is yours—and another besides—if you answer my questions."

A wary look crept over the lad's sharp, grime-streaked face. In age he could have been anywhere between eight and twelve; an appalling collection of rags hung on his thin frame, and his hair was matted into an indeterminate color somewhere between dung and mud.

"Questions?" said the boy, who gave his name as Waldo Jones. " 'Bout wot?"

Sebastian nodded toward the dead man's house. "You're familiar with Lord Ashworth?"

Waldo made a face and spit into the gutter. "The nob wot got hisself kilt? Course I am. 'E never give any of us nuthin'—unless it was t' be mean."

"Mean? How?"

" 'E liked t' drop a penny in a pile of fresh dung and then laugh when we'd pick it up."

"Charming," said Sebastian.

"They don't come much nastier than that bugger." The boy gave Sebastian a suspicious sideways glance. "Why ye askin' 'bout 'im? 'E a friend o' yers?"

"Not at all."

"Huh. Ye ain't no Bow Street Runner, that's fer sure."

"No, but I am interested in finding a housemaid who used to work for his lordship—a woman by the name of Jenny Crutcher. Did you know her?"

The boy's expression betrayed not a hint of reaction. But a muscle beneath his right eye began to twitch. "Wot ye want wit 'er?"

"She's missing, and I'm worried about her. Did you know her?"

"A bit," admitted the boy guardedly. "She was always real nice t' me and Ben."

"Ben?"

"Ben King. 'E used t' work the corner wit me."

"Oh? And where is Ben now?"

The boy shrugged one skinny shoulder and fiddled with his broom handle. " 'E moved on."

"Why? This must be a lucrative corner."

The boy's eyebrows drew together at the unfamiliar word. "I don't know 'bout that. But it's a good stand, ain't no denying that."

"Do you know where Jenny and Ben are now?"

"Jenny cleared out the day after the nob got whacked. I don't know where she went."

"And Ben?"

Waldo fixed Sebastian with a hard, steady stare. "Ye ain't never said why yer askin' all these questions."

"I'm trying to find out who killed Ashworth.

Not because I'm with Bow Street or because he was my friend," Sebastian added hastily when the boy took a quick step back. "But because I'm afraid his killer may be a danger to other people. People like Jenny Crutcher. And others."

Waldo brought up one arm to wipe his runny nose on his sleeve. "I told ye, I don't know where she went."

"What time did you leave your corner that night? The night his lordship was killed, I mean."

"I dunno. We usually quit when it's gettin' dark."

"So around nine?"

"There 'bouts, I suppose. Why?"

"Did you happen to see anyone go in or out of Ashworth's house that evening?"

"Not so's I recall."

"Was your friend Ben here that day?"

"Aye," said the boy, wary again. "Why?"

"Did he leave at the same time as you?"

The wind gusted up harder, thrashing the limbs of the plane trees that stood around a large detached house halfway up the block. The boy jerked and glanced toward the sound, his eyes widening as if he were afraid.

"Waldo?" said Sebastian.

Again that twitch of the shoulder. "I dunno. Sometimes Ben hung around a bit later."

"Any particular reason?"

Waldo shook his head, stony faced, trying

261

frantically to keep all his secrets and the roiling emotions they aroused within him tucked away out of sight.

Sebastian said gently, "I'm not a threat to either you or your friend, Waldo. I want to help him."

The boy's breath was coming fast enough now to jerk his thin chest, and for a moment Sebastian thought he might bolt. But the lure of that promised second shilling was too hard to resist. He licked his lower lip. "All I know is that Ben carried a message that night."

Sebastian felt a sick sense of dread settle low in his gut. Crossing sweeps often carried messages or parcels for people in the neighborhood they worked. Because the children were around day after day, often for years, residents grew to feel they could trust them. Householders and their servants too.

"Who gave Ben the message?" asked Sebastian.

"Digby." The boy said the name on a painful expulsion of air. "Him they found dead in an alley up the street. 'E was always payin' Ben t' carry messages fer 'im."

"He never used you?"

Waldo shook his head, and Sebastian thought it irked the lad a bit, that his friend had been entrusted with these lucrative commissions but he never had.

Sebastian asked, "Do you know where Ben carried the messages?"

"No. 'E never said. Always real secretive about it, 'e was."

Digby had obviously chosen his messenger well, Sebastian thought. He said, "I need to talk to Ben. I'm not a danger to him, but the killer might be. It all depends on where he took that message the night Lord Ashworth was killed."

"I told ye, I don't know where 'e took it!"

Sebastian studied the boy's wide, frightened eyes and anxious face. "Is that why Ben's not here, Waldo? Because he's afraid, and he's hiding? That's it, isn't it?"

The boy nodded slowly, his nose beginning to run again. "I ain't seen 'im fer days. I even went and asked at the Mount Street dead'ouse, thinkin' maybe somebody'd kilt 'im. But 'e weren't there." The boy's voice broke as he visibly tightened the muscles in his face to hold back the threat of tears.

Sebastian pressed two shillings into Waldo's hand. "If you see Ben, try to convince him that he can trust me."

"I told ye, I don't know where 'e is."

Sebastian nodded and started to turn away, but the boy stopped him, saying, "I did see that feller 'ere that night. Right before I left, it was."

Sebastian paused. "What 'feller'?"

"That tradesman wot's been givin' Ashworth 'ell fer weeks."

"You mean Lawrence McCay?"

263

"I dunno 'is name. 'E's an older cove, on the short side. 'E been comin' 'round, standin' in the middle o' the street, and shoutin' 'bout how Ashworth cheated 'im and owed 'im money. Bothered Ashworth somethin' fierce, it did. Ben and me'd always whoop and cheer whenever 'e'd come and start up about it."

"When did you say he was here?"

"I told ye—the night the bugger got hisself kilt. I noticed 'im just as I was leavin'. Standing over there by the trees, 'e was." Ben nodded with his chin toward the thick grove of rustling plane trees.

"He was shouting?"

"Not then, 'e weren't. Weren't sayin' nothin' at all. Just standin' there in the shadows, 'e was, watchin' Ashworth's 'ouse. Ain't never seen 'im do that before, which is why I remember it. Thought it was queer, I did."

Sebastian spent the next hour working his way up and down the street, talking to various members of that largely invisible league of laborers who kept the lives of Mayfair's wealthy residents running so smoothly: crossing sweeps from other corners, the barmaid at the White Hart on Clarges Street, a baker's boy, and a butcher's boy—anyone and everyone he could find. No one had anything of use to tell him. The barmaid didn't know Digby and confided that Ashworth considered himself too grand to ever be seen in such a relatively unfashionable public house. No one seemed to be hiding anything. With the exception of Waldo Jones, all were eager to talk about Ashworth's murder. But no one could remember having seen anything untoward the night of his death. Like Waldo, the other crossing sweeps said they also gave up and left at dusk. All knew Ben King had suddenly disappeared, but none would admit to knowing where he was.

Frustrated, Sebastian walked back to where he'd left Tom with the curricle. Leaping up to the high seat, he gathered his reins, then paused to look back at his tiger.

"What?" said Tom when Sebastian continued simply to stare at him.

"I have a job for you."

CHAPTER 29

Lawrence McCay was working his way through a plate of kippers in a tavern just off Long Acre when Sebastian came to slide into the opposite bench.

"Good morning," said Sebastian cheerfully, resting his forearms on the tabletop and leaning into them.

The furniture maker froze with his fork raised halfway to his mouth. He'd had his head down, his shoulders hunched, and had obviously been too absorbed in either his meal or his own thoughts to notice Sebastian's approach. Now he looked up slowly, like a man awakening from a bad dream to an even harsher reality. "What do you want with me?"

Sebastian gave him a hard smile. "The truth would be nice. For a change."

McCay dropped his fork with a clatter. "What are you accusing me of now?"

"Last Thursday evening at dusk, you were seen lurking in the shadows of Curzon Street. What the bloody hell were you doing there?"

Sebastian thought the furniture maker might try to deny it, but he didn't. Plopping back against the high, old-fashioned bench, he stared directly into Sebastian's face, his expression one of a man mesmerized by a looming horror from which

266

he could not look away and from which it was beyond his capacity to escape.

Sebastian said, "You told me you hadn't seen Ashworth since a day or two before he died. You told me you never left your shop Thursday night. You told me a lie. You were in Curzon Street on Thursday night. You were seen."

McCay blew out a harsh breath and tapped his linked hands against the tight line of his lips.

"Did you kill him?" Sebastian asked, his voice low.

"No! I swear it."

"Why the blazes should I believe you?"

McCay leaned forward and shoved away his half-eaten meal. "It wasn't exactly a lie. I didn't see Ashworth that night; I didn't even try."

"So you—what? Contented yourself with lurking in the shadows and watching the house? Do you realize how bad that looks?"

McCay nodded, his face morose. "I guess that's why I didn't tell you about it. I had no real reason for being there—I'd just confronted him and handed him my invoice the day before."

"Why were you there?"

"To be honest? I don't really know. It wasn't even the first time I'd done it. It was like this . . . this compulsion I had, sorta like picking at a scab when you're a kid. You know what I mean? You know it's wrong, and it'll only make everything worse. But you do it anyway."

"So you'd go there and . . . what?"

"Nothing. I wouldn't do anything. I'd just stand there and look at his house, thinking about the kind of man he was and about what he'd done to us. Thinking about what kind of society lets a man like him get away with anything he wants. Anything."

"I guess we know where your daughter gets her revolutionary ideals."

A new flare of fear leapt in the older man's eyes. "What you heard my Julie say the other day was just talk. Angry talk. She didn't mean it."

"Yes, she did. But never mind that now. How long were you on Curzon Street that evening?"

"I don't know. Fifteen, twenty minutes, maybe? Not long."

"And this was at dusk?"

"Yes. I was home by ten. I swear it."

"What did you see while you were there watching the house?"

"Nothing. I didn't see anything."

"No one came to the house or left?"

McCay frowned as if in thought. "Well, Ashworth's valet came out. He hailed a hackney and drove off. But that was all."

"When did he come back?"

"I don't know. I must've been gone by then. I told you I wasn't there very long."

Sebastian studied the furniture maker's tired, care-lined face. The man might be telling the

268

truth; but he could also be lying—and for more than one reason. If McCay had seen Digby come back with Sissy Jordan and then had hung around after that, he might well have seen the arrival of Ashworth's killer.

"There's something you're still not telling me," said Sebastian.

McCay stared beyond him into space, his eyes purposely vacant even as the pulse at the side of his neck throbbed with the intensity of his stress. But it remained impossible to discern what the true source of his anxiety was.

Sebastian was paying off his hackney back at Brook Street when a magnificent barouche with a crest emblazoned on the panel swept around the corner from Bond Street and drew up behind him.

"Dear Amanda," he said, walking up to his sister's carriage as her footman leapt to open her door and put down the steps. "What a pleasant surprise."

She threw a scornful glance after the departing hackney. "God save us. As if it isn't bad enough that you amuse yourself by behaving like some grubby little Bow Street Runner. Must you also take to showing yourself around London in a common hackney?"

"Fortunately, I'm not Beau Brummell, so I have no reputation for fashionable fastidiousness to maintain. And as it happens, my tiger is . . . busy."

She gave him her hand and condescended to allow him to help her alight. "Surely you employ a proper groom? You can't mean to suggest you are reduced to nothing but that scruffy little pickpocket."

"Ex-pickpocket. And he isn't terribly 'little' anymore, in case you hadn't noticed."

"Do you seriously imagine I concern myself with your servants?" She swept ahead of him up the front steps and into the house as Morey opened the door with a bow.

He followed her into the library. "Well, you do seem to concern yourself with my mode of transportation."

She drew up halfway across the room as Mr. Darcy, who'd been curled up on one of the armchairs by the fire, arched his back and hissed. "You still have that nasty cat, I see."

"We do. But then, he's only nasty to you." He gestured toward the chairs by the bow window overlooking the street. "Perhaps you'd prefer to take a seat over here. May I offer you tea? Or would you prefer a glass of Madeira?"

"No, thank you. I don't intend to be here long."

"Not to be rude, but why are you here, Amanda?"

She stiffened. "Everyone is still talking about this Ashworth business, and it's becoming

270

obvious that your investigation is much to blame. You need to either hurry up and catch his killer, or simply drop the matter and let people forget about it."

"You think they would?"

"In time, yes. They can't keep speculating endlessly. Without new fodder for their conjectures, they'll soon move on to other scandals."

"So what are they conjecturing?"

Amanda stood very still, her head held high, her nostrils flaring.

He said, "It might help if you told me, Amanda."

"Someone has started . . . whispers."

"About Stephanie?"

"Obviously."

"What about her?"

"There's a ridiculous rumor linking her with some common, lowborn builder."

"You mean Russell Firth? I suppose he is lowborn, but he's not exactly 'common.' He's brilliant at what he does, and he's extraordinarily successful. I suspect his name and his work will be remembered long after we are both forgotten."

"He's *Welsh*. His grandfather was a bricklayer."

"Was he? Then that makes his ascent all the more admirable."

"Good God. You sound like a republican."

"Thank you." He walked over to reach down

and scratch Mr. Darcy behind the ears. The cat glared up at him, as if holding Sebastian responsible for their unwanted guest. "So, what else are people saying? Surely they aren't limiting their speculations to Stephanie?"

Amanda waved one exquisitely gloved hand through the air in a dismissive gesture. "Just the usual silly nonsense. Last night at Lady Farnham's card party, Emma Townsend was trying to make herself sound important with some tale about a quarrel she overheard at the Pulteney between Ashworth and one of those Russian women."

"Princess Ivanna Gagarin?"

He said it so sharply that she looked at him in surprise. "I've no idea. Why?"

"When did this happen?"

"The quarrel? Supposedly the day he was killed. Or at least that's the story Emma was telling. But then, she does like to give herself airs and is always trying to make herself seem far more interesting than she is. I wouldn't put much stock in it if I were you."

"What made Lady Townsend think they were quarreling? Did she hear what they were saying?"

"I doubt it. Otherwise she would have added that to the tale, surely. She claims she saw Ashworth grab the Russian woman's arm before she pulled away from him." Amanda pressed her lips together in tight disapproval. "Please don't tell me you're planning to drag the Grand Duchess and her ladies into this investigation of yours. People will never stop talking about it, then."

"And that's the most important thing, is it?"

She readjusted the wispy shawl she wore artistically draped around her shoulders and tightened her grip on her reticule and fan. "I should have known better than to come here and try to talk sense into you."

"Yes, you really should have."

For one intense moment, her gaze met his, and he saw in those familiar blue eyes a lifetime of resentment and hate so fierce it still had the power to stun him, even after all these years.

Then she sailed regally from the room.

"What was that about?" asked Hero, coming down the stairs just as Morey was closing the door behind the Dowager Baroness.

Sebastian listened to her receding footsteps and sharp command to her coachman. "Amanda wants me to either find Ashworth's killer immediately or stop trying."

"Oh? Somehow I doubt her impatience is devoid of self-interest."

"It's not. Someone is spreading whispers about Stephanie and Firth."

"That is worrisome."

"It is. And while it might be a coincidence, it could also be an attempt to distract from a competing tale about Ashworth and Princess Ivanna Gagarin."

"You think Ivanna is behind the rumors?"

"Given what she said to me at Countess Lieven's ball, I'd say it's more than likely."

"That bloodstained gown pulled from the Thames would have fit her."

"It would, wouldn't it?"

CHAPTER 30

That afternoon, Sebastian drove through dreary, wind-scoured streets to Clerkenwell. This was an ancient section of London lying just to the north of the old city walls. In medieval times, it had been home to three wealthy monasteries: the nunnery of St. Mary's, the London Charter-house, and the English headquarters of the Knights Hospitaller of St. John of Jerusalem. After the Dissolution, the nobility turned it into an area of fine town houses, fashionable spas, and bowling greens. But the wealthy and their pleasure haunts were long gone. These days Clerkenwell was a crumbling warren of decrepit houses, straggling tradesmen and artisans, radicals, and prisons.

Sebastian left his groom, Giles, watering the horses at the old stone trough on Clerkenwell Green and walked up the Close to the church of St. James. Skirting the redbrick building that had replaced the ancient chapel of the long-vanished nuns, he cut across a churchyard crowded with lichen-covered tombstones. There near the far corner lay two graves so new that their mounds of earth had not yet sunk beneath the weight of time. One belonged to a murdered street child named Benji Thatcher; the other was the

275

communal grave of his friend Toby Dancing and the bones of more than a dozen other youngsters, most of them never positively identified. The names of the known missing still haunted Sebastian's dreams, and he'd had them engraved along with Toby's on a simple tombstone. IN MEMORY OF BRIDGET LEARY, JACK LAWSON, MARY CARTWRIGHT, EMMA SMITH, JENNY HOPKINS, BRADY BARKER, MICK SWALLOW, PADDY GANTRY . . .

He stood beside the two graves for a long time, his hat in his hands, the wind ruffling his hair and thrashing the limbs of a nearby row of maples and horse chestnuts heavy with the fresh green growth of spring. When he'd watched the children laid to rest last September, the trees' wet, dying leaves had painted the churchyard with yellow and scarlet. For seven months, he had sought to bring their second murderer to justice. But in the end, someone else had done it for him.

"Ashworth is dead," he told the children. He said it aloud, the wind snatching his words and blowing them away into infinity. "If there were any justice in this world, he would have paid for what he did with everlasting infamy. And even that would never have been enough."

Because there is no justice in this world. The response echoed through him as surely as if someone whispered it from beyond the grave.

No, he thought. *There is no justice. If there*

were, you wouldn't be here. You'd be alive and feeling the wind against your faces. You'd grow up to discover love and have children of your own the way you were meant to, rather than lying here forever beneath the cold, dark earth.

He could not have explained why he'd felt the need to come here. He had no illusions; he knew the children couldn't hear him, knew they had moved beyond hearing long ago. And yet somehow he felt he owed them this.

His society had failed these children both in life and in death. Did they rest easy now? he wondered. Did something of them linger somewhere still? Something beyond the bones swallowed by the earth? He wished he could believe it did. He wanted to believe.

But that comfort, like so much else, remained elusive.

South of Clerkenwell Green, in the ancient lane that once led to the priory of St. John, stood the worn, two-story sandstone house of secondhand dealer Icarus Cantrell. Built hard up against the crumbling old monastic gateway, the Professor's Attic sold everything from fine bejeweled snuffboxes and silk handkerchiefs to rusty old fire irons. Some were doubtless legally sourced. Most were not.

People called Cantrell "the Professor," both because of his establishment's name and because he'd once attended Cambridge. The road from

277

gentleman's son to dolly-shop dealer involved murder and transportation and seven years' penal servitude under the lash on a Georgia plantation. He was an old man now, somewhere between fifty-five and seventy-five. Those cruel years under a hot colonial sun had left his face a burned brown, and he had a thin white scar that curled like a lash around his neck to his cheek and hinted at other scars hidden beneath the old-fashioned velvet coats, lace falls, and powdered wigs he wore.

"Thought I might be seeing you," said the Professor when Sebastian walked down the lane to the crumbling old gate and pushed open his shop door.

"Saw the newspapers, did you?" said Sebastian.

The old man came from behind the counter to lock the door against the wind and put up a Closed sign. "Did you kill him?"

"No. Did you?"

The old man laughed and turned to lead the way into the narrow kitchen that stretched across the back of the shop. There they sat facing each other across a scrubbed table, two pewter tankards of cider on the worn boards between them. They spoke for a time of the hardships of the previous winter and the coming end of the long French war, and of Sybil Thatcher, the younger sister of one of Ashworth's victims whom the Professor was now sending to school.

"I thought you were going to train her to be a pickpocket," said Sebastian.

The Professor's eyes crinkled with amusement. "I might still."

"Gammon." Sebastian took a deep drink of his cider. "Think it's possible a family member of one of Ashworth's victims could have killed him?"

The old man sucked thoughtfully on his lower lip. "Most of those children were orphans. I haven't heard of anyone coming around looking for any of them. Apart from which, how would they know he was one of the killers?"

"You haven't voiced your suspicions to anyone?"

"Me? No. Next you'll be saying you've got me on your suspects list."

"I'll admit the thought crossed my mind. But Ashworth isn't the only one who has died. And I can't see you stabbing a fifteen-year-old child."

"Dear Lord." The old man stared out the window at the heavy gray clouds tossed about by the wind. "He was an evil man, that one. The world is better off without him. But not at the cost of another innocent's life. Too many have died already."

They sat for a time in companionable silence, listening to the bluster of the wind and the soft crackle of the fire on the kitchen hearth. Sebastian said, "Does Sybil know about Benji?"

"She knows where he is. Every week we walk up to the churchyard and put flowers on his grave. But she doesn't know exactly how he died. To be honest, I'm not sure I'll ever tell her. What would be the point in forcing her to live with the knowledge of the horrors that were done to him?"

"I can't think of any. Secrets that shield the wicked should be exposed. But why not hide an ugly truth that would only harm an innocent?"

The Professor nodded. "How is your niece? She did marry him, I take it?"

"She did. He made her life miserable, and now she is free of him."

"She's lucky. Does she realize that?"

Sebastian met the old man's gaze. "Yes."

"And you've no idea at all who killed the bastard?"

"Not really. But whoever did this also killed Ashworth's valet as well as the young girl from the Haymarket. And there's a missing crossing sweep and a parlor maid who could be additional victims."

"Doesn't sound to me like a dead street child's grieving parent out for revenge," said the Professor. "Sounds like someone nearly as sick and twisted as Ashworth himself."

Sebastian drained his tankard and set it aside. "I'm afraid you might be right."

CHAPTER 31

Why do people murder?

It was a question Sebastian asked himself as he drove south toward Mayfair with the wind buffeting his face and the clouds scuttling fast overhead. He knew the reasons for murder were as varied and idiosyncratic as the people who killed. But in his experience, most of their motives could be reduced to five common human emotions: greed, whether for money or power; love, or at least sexual lust; fear; jealousy; and revenge.

But there existed another breed of killer, and those were the ones Sebastian believed belonged in a category all their own: the men and women who killed for pleasure. Ashworth had been that kind, feeding off the helplessness and fear of his victims. And Sebastian couldn't shake the growing suspicion that he might be dealing with such a monster again.

The killer's primary victim had been Ashworth, which meant that the way the Viscount died must be telling. The other victims—Edward Digby and Sissy Jordan, and perhaps Ben King and Jenny Crutcher—all felt incidental, a matter of cleaning up loose ends and eliminating anyone who might threaten exposure. Their deaths told Sebastian much about the ruthlessness of the killer he sought. But it was that first murder—the bloody, savage hacking of Viscount Ashworth's naked, spread-eagled body—that surely defined this murderer in a way the others did not.

So, it wasn't simply a matter of asking, *Why kill Ashworth?* The question was also, *Why kill Ashworth in that particular way?*

Why not a quick, silent dagger thrust to the back? Sebastian could see Sid Cotton killing in that way, or even the furniture seller Lawrence McCay. But why would either man bother to tie his victim naked to his bed or—if they simply chanced to find him that way—utterly drench it with his blood? Sid Cotton might do such a thing out of pure meanness or spite, but surely not if it put his own life at risk—which sneaking into Ashworth's house undoubtedly would have done.

McCay was different. Sebastian would say the shopkeeper lacked a motive for that kind of flourish if it weren't for McCay's pretty young daughter. Had Ashworth abused Julie McCay the same way he had used Giselle Blanchette and so many others? It was possible. Would that drive her father to seek such a hideous revenge?

Perhaps.

What about the young Welsh architect, Russell Firth? Depending upon what Ashworth had done to Stephanie in the past and how much Firth knew about it, such a murder might make sense— again, as a twisted act of revenge.

And Marie-Claire Blanchette?

Sebastian considered the French cartomancer and decided the answer was, again, *Perhaps*. There was something almost ritualistic about the manner of Ashworth's death, something that suggested both a familiarity with Ashworth's erotic tastes and a desire for some reason to symbolically replicate or at least echo his past activities. And that was without taking into account the strange death of the Bond Street jeweler, Vincent.

The problem was, if McCay, Firth, or Blanchette was Ashworth's killer, then how to explain the blood-soaked gown and cloak plucked by chance from the Thames? Yes, the gown might have nothing at all to do with Ashworth's murder. And yet Sebastian found himself unable to discount it. Of those he already suspected, the gown pointed to two. One was Stephanie, the other Ivanna Gagarin.

While it pained Sebastian to admit it, he could see Stephanie driven to kill by fear and humiliation. And if she hated Ashworth enough, Sebastian could even imagine her thrusting a butcher knife again and again into her husband's chest while his blood sprayed in gruesome arcs around her. What he couldn't see was her then setting about methodically eliminating anyone who might possibly expose her, from Ashworth's venal valet to a frightened Haymarket girl and an impoverished young crossing sweep. If it weren't for Firth, he'd have crossed her off his list of suspects long ago. But because of Firth, he couldn't.

He knew his list of suspects could easily be incomplete, that the person or persons Sissy Jordan heard come to Curzon Street that fateful night might be utterly unknown to him. Yet he still found his thoughts circling back to Princess Ivanna Gagarin. The tall, slender Russian noblewoman's gowns had surely all come from Continental modistas safe from Bow Street's questioning. Her knowledge of sedating drugs and poisons was extensive enough to have led to whispers about her own husband's sudden death. She'd freely admitted she enjoyed the kind of games Ashworth played. She'd even laughed with casual indifference when Sebastian suggested Ashworth had diverted himself by killing street children. Such a woman might not need a motive to kill.

No reason beyond a desire for pleasure and a taste for watching others die.

By the time Sebastian reached the Pulteney Hotel, the wind had blown away most of the clouds, leaving the sky scoured clean of all but some high white streaks. A few careful questions directed at the staff led him to a harried chambermaid who was not at all fond of either the Tsar's histrionic sister or the thirty-seven servants and demanding members of the Russian and Oldenburg courts traveling with her.

What she had to tell him was damning.

Afterward, he paused on the hotel's front steps and stared across Piccadilly at Green Park. The plane trees were lifting with the strength of the gusts, for the day was still blustery. Despite the wind, two women stood beside the elongated oval reservoir that ran parallel to the street. One was a tall, slender gentlewoman wearing a wide-brimmed straw hat and a fine muslin walking gown trimmed with turquoise ribbons; the other the hatchet-faced middle-aged companion he remembered from before. Some ten or twenty feet behind them stood two men in the uniform of the Imperial Guard, their arms crossed, their glorious mustaches carefully waxed and curled.

As Sebastian watched, the middle-aged companion said something to her mistress, and Princess Ivanna turned to stare across the street toward the hotel. She went suddenly still, one hand coming up to catch the brim of her hat as the wind caught it. She stayed motionless, watching Sebastian as he walked down the steps and across the street toward her.

"Windy day for a stroll in the park," he said, coming up to her.

She glanced at the blue sky, the sun falling full on her face and her lips curling into a charming smile that made her look guileless and carefree and everything he knew she was not. "True. But it is a glorious spring day, yes?"

"It is, indeed."

They turned to walk together along the side of the reservoir, her companion and the two men following at a distance, the gravel path crunching beneath their feet. "And would you have me believe you are here by chance, my lord?"

"No."

"Ah. At least you are honest. It's about Lord Ashworth again, I take it?"

"You told me Ashworth came to see you the afternoon of his death."

"He did, yes. Why?"

"I'm wondering why you quarreled."

She gave a startled laugh. "What a curious notion. Whatever would we have quarreled about?"

"I don't know. That's my question."

Her smile never faltered. "There was no quarrel."

"He didn't grab your arm?"

Her brow wrinkled in a pretty little frown, then cleared. "Ah, now I know to what you refer. We encountered each other on the stairs and stopped to talk. But my heel caught on the flounce of my dress, and I would have tumbled headfirst down the steps had he not put out a hand to steady me."

"There were no harsh words?"

"But no. As I said, over what would we have quarreled?"

He might have believed her if all he had to go on was the tale told by the talkative Lady Townsend from Amanda's evening party. But the encounter had also been observed by the Pulteney's chambermaid. And while the maid couldn't understand the quiet, harsh French they'd spoken, she had no doubt about either the anger in which the words were said or the fact that the Russian noblewoman had jerked her arm from the Viscount's grasp.

"Actually, I can think of several possible reasons," he said.

Her eyes crinkled with her smile. "I fear you have a more active imagination than I." She turned her head, her gaze fixing on the vast Palladian-style house that stood on the far side of Piccadilly, set back behind massive iron gates and surrounded by acres of gardens. "Whose palace is that?"

Sebastian followed her gaze "It's not a palace. That's Devonshire House, the London residence of the Dukes of Devonshire."

"If it is the home of a duke, why is it not considered a palace?"

"I don't know why. We simply don't call them that here."

She gave a faint sniff. "The architecture is rather severe."

"The facade, yes. But the interior is as Baroque as anyone might wish."

"How very . . . English." She brought her gaze back to him, the sunlight shimmering on the wind-ruffled water beside them to reflect on her face, her eyes speculative in a way he could not follow. She said, "You've heard that the allied armies have entered Paris?"

"I hadn't heard, no." He felt oddly light-headed at the news, almost numb, as a surge of hope and elation warred with a wary incredulity. After so many years of war, it was difficult to believe peace could actually be close at hand. "Are you quite certain?"

"Oh, yes. Word reached Her Imperial Highness from her brother not long ago. No doubt the Regent has heard by now as well. A public announcement should be made soon." The wind gusted up, bringing them the smell of fresh grass and wet humus and a hint of sweetness from the French honeysuckle tumbling over the high garden walls of Devonshire House. She said, "Life marches on, and the world changes. What once seemed impossible is suddenly our new reality. We must strive always to adapt, yes? Or we die."

"Some die without being given the chance to adapt."

Her face lifted to his, her strange wintry eyes carefully emptied of anything he might have read

288

there even as her lips formed a moue of sorrow. "The death of Lord Ashworth genuinely does grieve me. I know you don't believe me, but it is true."

"Someone is spreading nasty rumors about his widow. You wouldn't know anything about that, would you?"

"I have heard the whispers. It is inevitable, is it not?"

"Is it?"

"They say she was seen recently in Howard and Mercer's. I hope she does not fear that her own life is in danger."

Sebastian studied the Russian noblewoman's smooth, beautiful face. Howard and Mercer's was an exclusive gun dealer on the Strand popular with members of the Upper Ten Thousand. He didn't want to believe what she was saying, except that he suspected she was far too clever to simply make up such a tale. Not to him.

He kept his voice calm. "Where did you hear that?"

Her brows drew together into a parody of a thoughtful frown. "That I cannot recall. But now that I think upon it, she is said to have bought the gun early last week. So it must not have anything to do with Ashworth's murder after all, hmm?" She turned her face into the wind, letting a gust catch her heavy fall of dark hair and blow it away from her face. "I met your Princess Charlotte at the Regent's Carlton House banquet. She is an extraordinarily beautiful young woman, but very sad, yes?"

"Her life has not been easy," said Sebastian, choosing his words carefully.

"And her mother, the Princess of Wales, was not invited. She is no longer welcome in society?"

"The Regent and his wife are estranged."

"So I am told." A gust caught the brim of her straw hat again, dancing a hatched pattern of light and shade across her face, and she laughed and put up a hand to catch it. "The wind is fierce enough that I believe it has defeated me. But I enjoyed our walk, my lord. Good luck with your investigation." Then she turned and strolled away from him, the sun bathing her back in a warm light, the turquoise ribbons of her hat fluttering behind her.

Plump and rosy-cheeked, the twins slept side by side in baskets lined with lace-trimmed muslin and set up on stands on Lindley House's stone-flagged rear terrace where the massive looming bulk of the house sheltered them from the wind. Their mother sat beside them, watching them. The peace and joy in Stephanie's face as she gazed down at her tiny sons caught at Sebastian's heart, and he was reluctant to break the moment. Then she looked up and saw him, and the smile faded away to something bleak and fearful.

"Uncle," she said warily.

He let his gaze drift over his sleeping nephews. Their hair was fair, their innocence as yet untouched, their little mouths making contented sucking movements in their sleep. "They're beautiful, Stephanie. I mean that."

A smile flashed across her face and then was gone. "Why are you here?"

He pulled out one of the chairs and sat beside her. "Last Tuesday morning, you purchased a French muff pistol with mother-of-pearl grips from Howard and Mercer's." He knew this because he had stopped in the Strand before driving to Park Lane. He searched her familiar, beloved face. "Why, Steph?"

"How did you find out?"

"Someone told me. Someone I'm afraid does not wish you well."

She pushed up and went to stand at the edge of the terrace overlooking the garden. The wind fluttered the blossoms of the neat eighteenth-century-style parterres of closely planted daffodils and tulips into waves of dancing color. She brought up a trembling hand to touch her forehead in a gesture he suspected she didn't even realize she was making. "But . . . how could they know? I wore a veil and left my carriage a block away."

"Your carriage might have been a block away, but the crest on the panel was plainly visible. You should have taken a hackney, Steph."

She made a ragged sound that might have been meant as a laugh but wasn't. "Now I know. I'll do better next time."

"Why did you buy a pistol, Stephanie? Steph? Talk to me."

She swung to face him, her eyes wide and glazed with a hopeless terror that reminded him of a trapped animal. "Why do people typically buy guns?"

"Generally, because they want to kill someone, or because they're afraid someone is going to try to kill them. Which was it, Steph?"

She pressed both hands flat against the midriff of her morning gown, accentuating the soft bump left from the recent births. "It was because of Ashworth. I was afraid he was going to kill me."

"Did he threaten you?"

She nodded. But her eyes slid away from Sebastian's face.

"Why now? Something must have happened."

"I always knew there was more to him than what he cared to show the world—that beneath that handsome, charming facade lurked something else, something dark and dangerous. But I never realized just how dangerous he was."

I tried to tell you, Sebastian thought. But then he knew only too well that the most brutal truths can only be learned the hard way, firsthand. "Did he find out about Firth, Steph? Is that what happened?"

"You asked me that before, and I told you no."

"And I don't believe you any more now than I did then."

"Believe this, Uncle: Anthony didn't need a reason to kill. He liked it."

Her words so echoed his own recent thoughts that his stomach wrenched. He said, "I'd like to talk to your abigail, Steph, if I may?"

She stared at him in silence for so long that he thought she might not answer him. Then she said, "Why?"

"It's important."

"I'm sorry, but no. She was so frightened by Bow Street's visit yesterday that she's still useless. I don't want her upset again."

He searched her beautiful, lying face. "You're hiding something, Stephanie."

She met his gaze and held it. "I'm not hiding anything." Yet even as she said it, the color drained from her face, leaving her cheeks pale and her lips looking bruised.

CHAPTER 32

Sebastian was crossing Lindley House's vast entrance hall, preparing to leave, when the Marquis himself came in wearing a heavy greatcoat and bringing with him all the scents of a windy spring day.

"Ah, I thought I recognized your chestnuts and curricle out front," said the old man, handing his hat to a manservant. "But I didn't see your young tiger."

"He's running some errands for me today," said Sebastian.

"You were leaving? Won't you step into the library for a moment, first?"

"Of course."

"I take it you've been visiting with Stephanie? Tell me honestly," said the Marquis, his voice tense with concern as they reached the library. "How do you find her?"

"Let's just say I'm glad she has the twins to focus on."

"Ah, yes." The old man sighed. "I've tried to get her to come with me on my constitutionals around the park, but she won't do it. I go out twice a day, you know. Don't want to turn into a doddering old man who can't walk across the room without getting winded."

The Marquis's cheeks were flushed from the exercise and fresh air, his eyes sparkling with pleasure. But as Sebastian watched, the light went out of his eyes, and Sebastian knew the old man's thoughts had returned, inevitably, to the brutal murder of his son. "Are you here to tell us you've discovered something about Anthony's death?"

"Not really. I'm sorry."

Lindley nodded, his hands shaky as he set to work removing his gloves. "I spoke to that Bow Street magistrate yesterday. He said the same thing. It's . . . it's very hard to accept."

When Sebastian remained silent, Lindley looked up, his eyes narrowing as if with speculation. "I've been thinking about what you asked me at the inquest—if I knew of anyone Anthony might have angered or frightened lately."

"And?"

"It might be nothing, but . . ."

"Yes?"

"A few days before Anthony died—I believe it was that Monday—I chanced to meet him on Bond Street. He turned and walked with me a ways, and I noticed a rather scruffy fellow who looked as if he might be following us. When I pointed the man out to Anthony, he laughed and tried to say it was nothing. But I know my son—know him well enough to suspect that he wasn't being honest with me."

"Was he afraid of the man, do you think?"

"Afraid? No. But he was annoyed."

"What did this fellow look like? Had you ever seen him before?"

"Good heavens, no."

"You're certain?"

"Oh, yes. He's not one you'd forget, once you saw him. Tall and lanky, with a strangely narrow, elongated head and a puckery mouth that makes it look like he's sucking on an invisible lemon."

Sebastian had automatically assumed Ashworth's shadow must have been McCay. Now he realized he was wrong. "What was this fellow doing?"

"Nothing beyond sticking close enough to be noticeable. If he'd actually done anything I'd have set the constables after him. I was tempted to anyway, but Anthony told me to leave it be."

"He never explained to you how he knew the man?"

"No. And the next time I looked around, the fellow was gone. To be frank, I completely forgot the incident until last night, when I was thinking about your question." He studied Sebastian's deliberately impassive face. "But it means something, doesn't it?"

"It might."

"It's getting dark," said Hero, watching Sebastian tie a coarse black kerchief around his neck.

He reached for a tattered coat from the rag fair in Rosemary Lane and shrugged into it.

She said, "You do realize you could wait until morning to go plunging into Seven Dials. That it would be safer. And wiser."

"I should have gone after Cotton last night and given him my opinion of shady characters who approach my wife."

"He didn't do anything to me."

"No." Sebastian set a slouch hat at a rakish angle on his ash-and-lard-drenched hair. "But that doesn't mean he won't."

Sebastian found the common room of the Black Swan thick with tobacco smoke and reeking with the usual foul combination of spilled ale, bad teeth, and rank body odor. The dim light from a scattering of guttering tallow dips flickered over a roaring throng of rough men, their faces shiny with a desperate kind of excitement or sunken into hopeless despair.

Sebastian ordered a pint and stood with an elbow propped on the battered bar, his gaze roving from one cluster of ragged men to the next. A couple of burly tradesmen, probably butchers from the looks of them, came in without glancing at him and quickly faded into the shadowy corners. This was a world of unshaven faces and furtive glances, of men who'd steal the pennies off a dead man's eyes and kill you for the clothes off your back if given a chance. As he watched a "blind" beggar laughingly remove the bandages from his head to reveal perfectly sound eyes, Sebastian found himself wondering, again, how Ashworth had connected with a man such as Sid Cotton in the first place. Or was this another service provided by the dead valet? If Digby had sourced prostitutes from the Haymarket, why not killers from Seven Dials?

Sebastian raised his tankard to his lips but was careful not to drink from it. He became aware of the barman watching him slyly. The man's beefy arms were crossed at his chest, his protuberant belly straining against his greasy leather apron, his balding head thrown back at a belligerent angle. Taking a shilling from his pocket, Sebastian slid the coin across the scarred surface of the bar toward him. "I'm looking for Sid Cotton. Is he upstairs?"

The coin disappeared. "Nah."

"You're certain of that?"

" 'E went out. Two hours 'n' more ago."

Sebastian slid another shilling across the boards. "Where did he go?"

The second coin disappeared. "Don't know."

"Or won't say?"

The barman's eyes narrowed to slits as his lips pulled back to display a mouthful of large, crooked teeth. Sebastian couldn't decide whether it was meant to be a smile. "I'll tell 'im yer lookin' fer 'im," said the man.

Sebastian briefly considered carrying his search for Cotton up the rickety narrow stairs at the back of the tavern, then decided against it. The menacing hostility in the room was so intense as to be palpable.

The bartender sniffed. "If I see 'im, who should I send 'im to?"

"He'll know."

Pushing the tankard away, Sebastian headed for the door. He was aware of the two husky men who had come into the Black Swan behind him rising to their feet and following him.

He was beginning to suspect they weren't butchers after all.

Outside, the night was cold, the air heavy with the stench of coal smoke, roasting meat, and overflowing boghouses. He drew up on the narrow pavement, his gaze seemingly focused on the old-iron monger's across the street even as his awareness was all for the two men pausing behind him. He'd never seen either man before and had no idea if their interest in him was driven by simple larceny or something more personal.

But as he stepped wide to avoid the refuse-clogged gutter, the two men fell in behind him.

CHAPTER 33

Sebastian pushed his way through the knots of ragged men, women, and filthy, scrawny children that clogged the intersection of the seven radiating streets. A mist was rolling in, blurring the already dim light cast by torches thrust into high wall brackets. Keeping one hand on the small double-barreled flintlock pistol in his greatcoat pocket, he turned north toward Broad Street. The two men kept perhaps seven or eight paces behind him.

There was no doubt they were following him.

Both were relatively young, one dark, the other fair, their clothes that of semiskilled workingmen rather than the motley assortment of rags worn by ruffians such as Sid Cotton. Unlike Cotton, these men would blend easily into any neighborhood, including Mayfair. Sebastian tried to recall if he'd noticed them earlier. But he'd been so focused on finding Ashworth's killer and proving Stephanie innocent that he'd been largely oblivious to anything else.

Dangerously oblivious.

He brushed past a stall selling smoked herrings in paper cones, past a decrepit, decaying hovel with missing windowpanes covered in old newspaper that crackled in the rising cold wind. With every step he took away from the district's starlike center, the lane became darker, and the crowds thinned until they disappeared. This was a good place to kill, and he suspected the men shadowing him had been sent to kill him.

Carefully slipping the flintlock from his pocket, Sebastian drew up abruptly and swung about, his pistol's twin muzzles coming up as he thumbed back the first hammer. "Do I take it you gentlemen wish to speak with me? Or did you intend to go straight for the kill?"

The men stopped, eyes widening and arms dangling awkwardly at their sides. Despite the cold, their coats hung open to display the flintlock thrust into one man's waistband and the knife strapped to his companion's side. The way Sebastian figured it, they now had basically three options: They could run away, laugh and try to claim it was all a mistake, or rush him. The dark-haired man said something to his companion—something Sebastian couldn't understand. The companion's response was guttural and decisive and sounded vaguely like *miyego-ubivayem.*

"Well?" said Sebastian.

The first man—the darker one, the one who seemed less sure of himself—stayed where he was on the narrow pavement while his fair-haired companion stepped sideways into the lane, putting distance between them. And Sebastian knew that if he didn't stop him, the men would soon have him sandwiched between them.

Sebastian shifted the muzzle of his flintlock to follow the moving man and said calmly, "One more step and you're dead."

The fair-haired man drew up, his lips pulling back in a smile. He was still smiling when his hand flashed toward the pistol at his waist.

Sebastian squeezed the trigger.

A roaring burst of fire exploded into the dark night. The bullet tore into the man's throat to send blood spurting in pulsing arcs. He staggered back, his body swaying as he continued bringing up his own flintlock and fired.

The brick wall beside Sebastian's head erupted in a shower of dust and sharp chunks of debris. He felt a jagged pain tear across his temple and the sting of grit in his eyes.

"Boris!" shouted the dark-haired man as his companion crumpled in the gutter.

Half-blind, Sebastian thumbed back his second hammer and pivoted to face the surviving assassin. "Your choice."

The man's gaze flickered from Sebastian's gun to his dying companion. Then he turned and ran.

Sebastian swiped a sleeve across his face, trying to wipe the blood and grit from his eyes. "Bloody hell," he swore, and let the man go.

His eyes and forehead hurting like hell, Sebastian went to crouch beside the man in the gutter. The assailant's eyes were half-open but glazed, the blood surging from his neck beginning to slow.

"Who sent you?" said Sebastian.

Lips slick with blood, the man stared silently back at him, his eyes vacant.

"Damn." Easing the man down to the pavement, Sebastian found himself looking at the empty flintlock that had fallen nearby.

Swearing again, he reached for it, his eyes narrowing at the sight of the familiar escutcheon on the grip.

Charles, Lord Jarvis, was crossing the torchlit forecourt of Carlton House when a tall, dark-haired young man in an appallingly ragged coat and greasy breeches fell into step beside him. Blood ran down the side of his face from a wound on his forehead and dripped onto his black neckcloth; a yellowing bruise showed on his chin.

"Good God," said Jarvis. "How ever did you get past the guards, looking like that?"

Devlin's teeth gleamed white out of his dirt- and blood-streaked face. "They recognized me."

"Commendable, I suppose." Jarvis nodded to the guards as he passed through the portal. "I assume you're here for a reason."

"There's something you need to see."

Jarvis's carriage was awaiting him at the kerb, and he paused to cast a disparaging glance at his son-in-law's clothes as a footman scrambled to open the door and let down the steps. "I trust those rags are not vermin-infested."

"Not too badly."

"Huh." He climbed into his carriage and watched silently as Devlin leapt up to take the backward-facing seat. "Drive on," Jarvis told the coachman.

The carriage rolled forward with a rattle of chains and the clatter of hooves on cobblestone. Jarvis kept his gaze fixed on his son-in-law. "So, what is of such pressing importance that you must offend my nostrils with such a malodorous and totally unsuitable rig?"

"This," said Devlin, holding out a brass-mounted flintlock.

"A pistol? Am I supposed to be impressed? It's rather ordinary-looking."

"Someone just tried to kill me with it."

"And they missed? What a pity."

Devlin laughed out loud, his lean body moving easily with the motion of the carriage. "You don't recognize it?"

"Should I?"

"It's a Russian pattern 1809, commissioned by Tsar Alexander and manufactured at Izhevsk in the Urals. They're carried by Russian mounted Dragoons and Cuirassier, Hussar, and Cossack troops, as well as by officers of other regiments."

Jarvis kept the same faintly derisive smile on his face, but he was curious enough to say, "How can you be certain it's Russian?"

"The Tsar believes in marking his own." Devlin

flipped the pistol to display a brass escutcheon mounted on the grip and engraved with Alexander's cipher: a florid "A" surmounted by a crown topped with a holy cross.

Jarvis shrugged. "Doubtless some English soldier picked it up off a battlefield somewhere and brought it home."

"I might think that if I hadn't heard one of the two men who jumped me say 'Kill him' to his companion in Russian."

"I didn't know you counted the ability to speak Russian amongst your many talents."

"I don't. But when you're in the army, you tend to pick up certain common words in a variety of languages. Generally, most are vulgar references to male and female body parts and related activities. But one also learns the word for 'kill.'"

Jarvis watched the light from the swinging carriage lantern dance across his son-in-law's bloody face. "And where is the original owner of this pistol now?"

"Dead."

"You killed him?"

"Yes."

"Inconvenient. The authorities have the corpse?"

Devlin shook his head. "By the time I returned with the constables, it was gone."

"Thank goodness for that, at least."

"Oh? Why is that?"

"Don't be stupid." Jarvis paused. "So, why are you here, precisely?"

Devlin tucked the pistol into the waistband of his disgusting breeches and swiped a forearm across his bleeding face. "You don't find it telling that the Russians should have such a lethal reaction to my investigation into Ashworth's death?"

"When you keep trying to implicate the Grand Duchess's lady-in-waiting—who happens to be the widow of a Russian prince and war hero? No, I do not. On the contrary, I would find it remarkable if they failed to show any interest."

"Bit of a leap from showing an interest in my investigation to trying to kill me, wouldn't you say?"

"Perhaps. But then, they do things differently in Russia." Jarvis drew his snuffbox from his pocket and opened it with a flick of his thumb. "I did warn you to stay away from the Pulteney. You ignored me."

"I did, yes. Although I wonder how you know that."

Jarvis lifted a pinch of snuff to one nostril and sniffed.

When he continued to remain silent, Devlin said, "Did you know the Russians were trying to kill me?"

"I did not. Presumably they see your activities as a threat."

"Obviously. The question is still why."

"That I cannot say."

"Actually, I suspect you could."

Jarvis closed his snuffbox and tucked it away. "You heard the allied armies have entered Paris?"

"Yes. And Napoléon?"

"Has been formally deposed by the Sénat. He could have saved himself by simply agreeing to accept France's original borders under the *ancien régime*. But he refused. And now he's on the run."

"With his army?"

"Unfortunately. But while the common soldiers would probably follow him to hell if he asked it of them, I suspect most of his officers have more sense. It will be over soon."

Devlin swiped at his cheek again. "I'll believe it when he's dead."

Jarvis frowned. "You're bleeding all over my carriage."

Devlin laughed and signaled the coachman to pull up.

Jarvis watched the Viscount jump down from the carriage, then said, "I meant it when I warned you to stay away from the Grand Duchess and her court. Ignore me at your peril."

Devlin glanced back at him, his strange yellow eyes glowing in the lamplight. "Or—what? You'll send someone to try to kill me next?"

"You don't understand what you're interfering in."

"Not yet. But I will."

CHAPTER 34

Sebastian was in his dressing room, dabbing at the blood on his face, when Hero came to stand in the doorway.

"One of the housemaids tells me my husband came home covered in blood. I assumed she was exaggerating. Obviously, I was mistaken."

"I don't know if I'd say 'covered' in blood."

"Look in the mirror." She watched him dip the cloth in the washbowl and squeeze, the gentle trickle of water filling the room's silence. He touched the cloth to his forehead and winced.

"Here, let me do that." She pushed away from the doorway and came to take the cloth from him. Her voice and face were both utterly calm. But when she dipped the cloth in the water again, he noticed her hands were not quite steady. She turned his face to the lamplight. "Shouldn't you have gone to see Gibson?"

"It's only a scratch."

"It's a bit more than that."

"I'll live."

She made an incoherent noise deep in her throat but kept her focus on the task of cleaning the raw, jagged furrows dug into the side of his scalp by the exploding brick. "And was it worth it?"

"I didn't find Cotton. But a couple of Russians found me."

Her hand fell. "Russians did this?"

"Mmm. I killed one of them, then beat a prudent retreat for reinforcements. By the time I returned with the constables, the body was gone. I assume his compatriot removed him."

"You're certain they were Russian?"

"Yes. I thought Jarvis might find their involvement interesting, but all he did was complain about my dripping blood on his carriage's upholstery."

"So, are you going to ask the lovely Princess Ivanna why she wants you dead?"

"Yes, but not until I understand it a bit better myself." He watched her soak a pad with alcohol. "Has Tom come back yet?"

She pressed the pad to his wound and waited while he let out a long hiss. "No."

Tom returned to Brook Street late that night.

He was dressed in a pair of ragged breeches so big he had to hold them up with a length of rope. Once his shirt might have been white, but those days were far in the distant, forgotten past. His coat was a motley collection of patches, and the hat he clutched was so battered that half the brim hung loose from the crown.

"Good God," said Sebastian when he saw him. "I'm surprised Morey didn't turn you away at the door, thinking you were some grubby beggar."

Tom grinned, his face so smeared with dirt that his scattered freckles were invisible. "Look the part, don't I?"

"It's amazing. Have you eaten?"

"Aye, gov'nor. I nicked some sausages with Waldo Jones."

"Bonding over theft? I suppose that's one way to gain his confidence—as long as you don't get taken up by the watch."

The boy looked vaguely affronted. "I ain't lost me touch."

Sebastian ducked his head to hide a smile. "What did you discover about Ben King?"

" 'E's definitely missing—took off scared the mornin' Ashworth was found dead. But I don't reckon Waldo knows where 'e is. Waldo's afraid 'e's dead."

"Any idea where the lad used to sleep?"

"Waldo says 'e'd get a pallet in one o' the flea traps near St. Martin's whenever 'e 'ad a couple extra pennies. I thought I'd go there tomorrow."

Sebastian thought about the stacks of corpses in the deadhouse of St. Martin's workhouse and felt a heavy weight of unease settle low in his gut. "Just be careful, you hear?"

Tom eyed the sticking plaster on Sebastian's forehead and gave him a jaunty grin.

Wednesday, 6 April

"I received a visit late last night from one Major Edward Burnside," said Sir Henry Lovejoy when he and Sebastian met in a coffeehouse near Bow Street early the next morning. "We're instructed to stay away from both the Grand Duchess's household and the Russian ambassador and his lady." Lovejoy paused. "I take it you're getting uncomfortably close to something?"

Sebastian took a deep swallow of his scalding coffee and grimaced. Major Burnside was one of Jarvis's most trusted minions. "You heard two Russians tried to kill me last night?"

Lovejoy nodded. "You're quite certain as to their nationality?"

"Yes."

Lovejoy nodded again. "The major expressed the palace's concerns over the recent rise in violent crime on the city's streets and suggested we might want to conduct a sweeping arrest of undesirable elements. Presumably one or more of them could then be charged with recent events."

"Tidy."

Lovejoy sipped his hot chocolate. "Have you seen Gibson since he completed the Jordan girl's autopsy?"

"Not yet."

Lovejoy let out his breath in a long, painful rush. "It's disturbing. Most disturbing."

Sissy Jordan lay pale and waxen on Gibson's stained stone slab. In the morning light streaming in through the outbuilding's open door, she looked even younger than she had in the dim horror that was St. Martin's deadhouse. Her nose was small and childlike, her chin firm, her eyebrows delicately arched. Looking at her, Sebastian was struck again by the tragedy of both her death and her short life. And he felt a rush of rage so all-consuming that he was practically shaking with it.

"You all right?" asked Gibson, watching him through narrowed eyes.

Sebastian turned away and went to slap his open palm against the doorframe as he stared out at Alexi Sauvage's dew-dampened garden. "*Damn*. Damn, damn, damn. She was only fifteen years old—thirteen when she had to start selling herself on the streets so she could eat. What the bloody hell is wrong with us? What kind of society turns its back on the neediest amongst them?" He flung his arm through the air in a sweeping motion that took in the awakening city. "They call themselves Christians; they smugly go to church every Sunday and pat themselves on the back for being so damned holy. And then they allow *this?*"

" 'For I was hungered and ye gave me no meat,' " quoted Gibson softly. " 'I was thirsty and ye gave me no drink; I was a stranger and ye took me not in.' "

Sebastian turned to look again at the dead child prostitute. "Can you tell me anything?"

Gibson stood with his hands tucked up under his armpits. His face was unshaven and sallow, his eyes sunken and bruised-looking in a way Sebastian had learned to recognize. "Well," said the surgeon, "she was stabbed, but not with as large a knife as Ashworth or Digby—probably more like a dagger. And unlike the other two, she fought back. There are cuts on her hands from when she tried to either grab the knife or at least deflect it." He picked up her nearest hand and turned it over to show the lacerations on her palm and fingers. "See?"

"Brave girl." Sebastian shifted his gaze to the bloody wounds in her chest. Sissy had been stabbed again and again, but not nearly as many times as Ashworth or Digby. "I wonder why the differences. Think we could be dealing with two different killers?"

"No way to tell, really. Perhaps your killer is simply gaining confidence as he gains experience."

"Now, there's a frightening thought."

The sound of a door opening drew Sebastian's attention to the ancient stone house where Alexi had appeared on the stoop wearing an old gown and a simple hat with a wide brim. Her gaze met his across the yard. Then she turned away to kneel at a patch of some dark green herb, a trowel in her hand.

Sebastian said, "I've discovered there's a boy missing too—a crossing sweep named Ben King who carried a message from Digby the night Ashworth was murdered. He disappeared the next morning."

Gibson reached for the sheet and drew it up over the dead girl's face. "Please tell me you're close to figuring out who's doing this."

But Sebastian could only shake his head, any possible reply he might have made lost in a swirl of frustration and fear.

Later, after Gibson applied a foul-smelling ointment and a fresh sticking plaster to Sebastian's head wounds, he walked across the yard to where Alexi Sauvage still knelt in her garden. Her hands were deep in the dirt, the sun warm on her back, her face a study of serene contentment. Then his shadow fell across her and she looked up. Her expression of peace drained away.

She said, "Paul tells me you were asking about soporifics. Something that might have been used to render Ashworth unconscious so he wouldn't fight back when he was killed."

"Do you know of something?"

She tugged at a stubborn clump of grass. "There are dozens of possibilities. Laudanum would do it, although he'd need to take it himself, because it would require too large a dose for someone to slip to him unawares. The same is probably true of herbs such as valerian and skullcap. Henbane can cause a stupor, but it usually also provokes convulsions, and Paul says he saw no evidence of anything like that on his body."

"What else?"

She thought for a moment. "Most plants that cause paralysis can also cause death if you're not careful and don't know what you're doing. Although given that your killer's plan was to then stab Ashworth, I suppose that wouldn't matter. So if you're not deterred by the fear of accidentally killing someone, the number of possibilities expands dramatically. There's a pretty yellow-flowering vine from America called Carolina jessamine that would do it. But many more-familiar garden plants can also be dangerous. I've heard of people falling unconscious from breathing in the smoke of burning oleander branches or even after eating food stirred with a twig. And simply chewing a foxglove leaf can cause temporary paralysis—or stop your heart if you're unlucky."

"Something as common as foxglove?"

"Yes. But if I were to pick the most likely culprit, I'd probably go with belladonna, or deadly nightshade as it is sometimes called. The wives of the Roman emperors Augustus and Claudius are said to have used it to dispose of their husbands, but it can also be used to create hallucinations or a stupor. It was supposedly a favorite of witches, but I don't know if that's true."

"And there's no way to detect it?"

"No."

"How common is this knowledge?"

"It's probably less common in London than in the countryside, where these things are passed down from mother to daughter. But the city is full of apothecaries who would know."

Sebastian blew out a long, harsh breath as he watched her set to work trimming a woody, upright shrub with long ovate leaves. "What's that?"

She looked up and smiled, her lips parting on a laugh he didn't understand until she said, "Nightshade."

CHAPTER 35

Sebastian was walking down Tower Hill toward where he'd left his curricle, when he spotted a lanky man with protuberant lips who was leaning against the front of one of the older houses.

"Why the bloody hell are you following me?" Sebastian demanded, stopping in front of him.

Sid Cotton straightened with a slow, insolent smile. "I'm hurt, I am, ye talkin' to me like that. And me thinkin' you'd be grateful I took the trouble to look ye up, seein' as how I'm told ye was askin' after me last night at the pub."

"Yes. Right before someone tried to kill me."

"I didn't have nothin' to do with that."

"If true, that's probably the first honest thing you've said to me."

Cotton splayed a hand over his heart. "I keep tellin' ye I had nothin' to do with that viscount's death neither, and that's the gospel truth."

Sebastian grunted. "You were seen following Lord Ashworth on Bond Street just days before he died."

Cotton's eyes crinkled with a grin. "Course I was followin' the bugger. I thought ye knew that."

"Not exactly."

" 'Twas my way of givin' him a friendly

reminder about how I ain't forgot what he owed me." Cotton squinted down the lane toward the soot-stained walls of the ancient castle. "Ye can learn a lot about a man, following him."

"Oh? Such as?"

"Seen some things, I did—seen 'em and heard 'em. Some things ye maybe don't know about. Some things ye maybe don't want to know about."

"Meaning?"

Cotton threw up his hands as if to ward off Sebastian as he took a menacing step toward the man. "Meanin' I'll tell ye, but ye gots t' promise not to take it out on me if'n you don't like what I got to say."

Sebastian rested his fists on his hips. "What the bloody hell are you talking about?"

Cotton sniffed and wiped the back of one hand across his nose. "That day I was following his lordship and saw him on Bond Street with his da? Well, I also seen him with another feller. A young buck."

"What young buck?"

"I dunno his name. But I heard some of what they was saying." Cotton's loose fish mouth pulled into a wide smile. "Accused this young buck of cuckolding him, he did. Said something about babies too, but I wasn't entirely clear on that part."

Sebastian studied the other man's strange,

mobile face. He was beginning to notice there were times when Cotton forgot to drop his "g's" and allowed his syntax and accent to slip into something considerably less in keeping with his affected persona. Something that suggested origins far from Seven Dials. "Where did this happen? It's hardly the sort of discussion one would have in public."

"There are ways to hear, even when folks think they're being private."

"You know who Ashworth was talking to?"

Sebastian wondered what Cotton saw in his eyes, because the man sidled a few feet away from him. "Said I didn't!"

"Well, at least your instincts for self-preservation are in order. See that your ignorance likewise remains intact."

"Whatever ye say, yer honor."

Sebastian grunted. "Why didn't you tell me this before?"

"Slipped my mind, it did."

"Right."

Sebastian knew Cotton's waxing and waning memory served his own purposes. But that didn't mean the information Cotton was feeding him was false.

Sebastian started to walk away, then paused to look back. "One more thing: Go anywhere near my wife again, and I'll have you taken up for murder. Is that clear?"

"But I ain't killed nobody!"

Sebastian gave a slow smile that showed his teeth, and shook his head.

"But I ain't," shouted Cotton as Sebastian walked away. "I ain't!"

Half a dozen workmen were tossing the last of the rubble from the dismantled Swallow Street pub into a wagon bed when Sebastian paused to ask about Russell Firth.

"Don't know fer sure where he's at," said one of the workers, a wiry, sun-darkened man who looked to be in his fifties if not older. "Ye might try lookin' down on Piccadilly."

"Piccadilly?"

"Aye. They're fixin' to put in a circus there."

"On Piccadilly? Where?"

"Right smack on top o' Lady Hatton's house and gardens," another of the men said with a grin. "Hear she ain't too happy 'bout it."

"Understandable," said Sebastian.

A busy thoroughfare that ran from the Haymarket in the east to Hyde Park turnpike and Knightsbridge in the west, Piccadilly was home to numerous fashionable pubs and inns as well as such venerable booksellers as Hatchards. Sebastian half suspected the workmen might be wrong—until he saw Firth standing beside Lady Hatton's garden wall, a notebook and pencil in hand.

"Here?" said Sebastian, leaving his horses with Giles and walking up to the young architect. "You're going to put a circus *here?*"

Firth's face broke into a wide grin that made him look likable in a way Sebastian found oddly troublesome. "It'll be grand. You'll see."

Sebastian grunted. "I'll believe it when it happens."

Firth nodded toward the Stuart-era church that stood farther down Piccadilly. "The Regent originally wanted his New Street to wipe out St. James's and its churchyard, but the uproar was too great. Turns out people object to having their loved ones dug up."

"Imagine that." Sebastian glanced down the street toward the church's brick bell tower. Madame Blanchette had said her daughter, Giselle, was buried in St. James's, Piccadilly.

Firth's grin widened. "Shockingly selfish of them, isn't it? I'm told the Regent is still having a hard time finding his way to understanding it."

Sebastian brought his attention back to Firth. "You do realize that if you're trying to protect Stephanie, the best way to do it is to be honest with me."

Firth's smile faded. "I beg your pardon?"

"Cut line. Ashworth not only knew you were in love with his wife; he suspected the twins might not be his. And it infuriated him enough that he confronted you about it just days before he died."

Firth cast a quick, anxious look around and lowered his voice. "I didn't kill him. I swear it."

"Did Ashworth threaten you with a crim. con. case?" Under common law, crim. con.—short for criminal conversation or adultery—was a tort. Husbands had been known to sue their adulterous wives' partners for as much as twenty thousand pounds. And they usually won.

"No," said Firth, not quite meeting Sebastian's eyes.

"Why not?"

"Presumably because he was too proud to tell the world he'd been cuckolded."

"So you admit you and Stephanie were lovers?"

Firth sucked in a quick breath. "No. Never."

Sebastian studied the younger man's even, strained features. "If you're innocent—which at this point is a big *if*—I'll do my best to keep this from coming out. But you should know I'm not the only one asking questions."

Firth's eyes narrowed. "How did you find out what was said that day? I mean, who could know? Surely Ashworth didn't tell anyone?"

"Your conversation was overheard."

"But that's impossible."

"Not really. Ashworth had a lot of enemies—and several of them were following him."

"Dear God," whispered Firth under his breath.

"If there is anything else—"

"No! I swear it."

"I don't believe you," said Sebastian. And then he turned and walked away before his desire to manhandle the bastard overcame his already beleaguered self-restraint.

Sebastian spent the next half hour prowling the crowded churchyard of St. James's, looking for a four-month-old grave.

Built of red brick with Portland stone dressings, the church of St. James's, Piccadilly, dated back to the days of Charles II and Sir Christopher Wren. Its extensive churchyard was divided into two sections, one to the west fronting Jermyn Street and another to the north, separated from Piccadilly by the rectory, a watch house, and a stable.

He finally found Giselle Blanchette's grave in the far southwestern corner of the churchyard. She was lucky her suicide hadn't condemned her to an ignoble midnight burial at the crossroads with a stake through her heart. But the rector of St. James's had nevertheless buried her as far from his church as he could. The grave bore only a small stone inscribed GISELLE MARIE BLANCHETTE, 1794 TO 1813. And, below that, EVIL SHALL SLAY THE WICKED, AND THEY THAT HATE THE RIGHTEOUS SHALL BE DESOLATE.

He stared at that inscription for a long time, his thoughts on the grief-stricken mother who had undoubtedly chosen it. "I'm sorry," he said aloud to the dead girl. *I'm sorry I didn't stop him in time to save you. I'm sorry someone didn't stop him long ago. I'm sorry, sorry, sorry.* And it came to him that he was doing a lot of apologizing to graves lately.

He lifted his head to stare across the jumble of graying, lichen-covered stones. The tragedy of Giselle Blanchette's death lay heavily on his heart. He thought about the child she'd carried in her womb, the child fathered by a dangerous, evil man. Giselle had died rather than allow that child to be born. He firmly believed that all children were innocent of the sins of their fathers. And yet . . .

And yet Sebastian found himself desperately hoping that Ashworth's suspicions had been right. That Stephanie's twin boys were not, in truth, the seed of his loins.

CHAPTER 36

Only a handful of noble London houses were grand enough to stand alone, surrounded by their own extensive gardens. Most of those were ducal residences such as Marlborough House and Devonshire House.

And then there was Lindley House.

A massive pile situated on several acres overlooking Hyde Park, it had been built a hundred years before, in the days of Queen Anne, for Ashworth's great-grandfather, who'd been a great favorite of Her Highness. Like Marlborough House, it had been designed by Wren and built of red brick with stone quoins. And it occurred to Sebastian as he mounted the house's broad front steps that when the current Marquis died, this grand house would pass along with his titles and the rest of the vast Lindley estates to a tiny infant who might not even be related to that long, august line of Ledgers.

Sebastian's knock was answered by a liveried footman who ushered him into a withdrawing room and then went off to ascertain whether Lady Ashworth was receiving. He returned to report apologetically that, according to her ladyship's abigail, Lady Ashworth had slept poorly the night before and was now resting. Sebastian didn't believe a word of it, but on the off chance it might be true, he asked to speak with her ladyship's abigail instead.

To his surprise, a young woman of about Stephanie's own age appeared to drop a nervous curtsy and said, "You wished to speak to me, my lord?"

"Do I take it her ladyship actually is asleep?" said Sebastian. He couldn't imagine Stephanie allowing the girl to speak to him if she were awake.

The abigail looked confused. "My lord?"

She was a small thing and slim, with a childlike nose, pretty brown eyes, and dark, close-cut curls. Discovering the color of her hair was the main reason Sebastian had asked to see her. He said, "What's your name?"

"Elizabeth, my lord. Elizabeth Holt."

Sebastian gave her a friendly, encouraging smile. "How long have you been with her ladyship, Elizabeth?"

"Three years, my lord."

"So since before her marriage?"

"Yes, my lord."

"When was the last time her ladyship saw Lord Ashworth?"

At the sudden, unexpected shift in topic, Elizabeth Holt sucked in a quick breath that jerked her chest. Stephanie had obviously warned the girl at some point to be very, very careful what she said to anyone. "My lord?"

Sebastian gave her a look that had once commanded men in battle and said, "It's a simple question, Elizabeth. I suggest you answer it. And don't even think of trying to pretend you don't know, because I will find out. You do your mistress no service with your evasion."

She laced her fingers together and held her hands tight against her ribs as if finding it difficult to breathe. "A week ago last Monday, my lord. In the evening." It came out as a whisper.

"He came here?"

The girl nodded, her eyes wide with panic.

"And the Marquis? Did he see his son that evening as well?"

"Oh, no, my lord. Parliament was sitting."

"How long did Ashworth stay?"

She hung her head. "Not long, my lord."

"Did he and Lady Ashworth argue?"

At that she looked up, her face pale and stricken. "I don't think I should say, my lord."

"I'm afraid you must."

She hesitated a moment and then nodded, her lower lip caught between her teeth.

"About what?"

"I didn't hear, my lord."

He suspected that was a lie. But he knew by the stubborn tilt of her head that she would tell him no more.

It didn't matter anyway. He already knew the answer.

• • •

"You think Ashworth went to Lindley House that night to accuse Stephanie of being unfaithful to him?"

Hero asked the question as they sat in the drawing room after dinner, Hero drinking tea while Devlin nursed a glass of port by the fire.

"That, and to demand to know if the twins were his," said Devlin.

Hero was silent a moment, then said, "Do you think they are?"

"I honestly don't know."

She let out a long, troubled sigh. "It's such a delicate subject for anyone to broach. Who told him, do you think? About Firth, I mean."

"If I had to guess, I'd say it was probably Cotton. But it could have been anyone." He turned his head, suddenly alert.

"What is it?" she asked, watching him. "Tom?"

He shook his head. "He already reported in."

"No luck finding Ben King?"

"Not yet."

"Then what do you hear?"

"Someone's on the front steps."

"But I don't—," she started to say, then broke off at the sound of the front-door knocker. "Your hearing is unnerving."

"Still?"

She gave a low laugh. "Still."

They listened to voices in the hall below; then

328

Morey mounted the stairs with a note on a salver. "From Sir Henry Lovejoy, my lord."

Devlin broke the seal and quickly glanced through the missive as Morey bowed himself out. "Ah. They've found Ashworth's missing housemaid, Jenny Crutcher."

Hero set aside her teacup and went to stand beside him. "Please tell me she's still alive."

"She was as of this afternoon. She's staying with her aunt—a widow named Travis—in Kennington."

"Kennington? Why?"

Devlin handed her the note. "According to the Bow Street constable who interviewed her, she left Curzon Street because the Viscount's murder frightened her."

"You say that as if you have reason to doubt her."

Devlin glanced at the ormolu clock on the mantel. Too late now to pay the elusive woman a call. "Someone was having hysterics the morning after Ashworth's murder, but according to the butler, that was the second parlor maid, Alice. Not Jenny. He said Jenny was made of sterner stuff."

"So why did she lie?"

He met her gaze. "Interesting question, isn't it?"

CHAPTER 37

Thursday, 7 April

The next morning dawned cool and misty white.

They drove to Kennington in Hero's smart yellow barouche drawn by a team of sleek blacks. "I take it the intent is to simultaneously overawe Jenny Crutcher with the grandeur of the carriage and reassure her with my presence?" said Hero as they rattled across Westminster Bridge.

"Something like that," said Sebastian.

Once a simple village a mile south of the Thames, Kennington had grown considerably in the decades since the construction of Westminster Bridge. But it was still an area of built-up roads separated by orchards and market gardens and vast open stretches of meadowland. Jenny Crutcher's aunt lived in a slate-roofed, white-washed cottage that overlooked Kennington Common. As they turned into Penton Place, they could see a middle-aged woman picking daffodils in the cottage's miniature front garden with a flaxen-haired little girl at her side. The girl held a bouquet of flowers in one fist and was laughing. But she looked around slack-jawed as the grand carriage drew up before her house.

"Look, Mama! They're stopping here. Whoever could it be?"

The relaxed smile on the older woman's face slid away into something apprehensive. "Go inside, Antonia. Quickly." The little girl ran for the cottage door while her mother stood straight-backed, her hands clenched in the black folds of her mourning gown as she watched Sebastian alight from the carriage.

"Good morning, madam," he said, touching a hand to his hat. "You must be Mrs. Travis."

The widow dropped a deep curtsy, her gaze flicking to the crest on the carriage's panel. "Yes, my lord."

Sebastian turned to help Hero alight. "Allow me to present you to my wife, Lady Devlin."

Hero gave the woman an encouraging smile. "How do you do, Mrs. Travis? Your garden is lovely."

"Thank you, my lady." The widow dropped another curtsy, her gaze straying for one telltale instant toward the cottage door left standing ajar by the child.

Sebastian said, "Your niece, Jenny Crutcher, is inside?"

The older woman nodded, her face wooden.

"We'd like to speak with her, please."

As the aunt hesitated, a younger woman of perhaps thirty or thirty-five appeared on the stoop. She had a sharp chin and the same flaxen hair as the child peeking around from behind her. "You're here about his lordship?"

"Yes," said Sebastian, meeting her gaze.

Jenny Crutcher gave a brisk, decisive nod. "Let me fetch my hat and gloves. I don't want Antonia hearing this."

They walked the overgrown paths of the common, the mist cool and damp against their faces, the air heavy with the smell of grass and wet earth and coal smoke.

"I don't know nothing about who killed his lordship," said Jenny in a tight, strained voice. "Truly I don't."

"Then what were you worried Antonia might overhear?" asked Hero.

The housemaid glanced over at her, her eyes widening as she realized her mistake. But all she said was "This talk of murder isn't good for the child. It gives her bad dreams."

"Who do you think killed Ashworth?" asked Sebastian.

"Me? I don't know. Truly I don't."

"But if you were to guess?"

Jenny stared off across the common to where some half-grown boys were playing cricket. Her eyes were dull, her face haggard. And it came to Sebastian that she must not be sleeping well. She looked exhausted. "I don't know," she said again. "But it must've been a woman, surely? Whoever tied him to the bed like that."

"That's the only thing makes you think the killer was a woman? The way Ashworth was found?"

"That and the bloody handprint."

"What bloody handprint?"

"I found it on the inside panel of the front door that morning. The constables were right peeved with me for washing it off, but how was I to know?"

"It looked like a woman's handprint?"

"Oh, yes. Right small, it was." She held out her own sturdy hand. Her hands were strong and work worn, but they were not large. "Smaller than mine, and real delicate-like. Almost like a child's."

Sebastian felt something twist in the pit of his stomach. Stephanie's hands were unusually small and delicate.

He managed to keep his voice steady. "Did you notice anything else when you cleaned the house that morning? I believe you said something to Bow Street about dirty glasses."

Jenny nodded. "There was two wineglasses in the parlor and two brandy glasses in the library."

"Brandy?"

"Yes, my lord."

Sebastian and Hero exchanged a quick glance. Women sometimes drank brandy, but it was more a man's drink. The presence of two brandy glasses in the library suggested that the person Sissy Jordan heard come to the door that night was probably male.

Unless of course the glasses had been used by some earlier, as-yet-unknown visitor who departed before Sissy's arrival.

"Anything else?"

"Well, there was the branch of candles that had been allowed to burn down on the chest in the entry. I thought it a strange and dangerous thing for Digby to have done, leaving them like that. But that was before I knew he'd gone off and never come back."

Sebastian said, "Fullerton tells me you're an unusually calm young woman."

"I try to be," she said cautiously. She was clever enough to wonder where his statement was leading.

"So why did you leave Curzon Street so quickly?"

She drew up abruptly, one hand pressing against her lips. They had reached a part of the common shaded by a thick stand of ancient oaks that looked as if they had been there since the days when Kennington was the site of a royal palace and villagers had grazed their cows and geese here.

"Miss Crutcher?" he prompted when she remained silent.

The pale skin of her face looked oddly

stretched across the bone, and despite the cool temperature, he could see a sheen of perspiration on her temples. "It was on account of Digby," she said on a harsh expulsion of breath. "The way he disappeared and never came back. I knew he must be dead too."

"How did you know that?"

"He was a sly one, Digby. Always going out at odd times without any reason. Sending messages by that crossing sweep."

"Do you know who he sent messages to?"

She shook her head. "Somebody was paying him, but I never knew who."

"So what made you assume Digby must be dead?"

She sucked in a quick breath that made her chest shudder. "It was on account of the letter."

"The letter?"

She nodded. "Just the evening before, he'd been bragging to me about how his lordship had given him a letter—a sealed letter he was to take to the *Morning Post* if something happened to him."

"If something happened to his lordship, you mean?"

She nodded again.

"You didn't tell Bow Street about this letter?"

"No one was asking about Digby that morning. I didn't even think about it until later, when he still didn't show up. That's when I knew something must have happened to him too; otherwise he'd have been playing that letter up for all it was worth. He did love to be seen as important."

"So why not go to Bow Street then? Why simply leave?" *Why not tell this to the constable who came to see you yesterday?*

Jenny's voice was now little more than a whisper. "I was afraid. Afraid somebody'd think maybe I knew what was in that letter and kill me too."

"Do you know what was in the letter?"

"No. I don't think Digby himself knew." She nodded across the common to a neglected area of half-dead trees and rank grass tangled with thistles and nettles. "See that? That's where they used to hang people," she said. "Hang them, and sometimes draw and quarter them too—or burn them alive if they were women. They say the first person ever put to death there was a woman burned for murdering her husband. I remember watching a woman burn here when I was a little girl. But they never burn men for murdering their wives. Why is that, do you think?"

Sebastian felt the damp wind cold against his face. They burned husband-killers because, under common law, for a woman to kill her husband was more than simple murder. It was also an act of treason—a rebellion against both God and King, who together had placed her husband above her as her master. As a desecration that threatened the God-ordained fabric of society, such an act was therefore seen as a threat—and punished as harshly as witchcraft.

"They don't burn women for murder anymore," he said. "Not for twenty years."

He was aware of Hero staring at the housemaid with understanding. "Antonia is Ashworth's child, isn't she?"

Jenny Crutcher's gaze flew to meet Hero's before skittering away. She swallowed hard and then gave a faint, quick nod.

Hero said, "Did he acknowledge her?"

"No. He never knew. Once he . . . Once he was tired of me, he lost interest and never looked at me again. It's like I wasn't even there—no more alive than the newel post or a door. And by the time I started getting really big, it was hunting season and he was in the country. He didn't come back to London till after Christmas, and I'd had her by then." She paused for a moment, and something about the angle of her head or some trick of the light made Sebastian realize she was younger than he'd first taken her to be, probably closer to twenty-five than thirty-five.

She said, "Fullerton was good to me. He let me stay on." Most housemaids who found themselves "in the family way" were summarily dismissed—even when their pregnancy was the result of seduction or rape by the master, one of

337

his sons, or some guest. "My aunt, she never had any little ones of her own, and she offered to take Antonia and raise her for me."

"No one ever told Ashworth?"

"No. Who would?" Her upper lip quivered with disdain. "Well, Digby would. But he didn't come till after that. And everybody else kept my secret."

"I imagine his lordship's staff kept a lot of secrets," said Hero.

Jenny Crutcher brought up a fist to dash away a tear rolling silently down one cheek. "I'm glad he's dead. He was a vile man who ruined the lives of more people than you'll ever know. I don't care who killed him. The world is a better place with him out of it."

Will you tell Antonia who her father was? Sebastian wondered, watching her wipe away another tear. Except she wouldn't, of course.

And he realized this was one of those painful truths best left untold.

CHAPTER 38

"I think she was telling the truth," said Hero as they drove away from Kennington Common with a clatter of horses' hooves and a rattle of trace chains.

Sebastian had his head turned, his gaze on the woman now standing in the cottage garden with her arms looped around her child—a child who would probably never know the real identity of either her mother or her father. "Yes. Although perhaps not all of it."

"What do you make of this 'letter' Digby claimed to have?"

He brought his gaze back to Hero's. "Seems out of character for Ashworth, doesn't it? He wasn't a man who scared easily—if at all. That type don't usually contemplate their own possible death."

"Yet both the timing and the murder of Digby are suggestive."

"They are, indeed."

She was silent a moment, then surprised him by reaching out to take his hand. "That poor little girl."

"Yes," said Sebastian. "In more ways than one."

Viscount Ashworth's aged butler, Fullerton, stared at Sebastian through bloodshot, watery eyes. "Edward Digby's things? You want to see his things?"

Sebastian studied the old man's haggard face and reddened nose. He looked like someone who still belonged in front of a fire with a nice warm bowl of chicken soup. "Do you have them?"

"Yes, yes. One of the footmen packed them up in case his family should come asking for them. But nobody's contacted us. Don't imagine they will, frankly."

Sebastian waited a moment, but when the butler continued to simply stare at him, he said, "May I see them, please?"

Fullerton gave a creaky bow. "Yes, yes, of course, my lord. I'll have George show you the way. The knees object to all those stairs these days, I'm afraid."

As befitted his status as the master's valet, Digby had had the privilege of a private room in the servants' quarters in the attic. But whatever personal touches he might have added to that Spartan space were now gone. There was only a stripped bed, an ugly chest of drawers, and a washstand. A ridiculously small bundle rested on the bare mattress.

"That will be all, thank you," Sebastian said to the footman, George. George hesitated a moment, then withdrew.

As he stared at that diminished pile of belongings, Sebastian found himself wondering whether George had been the footman assigned to assemble the dead valet's effects. Whoever it was had obviously helped himself to anything useful. Little remained beyond a few pairs of drawers, a silk stocking with a rent in it, a slim, well-worn book entitled *Helpful Hints*, and a broken pocket watch.

A more conscientious butler would have supervised the project and kept the dead man's room locked. Yet because it was of no apparent value and had been tucked out of sight inside the book, the letter Sebastian sought was still there, unaddressed but bearing Ashworth's seal in red wax.

Sebastian broke the seal, unfolded the single heavy parchment sheet, and began to read.

Charles, Lord Jarvis, was in Sotheby's auction rooms, studying a lot of particularly fine ancient Egyptian artifacts to be offered for sale, when Devlin came to stand beside him.

The auction rooms were otherwise empty, as they always were whenever Jarvis chose to patronize them. He frowned. "This is supposed to be a private showing."

Devlin kept his gaze on the ka statue before them. "Good. Because I suspect the palace wouldn't want anyone to overhear what I have to say."

Jarvis let his breath out in a pained sigh. "What now?"

"Last Thursday afternoon, Viscount Ashworth paid a visit to the Pulteney Hotel. The original reason for his visit is probably irrelevant. But the timing is important because he somehow chanced to overhear a discussion between Grand Duchess Catherine of Oldenburg and her lady-in-waiting, Princess Ivanna Gagarin. A discussion they assumed was private."

"You think this conversation should interest me, do you?"

"Considering the fact they were discussing the Russians' new scheme for scuttling the Anglo-Dutch alliance, I would think so, yes."

"I do hope in your naïveté you don't assume you have stumbled across something of which I am ignorant."

"Not entirely."

Jarvis studied the younger man's impassive features. "I see. So, tell me this: What have you discovered?"

"The Tsar's original plan was to set up a match between his sister and the Prince Regent—with the inconvenient current Princess of Wales presumably to be eliminated by either fair means or foul. But when that option was crushed by the two royals taking each other in instant and mutual dislike, the Russians moved on to their next alternative."

"By which I take it you mean their hopes of breaking Princess Charlotte's betrothal to the

Prince of Orange by flinging some obscure but handsome and charming European prince into the girl's path?"

"So you do know."

"Very little of importance goes on in London of which I am unaware," said Jarvis, shifting to the next display, a particularly fine sculpted head of Amenhotep III. "Do I take it you think I should be alarmed? The Russians won't succeed, you know. The marriage will take place."

A faint smile curled the younger man's lips. "Have you met the two princes I understand they consider the most promising? Prince August of Prussia and Leopold of Saxe-Coburg?"

"I have not."

"August is debonair, handsome, and charming, while Leopold cuts a most romantic figure. And while I myself don't care for either man, I can see them having a devastating effect on a young, impressionable girl who has been kept dangerously isolated. Both have apparently agreed to come to London with the Allied Sovereigns."

"The Princess is already betrothed. These machinations come too late."

"I'm told the marriage contract has yet to be signed."

"It will be. The Princess can only drag out the negotiations for so long."

Devlin let his gaze rove over a selection of

wooden tomb models from the Eleventh Dynasty. "When are the Tsar and his entourage expected to arrive in London? June?" Devlin smiled and started to turn away.

Jarvis put out a hand, stopping him. "The Grand Duchess had nothing to do with Ashworth's death."

Devlin paused to look back at him. "So certain?"

"Yes."

Jarvis was aware of Devlin studying him with an intensity and level of understanding he didn't like. Then the younger man shook his head and said, "I think you're wrong."

CHAPTER 39

Sebastian drove next to the Pulteney Hotel, only to discover that the Grand Duchess and her entourage were spending the day visiting some of London's most celebrated tourist attractions. He wasted a frustrating amount of time tracking the royal party from the wild beasts at the Exchange to the Tower and the Royal Mint before finally running them down in the Lady Chapel of Westminster Abbey.

It was a large party, with the Grand Duchess accompanied by her lady-in-waiting, Princess Ivanna Gagarin, as well as half a dozen or so other ladies, including the older, hatchet-faced woman no one ever bothered to introduce. Colonel Nikolai Demidov and two tall, imposing members of the Imperial Guard stood nearby. When Sebastian came upon them, all were gathered around a tattered, life-sized figure in faded robes of the Garter that Sebastian recognized as the funeral effigy of Charles II.

Posed upright, with eyes open wide, the effigy had been made to the King's exact measurements and with his facial features modeled in carefully tinted wax. The result was eerily lifelike and easily recognizable, with fine blue veins etching the monarch's familiar straight, prominent nose, the eyes pouched by years of excess, the long dark hair flowing about his shoulders. But the ermine edging the once-grand velvet was noticeably grimy, the point lace at the royal neck and wrists yellowed with age and nibbled by silverfish. A clump of bedraggled, dusty feathers drooped from the long-dead King's limp hat.

A living but obviously nervous young cleric in a rusty black cassock stood beside the effigy with a lamp, his voice high-pitched and shaky as he tried to explain Charles's history to the royal visitors.

"Ah, good," said the Grand Duchess, interrupting the cleric without apology when she spotted Sebastian walking toward them. "You."

"Your Imperial Highness," said Sebastian, bowing low.

"*Vraiment*, your arrival is most opportune. Perhaps you can explain to us why these things are here." She waved a hand in the direction of the Stuart King and turned her back on her guide. "This personage has been unable to do so."

"They're funeral effigies," said Sebastian with an apologetic glance at the cleric. "There was a time when the actual bodies of royals and great nobles were displayed in funeral processions. But when the death ceremonies became too long and elaborate for that to be practical, effigies were substituted."

"Yes, yes," she said impatiently. "I have heard

of such things in France and Italy. But why are they here?"

Sebastian himself had always found the effigies' presence in the Abbey vaguely troubling. Meticulously life-sized images of the dead, they'd been modeled as if still alive. The heads of the earliest examples were of wood and plaster rather than wax, but all had been dressed in the dead's own extravagant clothing and decked out with paste jewels and fake pearls now blackened with age. A few of the oldest effigies were lying down, but most were posed upright like giant articulated dolls, their painted or glass eyes wide and staring.

He took a moment to answer. "I suppose because they were set up here when the bodies were interred."

"Yes, yes. But why are they *still* here? I'm told the common people are allowed to view them for the price of a few pennies. It's like a—a puppet show, with these great kings and queens serving as entertainment for the vulgar to gawk at. It makes them appear worse than ridiculous; it makes them seem *ordinary*. And such a thing should never be allowed."

"We don't do it anymore," said Sebastian, although that wasn't strictly true. Somewhere in the Abbey was an effigy of Nelson dressed in the admiral's own uniform, complete with eye patch and sword—although it wasn't technically a funeral effigy since Nelson had been buried at St. Paul's. The Abbey had commissioned the figure in an attempt to compete with the Cathedral as a tourist attraction.

"Yet they are still here," said the Grand Duchess, as if the ragged royal effigies were a personal affront to her own exalted status. And he supposed that in a sense they were.

Up to this point, Princess Ivanna Gagarin had been silently listening to the exchange with a faint smile on her lips. Now she said, "Perhaps it became a matter of who was going to order them taken down once they'd been set up. And what would they do with them? Throw them out with the rubbish? Burn them?"

"Heaven forbid," said the Grand Duchess. Dark eyes smoldering with vicarious outrage, she moved to study a nearby effigy of a woman. This one was obviously older than Charles, her head made of wood and plaster. Once she must have been an imposing figure, standing almost as tall as Sebastian, her limbs gracefully composed. Now her once-fine clothes were mostly gone, her torso ripped and losing straw, her legs exposed. Even her head was bald, with only peg holes to show where a wig and perhaps a crown had once been attached. There was something almost obscene about seeing her like this—as if they were staring at the long-dead lady herself, stripped of all her finery and bared for all to see.

"*Mon Dieu*," said the Tsar's sister. "Who is this?"

Sebastian cast a helpless glance at the cleric, who cleared his throat and said, "Elizabeth of York, Your Imperial Highness. Wife of Henry the Seventh."

"A queen? This is a *queen?* And the riffraff are allowed in to see her? Looking like this?"

"If they pay their pennies," said Sebastian, who found himself thinking, inevitably, of the ancient Egyptian funerary statues and tomb models Jarvis had been viewing.

"I have seen enough," announced the Grand Duchess, and turned away with an affronted flounce.

"I assume you've taken the trouble to track us down for a reason?" said Princess Ivanna, falling in beside Sebastian as the party of Russians filed out of the chapel.

"As a matter of fact, yes. Two men tried to kill me last night. Two *Russian* men."

"Oh? Surely you aren't suggesting they were in any way connected to the Grand Duchess?"

"The Grand Duchess? Not exactly."

"Then what? 'Exactly'?"

Rather than answer, he said, "So, when do you expect Prince August to arrive in London? Or has the Tsar decided to place his hopes on Leopold instead?"

She gave Sebastian that wry, amused smile she did so well. "I fear I've not the slightest idea what you're talking about."

"Surely you haven't forgotten the handsome princes you and the Grand Duchess suggested the Tsar bring with him to London? With the Grand Duchess having abandoned her original scheme of marrying the Regent herself, I suppose sabotaging Princess Charlotte's proposed Dutch marriage is a rather obvious alternative. It's hardly a secret that the Princess is unhappy with this match her father is pressing on her."

Ivanna kept her gaze on the ornate carvings along the ambulatory as she considered her response. "Have you met Orange? Are you saying you'd like to see that poor girl married to him?"

"I have met him. And no, I would not like to see Charlotte married to him. Nevertheless, I find interference by a foreign power in such matters highly offensive."

She glanced over at Sebastian. "Why? If it achieves an objective you yourself desire?"

"I think most Englishmen would find the idea of St. Petersburg handpicking our future queen's prince consort an affront to our sovereignty."

"And the young Princess herself? Do you spare not a thought for her?"

Sebastian gave a soft huff of amusement. "You would have me think your pity for her sincere? When the Tsar hopes to subsequently marry Orange to the Grand Duchess's own younger sister? I wonder, will she be given any say in the matter? Somehow I doubt it."

Ivanna was no longer smiling. "Who told you of this?"

"Ashworth, actually."

She stared at him a moment, their footsteps echoing with those of the others as they moved up the ancient stone nave. Then she went off in what sounded like a genuine peal of laughter. "You mean to say he did write a letter?"

"You find that amusing?"

"I do, yes. He warned me he intended to do so, but I never believed he actually would."

"Why not?"

"Because, unlike you, Ashworth couldn't have cared less about violations of British sovereignty or the happiness of your silly little Princess."

"Yet presumably he did have a healthy interest in his own self-preservation."

She threw a thoughtful, telling glance back at the fiercely glowering colonel walking silently behind them.

Sebastian said, "Let me guess: The colonel threatened him, did he?"

"Perhaps. But men such as Ashworth are fearless."

"Then perhaps the letter was written more in anger and a desire for revenge than out of fear. So that if, in the unlikely possibility you did succeed in killing him, he'd still have the last laugh— even if it was from beyond the grave."

She looked thoughtful. "Yes, I can see that."

Her eyes narrowed. "I gather you now think we killed him?"

Her use of the word "we" rather than "I" was not lost on him. "Yes."

"And yet you have the letter. Its existence does rather prove that we weren't responsible, wouldn't you say? Why would we deliberately do something that might provoke the publication of the very thing we desired to keep secret?"

"As you say, you didn't believe he'd actually write the letter."

She gave a negligent shrug he found chilling. "Pain is a very effective persuader. Believe me, if we had killed him, we would have ascertained the truth of the letter's existence before we allowed him to die."

"You mean you would have tortured him into giving it up?"

"Colonel Demidov is very talented."

"I've no doubt he is. Except that Ashworth didn't have the letter; his valet did—the same valet who coincidentally died the same night as the Viscount."

"But without giving up the letter?"

"Obviously."

"Once more I remind you of the marvelous uses of pain as a persuader."

Sebastian let his gaze travel over her full, seductive mouth and strange, wintry eyes. How many men and women, he wondered, had died screaming in soul-destroying agony on this woman's orders? It was an effort to keep his voice even and unemotional as he said, "I am curious about one thing."

They'd reached the abbey's soaring west doors, and she turned to face him. "Oh? What's that?"

After the dim interior of the old church, the daylight was blinding. "Where were you Friday night?"

Her lips curled into one of her faintly derisive smiles. "With the Grand Duchess, of course." She nodded toward the Tsar's sister, who was allowing one of her ladies to fuss with the adjustment of her massive bonnet. "You can ask her, if you like. Although do you seriously think I'd do my own killing?"

"Of Edward Digby and Sissy Jordan? Probably not. But Ashworth?" He paused. "I think you might have enjoyed it."

Her smile never slipped. It was the confident, serene smile of a woman born to privilege and utterly convinced of the superiority of her own intellect and will; a woman who could lie without compunction and face danger or even death without flinching because she knew neither fear nor remorse.

A woman who was basically the female version of Ashworth.

She said, "Even if you came to the conclusion

that we had killed him, you could never touch us. You know that, don't you?"

He shook his head. "Bow Street and the palace would never move against the Grand Duchess's entourage. But remember this: You aren't the only one who can break the rules."

A fierce, ugly light blazed up in the depths of those cold, calculating eyes. And he had the satisfaction of seeing her smile tighten into something less confident—but more lethal.

CHAPTER 40

Sebastian sat in the Abbey's cold, ancient nave, his head tilted back as he stared up at the soaring vaulted ceiling.

Last night's deadly attack in Seven Dials had already swung his suspicions back toward the Grand Duchess and her sinister lady-in-waiting. But the revelations contained in the sealed letter found amongst Edward Digby's few remaining belongings were damning. As uncharacteristic as it seemed, Ashworth had obviously taken the threat from the Russians seriously. Perhaps not seriously enough to fear for his safety and take steps to protect himself, but enough to record what he'd overheard in case Ivanna should actually manage to have him killed.

Or kill him herself.

Had she done it? Sebastian was beginning to think it more and more likely. True, neither the Viscount nor his valet had shown signs of torture. Except how much torture would it take to convince a man like Ashworth to give up his valet? None, Sebastian decided. All someone would have needed to do was to hold a sharp blade to his throat or genitalia, and Ashworth would have given up friends, father, wife, infant sons—anyone. He wouldn't have hesitated to sacrifice Edward Digby.

Of course, Digby hadn't shown signs of torture either, nor had he surrendered the letter. That might seem to rule out the Russians, except that Sebastian had no difficulty envisioning several scenarios in which a plan to nab the valet had gone awry and ended in simple murder.

He was still pondering these possibilities when Colonel Nikolai Demidov slid into the pew beside him.

"Good," said the Russian in his heavily accented English. "You are still here."

"Have something you wished to say to me, do you?"

"You were warned to stay away from the Princess," said the colonel. Except that with his pronounced accent, it came out sounding more like, *You vere varrrned to stay a vay from dee Prrreencess.*

Sebastian settled more comfortably in his seat, crossing his right foot over the opposite knee in a way that brought the dagger he kept sheathed in his boot within easy reach. "And you assumed I would comply?"

The colonel's eyes narrowed. "You are amused?"

"Hardly. There's nothing the least amusing about a fifteen-year-old girl dying alone and afraid in an alley."

"What girl?"

"Sissy Jordan."

"I know not of what you speak."

"No? Initially I'd assumed that Ashworth's death must have been something in the nature of an accident—that perhaps the lovely Princess got carried away while playing one of Ashworth's erotic games—"

Demidov's breath came out in a furious hiss. "Speak of the Princess again in this manner and I will cut out your—"

"But now I'm inclined to suspect there was nothing accidental about it," Sebastian continued, ignoring the Russian's interruption. "If I'm right, then it—"

"—tongue and feed it to the—"

"—was a stupid thing to do. And the more you kill to try to clean up your mess, the worse you're making it."

The colonel's eyes were two narrow slits. "I have killed no one. Not yet."

Sebastian kept his hand resting by his boot. "You'd have me believe you had nothing to do with what happened last night in Seven Dials?"

"If you were wise, you would see it as a warning." *You vould see it as a varrrning.*

"Oh, believe me, I do."

"I think not. The next time, we will not miss." *Vee veel not mees.*

"The word you're looking for is 'miss.' *We will not miss.*"

"Still, you make the fun." The colonel leaned

357

in closer, his breath washing over Sebastian's face as he made a low *tssk-tssk*ing sound. Then he pushed up from the pew and walked away.

Sebastian stayed where he was, listening to the *click-click* of the Russian colonel's receding boot heels on the Abbey's ancient paving stones.

The pieces were finally beginning to fall into place, Sebastian decided. The angry confrontation between Ashworth and Ivanna Gagarin on the Pulteney Hotel's stairs had never quite made sense before. Why would a man like Ashworth—who didn't give a fig about either young Princess Charlotte or the new Anglo-Dutch alliance—quarrel with the Grand Duchess's lady-in-waiting over some secret Russian scheme he chanced to overhear?

The truth was he wouldn't, and he hadn't. But Colonel Demidov hadn't realized that. And so, the colonel had confronted Ashworth. Threatened him. And *that* was what had sparked Ashworth's anger and led to the confrontation with Ivanna Gagarin.

Was that when she'd decided to kill him?

Sebastian kept thinking of something Ashworth's friend and longtime companion, Sir Felix Paige, had said the morning after Ashworth's murder. "A dangerous woman" was how he'd described Ivanna Gagarin. And because it fit her so well, Sebastian had never thought to question the designation.

Now he found himself wondering whether

Paige actually knew more about Ashworth's last, fateful encounter with the Russians than he'd been willing to admit.

Sir Felix was leaving Angelo's fencing academy on Bond Street when Sebastian fell into step beside him. The Baronet gave him one swift glance and kept walking. "You do realize this is becoming tiresome?"

"Answer my questions and I'll leave you alone," said Sebastian.

"I was under the impression I had already answered your excessively tedious questions."

"Not quite all of them. I've discovered that not only did Ashworth see Ivanna Gagarin on the afternoon of the day he died; he actually had a rather heated and potentially dangerous confrontation with her. Do you know anything about that?"

Paige gave a faint shake of his head, as if puzzled. "Dangerous in what way?"

"Seems he overhead the Russians plotting to break up Princess Charlotte's betrothal to Orange with the assistance of a couple of handsome German princes."

Paige lifted his eyebrows in an exaggerated grimace and shrugged. "So that's the plan, is it? Clever—if they can manage it."

"But you knew nothing of it?"

"Ash never said anything to me, if that's what you're suggesting." He grinned unexpectedly.

"You're not thinking that's why he was killed, are you?"

"It did occur to me, yes. Yet you obviously find the idea unbelievable. Why?"

"Because it's ridiculous. Why would Ash have cared what they were plotting?"

"He'd care if his possession of such knowledge put his life at risk."

"Why would it?"

"Governments generally prefer their secret machinations to remain secret."

"It's not as if Ash were the type to go running to either the palace or Fleet Street with such information."

"Perhaps. But I'm not convinced the Russians knew that—or would be willing to take a chance on it."

Sir Felix threw back his head and gave a throaty laugh that sounded both genuine and oddly chilling.

"Something's funny, is it?" said Sebastian, watching him.

"Getting a bit desperate, aren't you?"

"Meaning?"

Sir Felix drew up and turned to face him. "Husbands kill wives and wives kill husbands all the time. Why keep chasing after phantom illusions of foreign 'sculduddery'? There are occasions when the obvious solution to a problem really is the correct one."

"Not this time."

The Baronet's smile was still firmly in place. "So certain? When I was in India, we had a fellow in my regiment by the name of Boyne—Lieutenant Lester Boyne. His father was a simple Shropshire vicar, but he thought he was better than the rest of us because he was heir presumptive to his cousin's earldom—that, and because he had an extraordinarily pretty little wife whom virtually every man in the regiment wanted. But then one day we learned that his cousin's wife had miraculously given birth to a child at the age of thirty-eight. A healthy boy child. Overnight, Lieutenant Boyne went from being an earl's heir to just another officer trying to survive on inadequate pay in a hot hellhole far from England."

"I presume there is a point to this tale?"

"I'm getting to it. Less than two months later, Boyne was dead. A 'fever,' was the official claim. But more than a few of us suspected his pretty little wife, Victoria, had actually poisoned him. Seems she numbered a startlingly detailed knowledge of plants and medicines amongst her numerous other talents."

Something about the other man's broad grin told Sebastian this tale was neither as random nor as innocent as it was made to seem. "Victoria, you say?"

"Mmm. I've been thinking about the incident because I chanced to see her a few weeks ago—

here, in London. Of course, she has a different name now. Married a lord's son who came into the regiment not too long before Boyne died. Hart-Davis was his name, John Hart-Davis. Son and heir of Lord Hart-Davis. Although, unfortunately for little Victoria, I hear Captain Hart-Davis got himself killed at the siege of San Sebastián before she managed to become Lady Hart-Davis or produce an heir."

Sebastian studied Paige's mobile, clownlike face. His mouth was still stretched into a wide, cheerful grin. But his eyes were hard and glittering with a calculated malice that told Sebastian the man was only too familiar with Victoria Hart-Davis's relationship to Hero.

"Deaths in a line of succession frequently do provoke ugly rumors," said Sebastian, also smiling. "You're lucky you were in India when all your male relatives died." Sebastian hesitated a beat, then added, "Or were you?"

Paige's smile slid into something ugly and revealing. "Meaning what?"

Sebastian met the other man's gaze and held it. "How did you put it? Ah, yes. There are occasions when the most obvious solution really is the correct one."

"So, was he?" Hero asked Sebastian later when he found her working on her article in the library and relayed the conversation with Paige to her. "In India when all his relatives died so conveniently, I mean."

Sebastian poured himself a glass of wine. "I looked into it, and the answer is no, he wasn't. From what I understand, his own father was the first to die—in his sleep, shortly after Paige returned to London to convalesce from his wounds. The father was a barrister—as was Paige's elder brother."

"Had he been ill?"

"Not at all. He was actually fairly young—just forty-eight. Paige's uncle, the baronet, died shortly afterward, at his estate up in Leicestershire. He'd had a long battle with bowel cancer, so presumably that death at least was natural."

"Let me guess: The cousin was next?"

Sebastian nodded. "His body was found in an alley near Birdcage Walk. He'd been stabbed in the back, but because his purse and watch were missing, the verdict was footpads."

Hero frowned. "I suppose it's possible, if suspiciously convenient. What happened to Paige's brother?"

"He appeared to have fallen from his horse and broken his neck."

" 'Appeared'?"

"I'm told some of the circumstances sur-rounding the incident were rather strange. The accident occurred up in Leicestershire while the new Baronet was surveying his recently inherited estate. Seems he made the mistake of taking Brother Felix with him."

"A mistake, indeed. And did no one find this run of sudden, convenient deaths suspicious?"

"Apparently not. From the sound of things, Paige played the grieving son-nephew-cousin-brother to perfection. And then, of course, he was said to still be quite ill—much more seriously incapacitated than was first thought."

"In other words, he could have been exaggerating his illness in order to deflect suspicion while he went on his killing spree."

"The thought had occurred to me."

Hero was silent for a moment. "I suppose it makes a certain kind of sense. Ashworth was a vile, dangerous human being. Anyone who could be friends with such a man since Eton must be of a similar type."

Sebastian nodded. "To be frank, I'm starting to wonder if he might not have been involved in some of the killings up in Clerkenwell last year."

"Dear God. Could Paige have killed Ashworth—and all the others?"

"If he killed his own father, brother, and cousin—which admittedly at this point is a big *if*—then he would certainly be capable of it. The main problem—apart from the fact that the Russian explanation seems far more likely—is that I can't come up with a reason why he would want to kill Ashworth. Particularly in such a spectacular fashion."

"Just because you don't know the reason doesn't mean he didn't have one. After all, how much do you know about Sir Felix?"

"Not nearly enough," Devlin acknowledged, draining the last of his wine.

Hero hesitated a moment, then said, "I could pay another visit to Cousin Victoria. I suspect she saw a side of Paige in India visible to few of his London cohorts."

"I thought you were making notes for a new interview you wanted to do today."

"I am. But the interview isn't until later this evening." She wrinkled her nose. "I've found a night-soil man who has agreed to meet with me before he begins his rounds."

"A night-soil man? Good God. You're a brave woman."

Her eyes crinkled with a smile. "Not really. If I were truly courageous, I'd have arranged to interview him in the morning *after* his rounds."

Later that afternoon, Hero went for a walk in Hyde Park with her cousin Victoria. The most fashionable hour for the promenade wasn't until early evening. But with the Season in full swing, the park was already crowded with throngs of equestrians and pedestrians as well as phaetons, curricles, barouches, and landaus.

"Any progress in Devlin's investigation into the death of his niece's husband?" asked Cousin Victoria as they walked along a grassy path.

"Not as much as one might hope," said Hero, choosing her words carefully. "Although he's recently taken an interest in one of Ashworth's friends, a former army officer named Sir Felix Paige."

Victoria glanced over at her. "Felix Paige? He was in my husband's regiment in India. I know him."

"I hoped you might. Can you tell me more about him?"

Victoria stared across the park, toward the noisy congestion of Rotten Row. "He comes across as pleasant and easygoing—a man with a ready smile and laugh and little guile or conceit. But . . ."

"But?" prompted Hero when she paused.

"He's not as he seems. I once found him forcing himself on a local girl who couldn't have been more than twelve or thirteen. At first, he simply laughed at me for being shocked. But when he realized I was inclined to take the incident seriously, he threatened me. Said if I dared to breathe a word about what I'd seen, he'd tell everyone that I'd killed Lester—my first husband."

"What did you do?"

"I went to the colonel. Unfortunately, the only thing he did was call the lieutenant in for a tepid sermon about how such activities damaged the regiment's relations with the natives. The next thing I knew, everyone was whispering that I'd poisoned Lester."

She was silent for a moment, her thoughts obviously lost in the painful past. Then she said, "You know that head wound he tells everyone he received at the Battle of Assaye? The one that led to his being sent home to recuperate? He got it at Assaye, all right, but not in battle. John—my second husband—challenged him to a duel over the things he was saying about me." She drew a deep breath. "Devlin thinks Paige could have killed Ashworth?"

"At the moment, it's just a theory. The thing is, Ashworth was his friend. Why would he kill him?"

"Who knows? Rivalry? Wounded pride? Men like Paige, they like to humiliate and hurt others—even those they call their friends."

"Yes," said Hero. "I can see that."

Victoria glanced over at her. "How did you know he was in my husband's regiment in India?"

"He mentioned it to Devlin."

"Along with the suggestion that I'd poisoned Lester?"

Hero met her gaze squarely. "As a matter of fact, yes."

Victoria gave a sharp little nod of her chin. "I thought so. I ran into him recently here in London, when I was visiting Madame Blanchette."

"The fortune-teller?" Hero was unable to keep the surprise out of her voice.

"Yes." Victoria's eyes narrowed. "That's significant for some reason. Why?"

"Was Lord Ashworth with him?"

"I didn't see him. But Paige did mention that he was there with a friend who was already closeted with Madame when I arrived. She has a separate door through which her clients can leave if they prefer, so I never saw him myself."

"Had you been to her before?"

"No. That was the first and only time. An acquaintance of mine found her readings so credible that I was curious to see for myself."

"And?"

Victoria gave a little shrug. "I believe she is a very astute, observant woman. But how much she actually 'sees' in her cards is open to debate."

"Do you know why Paige and his friend were there?"

"A lark, surely? I didn't know Ashworth, but I can't believe Paige would take such things seriously."

"Is that the way it struck you? I mean, did it seem they were there on a lark?"

Victoria frowned, her pretty eyes dark and thoughtful. "No, actually. Now that you mention it, I'd say rather that the visit was quite serious."

She paused, then added, "Deadly serious."

CHAPTER 41

"Ah, Lady Devlin," said Madame Marie-Claire Blanchette, personally answering Hero's knock at the door of the cartomancer's Golden Square rooms. "I've been expecting you."

"Indeed," said Hero, stepping into a strange, incense-scented space crowded with dark, exotic furniture and an array of crystal spheres, obelisks, and pyramids, some clear, others in a glorious spectrum of colorful hues. The Frenchwoman was as finely made as a child and wore an old-fashioned brocade gown with a stomacher that made her look like a vision from a painting of the court of Louis XVI and Marie Antoinette.

"I never saw King Louis," said the cartomancer, quietly closing the door. "Although I did catch a glimpse of Marie Antoinette in the cart on her way to the guillotine. Whatever one thinks of the regime of which the Queen was a part, one can't help but admire the woman's composure and courage in the face of death."

Her words so closely echoed Hero's thoughts as to be uncanny. Hero brought her gaze from a massive chunk of some shiny, faceted metallic ore to the Frenchwoman's face. "That's quite a trick."

Madame Blanchette's eyes crinkled with

amusement. "Party tricks are my stock-in-trade, remember?" She extended a hand toward an adjacent small chamber draped in red cloth and empty except for a collection of stuffed bats hanging from the ceiling, an articulated skeleton, a live owl on its perch in one corner, and a round inlaid table with two low stools. "Won't you come in and sit down?"

"I'm not here for a card reading."

The Frenchwoman kept her hand extended. "I know."

Hero hesitated another moment, then went to sit.

Limping badly, Madame Blanchette took the opposite stool. A deck of thick cards rested on the table before her, and she began to shuffle them, her gaze never leaving Hero's face.

Hero said, "Why didn't you tell Devlin that one of Ashworth's friends came for a reading shortly before Ashworth's death?"

"Not only Ashworth's friend, but Ashworth himself came that day. But they were not here for readings." The Frenchwoman neatened the edges of her cards in her hands. "Ashworth came to threaten me."

"And did he?"

"Oh, yes. He said that if I didn't shut up about Giselle, I would die."

"I suppose that explains why you didn't tell Devlin about the encounter."

"You think it gives me an added incentive to

370

have killed him? Kill him before he could kill me?" Her lips thinned into a hard line. "Believe me, I needed no added incentive. No one could have wished for Ashworth's death more than I. But I wanted him to suffer first. I had only just begun to torment him."

"Are you saying you didn't foresee his murder?"

The Frenchwoman set the deck of cards on the table in front of Hero and said, "*Coupé.*"

Hero hesitated a moment, then cut the deck.

Madame Blanchette turned over the revealed card and laid it faceup between them. In place of the crude image Hero was expecting, this was an exquisite painting of a moon rising over a star-spangled sea.

"*Encore.*"

Again and again, Hero cut the deck, until a pattern of beautifully painted cards lay spread across the table. Madame Blanchette folded her hands together in her lap and leaned forward to study them. She stared at them so long that Hero grew impatient and said, "Well?"

"Interesting."

"That's all you have to say? 'Interesting'?"

The Frenchwoman waved one hand over the layout. "You don't believe in this. So why would you want to hear?"

"Curiosity."

A corner of the woman's mouth quirked up with a hint of amusement. "*D'accord.*"

She tapped the third card in the first row, an image of a craggy mountain backed by dark swirling clouds. "This tells me you may have a powerful enemy—an enemy who is near to you. You must be wary of those who envy you."

In spite of herself, Hero felt a faint chill run up her spine. "Such as?"

"That I cannot say."

"Of course."

The Frenchwoman's hand skimmed over the cards to an image of a scythe in the bony hand of a cloaked skeleton. "The Viscount had this card in a similar position. It is a warning that you are in serious danger. You must be prudent in the places you go, the things you do, and the people you meet."

"Well, that narrows it down." Hero waited a moment, but when the cartomancer remained silent, said, "That's it? Out of all these cards, all you can tell me is that I am in danger and that I should be wary of someone near to me?"

The Frenchwoman gave a very Gallic twitch of one shoulder. "Most of the rest you know already—or it is not for me to tell you."

Hero leaned back on her stool, her hands resting on her knees. "You never answered my last question about Ashworth. Would you have me think you didn't foresee his death?"

"I don't know who killed him."

"That isn't what I asked."

Again that faint suggestion of amusement crinkled the older woman's eyes. "All is never revealed, no matter how 'talented' the one who asks. Nor should it be."

"Whoever is responsible for these murders should and must be revealed. Revealed and stopped. One could argue that Ashworth and his valet earned their deaths. But a desperate fifteen-year-old orphan by the name of Sissy Jordan was also a victim of this killer. And she may not be the last innocent to die."

A strange, pinched look came into the Frenchwoman's face. "The death of any innocent is always a tragedy."

Hero found her gaze falling, again, to the beautiful, disturbing images spread across the table before her. "You say Ashworth came here not for a reading but to threaten you. Does that mean you didn't read his cards?"

"No. I read them."

"What did you see?"

Madame Blanchette began to pick up the spread cards. "Normally I keep such things private, but under the circumstances, I believe an exception can be made. He also drew the mountain, and in a similar position to yours. I told him he was threatened by someone close to him—in Ashworth's case by someone who also saw Ashworth as a threat."

"So are we talking about a man or a woman?"

"Ashworth had many enemies, both male and female."

"Yet you say he was threatened by someone close to him, not an enemy."

Madame set the cards aside and folded one hand over the other to rest them flat on the table before her. "Some of our worst enemies are those near to us. But remember, just because someone close to Ashworth was a threat does not mean that person killed him."

Hero studied the Frenchwoman's calm, blank face, the features kept deliberately free of any betraying emotion. "You're not telling me everything you told Ashworth was in his cards."

"Perhaps. But then, you don't believe in the cards, do you?"

"I believe you know more than what you have revealed to me—however you came to know it."

The Frenchwoman reached out to tap the top of the tarot deck with one curled finger. "If you believe that, then believe my warning. The danger to you is real."

"Is that a threat?"

Madame Blanchette looked vaguely surprised. "From me? No. You asked what the other cards reveal. They show the possibility of a happy life filled with much joy, love, and accomplishment. But what I see is always a potential only, which means the danger is as real as anything else. Heed me and the good the cards foretell will be more

374

likely to come to be. But . . ." Her voice trailed off as a fey, flaxen-haired little girl appeared in the doorway to escort Hero out.

"But?" prompted Hero, rising to her feet.

The Frenchwoman rose with her, the old-fashioned brocade skirts swirling around her. "*Vraiment, c'est simple.* Ignore me at your peril."

CHAPTER 42

Later that evening, Hero was positioning an uncharacteristically plain bonnet on her head when Devlin came to stand in the doorway and watch her.

"I take it you're still planning to interview that night-soil man?" he said.

"Why wouldn't I?" She kept her gaze on her reflection in the mirror as she reached for a hat pin. "Surely not because of the cartomancer's warnings? Please tell me you don't believe that nonsense."

"Not exactly."

She glanced over at him. "Then what?"

He pushed away from the door and came up beside her. "No matter how she acquires her knowledge, there is no denying Madame Blanchette has formidable sources of information."

"About Ashworth, perhaps. She obviously made it her business to find out everything she could about him. But about me? I think not."

His brows twitched into a frown. But all he said was "You think she was simply trying to rattle you?"

"You don't?"

"I think she's an astute judge of character,

which suggests she should have been able to tell that you don't rattle easily."

"Perhaps she thought it worth a try. What I'm wondering is why Paige originally pretended not to know Madame Blanchette's name. Surely he couldn't have gone to Golden Square with Ashworth without knowing something of what happened to her daughter."

"Oh, he knew," said Devlin. "It's one of the reasons he told me about seeing Cousin Victoria—because she was bound to tell us where she saw him."

"But . . . why?"

"That's the part I can't figure out—although I certainly intend to press him for an explanation." His gaze drifted toward the window, where the waning daylight was already taking on the golden hues of approaching evening. He pressed his lips into a tight line, but he didn't say anything.

Laughing, she reached out to touch his cheek. "I know what you're thinking, but don't worry. I'm taking two footmen as well as the coachman, and I promise I'll be back before nightfall."

Sir Felix Paige was not at home.

His servants helpfully suggested Sebastian try Cribb's Parlor, Limmer's, or the Castle. But Sebastian searched first one Corinthian haunt, then the next without success. He kept trying to make sense of everything he'd learned in the past twenty-four hours, but it seemed to be pointing him in two entirely different directions.

Frustrated, he decided to pay another visit to Park Lane.

"Good God, Devlin, not now," exclaimed the Dowager Duchess of Claiborne when Sebastian bullied and cajoled her butler into allowing him upstairs. He found Her Grace clad in a splendid Chinese silk dressing gown embroidered over with red dragons and colorful butterflies. She was trying to decide between two gowns being presented by her abigail—one of lavender silk, the other of puce satin trimmed with blond lace.

"Answer my questions quickly and I'll be gone."

She raised her quizzing glass to one eye and stared at him through it. "What have you done to your face now?"

He touched his fingertips to the sticking plaster on his forehead. "It's nothing."

"Huh. You can't seriously think that if I knew anything more about Ashworth, I wouldn't have told you."

"You may know more than you realize."

She glared at him a moment longer, then shooed her woman out of the room and said, "From what Hendon has been telling me today, I sincerely hope not. Black leather whips and red silk bonds? Merciful heavens."

"You hadn't heard that part before?"

"No. Thankfully, they seem to have kept those lurid details out of the papers. Now, tell me what you want and go away."

"What do you know about Sir Felix Paige?"

"Paige?"

"Yes."

She drew her chin back against her neck and flattened her lips. "Bad *ton*, that one. But then, it stands to reason, does it not? Who else would be friends with a bounder like Ashworth?"

"Is he capable of killing, do you think?"

"You can't imagine I know the man, do you? All I know is that his father was a bounder, if ever there was one."

"He was?"

"He was. Now, go away and let me dress."

"One more thing. Were you by chance at Lady Cowper's ball last June?"

Henrietta shook her head. "Lady Cowper didn't give a ball last June."

"You're quite certain?"

"Of course I'm certain. Emily Cowper gives her annual ball in April."

"April? Every year?"

The Dowager raised her eyebrows. "That is generally the definition of 'annual,' is it not? Now, will you go away? My guests will be here before I'm even dressed."

CHAPTER 43

"We work in teams o' four," said the night-soil collector, a stout, middle-aged fellow with a whiskered face and bloodshot eyes who said his name was William Bell. He wore a battered slouch hat with a ragged, muck-smeared coat, waistcoat, and knee breeches of indeterminate color. The reek wafting from his person was stomach churning.

"And why is that?" asked Hero, who had positioned herself strategically upwind.

It wasn't helping.

"Need four," said Bell, taking a swig from what Hero realized was a gin bottle. He had agreed to meet with her near Dorchester House in Park Lane, which he'd explained was at the beginning of the route he planned to work that evening. "Need a ropeman, a holeman, and two tubmen. At first ye can jist scoop out the sh—" He broke off, looked flummoxed for a moment, then changed what he'd been about to say to "stuff."

Hero hid a smile as she glanced up from the notes she was rapidly scribbling. "What do you use to scoop it with?"

"Buckets, at first. Thing is, ye see, we can only do that fer so long. Then we gotta put a ladder down in there."

"You put a ladder right down into the cesspit or privy hole?"

"Aye. The holeman, he's the one who climbs down in there and shovels the sh—stuff into the bucket. Then the ropeman, he hauls up the bucket and empties it into the tub. When that's full, the tubmen carry it out t' the street and dump it into the cart."

"Why two tubmen?"

" 'Cause them tubs is heavy. Ye have'ta carry 'em on a pole between two men. Most houses 'round here, there's ways to get to the back without goin' through the house. But it can be right messy if the cesspit's in the basement, or if there ain't no other way to empty the privy 'cept by carryin' the tubs right through the house. They do drip, ye see."

"Good Lord," said Hero, staring at him.

"Now, some privies and cesspools are what we call a 'dry pit.' They ain't too bad, 'cause the liquid most all drains away pretty quicklike. But when it don't, it can be godawful."

"Why does it drain away sometimes but not others?"

William Bell gave a shrug. "Depends on the way the cesspit is built—that and the water table, I reckon. I've seen some overflowin' so bad, they're draining into the cellar of the house next door. Folks get irate when that happens. The worst is them cesspits what's hooked up to them newfangled water-flushing contraptions."

"Why?"

" 'Cause a cesspit, it ain't designed t' take all that water, that's why. So them things is always overflowin'. If ye ask me, what they oughta do is let them nobs who wants them danged patented washdown pedestals connect 'em to the sewer system."

London had long possessed an elaborate sewer system, but the sewers were intended only for stormwater and underground rivers. It was illegal to use them for the disposal of waste. Hero said, "The sewers empty into the Thames."

"Aye."

"We get our water from the Thames."

William Bell laughed, showing a mouthful of surprisingly even, healthy teeth. "Aye. So?"

Hero consulted the list of questions she'd prepared. "What do you do once your cart is full?"

"We drive t' the nightman's yard and empty it. They mix the sh—stuff with other rubbish like ashes and dung and rotting vegetables, and sell it t' farmers t' manure their fields."

"Lovely," said Hero under her breath. "How long have you been doing this?"

"Since I was a lad. Used to help me da, I did. In them days I was the holeman. Now I'm the ropeman."

"Did you ever think about doing something else?"

"No. Why would I? I make three times as much as yer typical journeyman. Can't beat that."

"You don't find the work . . . unpleasant?"

He laughed again. "Ye gets used t' it—as long as ye drink enough gin first. And it ain't too dangerous, although ye gotta be careful. I've known fellers suffocated from the gasses when a cesspool was too deep."

Hero thought about the possible danger posed by animalcules—tiny creatures invisible to the naked eye that some suspected could spread terrible maladies. But all she said was "How often are most cesspits and privies emptied?"

"In the poorer parts of town, they never empty 'em till they're overflowin'. But around here, folks have us in meybe two or three times a year—unless they've got one of them danged washdown pedestals. Then we gots to get in there every week or so."

"Do many people have them?"

"Too many, if'n ye ask me. The Pulteney Hotel's got eight of the danged things. We're always havin' to go there."

"Eight?"

"Aye. Chesterfield House has 'em too."

Chesterfield House was an elegant detached mansion built in the previous century by Philip Stanhope, the Earl of Chesterfield, on the corner of South Audley Street and Curzon just several blocks down from Viscount Ashcroft's town house. Hero looked up from her notes, her breath quickening with interest. "You empty the cesspits at Chesterfield House every week?"

"Aye."

"What nights?"

"Tuesdays."

"Ah," said Hero in some disappointment.

William Bell took another swig of his gin and smacked his lips. "You'd be surprised the things we see, workin' the streets at night. Why, I've found a good half dozen dead bodies in me day. Dead bodies and other things."

"Oh?" She hesitated a moment, then said with studied nonchalance, "I assume you've heard about the Viscount who was murdered on Curzon Street last week?"

"Oh, aye."

"Did you ever empty his cesspit?"

"Aye. Emptied it last December, we did. I remember 'cause it was durin' the Great Fog."

"Did you ever see anything unusual at his house?"

"Not when we was emptying his cesspit. But queer things was always goin' on around there."

"What sort of 'queer things'?"

William Bell leaned forward as if imparting a secret, and Hero felt her stomach lurch as the intensified stench of excrement and cheap gin washed over her. "One time we was drivin' down the street, headed fer Chesterfield House, and this woman come runnin' outa his lordship's house stark staring naked. Naked and covered in blood, she was."

"When was this?"

"While ago. Don't recall exactly. But there's been several times we've heard screamin' comin' from in there. Why, just last week we seen a lady standin' at his door with a gun in her hand."

"A week ago this last Tuesday?"

"Aye."

"What did the woman look like?"

"Couldn't see her face on account o' she was wearin' a hat wit' a veil. But she looked like a young thing—slim, she was, and tall for a woman."

"Could you tell if she was fair haired or dark?"

"Oh, she was fair, all right. The lantern was still lit over his lordship's door, and the light was shining right on her guinea gold hair—on her hair and on the gun in her hand."

"You're certain it was a gun?"

The night-soil man looked vaguely affronted. "Course I'm certain. Ain't nothin' wrong wit' me eyes."

"What did she do when she saw you?"

"Acted real startled, she did. Come down the front steps in a hurry and took off walkin' up the street."

"What made you think she was a lady?"

"Dressed real fine, she was. And she had that

air about her. There's jist somethin' about the way a gentry mort holds herself and moves. Ye can always tell, can't ye?"

It was a surprisingly astute observation from a man who'd spent his life cleaning out other people's privies. Hero said, "Do you remember what time this was?"

"Musta been about midnight. We always go to Chesterfield House first thing on Tuesday nights, and we ain't allowed to work 'cept between midnight and five."

Hero glanced at the watch she wore pinned to her bodice. "So what will you do between now and midnight?"

William Bell held up his gin bottle and grinned. "Prepare."

Hero arrived home to find Devlin seated cross-legged on the floor of the library with a number of rumpled newspapers scattered around him.

"What are you doing?" she asked when he looked up, a lock of dark hair falling across his forehead.

He raked his hair back from his face with splayed fingers, then linked his hands behind his neck as he arched his back. "When I spoke to Stephanie last Saturday, she described the way Ashworth was found in detail, right down to the clothes strewn around the room and the red silk bonds. Not just silk bonds, mind you, but *red* silk

386

bonds. I don't know why I didn't think about it before, but something Aunt Henrietta said tonight set me to wondering. So I was looking to see if any of the papers mentioned the color of the ropes."

Hero tugged off her gloves. "And?"

"And the answer is no. They didn't."

"So how did Aunt Henrietta know?"

"Hendon told her. And I told Hendon. But you can be damned sure he didn't divulge those details to Stephanie."

"Perhaps Ashworth always used red silk bonds. She would know that."

Devlin shook his head. "I sent a message to Lovejoy asking if his lads found any other color bonds when they searched the chamber. He said there were also lengths of black and gold cord in a chest."

Hero carefully removed her hat. "He could have always used the red ones with Stephanie."

Devlin drew a heavy breath. "That's ghastly to think about, but I suppose you could be right."

She went to the table holding the brandy decanter, poured a generous measure in a glass, and came back to hand it to him.

"What's this for?" he asked, looking up from neatening the papers into a pile.

"I suspect you're going to want it when you hear what I have to say."

CHAPTER 44

The night was blustery, with a cold wind that stirred the budding limbs of the trees in Hyde Park and tossed ghostly whispers of gossamer-fine clouds across a black sky.

Sebastian stood in the shadows of an elm, his gaze on the soaring classical facade of Lindley House. As he watched, an old-fashioned landau bearing the Marquis's crest on its panel drew up before the gate. A moment later, the Marquis himself emerged from the house, the light from the carriage lamps gleaming over his satin knee breeches and diamond-buckled formal shoes. He exchanged pleasantries with his driver about the weather, then climbed into the carriage and drove off.

Sebastian's gaze shifted back to the house. He felt a heaviness in his chest that was part sorrow, part something else he hated to acknowledge. He didn't want to believe that Stephanie might actually have killed her dangerous, dissolute husband, but he was becoming more and more afraid that she had. With Firth's assistance, she might even have been involved in the death of his valet, Edward Digby. But Sebastian refused to believe she'd had anything to do with the murder of the child prostitute, Sissy Jordan. Surely he couldn't be that wrong about the passionate, troubled niece he'd loved since her birth.

Could he?

But if Stephanie had killed Ashworth and Digby, then who murdered Sissy Jordan—and, in all likelihood, the missing crossing sweep, Ben King, as well? The obvious answer was someone who loved Steph and was utterly ruthless in his efforts to protect her from the repercussions of what she'd done. Someone such as Russell Firth.

It fit.

It all fit only too well.

Stephanie was embroidering a tiny baby cap in a high-backed chair by the hearth when Lindley's dignified butler showed Sebastian to the drawing room.

"Uncle," she said, setting aside her needlework and folding her hands in her lap.

He went to stand before the fire. "Thank you for agreeing to see me."

Her head fell back as she looked up at him. "Did you think I would refuse?"

"The idea had occurred to me."

She gave a little shake of her head. "My abigail told me you were here this morning."

"Did she happen to mention what we discussed?"

"She did."

"Tell me about Ashworth's visit the Monday night before he died, Steph."

She stared at him for a long moment, her chest rising and falling with the agitation of her breathing. And he wondered what she saw in his face, because she suddenly pushed up from her chair and retreated behind it. "So are you back to thinking I killed him, Uncle? Or did you ever stop?"

Rather than answer, he said, "When I spoke to you last Saturday, you mentioned that Ashworth was found tied to his bed with red silk cords. How did you know that?"

"I assume I read it in the newspapers."

"A logical assumption. Except that I checked, Stephanie. None of the papers' articles mentioned the color of the cords—or even the fact that they were silk. You also knew his clothes were strewn across the floor. How, Steph?"

"Lindley must have told me about it."

"Somehow I can't see Lindley dwelling on the lurid details of his son's erotic murder scene in his conversations with his newly bereaved daughter-in-law."

Her nostrils flared on a quickly indrawn breath. "Someone obviously told me."

"That's one explanation."

When she simply stared back at him, her head held at a stiff angle, he said, "The Tuesday morning before Ashworth was killed, you bought a muff pistol from Howard and Mercers'. I already knew that. But now I discover that Tuesday night, at midnight, you went to Curzon Street. You were seen, Steph. With the pistol in your hand."

"But no one—" She broke off, one hand coming up to touch her lips before falling again. "Dear God. The night-soil men."

"That's right."

She dug her curled fingers into the high back of the chair before her. "You can't prove it was me. No one can."

"Because you were veiled, you mean? No, I can't prove it—not that I had any intention of trying." He reached out to rest his hand over one of hers. "I wish you'd be honest with me, Steph."

She wrenched away from him and retreated to the far side of the room. "I didn't kill him!"

He stayed where he was, watching her. "I wouldn't blame you if you did, Steph. I wanted to kill him myself."

"Oh, God! How many times must I tell you I didn't do it?"

"Then be honest with me. Tell me what the hell happened that last Monday when Ashworth came here to Lindley House. I know there was a row. Was it over Russell Firth? Did Ashworth accuse you of being unfaithful? Did he threaten to divorce you?"

"Divorce me?" she gave a harsh, ringing laugh.

"Hardly. He needed a wife to keep Papa's money flowing, remember? But it seems that while he felt no need to honor his own marriage vows, he had no intention of allowing me any similar liberties. He came here to tell me that if he ever heard my name linked with Russell again, he'd kill one of the twins. He then illustrated the threat by holding a knife to first James's throat, then Adrian's. He said his father didn't need two young heirs; one would do. The choice as to which he killed could be mine."

"Good God," said Sebastian softly.

"I bought the gun the next morning and went to Curzon Street that night. What he said about killing one of the boys—it wasn't an idle threat, Uncle. Once he had an idea like that in his head, he wasn't going to let it drop. Whether he did it to punish me for some real or imagined transgression, or simply for the sheer pleasure of hurting me, he would eventually have done it. He was like that."

"I know."

"I meant to kill him that night. But the bar was already up on the door when I arrived. I was still deciding what to do when I saw the night-soil men's cart coming down the street, so I . . . walked away."

"And went back again on Thursday?"

He thought she might deny it. He knew by the sideways slide of her gaze that she thought about denying it. Then she sucked in a quick gasp of air and nodded. "But I didn't kill him, Uncle. I swear it. The door was unlatched and partly ajar when I got there. I thought it strange, but Ashworth always kept an irregular household, and it was a windy night. I assumed a gust must have blown it open."

She paused for a moment, her head cocked to one side as a strange smile played about her lips. She said, "Does that horrify you, Uncle? That I could calmly decide to kill my husband and then coldly set about doing it? What do you think I should have done? Let him kill one of the twins?"

"You didn't tell anyone what he threatened to do?"

She gave a ragged laugh that sounded more like a tearing of her soul. "Tell whom? Lindley? You think he would have believed such a tale? About his precious only surviving son?"

"He might have. I've heard he once paid off the parents of some innkeeper's daughter Ashworth raped up at Cambridge."

"Perhaps. But threatening to slit the throat of one of his own sons? Lindley would never have believed it of him. And, of course, Ashworth would have denied it—said I was hysterical. And you know what they do with 'hysterical' females, don't you, Uncle? Bedlam is full of inconvenient, unwanted wives."

"You could have told me, Steph." When she simply stared at him silently, he said, "So, what happened that night? The night he died."

"I pushed open the door and went inside. The library and dining room were dark, but a brace of candles was burning on a chest in the entrance hall, and I could see the glow of a lamp from the upper landing. I climbed the stairs to the first floor, but the drawing room and morning room were also dark, so I went up to the next floor. His bedchamber was ablaze with light."

Her voice quivered, but she pushed on. "I honestly don't know if I'd have had the courage to shoot him when the time came. I hope I would have. But in the end I never had the chance, because he was already dead."

She paused. Sebastian waited, and after a moment she went on. "He was lying in the shadows cast by the hangings of the bed, so I didn't realize he was dead until I'd drawn quite close to him." She brought up her hands to cover her nose and mouth, then let them fall and set her jaw. "It was . . . a ghastly sight."

"Yes, it was."

Her eyes widened as she searched his face. "You do believe me, don't you?"

"Honestly? I don't know."

She gave a little nod, as if he had only confirmed what she'd already suspected.

He said, "How did you come to be covered in blood, Stephanie? The clothes thrown into the Thames were yours, I take it?"

She nodded again. "I don't know. It's the oddest thing. I can remember walking up to the bed. I had the pistol in both hands, ready to shoot him. Then I realized . . . something was wrong. At first it made no sense. The candlelight was flickering over this strange, dark, wet sheen, and he was just lying there. I thought he was asleep. I remember saying his name—I wanted him to wake up and see me." She gave another of those odd little expulsions of breath that was not really a laugh. "It seemed wrong somehow to kill him in his sleep. But then I realized he wasn't sleeping; he was dead, and the dark gleam of wetness was his blood." She swallowed hard. "So much blood."

"What did you do then, Stephanie?"

"That's the part I don't remember very well. I think . . . I think I dropped the gun. I didn't mean to. And then . . . I couldn't find it. I suppose that's how I came to be so covered in blood—looking for the gun."

"But you did find it."

"I did. And then I ran down the stairs and out of the house. I ran all the way home. I haven't run like that since I was a child."

"How did you keep from tracking blood across the carpet? You must have been standing in it, but there were no bloody shoeprints leading back to the door."

"I took off my shoes and carried them. I don't know how it occurred to me to do it, except that I didn't want to leave any sign that I'd been there. I was terrified Ashworth's valet would see me and think I was the one who killed him."

"Did you see Digby?"

"No."

"If what you say is true, he was probably already dead."

A bitter smile curled her lips. " 'If,' Uncle?"

"What did you do then?"

"I told you. I came back here."

"How did you manage to get in and out of Lindley House without any of the servants seeing you?"

"I crawled out a window in the dining room, and I came back the same way."

"And then you bundled up your bloody clothes and threw them off Westminster Bridge?"

She nodded.

"With your abigail, Stephanie? Why the hell did you involve your woman?"

She stared at him bleakly. "I couldn't go all the way to Westminster alone in the middle of the night. Wandering around Mayfair was terrifying enough. Besides, Elizabeth was waiting for me in the dining room, so she saw the blood all over me. At first, she thought it was mine, that I was hurt. It was her idea to throw everything away. She said she'd never be able to wash the clothes without the other servants seeing and asking questions."

"And your shoes? Why weren't they in the bundle with everything else?"

"I don't know what happened to my shoes. By the time I reached Park Lane, they were gone. I must have dropped them without realizing it. I don't know why I didn't put them back on—I cut my feet dreadfully."

"And the pistol? Did you lose that too?"

She shook her head. "We threw it in the Thames—but separately." Her hands tightened into fists. "I should have tied it up in the clothes. Perhaps then the bundle would have sunk too quickly for that blasted wherryman to retrieve it."

"Perhaps. But if it didn't, he would have found it too. And the pistol would have been easily identified by Howard and Mercer's. You're lucky your modista didn't identify the gown."

"I had it made in Brighton last autumn."

"Do any of the other servants know?"

"No. No one."

"Your abigail could have told someone."

"No. She never would. She's not friendly with any of the servants here. She came with me to Park Lane from St. James's Square, and the Lindley House servants still treat her as an outsider." Stephanie hesitated, then said, "So, what are you going to do, Uncle? Tell Bow Street?"

"You know me better than that, Steph."

She searched his face, her incredibly blue eyes

shining with a glimmer of unshed tears. "But you still think I did it?"

When he didn't answer, she went to stand by the windows overlooking the park, one hand pushing aside the heavy brocade curtain so she could look out at the night. He could see her face reflected in the blackness of the glass. "I suppose I shouldn't be offended," she said. "After all, I did go there to kill him."

"Yes."

"And do you think I killed his nasty little valet too?"

"Possibly. But probably not."

"No?" She turned to look at him. "You surprise me, Uncle. And why are you inclined to acquit me of that?"

"Because whoever killed Digby also stripped him of his clothes and moved the body, and even if you'd had help, I can't think of a reason why you'd do that. And because there's been another murder—a fifteen-year-old Haymarket girl named Sissy Jordan, whose only sin was being forced to sell her body to stay alive."

"She was there that night?"

"Earlier, yes."

He could see the pulse beating in her throat, and he found himself wondering again just how much she knew about her dead husband and his activities. But all she said was "Ashworth did like them young."

"Yes, he did."

She stared back at him, her slim, elegant figure held with a poise and grace born of a noblewoman's lifelong training in hiding her emotions and true state of mind.

He said, "If there's anything else you know that you're not telling me—"

"What do you think? That I'm protecting the killer?"

"The thought did occur to me."

And then her composure broke. He saw the fear well up within her, catching her breath and draining any remaining color from her face as she realized the implications of his words. "Dear God," she whispered. "You can't think Russell . . ."

"Does he know? Does he know you went to Curzon Street that night to kill Ashworth?"

"No!"

"You never told him?"

"No." She stared directly into his face with an intensity so powerful, it was almost palpable, as if she could somehow will him to believe her.

He wanted to, desperately.

But he could not.

Sebastian spent the next several hours talking to an eclectic selection of individuals, including a group of workmen he found at a pub just off Swallow Street, three scholars at a meeting of the Royal Academy, and a classicist who'd been with Russell Firth at Cambridge. What emerged was an image of a hard-driving, quick-tempered, ambitious man who'd learned young to control his outbursts of anger and frustration. A man who was said to go out of his way to protect a friend. A man who'd once been set upon by a couple of thieves in the Roman forum and killed them both.

"Stephanie's story does sound believable," Hero said later that night as she and Sebastian lay in bed. "I can see Ashworth threatening his own child simply to punish its mother. And as a mother, I can understand Stephanie deciding that the only way to protect her children would be to shoot Ashworth. But I have a hard time imagining her hacking him to death in a wild frenzy."

Sebastian ran one hand up and down her arm, holding her close. "She says she can't remember much of what happened after she crept up to the bed."

"That's understandable, isn't it?"

"Yes. Unfortunately, it's understandable whether she simply found him dead or killed him."

"You can't think she also killed Digby and Sissy Jordan?"

"I can picture several scenarios that might lead her to kill Digby. But I can't think why she would then strip him naked."

"Why would anyone?"

Sebastian shook his head. "You have a point there. But I also can't believe Steph would trace Sissy Jordan to the Haymarket, lure her to an alley, and kill her."

"You think that could have been Firth?"

He looked over at her. "You don't?"

Hero let out her breath in a sigh. "I always liked him. I hate to think I could be such an abysmal judge of character."

"Some people are very good at presenting a false face to the world."

"You've met him. Do you think him capable of it?"

"Well, given what I learned tonight about his encounter with the two thieves in Rome, we know he is capable of killing under the right circumstances. So I can see him killing Ashworth and even Digby. But Sissy Jordan and Ben King?" He shook his head. "I don't know. I just don't know."

Friday, 8 April

"I can't find 'im," Tom told Sebastian early the next morning when he came to report on the search for Ben King, the missing crossing sweep. "'E ain't been back t' none of the flea traps around St. Martin's. I'm thinkin' if 'e's too scared to go anywhere near Curzon Street, then meybe 'e's stayin' away from anyplace 'e's known."

Sebastian studied his tiger's drawn features, the dispirited slump of his shoulders. "You can quit looking if you'd like."

Tom's nostrils flared as he tightened his lips into a determined line. "If'n it's all the same to you, gov'nor, I'd like t' give it one more day. I got some ideas I could meybe check out before I calls it quits."

"If you think it's worth it, go ahead."

Tom gave a determined jerk of his chin. "If 'e's still alive, I'd like t' find 'im."

I suspect he's dead, thought Sebastian. But he didn't say it.

Sebastian was sitting down to breakfast a short time later when a message arrived from Sir Henry Lovejoy.

A milkmaid bringing her cows to graze in Hyde Park at daybreak had stumbled upon the dead body of Sir Felix Paige.

CHAPTER 45

Sir Felix Paige lay sprawled on his back in an unscythed patch of fine-leaved fescues and ryegrass not far from a stand of gnarled oaks in a naturalized section of the park. His stiffening arms were flung out at his sides, and he had one leg bent awkwardly beneath him. His face was livid, his eyes bulging. The dark cord used to cut off his life was still embedded deep in the flesh of his neck.

"Strangled, obviously," said Lovejoy as Sebastian hunkered down beside the corpse.

Sebastian studied the dead man's blood-smeared lips. "Why the hell would our killer change weapons at this stage in the game?"

"Perhaps it's a different killer."

"God save us." Sebastian ran his gaze over the dead man's clothes—the fashionable dark blue coat, the white-and-indigo-striped waistcoat, the pale yellow pantaloons. Paige was lying on his back, but the knees of his pantaloons were noticeably stained with grass and dirt. "Gibson will hopefully be able to tell us for certain, but it looks to me as if he's probably been dead for hours."

Lovejoy hunched his shoulders against the cold morning wind. "The palace isn't going to like this. First a marquis's son, now a baronet."

403

Sebastian pushed to his feet. "The world is better off without either of those two men in it. Unless I miss my guess, Paige only succeeded to his title by murdering his father, cousin, and brother—in that order."

Lovejoy stared at him. "Good heavens. You think there's a possibility he killed Ashworth?"

"And someone has now killed him in revenge?" Sebastian let his gaze drift around the half-wild remnant of old heathland. "That would explain the shift in murder weapons, wouldn't it? The main problem with that theory is, I haven't been able to come up with a believable reason for Paige to have killed Ashworth."

"Perhaps an explanation will become clearer once we begin investigating his affairs."

"Perhaps," said Sebastian.

It was several hours later when Sebastian arrived at the dank stone outbuilding behind Paul Gibson's surgery on Tower Hill to find Sir Felix Paige's lanky, naked body lying on the surgeon's stone slab.

"This one's different," said the Irishman, looking up as Sebastian paused in the open doorway.

"It is, indeed. Any idea when he might have been killed?"

"Probably last night. Does that fit with what you know?"

Sebastian nodded, his gaze on the ugly purple line circling the dead man's throat. "I've just spoken to some of his friends who say he was supposed to meet them at the cockpit on Birdcage Walk at nine, but he never showed."

"The lads who brought him said he was found near there."

"He was. Coincidentally, it's also near where his cousin was found murdered a few years ago."

"You think that's significant?"

"Damned if I know. But it does nothing to explain what he was doing in the park at that time of night. Any chance the body was dumped there?"

"It's possible. But there are grass stains along with the dirt on the knees of his pantaloons. Someone hit him on the back of his head before strangling him."

"Oh?" Sebastian pushed away from the door and took a step forward. "Hard enough to knock him out?"

"Maybe. Definitely hard enough to stun him."

"Huh. So the killer hits him, drops him to his knees, and then garrotes him? I suppose it's a good way to hamper your victim's ability to fight back."

"It is, indeed. There aren't any fingernail scratches on his neck the way you'd expect if he were conscious enough to try to claw at the ligature. But then, when the windpipe is compressed hard and fast, they don't stay conscious for long."

"And you think Paige's was? Compressed hard and fast, I mean."

"Definitely." Gibson reached for a dark cord that lay curled up on a nearby shelf and handed it to him. "You don't see one of these every day."

Sebastian found himself holding a narrow garrote with a large knot tied in the center. "It's waxed."

Gibson tucked his hands up under his arms and leaned back against the edge of the shelf behind him. "Not only is it waxed, but the knot is strategically positioned to crush the larynx. Whoever killed Paige knew exactly what he was doing. Under normal circumstances, it's not easy to strangle a strong, healthy man to death. But wax your garrote and it slices right into the throat and does the job in half the time. Crush the windpipe with a knot and it's even better."

Sebastian brought his gaze back to the dead man's bloated, discolored face. "The killings of Ashworth, Digby, and the girl were messy—acts of either passion or desperation. But this . . . This was professional."

"Very." Gibson blew out a long, troubled breath. "So, know any professional killers?"

"A waxed garrote?" said Hendon as he and Sebastian walked along the gravel paths of the

Privy Gardens that had once formed a part of Henry VIII's now-vanished Whitehall Palace. "I've never heard of such a thing."

Sebastian kept his gaze on the Earl's face. "It's an assassin's weapon."

Hendon was silent for a moment, his eyes narrowed against the glare of the weak spring sun off the wind-ruffled river beside them. "You're thinking someone in the Grand Duchess's household might have killed Paige?"

"I'm finding it hard to come up with any other explanation. Can you?"

"Not really. But . . . why? What possible threat could Paige have been to the Tsar's sister?"

"A considerable threat, if he knew—or even simply suspected—that her noble lady-in-waiting had hacked to death the son of the Marquis of Lindley in the midst of some decidedly risqué sex games. Especially if Ivanna's motive was to protect the Russian royal family from having its machinations exposed."

"Yes, I can see that. The problem is, if it is true, how do you prove it?"

"I'm not sure I can. And the palace would never let me touch the Russians even if I could."

Hendon let out his breath in a heavy sigh. "The bodies are beginning to pile up, aren't they? I was worried at first that Stephanie might have killed Ashworth herself, but she couldn't have committed this kind of carnage." He paused, then added, "Even considering who her father was."

Sebastian looked over at the Earl. "Wilcox wasn't actually her father, you know."

Hendon's eyes widened. "You can't be serious."

"Not according to Aunt Henrietta. And I assume she knows what she's talking about."

"Good heavens," said the Earl, his jaw working back and forth in that way he had. Then he said it again: "Good heavens."

Sebastian was drawing up in front of his Brook Street house when he spotted Tom rounding the corner from Bond Street at a run.

"I found 'im!" shouted the tiger, his face shining with triumph as he jumped over a crate of live chickens and dodged a coalman with a bulging sack. "I done found Ben King, and 'e says 'e's willin' to talk to yer honor."

"He's still alive?"

The boy skidded to a halt, breathing heavily. "Aye. 'E's got 'isself a new corner near St. Andrew's in Holborn."

"Holborn? That can't pay very well—especially not when compared to Beau Brummell's neighborhood."

"It don't. 'E says 'is take is 'alf what it was on Curzon Street. 'E didn't want t' talk t' ye, but I told 'im that if 'e tells ye wot 'e knows, then maybe you'll be able t' catch the killer so's 'e can come back t' Mayfair."

"And he agreed?"

"Not right away. I told 'im ye'd give 'im a couple o' shillings, and 'e said make it 'alf a crown and 'e'll spill it all."

"*Half a crown?*"

Tom grinned. "I figured ye was good fer it, gov'ner."

Ben King turned out to be a short, sturdy lad of perhaps eleven or twelve with thick golden hair; even, attractive features; and bright, knowing eyes. Despite his recent fall in income, he was still cleaner than most crossing sweeps, and although his clothes were the usual assortment of rag-fair finds, he somehow managed to carry them off with an air of assurance and cocky good humor.

"I wants me half crown up front," said the crossing sweep when Sebastian and his tiger met the boy in St. Andrew's ancient churchyard.

Sebastian held up two coins. "Half now, half when you've finished telling me what I need to know."

Ben's eyes narrowed with suspicion. "How can I be sure ye won't cheat me?"

"My word as a gentleman."

The boy made a rude noise. "I know what that's worth." But he tucked the first coin out of sight and hopped up to perch on the edge of a nearby table tomb. "What ye want t' know?"

"I'm told you used to deliver messages for Lord Ashworth's valet, Digby."

"Aye."

"To whom?"

"Mainly his lordship's da."

"You mean, to the Marquis of Lindley?"

"Aye."

"How often?"

Ben gave a negligent shrug. "Often enough."

"Where else?"

"Meyer's, sometimes."

"The Conduit Street tailor?"

"Aye. And Hoby's."

Hoby was a fashionable bootmaker. "Anyone else not a merchant in Conduit, St. James's, or Bond Street?"

The boy looked thoughtful. "Well, sometimes he'd give me a message for Sir Felix Paige, him as lives in Cork Street."

"Lived, past tense. Paige was found dead this morning. Strangled."

Ben's features remained impassive, but he sucked in a quick breath that jerked his narrow chest. "I ain't heard that."

"I understand Digby gave you a message to carry the night Ashworth was killed."

"Aye."

"For whom?"

"Fer his lordship—the old Marquis."

"The message was from Ashworth?"

"Nah. It was from Digby hisself. The ones for Park Lane almost always were."

Whatever Sebastian had been expecting, it wasn't that. "How did you know?"

" 'Cause they didn't have Ashworth's seal on 'em, like the others."

Of course, thought Sebastian. "And were you given a response to carry back to Curzon Street?"

"No."

Sebastian studied the boy's small, upturned nose, well-formed cheekbones, and gracefully arched brows. "How long have you been a crossing sweep?"

"Ever since me da died four—no, five years ago. I don't even remember me mother, she died so long ago."

"Have you been on Curzon Street all that time?"

"Aye—up till last week. It's a good stand." The boy pulled a face. "A hellova lot better'n here."

"When did you begin carrying messages from Digby to Lindley House?"

Ben gave another twitch of his shoulder. "I dunno. Mabye six months or so after I started."

So, four and a half years. Edward Digby had been sending messages to his employer's father since shortly after he'd arrived at Curzon Street, and Lindley had never said a word about it.

Sebastian said, "Did you see Digby again

the night of the murder? After he gave you the message to take to Park Lane, I mean."

Ben shook his head. "I didn't go back that night. Had no reason to."

"Who do you think killed him?"

The question seemed to take the boy by surprise. "Digby? How would I know?" A faintly malicious gleam of amusement lit up his dark brown eyes. "Heard he was found stripped to the skin in that alley up by Chesterfield House. He wouldn't have liked that. He wouldn't have liked that at all. Proud and fussy, he was."

"Do you have any idea why the killer would take Digby's clothes?"

"What makes you think the killer done that? As long as they say he was left layin' there, I reckon somebody musta come along, found him, and took the clothes to sell. He was always a natty dresser, Digby."

It was a simple explanation that for some reason had never occurred to any of them, but it made sense. Even if the back of the valet's shirt, waistcoat, and coat had been bloody and shredded, their fine material would still have been worth a great deal to that desperate army of poor men, women, and children who scoured the streets for rags, bones, and dog droppings.

Sebastian said, "Why did you run away from Curzon Street?"

"Why d'ye think?"

"You know who killed Ashworth?"

The boy shook his head slowly from side to side, but Sebastian saw his sun-darkened throat work as he swallowed.

"Then what made you run, Ben?"

"I seen him," said the boy, his voice barely a whisper.

"Who?"

"That old man. The Marquis. He come to Curzon Street."

"You mean the morning after Ashworth's murder?"

The boy nodded.

"And that frightened you? Why?"

"I dunno. It was jist . . ."

"Just—what?"

"Somethin' I seen in his eyes. He was gettin' outta his carriage, and he looked over and saw me. Gave me the creepy-jeepies, it did. I learned a long time ago to trust me creepy-jeepies. I mean, he might be an old man, but he's still Ashworth's da, ain't he? And that Viscount, he was like one o' them things the vicar used to preach to us about on Sundays when I was little—you know, them things you think look like men, but they've really got shaggy hair and hooves, or maybe claws and wings like bats? They're always lurkin' in the shadows, tryin' to hurt folks. That was Ashworth, all right."

"You mean, demons?"

Ben gave a faint shiver that he tried to suppress. "Aye. That's it. You'd look at that lord, and he seemed all rich and handsome-like. But underneath it all, he was really ugly and evil. A demon."

CHAPTER 46

The Marquis of Lindley was taking his afternoon constitutional around Hyde Park when Sebastian fell into step beside him. The old man's gait was slow but steady, his face only faintly flushed by the exertion.

"If I might have a word with you, my lord?" said Sebastian.

A spasm that looked like hope flashed across the old man's features. "Yes, of course. Have you discovered something that will lead to the arrest of my son's killer?"

"Not exactly. But I have learned that Ashworth's valet used to send messages to you via one of the neighborhood's crossing sweeps. I'm wondering why you didn't tell me that."

Lindley was silent for a moment, his aged, lined face heavy with sadness. "Why? It's rather obvious, isn't it? It's not something I'm proud of—paying my son's valet to keep an eye on his employer and send me periodic reports."

"He sent you a report the night your son was killed?"

"As a matter of fact, he did, yes. But nothing of any importance, unfortunately."

"May I see it?"

"Sorry, I never kept them. I had no desire to

have such a record of my son's foibles fall into anyone else's hands."

"You knew what your son was like?"

Something painful glittered in the old man's eyes, something hidden by quickly lowered lids. "I knew he gambled too much, drank too much, even experimented with opium. And I knew his sexual tastes were . . . Let's just call them unorthodox, shall we?"

"That's one way of putting it."

Lindley's jaw hardened, his mouth pressing into a tight, pained line. He kept his gaze fixed straight ahead. "I'd hoped marriage and a family might settle him down. Perhaps in time it would have done so. But now we'll never know."

Sebastian gazed across the park's wide, open swath of grassland toward the shimmering waters of the Serpentine in the distance. "Was there anything in the reports from your son's valet that might give some hint as to what happened?"

"No. Nothing. If there were, I would have told you."

Sebastian wasn't so sure about that. But all he said was "I wonder, would it be possible for me to have another look inside the Curzon Street house?"

The Marquis stumbled, so that Sebastian had to put out a hand to steady him. "Whatever for? Bow Street went over everything."

"They might have missed something."

Lindley tugged at his lower lip with a thumb and forefinger. "Well . . . I'm in the process of closing the place up, you know. I've dismissed most of the staff except for Fullerton and a couple of housemaids I'm having drape everything in holland covers. But perhaps we could set up something next week. I'll let you know. I'd like to be there myself. I'm sure you understand."

"Yes, of course. Do let me know." Sebastian started to turn away, then paused to look back and say, "By the way, when did you start paying Digby to report to you?"

"A year, perhaps a year and a bit ago. No longer."

It was a lie, of course. Ben King said he'd been carrying Digby's messages to Park Lane for more than four years. It could mean nothing—a simple reluctance on the old man's part to admit how long he'd been watching his son's activities. But Sebastian suspected it was more than that. Far more.

"I see. Thank you, my lord." Sebastian touched his hand to his hat. "I'll let you know if I learn anything more."

He was aware of the old Marquis watching him as he walked toward his waiting curricle. And he wondered whether the chill that ran up his spine despite the warmth of the spring day would qualify as one of young Ben King's "creepy-jeepies."

• • •

After returning to his curricle, Sebastian sat for a time, his thoughts on the often tense, painful relations that could develop between fathers and sons. He considered the ways in which sons and fathers could differ, and the many ways in which they were sometimes startlingly similar.

Then he turned his horses toward Bethnal Green.

Bethnal Green was a wretched, impoverished hamlet on the eastern outskirts of London, an area of French weavers and market gardens, of brickfields and almshouses and lunatic asylums. Not too many years ago, Ashworth and his friend Sir Francis Rowe had rented a modest brick house there. The things they'd done in that house still haunted Sebastian's dreams.

He'd decided to drive out to Bethnal Green because he wanted to talk to an old man named Corky Baldoon. Fifty years before, in the days of the present Marquis of Lindley's father, Baldoon had been a farmer on one of the Marquis's estates down in Devon. But then the old Marquis and his son had pushed an Enclosure Act through Parliament, stripping Baldoon and others like him of their land and ancient common rights. That winter, Baldoon's wife and two of his children died in the poorhouse, and Baldoon drifted up to London.

Sebastian knew Baldoon's opinion of Lindley

was colored by the cruelties of those days. But he suspected the former tenant farmer's assessment of the nobleman was probably more accurate than that of those who knew Lindley only as a suave, gently smiling figure who moved sedately through London's best drawing rooms and gentlemen's clubs.

Corky Baldoon was feeding chickens in his dusty yard when Sebastian drew up his curricle before the old man's ramshackle cottage and hopped down. "I remember you," said Corky, his mouth pulling into a toothless grin. A white-haired, bony old man with bowed legs, he had pale, nearly lashless eyes and surprisingly nimble liver-spotted hands. The smile faded. "Yer the feller was interested in the Marquis of Lindley, God rot his soul forever."

"I'm still interested in him," said Sebastian, pausing out of pecking reach of the hens.

Baldoon cast a handful of grain to his chickens. "Heard that son o' his got hisself kilt the other day."

"Yes."

"That why yer here?"

"It is, actually. Most people think of the Marquis of Lindley as a charming, gentle old man. But as I recall, you had a somewhat different opinion."

Baldoon kept his gaze on the chickens squawking and jostling around his scuffed boots.

"Oh, he was always a smooth one, no doubt about that. Smiling and quiet-spoken and gentle-sounding as he could be. But he was a mean son of a bitch, for all that. Just like his da, the Marquis before him."

"Could he kill, do you think?"

Baldoon turned his bucket upside down and slapped the bottom, emptying the last of the grain. "Saw him kill, once. It was just a few days after he and his da posted their bloody Enclosure Act on the church door. One of the cottagers, a fellow by the name of Hugh Platt, he stopped his young lordship as he was riding through the village. Closed his fist around his lordship's bridle and called him all sorts of names. Said the bastard and his da weren't gonna get away with what they was tryin' to do. Lindley—or Ashworth, as he was then—pulled out a pistol and shot Hugh in the face, just as cool as you please." Baldoon sniffed. "Nobody never did nothin' about it, of course. 'Self-defense,' they called it, on account of Hugh grabbing his lordship's bridle. But it weren't self-defense. All Hugh done was challenge his high-and-mighty lordship, and he paid for it with his life."

Baldoon paused, his eyes becoming unfocused as his thoughts drifted in the past. Then he glanced over at Sebastian. "That answer yer question?"

"It does, yes. Thank you."

420

• • •

On the way back to Brook Street, Sebastian swung by Tower Hill, where he found Alexi Sauvage spreading a salve on an old woman's burned arm.

"Paul is at St. Bartholomew's," said Alexi, barely throwing Sebastian a glance.

"Actually, you're the one I wanted to see. You said foxglove can create a kind of stupor. Is it used for anything? Anything medicinal, I mean."

"It is, yes. An extract is prescribed for the heart. It can be amazingly effective." She looked up then, her eyes narrowing. "You have a suspect with heart problems?"

"I do, indeed."

He went next to Bow Street but had to track Sir Henry Lovejoy from the Public Office to the Brown Bear before finally running him down in a chandler's just off Covent Garden.

"My lord," said the magistrate, looking up in surprise. "If you'd sent word, I would gladly have come by Brook Street—"

"It's quite all right," said Sebastian. "Just one quick question. I've been thinking about the knife that was used to murder Ashworth. If the killer found the weapon in the Viscount's bedroom, it suggests a crime of desperation, or at least opportunity. But if the killer brought the knife with him—or her—then we'd know we

421

were dealing with a level of premeditation that completely shifts our understanding of what happened that night."

"Yes," said Lovejoy with a faint frown.

"So my question is: Did your constables find a cache of knives when they searched Ashworth's bedchamber?"

"No. But then, we were never able to conduct more than a cursory search of the premises before the Marquis put a halt to our efforts."

"He did?"

"Mmm. Said it was an unnecessary invasion of his son's privacy and a waste of time—time that could be better employed elsewhere. My lads had only searched perhaps half the chamber when they were forced to leave."

"You didn't find that curious?"

"Not really, no. The lads had just come across Ashworth's collection of bonds and whips. I could understand a father's reluctance to allow us to discover more evidence of his son's depravity."

"That is one explanation," said Sebastian.

Lovejoy looked at him in surprise. "You're suggesting there's another?"

"You think *Lindley* killed Ashworth?" said Hero, who was kneeling on the nursery floor with Simon and his blocks when Sebastian came upon her. "His only surviving son? But . . . why?"

Sebastian hunkered down beside his wife and

child. "He told me at Ashworth's inquest that he has dedicated his life to protecting the Ledger name and expanding the estates entrusted to him by his own father, with the aim of someday passing that proud inheritance on to his son. The problem is, between his nasty sexual tastes and his gambling habits, Ashworth was a threat to both the honor of the family name and the family's wealth."

Hero was silent for a moment, her arms creeping around Simon to hold him so close, the boy fussed and she had to let him go. "Could Lindley have known about the houses in Bethnal Green and Clerkenwell?"

"With Digby sending him regular reports for the last four-plus years? Oh, he knew, all right. In fact, he's known what his son was like for a long time. Remember the whispers about Ashworth and Rowe's exploits up in Cambridge—the ones Lindley paid to keep quiet?"

"But to kill his own son?" She watched Simon begin to load his wooden blocks into a bin with studied care. "It's . . . unthinkable."

"For you or me, yes. For someone like Lindley? Perhaps not."

"But why now? Why kill Ashworth now if he's known what his son was like for the past fifteen or more years?"

"Because, thanks to Stephanie, he finally has another heir. Two, in fact."

"Dear God," she said softly. "It makes an awful kind of sense."

"It does, indeed."

"You think he's been planning this? That it's why he pushed Ashworth to marry and beget an heir? So he could kill him?"

"I wouldn't be surprised."

"Surely no one could be so diabolical."

"This is Ashworth's father, remember."

She was silent for a moment. Thoughtful. "Could Digby have been in on Ashworth's murder?"

"He must have been. The events of that evening were very carefully timed and orchestrated. I suspect Lindley arranged to have Digby send word the next time Ashworth was 'entertaining' one of his *filles publiques*."

"So it was Lindley who came to the door when Ashworth was plying Sissy Jordan with wine and charm?"

"I think so. By that point, the old butler and the rest of the servants had retired to their rooms for the night—and they'd learned long ago to ignore any strange sounds they might hear coming from below. So the only person around at that point was Digby, who showed his lordship to the library and then went upstairs to tell the Viscount that his father was there wanting to see him."

"That's why Ashworth was annoyed but went down anyway," Hero said quietly. "His father was the one person he didn't dare refuse to see."

Sebastian nodded. "Ashworth told the girl he'd be right back. But Digby went to the drawing room, paid her off, and told her to leave. Meanwhile, in the library, Lindley probably poured his son a brandy and, unless I am mistaken, added something to the drink."

"Would he have that kind of knowledge?"

"Stephanie told me he has a heart condition. I wouldn't be surprised if we discover someone prescribed him a tincture of foxglove—and warned him of the dangers of accidentally overdosing with it."

"So then what?"

"The way I see it, Ashworth begins to feel unwell. He probably asks his father to ring for Digby. But Digby doesn't come, so Lindley himself offers to help his son up the stairs and into bed."

"At which point Ashworth passed out?"

"Or was too incoherent to understand what was happening. With his son essentially unconscious, Lindley stabbed him—"

"Over and over again? Why?"

"Perhaps he wanted to be certain Ashworth was dead. Or perhaps he wanted to make it look as if the killer were caught up in a passionate frenzy. Once Ashworth was dead, Lindley must have searched the room for his son's erotic paraphernalia, tied him up, and scattered his clothes in a line from the door to the bed to make it look as if they'd been torn off in the heat of sexual desire. Presumably he also planted the woman's stocking under the bed. That was an inspired touch."

"He brought it with him? And the knife too? It was all that carefully planned?"

"It had to have been. That room was an elaborate tableau of deliberate misdirection—a stage set. And I fell for it."

"Not entirely," said Hero. "You noticed that the knots in the cords hadn't been pulled as tightly as they would have been by a man desperately straining against his bonds."

"Yes. But there were other explanations for that."

"So then what?" she said quietly as Simon began taking his blocks out of the bin again.

"I suspect Lindley cleaned himself up with Digby's help, then asked the valet to walk him home. Park Lane isn't far, and despite his age and failing health, the Marquis takes a morning and afternoon constitutional in the park, so he's surely capable of it. At some point between Ashworth's house and the alley where he was found, the valet must have divulged Sissy Jordan's name and direction to Lindley. For all we know, Lindley was annoyed with the man for paying the girl off. At any rate, once he had the information he needed, Lindley killed him."

"By stabbing him in the back," said Hero.

"What a ghastly man. But . . . why go through the trouble of stripping him?"

Sebastian shook his head. "He didn't. All he did was maneuver the body into the alley—probably as the man was still dying—and leave him there covered with rubbish. Some rag-and-bone picker must have come along, poked through the trash, and found the body."

Hero's eyes widened. "And took the clothes! Good heavens. Why didn't I think of that?"

"Because neither of us has ever been so desperate as to see the clothes of a murdered man as valuable, let alone something like a bone or a dog turd. Ben King was the one who suggested it to me."

Hero watched Simon toddle over to a stack of books. "And then Lindley tracked Sissy to her lodgings and killed her too? He's killed anyone who could possibly identify him."

"Everyone except Ben King. And I suspect the only reason the crossing sweep is still alive is because his 'creepy-jeepies' warned him he was in danger."

"But why kill Sir Felix Paige?"

"Paige is the one part of all this that doesn't seem to fit. I'm half inclined to credit his murder to the burly Russians around the Grand Duchess and her lovely lady-in-waiting, although I'm having to work to come up with an adequate explanation for it."

Hero said, "You can't prove any of this. Lindley has a perfectly understandable explanation for his arrangement with Digby, and everything else is simply . . . conjecture."

"So far. But I've just learned from Lovejoy that Lindley stopped Bow Street from conducting a thorough search of the Curzon Street house, and I know from Fullerton that the Marquis ordered his son's room closed and locked. Everyone assumed he was driven by a father's grief, combined with a desire to protect the reputation of his nasty son. But he may simply be hiding something— something that points to his own guilt."

"Like what?"

"That I don't know yet. I need to have another look at that room."

She narrowed her eyes. "You're planning to break in there, aren't you?"

He gave her a slow smile. "Tonight."

CHAPTER 47

Saturday, 9 April

The hours before dawn were moonless and so unseasonably cold that Sebastian could see his breath as he cut through the shadowy rear gardens of Ashworth's Curzon Street residence. The house loomed dark and silent before him; the aged butler and the two remaining housemaids would long since have retired to their rooms.

Slipping a housebreaker's tool known as a picklock from the pocket of his greatcoat, Sebastian paused at the edge of the flagged terrace, his preternaturally keen hearing alive to every faint rustle in the shrubbery, the distant bark of a dog, the echoing cry of the watch.

"Two o'clock on a cloudy night and all is well . . ."

Except Sebastian had the vague, niggling sense that something wasn't quite right. He drew a quiet breath, hesitating longer than he'd intended as he sought to identify the source of that elusive, prickly sense of danger. But he heard only the pattering of some four-footed creature in the night and the thump of his own heart.

Moving quickly, he crossed the terrace to flatten himself against the stuccoed wall beside the rear door. That was when he realized what was wrong: A faint but unmistakable scent of beeswax hung in the cold night air, and it came from the door that stood unlatched and cracked open perhaps an inch. Listening closely, he could now hear distant voices speaking quietly— first a woman's whisper, then a low baritone he recognized as Colonel Nikolai Demidov's.

What the devil?

Easing his knife from its sheath in his boot, Sebastian slowly pushed open the door. He waited, listening, alive to the possibility the Russians might have left a guard at the door.

Nothing.

Stepping into a rear service corridor, he moved easily through the darkened house to the front entrance hall. He could hear the Russian colonel and his female companion—*Ivanna?*—moving stealthily overhead. He thought at first they must be in the drawing room, then realized they were actually two floors above, in Ashworth's bedchamber.

Why? he wondered. *Why, why, why?*

He gazed thoughtfully at the main staircase, which rose from the entrance hall in a long straight line before taking a short jag to empty onto the first floor's corridor. If Demidov had posted a lookout above, Sebastian would be an easy target the moment he started up the steps. He considered going back to take the narrower, steeper servants' stairs that lay behind the green baize door at the rear of the house, then reasoned that the Russians were more likely to fear being disturbed by the servants than by someone from outside. That meant a guard was more likely to be posted at the back stairs than here.

Although there could always be two guards.

Clenching his knife for a moment between his teeth, Sebastian jerked off his boots. Then, the knife in one hand, his boots in the other, he started up the main staircase in his stocking feet. He was careful to stay close to the wall, avoiding the center of the treads to minimize the chance of a betraying creak. He'd almost reached the first floor when he heard Demidov grumble above, "It's not here."

Sebastian crept up the next flight of stairs.

"Hush," whispered the woman. "You speak too loudly." The colonel's French was even worse than his English, but the woman spoke with a flawless Parisian accent untouched by any Russian overtones.

"It's not here," Demidov repeated, lowering his voice.

"It must be."

"One of the servants could have found it and taken it."

"Don't be a fool."

As he reached the top of the second flight of stairs, Sebastian could see a faint glow of light spilling down the corridor from Ashworth's chamber overlooking the street. The rest of the house lay in darkness. He paused, quietly listening and watching. And from the archway that separated the front corridor from the narrow rear servants' passage came the faintest of sounds: the click of a boot heel on polished floorboards, the brush of cloth against cloth.

So Demidov had brought a lookout after all, stationing him at the narrow back stairs that would be used by any servants venturing from the attics or basement to investigate.

His grip tightening on the knife in his hand, Sebastian moved stealthily toward the guard. He could see him now, turned half away, a heavy Russian pattern 1809 flintlock held loosely at his side, his attention all for the door to the servants' stairs. There was something familiar about the shape of the Russian's head, about the angle of his jaw, and Sebastian realized he had seen the man before, in Seven Dials.

Then a faint betraying *creak* cut through the stillness as Sebastian's foot trod on a loose floorboard. He froze. The Russian turned, sucking in a quick, startled gasp as he jerked up the pistol and thumbed back the hammer. But Sebastian was already cocking his own arm to snap it forward and release his dagger in a fluid motion that sent the blade whistling through the air to sink into the Russian's throat. The man gave a faint gurgle and dropped to the floor.

"What was that?" Sebastian heard the unknown woman say as he darted forward to retrieve his knife.

"I didn't hear anything," said the colonel. "You're imagining things."

"I heard something. Go check."

Quickly yanking the blade from the dead Russian's body, Sebastian quietly set down his boots and flattened back against the green baize-covered door just as Colonel Demidov started down the corridor. He paused for a moment at the base of the main flight of stairs leading up to the third floor, his head cocked, listening. Then his gaze shifted toward the alcove of the servants' stair, and he said, "Vlad?"

Sebastian held himself very still, wishing his knife's handle weren't so damned blood-slicked. Impossible to accurately throw it now.

"Vladimir?" Drawing a sleek dueling pistol from his pocket, the colonel advanced cautiously toward the archway, obviously struggling to see in the darkness.

Sebastian waited. Waited until the colonel was almost opposite the baize-covered door. Then Demidov must have finally spotted the shadowy outline of the crumpled guard, because he gave a smothered oath and drew up.

Sebastian lunged forward, closing his left fist around the Russian's gun hand and yanking it up in an old street fighter's trick that both eliminated the gun's immediate threat and cleared a path for Sebastian to drive his dagger toward the man's heart.

Demidov pulled uselessly against Sebastian's grip. But by pivoting away and bringing his left arm down in a sweeping block, he managed to knock Sebastian's knife off target. The blade skittered across the colonel's side; then its hilt snagged on the colonel's gold-trimmed tunic in a way that pulled the dagger's slippery handle from Sebastian's grasp.

"Bloody hell," he swore softly.

"You!" roared the colonel. Drawing his chin down against his chest, he rammed forward like a butting bull, smashing the top of his big head into Sebastian's face and sending blood spurting everywhere.

Temporarily blinded by the explosion of pain and blood, Sebastian felt a beefy fist close around his throat and tighten. Knowing he didn't dare relax his grip on the Russian's gun, Sebastian clawed with one hand at the deadly hold that was squeezing, squeezing. It was useless.

Desperate, he gave up and fumbled instead for the dagger he knew he hadn't heard fall. Where the hell was it? He felt his fingers slide over the bloody hilt and closed his fist around the handle. There was a roaring in his ears as he yanked the knife free and shifted its angle to plunge the blade up under the Russian's left arm, thrusting straight into his heart.

Demidov let out a breathy *"Oof,"* his gun making a dull thump as it hit the floorboards. But somehow he still managed to keep his grip on Sebastian's throat. Gritting his teeth, Sebastian twisted the knife deeper and heard the rattling gurgle of the dying man's breath. Then the colonel collapsed against him. Sebastian barely managed to catch his weight and ease the Russian quietly to the floor.

"Demidov?" he heard the unseen woman call. *"Qu'est-ce que c'est?"*

Yanking the knife from the Russian's chest, Sebastian jammed his feet into his boots, thrust the blade back into its sheath, and snatched up the colonel's gun. He had his own small double-barreled flintlock in his pocket, but the colonel's pistol had a better range, and he was beyond worrying about waking the servants with noise.

Trotting back toward the front of the house, he could see Ashworth's chamber faintly illuminated by a shuttered lantern and a small brace of candles that rested on a bombe chest near the door. But the unknown woman had gone silent and was nowhere in sight.

He was still deciding how best to deal with her when the hatchet-faced older woman he'd seen so often at Ivanna's side came through the doorway at him, the long, oaken handle of a brass bed warmer clutched in both hands. *"Salaud,"* she hissed, and swung the bed warmer's brass pan at his head.

He flung up his right arm to block her blow. He managed to protect his head, but the impact of the heavy brass pan against his forearm sent waves of pain radiating down his wrist to his hand. The colonel's pistol slipped from his suddenly numb fingers and went spinning across the floor.

"I don't want to hurt you," he said, wiping a crooked elbow across his bloody face. "Just stop."

She backed into the room, then drew up and swung the bed warmer to one side, intending to hit him again.

Lunging forward, his foot kicked the fallen pistol and he stumbled, but somehow managed to close one hand around the bed warmer's handle just below the pan. Then he balled up his still-throbbing fist and punched her in the face.

He expected her to go down. She didn't.

Staggering sideways, she slammed into the bombe chest near the door, rocking the blazing candelabra and sending a glass figurine and a black satin reticule he realized must be hers tumbling to the floor. He punched her again. This time she went sprawling.

Stepping back well out of her reach, Sebastian yanked his own small double-barreled pistol from his pocket and leveled it at her. "*Ne bougez pas*," he said as she shoved herself up on all fours, shaking her head as if to clear her senses. "Don't move, and I won't hurt you."

436

She shifted around so that she was sitting on the floor facing him, her breath coming shallow and quick. "Why?" she said in English, bringing up a hand to swipe at the line of blood trickling from her nose. "Are you afraid of me?"

Sebastian thumbed back the first hammer of his flintlock. "A woman can kill as easily as a man."

She gave a faint smile. "True."

He was aware of the chaos of the room around them, the furniture overturned, the covers of the still-bloody bed torn asunder. He said, "What were you looking for?"

He didn't expect her to answer, but she did. "Madame left something she wanted back."

"The night she murdered Viscount Ashworth, you mean?"

The woman shook her head. "She lost the bracelet here that night, yes, but she did not kill him."

He gave a faint laugh. "Of course not."

"You don't believe me? You're a fool. I have the bracelet in my reticule. Here, I'll show it to you."

"Don't touch it," warned Sebastian, thumbing back the second hammer.

Her jaw tightening, she grabbed the black satin reticule and thrust her hand inside. Sebastian squeezed the first trigger, and the flintlock's muzzle belched an explosion of flame and smoke.

The shot caught her high in the shoulder, but she barely flinched. Rather than try to draw her own small muff gun from the reticule, she simply fired at him through the black satin bag.

He felt her bullet slam into his side. She was staggering to her feet when he fired the second barrel.

This time he hit her dead center, a new dark sheen of blood blooming across the black silk bodice of her mourning gown. But it didn't stop her. Surging to her feet, she caught up the candelabra from the chest and swung it at him.

He felt hot wax splatter his face and smelled singeing wool as the smoldering wicks crushed against his greatcoat. Grabbing her arm, he twisted it behind her back and slammed her against the nearest wall.

"*Bâtard*!" she snarled, bucking against him. Then she went limp in his arms.

"Jesus Christ." He took a step back, letting her go, and watched her slide down the wall, leaving a bloody trail against the elegant champagne-and-gold-striped wallpaper.

For a moment he wavered, holding himself tense, ready for her to come at him again. But her eyes were blank and staring. She was dead.

"Jesus Christ," he said again, sinking to his knees. Then the world went black, and he pitched forward onto his face.

His first awareness was of pain.

His side was afire with a wet burning that all

but eclipsed the throbbing pain in the middle of his face and the ache in his forearm. He realized he was lying on his back on something hard. The floor. Memory returned, and he knew where he was, except that there was too much light visible through his closed eyelids. Could dawn have come?

He opened his eyes slowly, peering cautiously through lowered lashes. He was still on the floor of Ashworth's bedchamber, but dawn had not yet arrived. Someone had set the candelabra back atop the bombe chest and lit its broken candles, along with the candles flanking the hearth and an oil lamp beside the bed. He could see the hatchet-faced woman still sprawled against the wall, her dead eyes wide and staring, her mouth agape.

He thought at first the gunshots must have brought the household to investigate. But even if Ashworth's servants hadn't been trained to ignore anything they heard, Fullerton was old and half-deaf and doubtless slept three floors below in the basement beside the silver and wine. The two remaining housemaids were probably cowering alone in the attic, too terrified to investigate. They had not come. Instead, someone—presumably the same person who'd lit the candles and lamps—had lashed Sebastian's wrists together with golden silk cords.

"Ah," said the Marquis of Lindley. "You're awake."

CHAPTER 48

"I see I was wise to tie your hands," said the old man.

Sebastian shifted his head. Ashworth's father stood near his son's overturned mattress, a flintlock pistol in one hand. At first, Sebastian assumed he had picked up the colonel's dueling pistol. But the weapon was too heavy, too graceless, and he realized the Marquis must have retrieved the gun from the fallen guard in the corridor. Which meant the colonel's pistol could still be—*where?*

"I thought you might come tonight," continued the aged Marquis in that same soft, deceptively gentle voice.

"How could you know?" said Sebastian, twisting his wrists, testing the knots. They held tight.

"I saw it in your eyes yesterday in the park, when you asked to search the house and I put you off. You're not a man who likes being told no, are you? And you have something of a reputation for unorthodox behavior. I looked into you when Sir Henry told me you'd be helping Bow Street with the investigation into my son's death. Did you think I would not?"

Sebastian tried to remember where he had dropped the colonel's gun, but his head was splitting, and he felt both nauseated and dangerously faint. He'd been near the chamber door, hadn't he? He had a vague memory of kicking the thing when he struggled with Ivanna's woman. So where was it now?

"Of course," Lindley said with what sounded almost like a laugh, "I wasn't expecting the Russians. It was most generous of you to eliminate them for me."

Sebastian twisted his wrists again, assessing the play in the cords and the range of movement it gave his hands. "You know why they were here?"

A pained expression of disgust flitted across the old man's face and then was gone. "The *putain* who calls herself a princess was with him earlier that night. I take it she left something she feared might incriminate her?"

"She was here?" Sebastian repeated, his head throbbing as his understanding of that night's events spun about and attempted to realign itself.

"She had been, although she'd left by the time I arrived. I expected to find him entertaining some vile streetwalker. Instead, he was sprawled in his bed, lost in an opium-induced haze after playing his nasty games with that highborn whore."

Sebastian could see the colonel's gun now, lying almost hidden by the folds of the dead woman's black silk skirts. "And so you killed him?" he said, surreptitiously working his wrists back and forth, back and forth. "Your own son?"

Lindley's lips pursed. "The Lord teaches us that if a man has a son who will not obey his father, then the father must lay hold of him and say, 'Our son is stubborn and rebellious. He will not obey our voice, but is a glutton and a drunkard.' "

" 'And all the men of his city shall stone him with stones, that he shall die,' " said Sebastian softly, continuing the quote from Deuteronomy. " 'So shalt thou put evil away from among you.' Except that you didn't deliver Ashworth to the 'elders of the city.' You killed him yourself."

"It was better that way."

Sebastian studied the Marquis's clear gray eyes. His words might be chilling, but Sebastian had no doubt the man was utterly sane—or at least as sane as his arrogant, self-absorbed son had been. "And the others? Digby? The girl? Paige? How do you justify their deaths?"

"Digby betrayed the man he served."

"Not to mention that he would have been in a position to blackmail you," said Sebastian. "But Sissy Jordan? She didn't know anything. Why kill her?"

"The girl was a whore. Plus, I couldn't be certain how much she knew, or what Digby might have let slip around her. I don't like loose ends."

"I'm surprised you didn't kill Ivanna."

"I'm still considering it. But her situation in the Grand Duchess's household does make things difficult." The old man shifted his weight.

"Unfortunately, that wretched little street sweeper ran away before I could deal with him."

"And Paige?"

"I didn't kill Paige."

"No?"

"No."

"So what's your justification for killing me?"

Lindley's mouth pursed again. "You have interfered in what is none of your affair."

"Oh? And is there a convenient biblical quotation for that as well?"

The Marquis pushed away from the bed and took several angry steps toward him, the gun held out in a shaky two-handed grip. "You mock the Lord?"

Sebastian knew he was playing a dangerous game. But he needed the man to come a little closer. "Not the Lord. I was thinking along the lines of—I believe it's in Mark, is it not? 'These people honor me with their lips, but their hearts are far from me.' "

"You shut up," hissed Lindley, his hands tightening on the flintlock just as Sebastian shifted to hook one foot around the old man's ankle and yank it forward, hard.

Lindley staggered, arms flinging wide as he fought to keep his balance. Kicking out, Sebastian smashed his heel into the Marquis's shin, then rolled to where the colonel's elegant dueling pistol lay beside the dead woman.

Grabbing the gun awkwardly with his lashed hands, Sebastian thumbed back the hammer and squeezed the trigger just as Lindley fired.

The Marquis's shot hit the wall with an explosion of plaster dust and lath splinters. But Sebastian's bullet slammed into the old man's chest.

He stumbled back, a vague look of surprise on his age-lined face. Then he crumpled beside his son's bloodstained bed and lay still.

"You're lucky," said Gibson, wrapping a roll of bandages around Sebastian's bare torso. "You've lost a lot of blood, but nothing vital was hit, and the wound looks clean. If you don't do anything stupid, you should live."

Sebastian grunted. They were in his dressing room before a roaring fire, but he still felt bone-cold. He brought up a hand to gingerly explore his face. "My nose feels like it's broken."

The surgeon tied off the bandage and squinted up at him. "Could be, but I doubt it. You've the makings of a couple of grand black eyes, though, and you may have a wee bit of a concussion. From the sounds of the carnage I'm hearing you left in Curzon Street, I'd say you got off lucky. I still can't believe it took four gunshots before Ashworth's old butler bestirred himself to investigate."

Sebastian reached for a clean shirt and pulled it over his head. "Given what typically went on in that house, I'm amazed he came at all."

444

• • •

Later, Sebastian had a long, tense conversation with Sir Henry Lovejoy and Lord Jarvis. Jarvis announced that the papers were being told Digby had killed his master, only to then fall victim himself to footpads. Footpads would also be blamed for Paige's death. There would be much official tut-tutting over the sudden alarming rise in violent crime; a few habitual offenders would be apprehended and hanged; and soon all would be forgotten.

Sissy's death was considered too commonplace and inconsequential to even require explanation.

After his lordship's departure, Lovejoy said, "It goes against the grain with me, this insistence that the sins of the 'better born' be covered up and hidden from public knowledge. It simply perpetuates the idea that rank and wealth are the result not of some accident of birth and luck but the mark of an innate superiority and divine favor."

"You mean to say you don't believe that they are?" said Sebastian with a smile.

Lovejoy rarely smiled himself. But Sebastian saw a twinkle of amusement in the magistrate's eyes before he lowered his chin and gave a faint shake of his head.

"You sort of had it right," said Hero as they sat together before the library fire, Sebastian with a glass of brandy cradled in one hand.

He looked over at her. "Only 'sort of.'"

She smiled. "Why did Ivanna go to Curzon Street that night, do you think? She and Ashworth had just had that awful row at the Pulteney, and she knew he was furious with her for letting one of her goons threaten him."

Sebastian tipped his head back against the chair. "I suspect she went to coax him out of the sulks and make certain he intended to keep quiet about the Russians' little scheme. One assumes she succeeded; otherwise she probably would have killed him before Lindley had the chance."

"She and Ashworth deserved each other."

"They did, indeed. We know from Sissy Jordan that he was annoyed when Digby came to tell him she was there. But he was obviously intrigued enough to go see what she wanted."

"I'm surprised Digby let her in, given that he knew the Marquis was coming."

"No lowly valet is going to turn away a princess. Besides, he probably figured one woman would serve Lindley's purposes as well as the next." Sebastian raised his brandy to his lips and took a sip. "I thought it was all a stage set— the scattered clothes, the whip, the silk stocking kicked under the bed. But it was real. Lindley simply took advantage of what he found."

"It makes you wonder if he'd killed before, doesn't it? I mean, someone besides that cottager down in Devon that Corky Baldoon was telling you about."

"As Lovejoy said, rank and wealth can cover a multitude of sins."

She was silent for a moment, her gaze on the fire. But he knew the drift of her thoughts and wasn't surprised when she said, "Do you believe Lindley was telling the truth when he said he didn't murder Sir Felix Paige?"

He met her gaze. "Given that he thought he was about to kill me, I can't think of a reason why he would lie."

"So who did kill Sir Felix? Demidov?"

Sebastian saw the worry in her eyes and said, "Probably. Paige knew Ashworth was involved with Ivanna. Demidov was probably worried about what else he knew."

He said it to reassure her. But he wasn't entirely convinced.

Ivanna Gagarin was eating an ice at Gunter's in Berkeley Square when Sebastian came to stand beside her, his left arm in a sling. The sun was shining warm and bright, and the afternoon was glorious.

"Beautiful day, is it not?" she said, looking up at him with one of her brilliant, utterly false smiles.

"It is." Reaching into his coat, he brought out a gold bangle studded with sapphires and diamonds and handed it to her. "I believe this is yours?"

She hesitated a moment, then took it from him to slip onto her wrist. "Thank you. I read of the

Marquis's death in the papers. They're saying he suffered a heart attack while visiting the site of his son's murder. How terribly tragic."

"Tragic, indeed. And what will the relatives of Colonel Demidov and his female companion be told?"

She flashed another of her dazzling, artificial smiles. "That London is a frightfully dangerous city, of course. Their murders will be seen as a warning to all visitors from Russia to avoid the more dangerous sections of the metropolis. I've heard the Regent is so concerned that he has ordered a sweep of the most undesirable elements."

"I take it the Prince hasn't yet heard of the Grand Duchess's plans for his daughter?"

Rather than answer, she tipped her head to one side and said softly, "I told you I didn't kill Ashworth."

"Yes. Although I suspect you would have if you hadn't been satisfied with whatever he said to you that evening. And you did try to kill me."

"That was Colonel Demidov."

"Was it? And did the good colonel also kill Sir Felix Paige?"

Her brows puckered together in a pretty frown. "Of course not."

When Sebastian remained silent, she said, "You don't believe me, do you?"

"No."

She gave a light laugh and held up her wrist so that the diamonds in the bracelet sparkled in the sun. He was turning to leave when she said, "Where was it?"

He paused to look back at her. "Behind the cushions in the library."

Later, Sebastian and Stephanie sat on a sunny bench in Hyde Park not far from Lindley House.

"Does your wound hurt terribly?" she asked.

"Not as much as my face."

She laughed. "You look terrible."

"Thank you."

Her smile faded as she gazed out over the sun-dazzled, undulating grass of the park. "I knew Lindley could be a hard man. But I had no idea he was capable of . . . that."

"He was far better at hiding his true nature than his son." They sat in a companionable silence for a time; then Sebastian said, "I've discovered Lady Cowper's ball was in April last year, Steph. April. Not June."

She looked over at him, her pulse beating visibly at the base of her throat. "I might have lied about the date of the ball," she said, her voice hoarse, "but not about what happened there."

"I never doubted that."

He watched her swallow. "I was lucky; there were no repercussions from what Ashworth did to me that night. But later, that summer, when I realized I was, as they say, in a 'delicate situation,' I was desperate."

"Did you tell Firth?"

"That I was carrying his child? No. Why would I? He couldn't marry me. His wife was still alive then, remember?"

"So you—what? Seduced Ashworth and then told him a few weeks later that the child you were carrying was his?"

She lifted her chin. "You think it horrible of me? Well, what he did to *me* was horrible. I think it served him right. I planned to tell him the baby came early. Except it was twins, and they really did come early. It made things . . . awkward."

"So he knew the boys weren't his?"

"Not for certain. But he suspected."

"He might have killed you, Steph."

"I know that now. I didn't then."

"I wish you'd come to me. I will always help you in any way I can. Please believe me."

She gave him a shaky smile, then turned her head toward the river as a series of booms filled the air in a rolling barrage of artillery fire. They could hear cannons up and down the Thames firing one after another, over and over again. *Boom, boom, boom.* "What is it?"

A cheer went up in a cascading wave that was like a sustained roar as all of London cried out at once in delirious excitement. Sebastian called to a lad running past. "What's happened?"

"It's Boney!" shouted the boy. "He's surrendered! The war is over. It's over!"

"Dear God," said Stephanie. "Is it possible?"

"Listen to that. It must be."

The church bells began to ring, first one, then the next, until every church in the city joined the celebration in a glorious peal of thanksgiving. Stephanie laughed out loud, and Sebastian felt his heart swell with joy and relief. . . .

Joy and relief, but something else too. Something he realized was a niggling sense of foreboding that Stephanie must have shared, because her face tightened and she grew serious.

"I hope that boy is wrong," she said. "I hope Napoléon hasn't simply surrendered but is dead. How can we believe this endless, wretched war is truly over as long as he's still out there? How can we know he won't come back again?"

Anyone else would have told her that her fears were groundless, that of course Napoléon could never come back to threaten them again. But Sebastian reached out to take her hand in his, and he held it as the clanging church bells and shouts of joy went on and on.

"We can't."

AUTHOR'S NOTE

Grand Duchess Catherine of Oldenburg, younger sister of Tsar Alexander I of Russia, did come to London in the spring of 1814, months ahead of the rest of the Allied Sovereigns invited by the Prince Regent for a grand victory celebration. She did rent the entire Pulteney Hotel for her enormous retinue. Letters from the time make it obvious that her goal was indeed to snare the Regent as her new husband, thus breaking up what Russia saw as a dangerously cozy Anglo-Dutch alliance. The two spoiled royals did indeed take an instant dislike to each other for the reasons Cousin Victoria explained. There is also little doubt that she and the Tsar schemed to break up the betrothal of Princess Charlotte to the Prince of Orange by throwing several handsome European princes into Charlotte's path; Prince Leopold was brought to London for that express purpose. (Spoiler alert: It worked.) Once the Princess's betrothal was broken, the Tsar then married his own younger sister to the Prince of Orange.

The Grand Duchess's looks and personality were much as described here. She did claim to hate music and made the Regent order his musicians to stop playing at the banquet held in her honor (the Prince boasted that he had personally selected the pieces to be played with each course, so she may have done it simply to annoy him). She did popularize the "Oldenburg bonnet," which was named after her. Incidentally, the title of grand duchess ranked in order of precedence below emperor and king but above sovereign prince and duke.

Ivanna Gagarin is a fictional character, although the Grand Duchess did bring a very-much-alive Prince Gagarin in her retinue. (He was not a nice person, and interestingly had once gone through a bigamous marriage ceremony with an impoverished English widow who was a longtime and much-loved member of Princess Charlotte's household. It was a small world.)

Cartomancy, crystallomancy, palmistry, necromancy, and astrology all became popular in the nineteenth century. There really was a colony of astrologers in Seven Dials, attracted by the symbolism of the streets' layout. Madame Blanchette is fictional but loosely inspired by the real-life French fortune-teller Marie Anne Adelaide Lenormand (1772–1843), who did indeed advise everyone from Josephine and Napoléon to Marat and Robespierre. Madame Lenormand used a thirty-six-card deck of her own design, said to have been lost. After her death, her name was attached to a popular nineteenth-century style of cards, still known today, which was actually created by someone else.

For most of the twentieth century, Westminster Abbey's funeral effigies were displayed in a museum in the undercroft (they have now been moved to a specially prepared museum in the attic). Before that, they could be found in glass cases in a gallery in the Islip Chapel. But in Sebastian's time, they still stood scattered about the Abbey itself. With the rise of tourism in the eighteenth century, they became curiosities and were used by the Abbey as a source of income, although little was done to preserve them. Production of wax figures was seen as "second-rate art," and so the effigies were typically made by women who were dubbed "modelers" rather than "artists." Nicknamed "the Ragged Regiment," many of the effigies were destroyed or damaged in World War II, so that only eighteen now survive. Particularly because they were dressed in the dead's own clothing, they have proved to be a valuable source of information. The earliest surviving example dates from the fourteenth century.

The construction of what would become Regent Street was only just beginning in 1814, after several years of planning. At the time, it was simply known as "the new street." Russell Firth is a fictional character, but he is modeled on the young architect James Burton and others.

The problems associated with the introduction of flush toilets described to Hero by the night-soil man were real; the cesspits used at the time simply could not handle the volume of water produced by the toilets, with the result that they were constantly overflowing into the basements of neighboring houses. Eventually, in 1815, the laws prohibiting flushing waste into London's famous storm sewers were repealed. The resulting flood of human waste, combined with the new gasworks, killed the river. In Sebastian's youth, half the salmon consumed in London came from the Thames. By the 1830s, the salmon were gone, and the river became famous for its horrific smell. It wasn't until Victorian times—after the summer of the famous Great Stink of 1858, when the smell grew so horrific that Parliament couldn't meet—that something was done about the problem.

The Pulteney Hotel did have eight flushing toilets in 1814. And yes, a drunken Byron really did once relieve himself in a potted plant in a hotel lobby.

Center Point Large Print
600 Brooks Road / PO Box 1
Thorndike, ME 04986-0001 USA

(207) 568-3717

US & Canada:
1 800 929-9108
www.centerpointlargeprint.com